D1263846

HEIDI HOSTETTER

Things We Keep

A LOWCOUNTRY NOVEL

For Laurie, Sandy, Heather, Liz, and Ann.
Thank you for everything.

CHAPTER 1

Eudora Grace Gadsden crossed her ankles and rested her hands in her lap as she waited for the man who would decide her fate. To keep herself occupied, she studied the framed portraits of past college presidents lining the dark paneled walls of the outer office. There were twenty-eight framed portraits evenly spaced around the perimeter of the room, with expressions so similar they could have been different iterations of the same man. The portrait of the current college president, slightly larger than the rest and lit from above, was in the center of the room, beside a portrait of the current President of the United States, Mr. Harry S. Truman. Eudora assumed President Truman's portrait would be replaced with General Eisenhower's, whose swearing in would be this coming January.

The chill of the outer office raised goosebumps on Eudora's arms. She'd begun to regret her decision to swap her green wool uniform cardigan for one of her mother's more elegant cashmeres. Whenever Eudora's mother wanted to make a good impression she'd wear a cashmere twinset, a pencil skirt and the Gadsden pearls, so this afternoon, Eudora did the same. Eudora might have been warmer in the sturdy green wool of her school uniform, but the gold crest on the front would have been a reminder that Santee girls were not welcome here.

With a sigh, Eudora turned her attention to the secretary stationed just outside Mr. Hendricks' office. The staccato of typewriter keys hitting the cylinder filled the otherwise quiet room. The sound was steady, efficient, much like the woman behind the desk, whose name Eudora could not recall. In the twenty minutes Eudora had been kept waiting, she'd watched the woman answer the telephone with a crisp professionalism, cradling the receiver on her shoulder while she jotted messages on a spiral pad at her side.

This would be exactly the kind of secretary Eudora would hire when the time came.

The desk intercom beeped, and the secretary lifted the receiver.

After a brief conversation that Eudora could not hear, the secretary rose from her desk. "Mr. Hendricks will see you now, Miss Gadsden."

As they entered the Admissions office, Mr. Hendricks pushed back his chair and stood. Eudora extended her hand, and while he seemed surprised at the gesture, he shook it anyway. "Miss Gadsden, thank you for waiting."

"I appreciate you meeting with me, Mr. Hendricks," Eudora replied automatically.

It was a lie, of course. Eudora would much rather have met with Mr. Whiting, the college president. Mr. Whiting had been a guest in the Gadsden family home several times over the years, and Eudora had the idea that when it came time for her to attend college, she would meet with him to discuss her options. So it came as a bit of a shock to have Mr. Whiting refer her to Admissions.

"Mr. Hendricks, the letters you requested are ready." His secretary opened a folder. "You mentioned they were urgent. If you sign them now, I will see to it they go out in the afternoon mail."

"Yes, fine." As he extended his hand to receive the folder, he glanced at Eudora. "Please excuse me for one moment, Miss Gadsden."

"Of course." Eudora glanced at the wall behind Mr. Hendricks' heavy mahogany desk. Hanging in the center of the wall was his degree from Charleston College. The document was framed in dark wood and double-matted in colors that highlighted the gold seal. Eudora noted that Mr. Hendricks had majored in business, like her father, and she wondered, idly, if the men had known each other as students. If they had, maybe she could use that connection now to speed this process along.

"Dory, where are the minutes from yesterday's committee meeting? I don't see them here." His voice was edged with impatience as he riffled through the pages on his desk.

Eudora cringed at his tone. Her father would never speak to a subordinate that way.

"You didn't say—" The woman began, then stopped. Eudora saw a hint of pink rising in her cheeks, then glanced away to allow the woman a bit of privacy. The secretary drew herself up and headed for the door. "I'm sure I have a copy on my desk. I'll get them right away."

"Never mind bringing them back," he called after her. "Send copies to every committee member. I need them out by the end of the day."

He settled back in his chair, smoothing his necktie with the palm of his hand.

"Let's get down to business, shall we?" He opened Eudora's folder and scanned the contents. "It says here that you're a senior, currently attending Santee Academy, and that you are applying to attend our business program in the fall?"

"Yes, that's right. Freshman class of 1953."

"I believe yours is the first application we've received this year. Most students apply in the spring, and here it is, not even Thanksgiving." He tilted his chin as he chuckled, as if she were a child and would not be taken seriously.

Eudora bristled.

Then she drew upon five years of Wednesday afternoon cotillion classes and produced a smile that even Miss Emily would approve of. She heard her teacher's voice in her head, reminding her that spitefulness was ugly and ugliness would not be tolerated.

Her voice softened. "Mr. Hendricks, I'm sure you are aware of the fact that Gadsdens have always attended Charleston College, though we have the choice to attend many other colleges. My family's roots are in Charleston. We love this city and wouldn't dream of living anywhere else."

And it was true. Eudora's father was a Gadsden. Her mother was a Moultrie. Together her parents were the closest thing Charleston Society had to royalty, and Eudora was their only child.

The Gadsden family was one of the first to settle the peninsula. Their land grant awarding them three hundred acres of fertile land along the banks of the Waccamaw River was signed by the king and sealed with wax. At first, the Gadsden men planted rice and the family prospered. For two hundred years, they cultivated a reputation for growing the best Carolina gold rice in the country. But when the nation went to war the men fled to safety. Years later, they returned to their home to find their possessions looted, their fields salted, and every building on the property burned to the ground. Broken-hearted, they could not bring themselves to start over. Instead, they directed their attention toward neighboring planters who *were* willing to try again. They saw opportunity where others saw despair, and they offered to broker the rice crops from area harvests – for a price. All during the summer, while area planters toiled in the fields, the Gadsden men traveled north, bringing rice samples to restaurants and shops and collecting orders for fall shipments. They kept a healthy percentage for themselves, of course, but were wise enough to spend their money publicly, on projects intended to rebuild Charleston. Now, almost one hundred years after the war's end, the Gadsden wealth and reputation for philanthropy had opened doors and invited opportunity that would not have been possible had they kept their land and farmed it.

What Eudora didn't say – what would have been vulgar to say – was that the Gadsden family wealth had helped start, and continued to support, Charleston College. She was sure Mr. Hendricks was aware of it, just as she was sure that had she been a son, her acceptance would have been automatic, regardless of grades or recommendations.

As a Gadsden woman, her life's path was very different, but she planned to chart a new course. She just needed Mr. Hendricks' help to begin.

He closed the cover of her file. "Have you considered other options? We have a fine secretarial program that could prepare you to enter the business world, if that's your goal.

I'm sure the Admission Board would have no objection to that."

Eudora raised an eyebrow slightly, as if the very question surprised her. It was something she'd seen her father do in business meetings a thousand times before. "Mr. Hendricks, my father employs a secretary already and doesn't need another." She gestured toward the folder he'd just closed and he opened it, as she knew he would. "As you can see from my application, I've worked for my father's company for the past several years. I have practical experience in billing, scheduling, correspondence—"

"Secretarial." He finished for her.

"I'm sorry?"

"What you've just described is secretarial work." He flicked his chin toward the door. "Dory does exactly that for me. She keeps track of details, leaving me free to attend more important matters." He crossed his arms in front of his chest and frowned. "Miss Gadsden, I feel I must be honest with you. This interview has been a courtesy, a favor to your father, but I'm afraid you've wasted your time. If your father is indeed aware of your interest in Charleston College..." He paused, allowing an opportunity for Eudora to speak.

"He is aware." Eudora lifted her chin as if she were offended that he would question her word. "Of course he's aware," she added again, just for good measure.

"Then I'm afraid he's made it more difficult for you," Mr. Hendricks concluded. "Your father should have mentioned that we don't admit Santee girls to programs other than secretarial. Further, we have found Santee's curriculum lacking in subjects we consider to be good foundation for college instruction."

The one objection Eudora couldn't argue with.

As the most exclusive private girls' schools in all of Charleston, Santee Academy's mission was to prepare their students for the life they would lead as young wives and mothers after graduation. Daughters from the most prominent families were enrolled at birth. Friendships begun as students carried into adulthood. And because parents expected a certain level of comfort for their daughters, the school provided lavish dormitories for boarding students, stables for their horses, music rooms for instruction and ballrooms for receptions. Santee administrators might not be able to control the changing world outside the halls of the school, but inside traditions were observed, cherished and strictly followed.

As a Gadsden, Eudora's attendance at Santee was part of her birthright. Eudora's parents were preparing her for a life in Society. Upon graduation, Eudora would be expected to pick up the mantle of generations of women before her. She would be expected to staff and run a large household of her own, leaving her days free to be spent in the company of other like-minded women. There would be afternoon bridge games to arrange and details to remember, such as knowing the chairwoman of the hospital committee didn't care for pecans in the chicken salad, or who can be depended upon to keep score accurately. The evenings belonged to her husband, and it was understood that Eudora would use her training as a proper hostess to host dinner parties to impress his boss or clients. Children, when they arrived, would be hers to care for and his to discipline.

The only piece of Eudora's future that Santee Academy couldn't guarantee was a suitable husband and a productive marriage. Eudora's parents helped the process along by filling in the gaps with private tutors and supplemental instruction. Summers were spent with her maternal grandparents on their horse farm in Aiken for the sole purpose of teaching Eudora to hold her seat on a horse, because one never knew when one will be called to a country shooting party. Additionally, there were tutors for dance and cotillion classes every Wednesday afternoon to prepare her for her formal debut into Society.

Reaching into a silver box on the corner of his desk, Mr. Hendricks selected a cigarette and tapped it on the surface. "Your initiative is impressive, Eudora, but I'm afraid your schoolwork has not academically prepared you for a typical college course load."

"Which is why I've been preparing on my own." Eudora reached into her bag and removed a textbook. "This calculus text is a required freshmen class for the business school." She opened the cover and flipped through the pages. "At first the material was challenging, but I've hired a tutor to help me. I've mastered the material in the first eight chapters—"

"'Mastered' is a strong word, Miss Gadsden. Perhaps you overstate?"

Many replies came to Eudora's mind, but none of them would serve her now, so she chose to say nothing.

Mr. Hendricks flicked his lighter and held it to the tip of his cigarette, drawing a breath as he spoke. "As a matter of curiosity, where did you get that textbook? It's Charleston College policy not to sell books to anyone but registered students."

. "I asked Miss Chessman, our school librarian, to request them for me. You won't sell books to non-students, but apparently anyone can borrow them."

"Interesting loophole." He exhaled, blowing a stream of

gray smoke above his head. "And you've studied the chapters, you say?"

"Yes. I have." Eudora straightened. "Passing each chapter test with a perfect score. As I mentioned, I've hired a tutor to explain what Santee doesn't."

"And the work you do for your father, it's substantial?" His eyes were sharp, watching.

"Yes." Eudora lifted her chin as she spun the lie. "In fact, I was the one who suggested he expand his market to include northern states. Specifically restaurants and specialty shops in Philadelphia, Hartford and Boston."

"Your research must have been extensive."

"It was." Eudora swallowed, uneasy with his line of questioning. "Of course, it was based on proprietary information, so I can't share my methods."

"I wouldn't expect you to." Eudora thought she saw the slightest smirk cross Mr. Hendricks' face as he flicked the ash from his cigarette. "As I said, it's very unusual for a Santee girl to apply to our college, something I'm sure your father must be aware of. Does he know your intention to apply?"

He'd asked that question before, and Eudora had answered it. It seemed odd that he'd repeat himself.

"Of course," she said again.

"I see." He frowned as he reached for one of the papers Dory had left on his desk. "Where is your father now; did you tell me and I've forgotten?"

"I believe he's still in Philadelphia, if the trip has gone well. I won't know for sure until I speak with him tonight." The lie fell easily from her lips. Truthfully, she had no idea where her father was. He never checked in when he was away on business, except on the last night to tell his family when to expect him home.

He glanced at her as he returned the paper to the edge of his desk. "I ask because, as I mentioned, I'm chairman for the Alumni Auction this year and I don't see his name on the list of donors. Or on the guest list, though we've attempted to contact him several times." His gaze sharpened. "I'm sure it's an oversight, but if you do as much work for him as you say, I thought perhaps you might shed some light on this?"

"As I said, he's traveling."

"You did mention that, yes. That would explain the unanswered letters. But we've also left messages with his secretary." He leaned back in his chair, twisting the gold college crest of his tie pin with his fingers as he paused to think. "Your father has been a generous donor in the past, and I'm sure this is just an error."

"I can say for certain that it is, Mr. Hendricks."

"Because you work so closely with him."

"Yes."

"So he *does* plan to attend our Alumni Auction this spring? I'm so glad to hear it." He pressed the intercom button on the corner of his desk.

The outer door opened and Dory appeared almost immediately.

"Yes, Mr. Hendricks?" She flipped the cover of her spiral stenography pad. "Did you need something?"

"Make a note to include Mr. Gadsden with the dignitaries at the head table this year." He crushed his cigarette against the glass as Eudora's heart thumped in her chest. "I'll dictate a letter later, reminding him of the dates and the deadlines for filling a separate table. Apparently, our paths have crossed."

"Will that be all?"

"No. Find the date for the mid-term calculus test. It should be sometime in December, before the boys leave for

Christmas break." He paused while Dory scribbled on her pad. "Tell Evans to expect Miss Gadsden and to have a final exam ready for her to take."

The secretary glanced up from her pad. "A final exam, sir? Do you mean a mid-term exam? That's what the other students will be taking."

"I mean a final exam, Dory." His glance cut to Eudora. "Miss Gadsden has just informed me that she's mastered the material in the textbook. I'm sure the final exam will present no problem for her at all. Mail a letter to Miss Gadsden's home with the details."

The woman glanced at Eudora with a look of concern. "Very good, Mr. Hendricks."

"That'll be all, Dory."

As the secretary withdrew, the door closed softly behind her, and Eudora felt the trap close.

Mr. Hendricks rose from his desk, signaling the meeting was over. "If you can prove mastery, passing with a ninety-five percent or better, I will speak to the Admissions Committee on your behalf. You shouldn't have a problem with acceptance, especially since your father is such a distinguished alumnus."

"Thank you, Mr. Hendricks. You won't be disappointed." Eudora rose from her chair and headed for the door, her mind racing.

She *had* demonstrated a mastery of the material – the first eight chapters. There were twenty-three chapters in the book, along with supplemental material and extra formulas to memorize. If the test was offered just before Christmas break, that didn't give her much time to study.

"One more thing, Miss Gadsden."

Eudora turned.

"I'd like to speak to your father personally, if I may," he continued, "to extend my best wishes on behalf of the school. If Charleston College is as important to him as you say, then we have a strong foundation to build on. I'd like to get to know him better, maybe partner with him on a project or two. Can I count on you to arrange a meeting?"

"Of course." There would never be a meeting because Eudora would never arrange it. For one thing, her father kept his own calendar and would not appreciate her adding to it. But Eudora didn't anticipate a problem. All she had to do was delay. "My father is traveling now, but I'll ask him to telephone you when he returns. After Christmas?"

If she passed the final exam, she'd have her acceptance letter by Christmas and it wouldn't matter if her father refused a meeting.

Mr. Hendricks regarded her for a long moment. "Surely he'll be home by Thanksgiving? I'll have my office contact him."

Eudora's smile didn't waver. "I'm sure he'll be delighted."

"One last thing," he said, his hand on the doorknob. "Because your situation is unique, I think it would be very impactful if your father would write a quick note to explain his support of your decision to attend Charleston College."

"A letter of recommendation?"

"Yes."

"From my father?"

"Is that a problem?"

"Of course not. I'm sure he'd be delighted."

"Good." Mr. Hendricks stepped back from the door. "I'll look forward to hearing from him."

CHAPTER 2

ONCE OUTSIDE THE BUILDING, Eudora stopped to pull on her gloves, her fingers trembling as she smoothed the kid leather across her palms.

That interview did not go according to plan. She knew her academic credentials wouldn't be enough to admit her to the business school, so she made a point to mention her family's friendship with Dr. and Mrs. Whiting and her father's business connections in the community on her application. But when Dr. Whiting's office redirected her to the Admissions office, it was clear that she needed another approach. She turned to her friend Jackson Legare, whom she'd known since they were children, because he knew how things worked. Together, they had rehearsed every possible question that Mr. Hendricks might pose, but neither of them could have predicted the outcome.

And there was the problem of her father.

Eudora couldn't remember a time when she didn't want to work in the family business, Palmetto Exports. When she was a little girl, her father brought her with him to work on Saturday mornings while her mother was out. Eudora had a little desk in the corner of his office and she spent her time on tasks that needed attention, like adding columns of numbers and checking her total against the clerk's total. As she got older, Eudora planned her father's business trips, booking hotels she knew he liked and private transportation whenever possible. And while Mr. Hendricks was correct about one thing – her father's personal secretary could have seen to these arrangements herself – he was wrong about Eudora's contributions in general. It had been Eudora's idea to expand the family's market further north. And Eudora was the one who suggested her father visit the Bollmann farm over in Augusta to persuade them to plant a crop more easily salable in the northern states.

A secretary wouldn't have known to do that.

By the time Eudora had turned thirteen, her mother had taken charge of her Saturdays and things changed. Quiet mornings spent at her little desk in the corner of her father's office were the first thing to go and it was harder to find time to do the work she'd come to love. Caroline Moultrie Gadsden's plans for her only daughter were specific and unwavering. On the afternoon of her fourteenth birthday, Eudora was taken to Chastains and fitted for her first girdle and was told to wear it every day thereafter, shedding it only to sleep. As she grew older and the date of her debut into Charleston Society approached, her mother's attention sharpened. There were frequent trips to the hair salon and nightly beauty treatments, dress fittings and dance instruction, club meetings and matrons to meet and impress.

The world her mother lived in was very different from her father's, and the more Eudora saw of the former, the more she preferred the latter. But she couldn't seem to reach her father to tell him; he seemed content to let Caroline manage Eudora's life.

So not only did her father not know about her application to his alma mater, but Eudora wasn't entirely sure that he would support her decision to go. Which made his letter of recommendation a bit harder to obtain.

Wishing wouldn't make it so, so Eudora forced herself into action. She descended the stairs, pausing for a moment to look across the quad, imagining what it would feel like to attend. The afternoon shadows lengthened across the blue stone path and the air smelled like fall, with the earthy scent of freshly planted mums and the sharpness of burning leaves. Clusters of students navigated the bricked paths crossing the grounds, clutching their books to the chests, head bent against the chilly air. In the distance was a stand of gnarled live oak trees veiled with Spanish moss, so old they may have pre-dated the college. In the back were the arches of the old porter's lodge. Every student at Charleston College passed through that arch – freshmen on the way in to be educated and seniors on their way out to the world.

Every man on both sides of Eudora's family tree, the Gadsdens and the Moultries, had graduated Charleston College before making their place in the world, and Eudora intended to do the same.

After all, it was 1952 and the world was changing, despite what Mr. Hendricks said.

With a new resolve, Eudora descended the last few steps into the courtyard, determined to put the experience with Mr. Hendricks out of her mind and enjoy the rest of the day. For the past few weeks, Charleston had been enjoying near-perfect weather, with crisp air and a deep Carolina blue sky, unusual this close to Thanksgiving. But the setting sun would bring a chill to the air so it was best to go directly home. And her mother would be expecting her.

"Hey – Eudora. Over here." The familiar pull of a Brooklyn accent made Eudora smile. Turning toward the voice, Eudora saw her friend Maggie O'Hanlan lounging on a slatted bench in the courtyard, her winter coat tossed aside, her face lifted toward the last bit of afternoon sun.

Maggie looked effortlessly chic, but then she always did. Everyone said she could have been a model if she wanted to be, with her clear skin, red hair, and sharp green eyes, but that wasn't what she wanted. The stack of magazines that littered the floor of her bedroom weren't collected for the models but for the dresses they wore. Maggie had an eye for what looked good; she always had. The Santee Academy school uniform, for example. The muddy-green plaid skirt, basic white Oxford blouse and thick wool sweater were standard issue and the same for every girl at Santee. But Maggie had found a way to transform the look somehow. She folded the cuffs of the Oxford and cardigan together and rolled both to her elbow. She pushed her knee socks down to her ankles and smudged away the white glare from her new Oxfords with carefully placed scuff marks. She got away with it, too, which made her a bit of a hero with the other girls.

And Maggie O'Hanlan had been Eudora's best friend since fifth grade.

When the O'Hanlan family moved to Charleston from Brooklyn in 1943, Maggie's mother decided that public school was good enough for her four unruly sons, but she wanted more for her only daughter. After carefully considering her options, Mrs. O'Hanlan decided that Santee Academy would be just the place for her Yankee-born daughter to acquire Southern charm. The years-long waiting list for admission at

Santee Academy posed no challenge at all for Marie O'Hanlan, and when the dust settled, Maggie was scheduled to begin that very September. Not coincidentally, a generous donation of building materials from the lumber company that Mr. O'Hanlan had recently bought allowed construction to begin almost immediately on the school's brand-new music building.

As Eudora approached, Maggie stood and stretched with a groan. Long and lean, she had a tumble of fiery red hair inherited from her mother and tied back with a green silk scarf. "Took you long enough. I was beginning to think this place had accepted you on the spot and you had moved into a dorm already."

"I wish. That would certainly make my life a lot easier," Eudora replied easily as she walked over to meet her friend. "What're you doing here?"

"Meeting you, of course." Maggie pulled on her coat and turned up the collar. "We had a sub for last period and half the class left because she forgot to take attendance. I don't think anyone except Posey and them are all that interested in the Senior Class Needlework Project, anyway."

Eudora linked arms with her friend and she wondered what Marie O'Hanlan would think of her daughter now. Before Maggie arrived at Santee, no one would have dreamed of skipping class; now they did it all the time. So really, it was Maggie who'd changed Santee.

As they walked the bricked path across the quad toward the gates of the college, Maggie said, "Ma gave me money to pick up dinner, do you mind if we stop at the train depot?"

"For chicken?"

"Yep," Maggie confirmed. "Da can't get enough of it and Ma says there's no way she could ever learn to fry a chicken as well as the ladies at the depot." Maggie tapped her pocket and the coins clinked together. "I have enough money to buy extra for us to eat on the way home."

Eudora imagined the look of horror on her mother's face had she seen Eudora walk the streets of Charleston while gnawing on a chicken bone. "Sounds good to me. Let's do it."

As they left the sheltering branches of the live oak trees, they felt the wind pick up. Eudora tucked the edges of her scarf into her winter coat and suppressed a shiver.

"So what did the college man say?" Maggie and Eudora turned the corner toward George Street and headed for the train depot. "You were in there a long time."

"It didn't go as well as I hoped."

"What happened?"

As they walked, Eudora told her about the meeting, how she'd prepared answers to questions that were never asked and how she was blindsided by unexpected questions about her father and his travels.

"Things kind of got away from me."

"Wow." Maggie let out a low whistle. "How did you leave it?"

"Well, Mr. Hendricks strongly suggested I apply to the secretarial program instead of the business school." The words felt like brine in Eudora's mouth. "He predicted a bright future as a secretary."

"There are other colleges," Maggie began as they turned into the wind blowing in from the harbor.

It was a point she'd made many times before, and Eudora answered as she always had. "My father requires a college degree from all his employees, so I need one to work for him. And every man on both sides of my family are Charleston

College alumni. I want that too, and there's no reason I can't have both."

Maggie squeezed Eudora's arm in response, and Eudora understood the implication. Maggie had been trying to get Eudora to move to New York City with her after graduation. She said the opportunities were better, and Eudora would have freedom to do whatever she wanted. But Eudora loved Charleston and didn't want to leave it.

"Do you have any idea how lucky you are that both your parents support what you want to do?" Eudora asked.

"I am lucky," Maggie agreed. "But sometimes it's okay not to do what your parents tell you to do," Maggie declared. "My Gramma threatened to wither away and die if Da moved her grandchildren from Brooklyn. But he couldn't see a future at the Navy Yard and wanted a fresh start. He moved down here with nothing more than hope and hard work."

The story of how Carl O'Hanlan revived a floundering business was impressive. Eudora thought of it often, as inspiration of what could be.

Maggie was ten years old when her father decided that he wouldn't put his family through another New York winter of ice and snow. A buddy of his mentioned a struggling lumberyard for sale just outside of Charleston, SC, a place Mr. O'Hanlan had never been but assumed was far enough south to not see winter snow or ice. He contacted the owner and bought the business, sight unseen. The following month he moved his wife and five children from a rented brownstone in Brooklyn into a brand-new tract house in a new development on the west side of Charleston, near Colonial Lake. That was eight years ago. In that time, Carl O'Hanlan had built his business into one of the biggest millworks in the city.

Eudora slowed her pace as she remembered a bit of information. "I might have said that Daddy is aware of my decision to attend Charleston College in the fall and that he fully supports it. Also that he'd be delighted to fund a table at the Alumni Auction in the spring."

"You said what?" Maggie stopped.

"It'll be fine," Eudora replied quickly. She'd given voice to her doubts but now looked for a way to push the genie back into the bottle. "It'll be fine," she repeated, her mind grasping at solutions. "I'll just explain to Daddy what working for the business means to me, and he'll find a way to get me in. I'll figure the rest out later. He might be impressed with my initiative."

"He might be," Maggie agreed. "But your mother won't. Does she know where you went today? What would she say if she found out you cut last period to go to the interview?"

"Today's Thursday," Eudora said by way of explanation. On Thursdays, Eudora's mother entertained members of the library committee and relied on Annie to look after Eudora. No matter what time Eudora returned home, Annie would keep Eudora's secrets. She always did.

Thinking about Annie made Eudora feel a bit better, so she put the meeting with Mr. Hendricks out of her mind. Things would work out for her.

They always did.

The walked in silence for a while, across Laurens Street, toward the train depot. The days were growing shorter as winter approached. Already, the yellow afternoon light was fading, giving way to a bit of blue twilight smudging across the horizon. As the streetlights flicked on, bare branches on overhead trees cast thin shadows on the cobblestone street. One of the homes along the street had a fire going in the hearth – the woodsmoke from the chimney curled in the air and was carried on the breeze. Window boxes were set with one last fall planting before the winter, with orange flowers and sturdy green trailing ivy.

"I love this city, don't you?" Eudora said.

"It's different from what I remember of Brooklyn," Maggie remarked as she shortened her stride to match Eudora's. "Quieter."

As they neared the train depot, they slowed to watch the activity. The evening train to Atlanta was at the station, waiting for passengers to board. A long column of gray smoke rose from the diesel engine and settled like fog overhead. Most of the passengers were businessmen, their overcoats and neckties flapping behind them as they ran across the street to board the train. This time, a few travelers were women, gathered on the platform in groups of three or four, probably headed to Atlanta for last-minute shopping before the Season began.

"They're here." Closing her eyes, Maggie lifted her chin and inhaled. After a moment she turned to Eudora with a smile. "I hope they have chicken left."

One of the best kept secrets of the Holy City was the women selling food at the train depot. As one of the smaller stops on the way to Atlanta or Charlotte, the entire Charleston depot consisted of a ticket booth and a seated waiting area. It was only after construction was completed that city officials realized that passengers who made the five-hour trip to Atlanta might need food for the trip. So a group of enterprising women stepped up to fill the need. They cooked food at home, boxed it into meals and sold it to passengers. They became known as 'waiter carriers.' Twice a day, every day, these women walked the length of the train – on the track side because they weren't allowed on the depot –

carrying sweetgrass baskets piled with packets of food. Passengers on board opened their windows and leaned out, waving dollar bills and accepting meals. Fried chicken and sweet potatoes were the most popular, but occasionally there were other offerings, like ham biscuits with a side of dirty rice or pimento cheese sandwiches and corn. When passengers *returning* to Charleston bought their meals to take home to their families, nearby restaurant owners began to complain. Bitterly.

While most of the waiter carriers were adult women, it wasn't unusual to see younger girls helping the adults with tasks like collecting money or making change. It was one of these girls who caught Eudora's attention, because she seemed to be working alone. She was dressed like the other women, in a gray shirtdress moist with perspiration and sturdy shoes that appeared to have walked the length of the tracks several times over. Her sleeves were hastily rolled and pushed above her elbows as if she couldn't spare a minute to smooth away the wrinkles. Her headscarf was bright yellow and anchored with a twist behind her ear. The load she bore must have been heavy; her sweetgrass basket was stacked with waxed-paper packets and a large tin thermos was tied around her waist with a length of rope. But it was the look of determination on her face that captivated Eudora, such an adult emotion on a girl who appeared younger than Eudora by several years. Eudora found herself drawn to such strength, wondering who this girl was.

From the platform a police whistle blew, shrill and loud, then the sound of running feet and angry voices.

Startled, the girls watched the waiter carriers gather their things and scatter, melting into the underbrush along the tracks as uniformed men poured into the depot.

"What is this?" Maggie stepped back. "Who are those men?"

"Health Department," Eudora answered. "The Health Inspector is trying to stop these women from selling their food."

"Why?"

"The inspectors said they can't guarantee their food is safe to eat."

"Is that true?" Maggie frowned.

Eudora shook her head. "Annie doesn't think so. Said restaurant owners around here have been trying to shut these ladies down for months because they're losing customers."

"Well, that makes sense," Maggie scoffed.

As quick as it started, it appeared to be over. The uniformed men returned to the depot empty-handed and chests heaving. Eventually, the platform quieted and the train began its journey to Atlanta.

"I've had enough." Maggie stepped forward. "Let's go."

Eudora followed, though she was lost in her thoughts. Despite what Annie had told her, the newspaper's editorials had made the decision to crack down on these women seem so logical. People were getting sick and these women were the cause. Of course they'd have to be shut down; they were a threat. But these women didn't look like a threat. They looked like every other business owner in the city, earning money for their family by selling something people wanted.

Eudora and Maggie turned the corner, making their way home.

"Will your father be upset if he doesn't have his chicken for supper?" Eudora asked the first question that came to mind, just to break the silence.

"Nah," Maggie kicked a pebble on the sidewalk. "I'll come back tomorrow. Surprise him then."

Eudora nodded, but her thoughts turned to the girl in the bright yellow headscarf. Eudora hoped she'd gotten away. And she wondered where the girl was now.

Maggie bumped Eudora with her shoulder, breaking into her thoughts. "You're going to be all right, you know. You always are."

"What do you mean?"

"I know you're worried about the test they're making you take, but you shouldn't be. You've been studying with Jackson for the past—" Maggie paused for a moment, then threw up her hands. "I don't know how many months."

"Six," Eudora supplied.

"Using the college book from the library *and* Jackson's school textbook," Maggie pointed out. "You'll be fine."

"I hope so."

A maze of cobblestone streets and hidden alleys shortened their trip across town by several blocks. One of Eudora's favorite alleys was tucked away from street noise and pedestrians. The entrance was obscured by a tangle of wisteria vines and easy to miss unless you knew exactly where to look. Inside, a canopy of tree branches stretched across the alley, casting dappled shadows on the path below. Fiddler ferns, sheltered from the cold and stubbornly green, grew from crevices in the bricked wall, and tufts of moss grew in the shadows.

This was the Charleston she loved. There was nothing like it anywhere else. Not in Atlanta, or Raleigh, or Columbia, or any of the cities her mother brought her to shop for gowns for her upcoming Season. If Eudora had her way, she'd stay in Charleston and never leave.

"This is me," Maggie announced when they came to Queen Street.

"See you tomorrow," Eudora started to say, then called Maggie back. "Thanks for waiting for me at the college, Maggs. It meant a lot."

Maggie scoffed. "What are friends for?"

CHAPTER 3

THE GADSDEN HOME was one of the oldest on the peninsula. Built as a city home for the family, it was used for entertaining during Charleston's social season. Over the years, several of the Gadsden women had made small improvements to the house, like moving the kitchens from the outbuildings to the main house or planting roses in a corner of the garden. But for the most part, the house looked the same as it did when a Gadsden ancestor scribbled his thoughts on an old bill of lading and instructed his wife to interpret for the architect while he returned to work.

Like many of the strong Gadsden women before her, Lucille Gadsden changed a few things while her husband's attention was elsewhere.

The front of the Gadsden house faced the street, for one thing. Many of the homes in this area of Meeting Street had been turned sideways to fit a narrow parcel of land, but the Gadsden home boldly faced the street. Lucy Gadsden happened to like gardening, so she ordered the house positioned in such a way as to allow room for a generous front garden and a second, informal garden on the side. To the interior of the house, she added a third-floor ballroom, a large formal dining room and a widow's walk so she could always see the harbor. Eudora's ancestor designed the formal gardens herself, though she was savvy enough to give credit to the landscaper her husband had hired to do the job. As a final reminder of her contributions to the Charleston home, Lucy Gadsden requested that her portrait be mounted above the fireplace in the ladies' sitting room as an inspiration to those who came after her.

Eudora unlatched the wrought iron gate that led from the sidewalk into the courtyard and onto the formal garden. She paused at the collection of cars parked beside the house, not understanding why her mother's company had stayed past the dinner hour. Every woman knew to be home by five o'clock in order to have supper on the table for her husband's arrival at six o'clock. It was already a quarter past four.

Eudora eyed the back of the house, hopefully. Beyond the side garden was a staircase that led to the back piazza and into the kitchen. It was possible for Eudora to escape her mother's party by using the narrow back staircase that led from the kitchen to a butler's pantry on the second floor. She'd done it before, without consequence. Certainly Eudora's mother would never hear her enter the house. Her mother's parlor was at the end of the grand hallway, on the other side of the house. The only room beyond her mother's parlor was her father's office, situated and unchanged since the house was build two hundred years before. When it came time for Eudora to join her father's company, Eudora would have an office just like it.

Eudora knew what she was supposed to do: go into her mother's parlor and greet her mother's guests.

But she didn't want to.

What she wanted was a hot bath, warm pajamas, and an early bedtime. Eudora's head was filled with empty check boxes that needed attention: call Jackson to arrange more study time, review the remaining chapters in her textbook, manufacture an excuse to slip out of the house for the final exam in December. She looked again at the house, brightly lit and filled with people, and her heart sank. All those things would have to wait. She was Caroline Moultrie Gadsden's daughter, and that meant she would be required to make an appearance at whatever party her mother was hosting.

Before going inside, she allowed herself a few minutes to linger in the garden because the setting always calmed her. The white gravel path crunching under her feet, the scent of freshly turned earth, the colors of newly planted flowers. The gardeners had replaced scraggly summer flowers along the border with smart choices for fall: warm yellow chrysanthemums, purple and green flowering kale, and tufts of orange asters scattered along the path. As she approached the stairs to the kitchen a fish broke the surface of the water in the reflecting pond and the last of the summer crickets started their chorus. She felt the tension lift from her shoulders.

Everything would be okay.

There would be a lot of studying to do to prepare for the calculus final, but she was ready for a challenge. If she budged her time wisely, and if Jackson was generous with his time, she'd be fine.

She took a moment to adjust her book bag and the package she'd picked up for her mother on the way home from the college interview, then climbed the stairs and entered the kitchen.

At first she didn't recognize it – every available surface

was piled with dirty dishes. There were lipstick-smeared teacups stacked in the sink, overflowing ashtrays piled on the stove, and the entire countertop was cluttered with cake plates and serving trays. Overhead cabinet doors were open and a jumble of baking ingredients were scattered across Annie's pastry table.

In the middle of the chaos was Annie herself, the house-keeper, cook, and heart of the Gadsden family. She'd been part of the Gadsden family since before Eudora was born and could be counted on, equally, for a kind word or a swat, depending on circumstance. Petite and plump with dark skin and sharp brown eyes, she favored brightly colored head wraps because she said colors were how God showed His favor. Annie noticed everything that went on in her house but held tight to every secret, and Eudora couldn't imagine life without her.

Annie stood now, with one fist planted firmly on her hip and the other holding open the refrigerator door, as she stared down the contents inside. "What in the world am I supposed to feed these ladies? Most 'em eat like birds anyway – nothing but cottage cheese and lettuce leaves. They 'pect fancy when they get together, even if it's just for lookin'." She slouched against the door. "And there ain't a thing in this house to fix."

"Hi, Annie." Eudora slipped off her shoes and kicked them under the table. They landed with a thump.

Startled, Annie stepped back. "Land, child. I didn't even hear you come in. You remember to get your mama's package?"

Picking up her mother's gloves from Chastains was the reason Eudora gave for saying out so late after school. Though she didn't need to. Her mother's attention was on her guests today, and Annie wouldn't mind if Eudora was late. The truth was that Chastains had been empty of customers when Eudora went in. She was in and out in less than three minutes, even after greeting Gus the doorman and chatting with Mrs. Tweedy. But no one needed to know that.

"They're on the table." Eudora swiped a green apple from the bowl on the counter and polished it against the front of her school cardigan. She'd remembered to exchange her mother's cashmere for her own wool before she entered Chastains. "Who's here? Still Mother's bridge company?"

"No, that ended hours ago." Annie turned her attention back to the refrigerator. "These ladies here showed up just after the bridge group left. I was sure they'd be long gone by now. I just hope they don't stay to supper." Annie heaved a sigh. "Grocery boy comes tomorrow, so there's not much for me to serve."

"I can run to the store for you." Eudora offered as she crunched her apple.

"Thank you, baby girl, but I can manage. I'll send Carter if something needs gettin." Annie closed the refrigerator door and crossed the kitchen to the pantry.

Eudora bit into her apple, feeling a little more optimistic about that hot bath. With both Annie and her mother occupied, no one would notice if she slipped away. "Any word from Daddy yet?"

Annie frowned. "You know better than anyone your daddy's schedule. You practically wrote it y'own self." Her eyes narrowed. "And don't you think for one second that I don't see what you're doing – stalling so you don't have to go out there." She gestured toward the hallway. "G'on now. Go say hello to your mama's friends."

Eudora heaved herself to her feet with a deep sigh.

"Don't you dare roll those eyes at me, young lady." Annie's voice, from behind the pantry door, was muffled. She couldn't possibly have seen from where she stood, but she knew anyway. She always did.

As she had done many times before, Eudora began the transformation from a normal high school student to Caroline Gadsden's daughter. She unrolled the sleeves of her Oxford shirt, smoothed the wrinkles, and buttoned the cuffs. Then she tucked the tails of her shirt into the waistband of her skirt and shook out the pleats so they hung perfectly. After finger-combing the tangles from her wavy brown hair, she checked herself in the hall mirror and turned back to Annie. With a smile, she dropped into an exaggerated debutante curtsey that even Miss Emily would envy.

"Shoes." Annie pointed to Eudora's feet.

Eudora had forgotten about her saddle shoes. She'd never worn the pair her mother bought for her at the beginning of the school year because it was deeply unfashionable to wear shiny white saddle shoes. Eudora had wrapped last year's pair in waxed paper and hidden it under a bench in the rose garden. She wore the new pair for her mother's occasional inspection and changed into her old pair on her way through the garden. A few times she'd forgotten to bring the box inside and a spatter of overnight rain had warped the leather, but Annie helped her dry them with newspapers and old towels. So far she'd avoided her mother's critical eye, but this was a close call.

Eudora turned toward the door, but Annie stopped her. "No time to go back for your shoes. You late already." She pointed toward the table. "Just leave those nasty ones under that table and hope none of your mama's friends looks at your feet."

~

Inside the sitting room, two dozen women, who would not otherwise have had opportunity to see the inside of the Gadsden home, gathered in Caroline's formal parlor. They clustered together in groups of three and four, sipping tea from the Gadsden bone china service. They dabbed the corners of their mouths with monogrammed linens and spoke in hushed tones, as if they weren't quite sure what to make of their good fortune.

Caroline had invited them to celebrate the opening of the 1953 Debutante Season, which, ironically, many of them would not be allowed to participate in. It was a delicate distinction, the difference between cotillion and debutante, and Caroline suspected that not all the woman present understood it, even after years of broad hints. Every ten-year-old girl with good breeding and background could apply to join Miss Emily's Wednesday afternoon cotillion, but only those whose fathers held membership in the St. Cecilia Society would be permitted to debut at Hibernian Hall at the end of December. The idea to include cotillion girls at a debutante tea started years ago, and it was Caroline's firm opinion that the practice should stop. But no one seemed brave enough to cull the guest list, so it seemed that everyone was invited.

The invitation itself lay unopened on a silver tray atop a mahogany table, both of which had been brought down from the attic and polished for just this occasion. As was custom, the invitation had been hand-delivered this morning, and it was impressive. A thick envelope of cream-colored linen, hand-calligraphed in perfect script, the flap edged in gold foil and sealed with deep burgundy wax. Of course Caroline knew what the text of the invitation said – they all did.

They'd been talking about the first Thursday of December for months.

Dresses had been bought months ago.

Beauty salon appointments scheduled weeks ago.

However, the debutante mothers gathered in the Gadsden home knew the contents of the envelope was secondary to the ceremony surrounding its opening. Circumstances had prevented Caroline from being present at the opening tea for her own Season, so she was determined to make this tea memorable for Eudora. This afternoon, Eudora would have the attention of every woman in Charleston Society, some-thing Caroline wished she had had for herself. The women present would decide Eudora's social position after her marriage, so this tea was a singularly important opportunity to demonstrate poise and confidence.

Caroline could see the events unfold very clearly in her mind: with the envelope in hand, Eudora would express excitement for the upcoming Season, gratitude for the support of the women gathered, and would end by asking for her mother's continued guidance and wisdom as they navi-gated the upcoming Season together. *Then* Eudora could slit open the envelope and delight in its contents. Because there was no room for mistakes, Caroline had taken a moment to jot down a few thoughts of her own for Eudora's speech. She'd insisted Eudora memorize and practice, because appearing spontaneous was important.

However, Eudora seemed hesitant to accept Caroline's guidance, and that worried her a bit. Then again, Caroline had never really understood her daughter. What was impor-tant was that Eudora knew what was expected of her, and Caroline felt sure that Eudora did.

Caroline surveyed the party and was satisfied with what

she saw. The formal parlor was a perfect setting for the tea. She'd decorated it herself, choosing shades of green and gold to compliment the winter view from the large windows in the front of the room. The couches and chairs had been newly upholstered in a matching fabric, the heavy damask draperies recently cleaned, and the antique mahogany tables polished with beeswax. On the whole, this room spoke of a family well-satisfied with their place in Charleston Society, which the Gadsdens were. And though he'd never voiced his approval, the fact that her husband had chosen to entertain his clients in this room several times was validation enough for her.

Though her lineage was better than anyone's, securing her rightful place in Charleston Society had not been easy for Caroline. Her father was a Moultrie – a family, it could be argued, that predated even the Chalmers' arrival to the peninsula. But instead of claiming his birthright as he should have, Caroline's father married beneath himself, choosing a nobody from Spartanburg. His family had no choice but to cut him off and he retreated, with his wife, to a horse farm in Aiken County. That he eventually built a thriving business breeding and training the best field hunters in the midlands mattered not at all to Charleston Society. In the interest of finding the best horseflesh, of course they would venture to the farm, grooms in tow, but they wouldn't return for entertainment. Nor would they invite Caroline's family to parties in Charleston. In retaliation, Caroline's father turned his back on Society entirely, cancelling memberships in every club and association that would have aided his daughters' entrance into Society. He kept only the membership to the Charleston County Hunt Club because it was good for business.

Both Caroline's father and his horse-loving wife would

have been content to raise their family in obscurity, but Caroline and her older sister had refused to allow it.

The battle to reenter Society started when Caroline's sister Evelyn was eight years old and Caroline was six. Horrified to learn their parents expected them to attend public school with local children while their Charleston cousins enjoyed the amenities of Santee Academy, the girls protested by locking themselves in their room. For three days they refused to come out, living on a stash of saltine crackers they replenished on nightly raids to the pantry. Help arrived in the form of Great Aunt Addie, coming to the Aiken farm in a sleek black car, driven by a uniformed chauffeur. To the girls' surprise, Great Aunt Addie took their side, berating their father and reminding him of his obligation to his children, even though he'd turned his back on it himself. His Spartanburg wife, she ignored entirely.

Two weeks later the two oldest girls were successfully enrolled in school and outfitted with uniforms and city clothing. Neither Caroline nor Evelyn shed a tear as they were driven from the horse farm into town. In fact, the only sadness they felt was on Friday afternoons as they were driven home to their parents. Very quickly, the Friday afternoon drive from Charleston back to Aiken became become a point of contention. Both girls were mortified by their father's red farm truck. Great Aunt Addie intervened again, insisting the girls be allowed to spend weekends with her, in her Charleston home. Surely Caroline's parents could see the advantages of allowing social interaction with their classmates?

As a final service, Great Aunt Addie took charge of the Moultrie daughters' debut. Only the youngest, Dorothy, seemed content to accept what life had offered her, choosing to spend her days in the stables on her parents' farm. In the end, Dorothy married a nobody too. The last Caroline had heard, Dorothy lived in student housing near the Medical College, while Evelyn had been clever enough to marry a state senator from Columbia and Caroline married a Charleston Gadsden.

"You've changed this room since I've seen it last." Camille Bradforth brought a cigarette to her lips and drew a delicate breath. "Was it recently done?"

"Last spring," Caroline replied, with just the right tilt of her head and the hint of a satisfied smile. "I decided it needed a refresh."

"I must say, I'm surprised Edward had no objection. Edward's mother was the one who chose the yellow and blue color scheme, wasn't she? In fact, when Edward and I were keeping company, I remember his mother being particularly proud of the Wedgwood plates displayed above the windows." She exhaled a ribbon of smoke through the corner of her lips. The motion reminded Caroline of the flicker of a snake tongue. "But I don't see her plates displayed. Have you stored them?"

"A few things have changed over the years, Camille." Caroline's smile didn't waver, though her gaze flicked to the grandfather clock near the door.

Eudora was told to enter the party at four o'clock, and it was almost ten minutes past. She was late, though none of the women had seemed to notice the time. Yet.

Camille gestured toward the envelope on the sterling letter tray. "The invitations are beautiful this year. Sissy really should be commended."

"I don't know how she kept track of everything," Caroline replied, not yet understanding where this conversation was headed.

"That was such an ordeal," Camille stubbed her cigarette into an ashtray and adjusted the gold bracelet on her wrist so it glinted in the sunlight. So that was it: a new gold bracelet. Caroline wondered what Camille had done to deserve it. Or what her husband had done to buy it. "I had lunch with Sissy just the other day at the club. She was concerned about finding a reliable calligraphy service."

"It turned out to be nothing." Caroline tucked a strand of hair behind her ear with her left hand, pausing for a beat longer than necessary. Her wedding set was already impressive, and she'd recently persuaded Edward to add an anniversary ring to it. The stack of gold rings was thick and a bit cumbersome, but the flicker of surprise on Camille's face when she saw it made it worthwhile. "Sissy was here just yesterday, finalizing the guest list."

Really, she had begun to wonder why Camille tried anymore. Twenty years ago it mattered; she and Camille had been pushing against each other like flint and steel as they shared the stage at St. Cecilia's ball in 1935. When her name was called, Camille had glided across the stage in a hand-beaded gown, heavy with seed pearls and edged with lace, and executed a curtsey that would have made a Texas girl weep with envy. Camille's parents beamed with pride as Camille's escort waited for her to cross the platform, then offered his arm to lead her into the ballroom. They entered the ball as if they were royalty.

But it was Camille's misfortune to have been called first.

When it was Caroline's turn, she presented the committee

with a dazzling smile as she sunk to the floor, not stopping until she felt her forehead touch the cool of the wood. She held the pose longer than was necessary, simply because she could. She'd not be able to walk comfortably for weeks afterward, but the reaction from the host committee made it worthwhile. Of course, her own parents weren't there to see her triumph. Her father had joined his friends at the bar immediately after signing the register, and her mother remained on the farm. Caroline's escort, a distant cousin, had been strong-armed into attending and abandoned her soon after the first dance.

However, her hard work and determination had paid off. By the conclusion of the Season, it was Caroline who had married Edward Gadsden. Caroline who would move into the Gadsden home and made it her own. And now, it was Caroline who had been chosen to host the invitation party, with Camille standing before her wearing faded lipstick and last year's hat.

A smile curled Camille's lip. "Really, Caroline, you should be commended. You've come so far from where you started. And to think: if Eudora had been born just a year later, you would have been hosting the Debutante Tea, instead of just the Invitation party."

The barb was meant to sting, and it did, though Caroline didn't show it. While it was true that the Gadsden family was one of the oldest in Charleston, the Chalmers' ancestors arrived just slightly ahead of them. The Chalmers family was one of the original few who received a land-grant from King Charles II's own hand. There were even whispers of a Chalmers family coat of arms and a distant ancestor listed in Burke's Peerage.

Thad Chalmers was a senior partner at a law firm on Meeting Street and had connections in both business and politics. Sissy served on the board of the newly formed Historic Society and chaired the membership committee of the Lowcountry Women's Club. No woman was extended an invitation to join without Sissy's express approval. The eldest son in the Chalmers family, Heyward, would have been a possible match for Eudora, but it seemed Eudora had her eye on Jackson Legare, which was fine with Caroline. Heyward had a bright future ahead of him; he was a distinguished cadet at The Citadel and his prospects looked strong. Younger son Anderson was a possibility too, but would be more of a stretch because the age difference between he and Eudora. In any case, he was away at Clemson University, studying politics, with an eye toward joining his father's law firm. Finally, there was Posey, the Chalmers youngest and only daughter. She was very close to perfect, and comparisons were bound to be made between the girls, with Eudora falling short.

This tea would make up for that, though. Every woman in Charleston, every woman who mattered, was gathered here today, and Caroline was certain they'd be impressed with Eudora's poise.

"Oh, don't be silly." Fully aware that whatever she said would be reported back to Sissy, Caroline replied with forced gaiety. "I'm honored to be a part of the process. I'm sure Sissy's tea will be perfect."

The Chalmers were a powerful family, deeply entrenched in the social fabric of the peninsula, and it would have been social suicide to offend any one of them.

"Still," Camille pressed, "don't you think we could have changed things a bit?" She gestured to the green walls they'd discussed earlier. "Being such an advocate for change and all."

"What do you mean?"

Camille reached toward the cigarette box Caroline had placed on the side table and withdrew a cigarette. She brought it to her lips and lit it. "Be honest, Caroline," she said as the smoke curled above her head. "Isn't it a shame Sissy is forced to invite *all* the girls from cotillion, not just the one who plan to debut?"

Caroline pictured the Chalmers home on East Bay, one of the grandest in the city. There were five floors, with the fifth floor, the attics, reserved for house staff. On the first floor was a formal dining room with expanded seating for dinner parties, a drawing room for entertaining, and a ladies' receiving room for teas. The upper floors contained guest bedrooms and a family library. The ballroom and a deep piazza claimed the third floor, and there wasn't an inch of green space that hadn't been blueprinted and landscaped.

Most of Charleston Society could be, and had been, easily accommodated in the Chalmers home.

Space wasn't the point. Exclusivity was. Caroline decided not to take the bait. The expression on Camille's face showed that Camille had noticed and was disappointed.

"Did you happen to notice the time?" Camille tried again, grounding her cigarette into the crystal ashtray and twisting the slim gold watch on her wrist. "I'm surprised Eudora's not here. Isn't she excited about the tea? My Anabelle certainly is; we've been ready for weeks."

"I'm sure it's slipped her mind; you know how busy the girls are this time of year." That barb hit Caroline's only weak spot: her inability to control her daughter.

The afternoon had crept dangerously close to the dinner hour, and her guests would expect to be home before their husbands returned from work. Caroline signaled to the maid to refresh both the tea and the coffee service, making a mental note to speak with Annie about making more of an effort to supervise the staff. Caroline disliked being distracted during a party.

As she crossed the room to give her attention to the debutante mothers, a cotillion mother placed her gloved hand on Caroline's arm. Caroline's benign smile didn't waver as she took the woman's measure. Her gloves were too heavy for afternoon tea, her dress too bright, her pumps too high. She was a peacock in a room full of swans, calling attention to herself when she should be trying to blend.

"I'm sure you don't remember me, Caroline – our daughters both attend Miss Emily's cotillion class." She lifted her gloved hand to rest on her imitation pearl necklace. "My Clemmie has learned so much these past few years, and I know she's disappointed not to be allowed to debut at St. Cecilia after Christmas. I know this is forward of me, but is there anything I can do?"

At least the woman had the decency to blush.

"I wish there was." Caroline frowned. "But the ball was planned months ago, and I believe the invitations are already at the engraver. But there are other balls Clemmie can attend. I'm sure Miss Emily can direct you."

"I've asked," the woman pressed. "But Clemmie has her heart set on it. Frank and I are happy to make a generous donation to the Society. I understand your husband sits on the board. Will you mention it to him?"

Caroline was stunned at the woman's horrifying lack of

manners. She allowed her smile to slip. "I'm sorry, but I can't help you."

Even if she wanted to, which she didn't, she couldn't help this woman. Rules governing membership at the St. Cecilia Society had been in place for hundreds of years, to restrict people just like this woman from joining. Imagine, trying to buy your way in.

Their conversation was cut mercifully short as the parlor opened. Fifteen minutes late and still dressed in her Santee uniform, apparently Eudora had ignored Caroline's instruction to freshen up before joining the party.

Caroline felt the press of her girdle against her ribs as her chest filled with anger.

Eudora favored Edward's side of the family, with her dark hair and eyes, stocky build, and her tendency to put on fat. Most of the shortcomings to her daughter's appearance could be managed with girdles, chin strapping, or a seamstress who knew how to hide flaws, but even that could only do so much. There seemed to be a constant battle between Caroline's offer to help and Eudora's rejection of it, and Caroline didn't understand it. Eudora's future depended upon the good will of the women gathered, but she didn't seem to care.

Caroline cringed as she watched her daughter lumber across the room like a plow horse.

Honestly, anyone would be at their wit's end with this child. Nevertheless, the room was watching and it wouldn't serve either of them to be the subject of tomorrow's gossip.

"Eudora, darling." Caroline lifted her hand languidly and gestured for her daughter as if she were delighted to see her. "We were beginning to worry."

As Eudora approached, Caroline lifted her chin to receive a kiss on her cheek. "Hello, Mother."

Conversation stilled as the women waited, but Eudora remained in her spot, seemingly unaware of what was expected of her.

"Eudora, look what arrived this morning; isn't it exciting?" Caroline willed her daughter toward the sterling tray on a mahogany side table near the entrance of the room.

Skipping over the speech and ignoring Caroline's friends, Eudora blithely picked up the monogrammed paper knife. She glanced at the paper briefly before handing it to her mother.

In one slight, Eudora had dismissed the matrons of Charleston Society and embarrassed the entire Gadsden family. How was Caroline expected to recover from that?

Caroline seethed at the slight but had the presence of mind to gracefully accept the invitation from her daughter and read the script aloud.

Mrs. Thaddeus Chalmers
Mrs. Thaddeus Chalmers Jr.
Miss Posey Chalmers
request the pleasure of
Mrs. Edward Gadsden and Miss Eudora Gadsden's
company at afternoon tea
On Thursday, the fourth of December
at two o'clock
at the Chalmers home on East Battery, Charleston

"Excuse me, Miss Caroline." Annie appeared at the door.

"Yes, Annie?" Caroline's tone was unintentionally sharp,

something unforgivable in front of guests. Had she and Annie been alone, Caroline might have apologized, but doing so now would have been awkward. Instead, she adjusted her position, folding her hands gracefully in her lap. "What is it?"

"There's a telephone call for Miss Eudora."

CHAPTER 4

GRATEFUL FOR THE reprieve from the oppressive rules of her mother's party, Eudora followed Annie to the kitchen. Annie had rescued her from what had become her mother's favorite topic: The Season. Not that Eudora wasn't looking forward to her debut. She was. After all, she'd spent the last seven years of her life preparing for the moment she would walk onto the platform at the St. Cecilia Ball. But her mother had other ideas about what it meant to 'be ready.'

Back in September, they'd traveled to Atlanta, Eudora, her mother and her Aunt Evelyn, to select the 'perfect' debut gown. They'd stayed in a hotel for a week, spending every day in this boutique or that, comparing the merits of each gown. Eudora had cooperated fully, with the hope that doing so might shorten their time in Atlanta. But it hadn't. By the end of the week, they'd bought so much that Eudora's mother had to summon Carter, the family driver, to drive to Atlanta and take their packages home.

But even that didn't satisfy her mother.

Nothing ever satisfied her mother.

Once in the kitchen, Eudora grabbed the things she'd

hidden under the table and turned to leave. "Thanks, Annie," she said.

"Not so fast, missy. There really is a telephone call for you." Annie gestured toward the telephone on the hallway table, the receiver off the hook. "Best not keep her waiting."

Once again, Eudora set her things down, postponing her studies just a little bit longer. "Hello?"

"Eudora!" Maggie's voice hummed with excitement. "It came – the invitation. Did you see it yet? It has a *wax seal*," Maggie breathed. "None of Miss Emily's example invitations had wax seals – have you ever seen anything so beautiful?"

The seal on the invitation was the Chalmers family crest and, in fact, Eudora had seen it many times, on cocktail napkins and personal stationery. Mrs. Chalmers was very fond of using and displaying it. But Maggie didn't need to know that.

"It is beautiful," Eudora agreed. "And the tea will be elegant."

"I changed the dress I'm planning to wear, dropped the hemline and lengthened the sleeves. You have to tell me if it's still okay."

"Your dress was fine. Why did you change it?"

"I got bored."

"Okay." Eudora sighed. "I'll come look. Tomorrow after school?"

"Nothing doing. The tea's next week and I need time to change this dress again if it's not right," Maggie reminded her. "Besides, I already told Ma you're coming now, and she's delighted. I think she's in the kitchen right now, making cookies."

If Maggie had known how nervous Eudora was about the final exam Mr. Hendricks had arranged, she would have insisted that Eudora stay home to study. But she didn't know because Eudora didn't tell her about the test she was required to take. This tea was the first of many for Eudora, but it was the only event of the Season Maggie would be allowed to attend, so Eudora wanted it to be special.

"You know," Eudora began, shifting the receiver to her other ear, "this preoccupation of yours for finding the right dress is mental. I blame that movie we saw a couple of years ago, Cinderella. You've never been the same after seeing the Fairy Godmother transform that girl."

"You are aware that you and I were switched at birth, aren't you?" Maggie declared with an exaggerated sigh. "Your mother and I know it's the glamorous things – the perfect outfit and a fashionable party – that makes life interesting. This tea invitation just proves it." She paused, then added, "But I need your help with my dress. I may have changed it too much."

"Fine, I'll come over now." Eudora groaned. "Give me a minute to change."

"I'll be waiting," Maggie said, suddenly cheerful. "But don't take forever – the tea's a week from Thursday."

Upstairs, Eudora shed her school uniform and dropped it on the floor, then chose a soft pair of dungarees, rolled the ankles, and pulled a soft gray sweatshirt over her head. Her mother would not have let her leave the house in this outfit, but her mother's attention was elsewhere.

On her way out, Eudora found Annie in the kitchen, stacking a platter with ham biscuits. "Do me a favor and take these out to the drivers. Tell them I got hot coffee coming directly and remind them to leave room for pie later."

"You baked a pie?"

"Ordered a few of them from Mrs. Marsdon when it

looked like them women weren't leaving anytime soon. Biscuits came from there, too." Annie shook her head as she wiped her hands on her apron. "She said she'd send me what she had left, and the delivery came while you was upstairs. Them ladies' drivers been outside waiting so long they won't care what I feed them, long as the food's hot." She smiled as she glanced at Eudora. "I may have ordered a few more pies than were strictly necessary, so you take a few outside. The men who have families may 'preciate a little extra to bring home, after staying as long as they do."

"Shouldn't everyone be leaving soon? Don't those women have families of their own to go home to?"

"Usually they do, but not tonight." Annie frowned. "Ever since that invitation came, your mama's friends been reminiscing 'bout their own Season. No one seem to be leaving anytime soon, no matter who's waiting at home." Annie opened the second-best silverware drawer and pulled out a handful of forks. As she turned away from Eudora, her voice dropped to a grumble. "Would have been nice to know these ladies was coming to stay. Least 'fore they showed up."

Eudora reached for the tray of food. "Can I go to Maggie's?"

"She going to the fancy tea, too?"

"Yes." Eudora added a stack of napkins to the platter. "Maggie was invited because she was in Miss Emily's class and the invitation has to include everyone."

Annie stopped. "Maggie know that?"

"She does," Eudora confirmed as she reached for a stack of coffee cups. "She wants to go to the tea for the glamor, but she thinks debuting is too much work."

"Make two trips," Annie said as she swatted Eudora's

hand from the coffee cups. "Maggie need help finding a dress?" Annie concluded.

"She made her own dress, designed it herself." Eudora hesitated, wondering how much she should tell Annie. She hadn't seen the dress yet because Maggie had wanted it to be a surprise.

"You make sure that baby gets what she needs." Annie's voice was sharp. "Some 'them girls are vicious, despite their fancy upbringing, and I don't want that baby getting a taste of their venom."

"I'll make sure." Eudora picked up the platter heavy with biscuits and cradled it in her arms. "Maggie's been working on this dress for months, so I'm sure it's fine."

"Never mind this." Annie shoo'd Eudora away from the percolating coffee. "Take the biscuits out then you g'won and see to your friend. Tell Carter I need his help; he's just jawing out there anyway."

"Okay." Eudora pushed open the door with her hip. "Thanks, Annie."

"Maggie's parents ask you to stay to supper, you tell them yes," Annie called after her. "Everything we got to eat in this house is stacked on that plate. Or in with those women. Nothing left in here for you t'eat."

CHAPTER 5

THE STORY of how Maggie's father moved the family from Brooklyn, NY, to Charleston, SC, had been told so many times that Eudora could recite it from memory, but she still loved hearing it.

It would not be an easy thing to move his wife out of Brooklyn, away from friends and relatives, so the first thing Carl O'Hanlan did was buy his wife a house of her own. She'd never had a house of her own before. The family of seven lived in a third-floor walk-up in Brooklyn, with three small bedrooms and a temperamental boiler because the building was rent-stabilized and Carl O'Hanlan was careful with money. The real estate agent had mentioned a brand-new development on the west side of Charleston called Colonial Lake, and Carl thought his wife would love the location. He splurged on the kind of home his wife had always talked about owning, with large bedrooms upstairs for the boys to share, a quiet master bedroom at the back of the house, and a kitchen with modern appliances to pamper his wife. Pictures were sent through the mail, contracts were notarized, and the deal was done.

The black paint on the outside shutters was barely dry when the moving van pulled up, but that didn't matter. The house was perfect for them. Certainly it was an improvement from their rented apartment in Brooklyn.

Leaving the domestic details for his wife to sort out, Maggie's father turned his attention to the company he'd bought and planned to modernize. Now, years later, Marie O'Hanlan would not hesitate to say that it was luck and years of hard work that transformed O'Hanlan Millworks into the success it was. And more often than not, Carl would laugh and agree, kissing his wife of twenty-one years soundly and declaring that he really was the luckiest man in the world.

But Eudora knew better. She and Mr. O'Hanlan had had a few discussions over the years, and he told Eudora that Charleston was not his first choice. Florida was. He changed his mind when he happened to come across newspaper articles about the city's progress: their plans to drain marshland on the west side of the peninsula to make room for new housing or to plant palmetto trees on either side of newly paved roads just because it was pretty, and finally, he read about their discussions on where to place the new medical center to best serve the community. All of that got him thinking about Charleston in a way he hadn't before, he said. In the end, he'd bought the lumberyard because a company that sold building supplies couldn't help but be successful in a city that welcomed progress as much as Charleston did.

There was no luck involved.

Eudora approached the O'Hanlan house, pushed open the white picket fence and latched the gate behind her. Maggie waited for her at the top of the steps, her usual spot. Like Eudora, Maggie had also changed from her Santee uniform, but Maggie looked like a movie star with cuffed jeans, sneak-

ers, and one of her father's blue work shirts knotted care-
lessly at her waist.

"You didn't tell me this wax seal is actually the Chalmers
family crest." Maggie waved the invitation in the air as
proof.

"I thought you'd figure it out, once you'd had a chance to
look at it," Eudora replied, slipping into place next to her
friend on the top step. "What did your mother say?"

"She hasn't seen it yet. At least, I don't think she has. It
was on the hall table when I got home from school," Maggie
answered, flipping the envelope over. "Why isn't there a
stamp on this envelope?"

"Mrs. Chalmers had them messengered to all the cotillion
girls this morning."

"That explains it," Maggie said as she pushed herself to
her feet.

They climbed the front stairs to the house, screen door
slamming the door behind them. "Ma, I'm home," Maggie
called out as the girls kicked off their shoes in the front entry.
"Eudora's here, too."

The O'Hanlans had brought a little piece of Brooklyn with
them when they moved. They saw no reason to change their
way of life just because they'd moved south. They shouted to
each other from across the house, they pounded up and down
the stairs, and sometimes had mud-fights over the back fence.
But at the end of the day, they always gathered around the
table for a family dinner. It didn't seem to matter what food
was served or who sat around the table; the O'Hanlans ended
the day together, and Eudora was always happy to be a part
of it.

Maggie's mother emerged from the kitchen with a bright
yellow apron wrapped around her ample waist. She carried a

deep ceramic mixing bowl overflowing with bags of flour, sugar, and chocolate chips.

"Enough with the shouting," she said. "I'm right here." The girls followed her to the kitchen as if she were a pied piper. They waited while she set the bowl on the countertop and accepted the hug she gave them. "How was your day, lovies?"

Born and raised in Brooklyn, New York, Marie O'Hanlan was one of five children born to a New York City fireman and an Irish mother. She met her husband at a USO dance for enlisted men stationed at the Brooklyn Navy Yard. They dated exactly three times before Carl proposed. They married a month later in a New York courthouse, with dozens of relatives in attendance. Smart and tough, she had deep auburn hair and a scattering of freckles on her face, which she refused to hide with powder. Marie knew the names of all her children's school friends – the ones she liked and the ones she didn't. She checked homework every night, sometimes with a word of praise, sometimes with a swat. Despite having help with housework, each of her children had chores and were expected to do them with a helpful attitude.

Marie was the sun of the O'Hanlan family solar system.

"Awful." Maggie groaned as she slipped from her mother's grasp and dropped herself dramatically onto a kitchen stool. As soon as her mother's back was turned, Maggie reached for the opened chocolate chips. She tossed a palmful of chips into her mouth, then slid the bag across the counter to Eudora, who also managed to sneak a few unnoticed. "We had a math test at school today and an English paper due on Monday. They're working us to death, Ma. And it's only November."

"I expect you'll survive." Her mother pulled eggs and butter from the refrigerator and laid them on the countertop.

Maggie reached for the bag of chips again, but this time she wasn't fast enough. Her mother batted Maggie's hand away. "None of that now. You'll spoil your appetite."

Sliding from her stool, Maggie produced the Chalmers' invitation for her mother's inspection. "The invitation for Posey's tea came, Ma, by *messenger*."

"I know it did. I'm the one who signed for it. Early this morning, a man in a blue uniform rings the bell and hands me an envelope. Tells me I have to sign for it. I was afraid someone had died." Mrs. O'Hanlan shook her head. "Imagine that, with a post box on every corner in this city, someone pays for hand-delivery. I've never seen anything like it."

"It's the way families like the Chalmers do things, Ma."

"Is it now?" Maggie's mother wiped her hands on her apron, then glanced at Eudora. "Is that how your family sends invitations, too, Eudora? By messenger?"

Mrs. O'Hanlan's question was completely without guile. It was her daughter who was interested in Charleston Society; Marie O'Hanlan was perfectly content to help her husband with his work, to raise her family, and when she had time, to volunteer at the library.

"Sometimes," Eudora answered simply.

Maggie's mother turned to preheat the oven. "If it's important to you, Maggie-girl, then I'm glad for you to go."

"It is, Ma, especially since I can't debut at St. Cecilia with Eudora."

Marie paused. When she turned back, her expression had changed to one of determination. "What'da mean you 'can't debut with Eudora'? Why can't you debut if that's what you want?" her mother challenged, her palms flat on the countertop. "We got you into Miss Emily's, didn't we? That was a project in itself, my girl. Forms, and permissions – everything but a secret handshake just to get in. This St. Cecilia – or whatever – can't be any harder than that."

"Well, we'll sort this later." Maggie's mother straightened; she'd seen it too. "Maggie, go call your brothers inside, willya? Your da'll be home soon, and I'm behind with the supper."

Eudora rose to help, but Mrs. O'Hanlan called Eudora back. "Eudora, would you mind giving me a hand with this tray? It won't take but a minute."

"Sure, Mrs. O'Hanlan."

The moment they heard the back door slam, Mrs. O'Hanlan turned to Eudora. "Tell me about this St—" She waived her hand in the air, as she searched for the word.

"Ceclia," Eudora supplied.

"Why can't our Maggie go to this dance?" she continued. "I'm the first to admit that I don't understand your ways, but it seems she might want to go after all."

Eudora drew a breath, giving her a moment to consider her words, but Marie would have none of it. "We don't have much time before Maggie comes back with the boys, lovie. Tell me straight-out: is it money? We can pay, and we will, if this is what Maggie wants."

Despite Marie's request for a blunt truth, Eudora was sure she wasn't ready for it. The truth was that money mattered very little to those within Charleston Society. What they valued was lineage and family history, which was why Betsy Fletcher, even with frayed cuffs and last year's shoes, would always be accepted and tradespeople from New York City would never be.

This truth was unchangeable.But she owed Mrs.

O'Hanlan an honest answer, so Eudora tried her best to explain rules that had been in place for generations. "The ceremony for formal entrance into Charleston Society is at the St. Cecilia Ball at the end of December. The dance is for members only, and Mr. O'Hanlan isn't a member of the St. Cecilia Society, so Maggie can't go. She won't be allowed inside."

Maggie's mother sat on the stool next to Eudora. "I'm sure Mr. O'Hanlan wouldn't mind joining if it made our Maggie happy. Just tell me who to telephone."

"For Mr. O'Hanlan to be a member, his father would have had to be a member. The committee is very strict."

"Well, that's it, then." Mrs. O'Hanlan sighed and rose from her place. "Maybe it's for the best, anyway. Maybe I was wrong to encourage Maggie's interest in all this fancy stuff. That's not who we are."

All at once, a commotion rose from the back yard: shouting, thumping, and the sound of running feet pounding up the back stairs.

Mrs. O'Hanlan glanced at the back door, then at Eudora, her words rushed. "Girls can be mean, Eudora, especially to ones they think are beneath them. You've always been a true friend to our Maggie, and I'd like you to watch out for her. Protect her, if you can."

Eudora didn't hesitate. "Of course I will."

Maggie entered the kitchen first, cheeks flushed from running and a spatter of mud on her pants. "They were by the creek again, Ma."

"And so it begins." Marie straightened, her expression returning to normal. "You girls better get going while I see to your brothers. Go see if you have something suitable to wear to that fancy tea of yours. Eudora can help you." She gestured toward the envelope on the countertop. "And take that letter with you."

The girls ran up the narrow wooden steps to the attic, closing the door behind them. Shortly after they moved in, Mrs. O'Hanlan convinced her husband that the only girl in the family required a bedroom of her own, and he chose the only available space: the attic. Set on the third floor, Maggie's room was cozy, tucked into the eaves of the house, with a half-bath all her own. On summer days, the windows on both sides drew cool breezes from the lake, and on a clear day, you could see the shimmer of the sun's reflection on the water.

But tonight, the air had cooled and the sky rolled with rainclouds. A distant clap of thunder signaled the beginning of a storm. Maggie crossed the room and opened the window wide; the lace curtains fluttered as the breeze entered the room.

The girls flopped onto the bed. Maggie propped the invitation on her bedside table, next to her favorite things: a photograph of Vivien Leigh torn from a fan magazine, and the watch she received last year on her sixteenth birthday.

"I don't know why you're so excited about this stuff, Maggs."

"I don't know why you're not," Maggie countered. "What girl wouldn't want to dress like Grace Kelly and go to a ball thrown in her honor?"

"I thought you didn't like all this stuff, Maggs? You told me you can't stand Posey Chalmers."

"Still can't. That doesn't mean I don't like the dresses or want to go to the ball."

Eudora adjusted the pillows behind her. "Honestly, Maggs, from the outside, it looks glamorous, but it's a lot of work. So much is expected of me that sometimes I can't breathe under the weight of it all. From Posey's tea next week to the St. Cecilia ball at the end of December, every second of my time is accounted for."

"What about your math test? The one at the college?"

"Jackson said he'd help me study. We'll have to spend afternoons and some evenings together, because that's the only free time I've got."

"And that's okay?"

"It helps us both. My mother thinks we're dating."

"Does she know—" Maggie began.

"I don't think so." Eudora waved her off. "But even if she did, it wouldn't matter. Caroline sees what she wants to see."

"Tell me again why you're only going to one ball?" Maggie rolled over on her stomach. "Didn't Miss Emily say that a Season lasts six months?"

"For girls like Posey and Joannie and Martha, it does. Their mothers have arranged a full five-city circuit for them, beginning with Charleston's St. Cecilia in December and ending in Greenville in May. In between are receptions in Columbia, Orangeburg, and Florence. But it's not just the one dance they have to prepare for; there are teas, receptions, and cocktail parties in every city before and after the debutante ball. It's a lot of work."

"What about school? Won't they miss a lot? How can they graduate?"

"Santee 'makes allowances' for girls on the circuit." Eudora rolled her eyes. "It's not well-known, but it's understood. After all, a Society wedding is what the school wants for their students, too."

"How do you know so much about the circuit if you're not going?"

"Because my mother did the whole circuit," Eudora

explained. "My Aunt Evelyn did too. I've heard their stories my whole life. Trust me, Maggs. The circuit is a career in itself, and the only goal is to be engaged by the end of it. I don't have time for that, and neither do you."

Outside the rain had started slowly, with a gentle patter on the roof and a breeze that ruffled the curtains.

"Okay, then. If I can't be a debutante, at least tell me about it." Maggie rolled over onto her stomach, elbows on the bed, chin cradled in her palms. "Everything."

"The debutante's father escorts her down the grand staircase—"

"Start with the dress," Maggie directed as she pulled a quilt from the foot of her bed and tossed it across their legs. "And don't leave anything out."

Eudora heaved a sigh. "Every dress is the same: white, tea-length, with maybe a subtle difference like a pastel sash or a short cape. Heels are low and match the dress—"

"Until they've debuted," Maggie finished for her.

"After they've formally entered Society, she can wear *almost* anything she wants, but for her debutante year, her mother decides – or at least, mine will."

"Then comes the Grand March," Maggie prompted.

"I've told you this a million times already, Maggs. It's not that interesting."

"It is to me, Eudora," she said as she settled back on the bed. "Just one more time."

Outside, rain pounded against the roof and lightning flashed across the dark sky.

When a clap of thunder boomed just a moment later, Maggie slid off the bed and crossed the room to close the window.

Eudora dug her bare feet deeper into the soft warmth of

the quilt and settled into the conversation. "When the debutante's name is announced, she ascends the platform in front of the host committee. She thanks them for the honor and drops to a curtsey – the deeper the better. When she rises, she crosses the platform and joins her escort on the other side. He greets her with flowers and leads her to the ballroom. After the debutante has been received, the first dance starts. Fourteen dances after that, they break for a midnight supper. When supper is over, the orchestra plays one final dance and everyone goes home. It's been the same way for generations."

"Seems like a lot of preparation for just one night. I can't believe your mother agreed to St. Cecilia's and that's all."

Technically, she hadn't. Eudora had only assumed it because they'd bought only one white gown on their trip to Atlanta, and her mother hadn't mentioned going back for another. And because Eudora didn't want to participate in anything beyond St. Cecelia, she didn't ask.

Maggie seemed content to let that part of the discussion drop. She walked to her closet and pulled open the door. "Tell me what you think of the changes I made to the dress for Posey's tea."

Maggie pulled the dress from her closet and turned.

"Wow." Eudora let out a slow breath.

Maggie's gaze shifted from the dress to Eudora's face. "Too much?"

Eudora pushed herself from the bed and went to take a closer look. The outfit itself was beautiful – Maggie had taken a simple beige sheath dress and had transformed it into something else entirely. She'd added a red wool swing coat with a wide lapel and three-quarter cuffed sleeves. And she changed the dress, too, sewing red piping around the neckline and adding a wide belt around the waist. The overall effect was elegant and unlike anything Eudora had ever seen in her mother's closet. Any woman would have been thrilled to wear Maggie's design to a restaurant, to a cocktail party, or to a formal luncheon.

It was, however, completely unsuitable for a debutante tea.

Maggie let her arm drop. The outfit puddled to the floor and Eudora moved to retrieve it. She opened the closet door and hooked the hanger over the top.

"It's the red, it's it?" Maggie asked.

"It's beautiful, Maggie, but I don't know why you changed it." She lifted a corner of the red wool coat to look at the stitching. Clean corners and tight seams, some of the best tailoring work she'd ever seen. Maggie would be celebrated as a clothes designer in New York, where they would appreciate unique design. In Charleston, however, especially at a debutante tea, women tended to embrace tradition over fashion.

Remembering her promise to Mrs. O'Hanlan about protecting Maggie from bullying, Eudora turned to face her friend. "Let's find something more subdued for Posey's tea." She pushed open the closet door and stepped aside to allow Maggie access. "What have you got?"

"Fine," Maggie conceded as she returned the outfit to the closet. "Posey doesn't deserve anything that fabulous, anyway."

"That's the spirit." Eudora laughed.

The metal hangers slid across the wooden bar as Maggie sifted through her choices. "How about the blue dress I wore to the cotillion tea? I like that one."

Eudora shook her head. "Posey's party is the first of the

Season, so you need to wear something more formal You'll
need gloves, too – how many pairs do you have?"

"Just the one." Maggie dug into a dresser drawer and held
them up. She'd worn the same pair every Wednesday afternoon for the past three months.

"Not those." They were smudged on the fingertips and
creased at the wrist. "Never mind – you can borrow a pair of
mine."

"How many do you have?"

"Enough to wear a fresh pair of gloves at every event. I've
been told to tuck an extra in my purse, just in case." Eudora
shrugged. "Most debutantes order them by the dozen before
the Season starts."

Returning to her closet, Maggie flicked through the last of her
dresses. Her voice was muffled as she looked. "There's nothing
here." She turned, exasperated. "What are *you* wearing?"

Eudora shrugged. "Something my mother picked out
months ago." She peered inside the closet at the rest of
Maggie's dresses. It was late to expect to find a suitable dress,
and what if it needed to be altered? "We might be able to find
a dress at Chastains. I can go with you."

"Chastains? Really? How very posh."

Chastains was a staple of Charleston Society, catering to
discerning taste of the oldest families, offering everything
from hand-laced baptism gowns to custom wedding and
bridesmaid dresses. It was a rite of passage for a new Society
wife to open a house account at Chastains because the shop
was so exclusive. A new bride could set up a house account
and shop in the store her whole life, which was exactly the
point. When she was little, Eudora's mother brought her to
Chastains for her Easter dress, gloves, and hat. Every one of

Eudora's cotillion dresses came from Chastains, as did many of her tea dresses and the gown she wore to her father's formal business receptions. The only exception was the white gown she'd wear to St. Cecilia, and the gown she'd wear for her wedding because her mother insisted on couture.

"If you want the right dress, we go to Chastains," Eudora replied.

Maggie shut her closet door. "Let's go ask Ma."

In the kitchen, Maggie's mother was putting the finishing touches on dinner, and it smelled delicious. Cooling on a rack on the counter was a tray of brownies, and in the sink was a colander of iceberg lettuce. On the table already was a plate of sliced tomatoes and a basket of bread.

Not for the first time, Eudora wished her mother was more like Mrs. O'Hanlan. She'd never seen her mother do more than boil water for tea and even that, reluctantly. The Gadsden family employed a full staff of help. In addition to Annie, there were housemaids for upstairs and down, two gardeners to look after the grounds, and Carter, the driver who sometimes ran errands for Annie. But even with that many people around, the house was always quiet as a crypt. Eudora preferred the chaos of the O'Hanlan house.

"I thought you were making cookies, Ma."

"Ran out of time." Mrs. O'Hanlan turned on the faucet and rinsed the lettuce. "And what can I do for you girls?"

While her mother's back was turned, Maggie snatched the edge of a brownie from the cooling rack, broke it in two, and offered half to Eudora. "I can't find anything to wear to the tea, Ma. Can I buy a new dress?"

Maggie's youngest brother, Danny, wandered into the kitchen and made a face at his sister. Then, seeing what his sister was eating, reached across the counter.

Mrs. O'Hanlan swatted his hand away. "Nothing for you until supper."

"But Maggie's got one," he protested. "And I'm *hungry*."

"Maggie didn't give her lunch away, now did she? Might explain why you're hungry now," Maggie's mother countered.

Danny scoffed. "I didn't 'give it away', I sold it. Reed Walker loves your sandwiches, especially the salami ones with peppers and onions. Can you make one tomorrow? He said he'd pay."

"You're not to sell your lunch, Daniel Patrick. I'll not tell you again," she admonished, then, after a moment, she softened her tone. "Bring the boy over after school, tell him that I'll make him one fresh."

That sorted, she turned to her daughter and picked up the thread of their conversation.

"Are you sure you've nothing appropriate...?" Mrs. O'Hanlan glanced at Eudora, who gave a quick shake of her head. "Well, I won't have you looking like country-come-to-town. We O'Hanlans may not be Society, but we know what's what." She opened the pantry door, seemingly oblivious to the fact that her comments made no sense at all. It was one of the things Eudora loved about her friend's mother: she seemed to have a phrase for every occasion.

Maggie's voice rose with excitement. "So is it all right if Eudora and I go dress shopping at Chastains?"

"Chastains?" Maggie's mother turned, her hand still holding the cabinet as she turned toward Maggie. "Does it have to be as grand as all that?"

"For this, it does," Maggie answered as she reached for another brownie corner.

Mrs. O'Hanlan frowned. She opened the refrigerator and disappeared behind the door.

"Can we?" Maggie called after her.

Her mother groaned, a sure sign she was about to give in, and it surprised Eudora again how easily Maggie spoke to her mother and how her mother seemed to really listen. In her whole life, Eudora had never asked for anything more than once, because the first answer Caroline Gadsden gave was always the final answer. In fact, Eudora couldn't remember a time her mother had ever changed her mind, so it would never occur to Eudora to ask twice.

Maggie's mother reappeared with a carton of milk. "I'll have to ask your father what he thinks. You'll have to wait."

"But Ma, the party's a week after Thanksgiving. I want to find the perfect dress." Maggie slid from her place at the counter and reached for her mother's hands. "It's important to me, Ma. It really is."

Mrs. O'Hanlan regarded her daughter for a moment, then she nodded. "I'll speak with your da tonight. If he agrees, I'll call the shop tomorrow and open an account."

Maggie twirled in place and kissed her mother on the cheek. "Thanks, Ma. You're the best."

But Mrs. O'Hanlan shoo'd her away. "I haven't said yes now, so save your celebrating for later." She addressed her next comment to Eudora. "Nothing crazy, you hear? One dress for one party, that's all. I'm saving for a television, so I'm not spending good money on a dress our Maggie can't even wear to church."

"Nothing crazy," Eudora repeated. "I promise. But there probably won't be time for you to open an account before tomorrow," she ventured. "It might be easier to charge the dress on my family's account."

Mrs. O'Hanlan's expression flickered as she understood. They would need to use the Gadsden house account because Chastains would not offer the O'Hanlans a house account of their own. "Well, then. I guess that's all right. Save the receipt, Maggie, and we can give the money to Eudora tomorrow. It's nearly six o'clock." Mrs. O'Hanlan pulled a casserole from the oven. "Danny, go wash your hands and call your brothers. Your da will be home any minute and he likes his supper on the table."

Danny planted his feet and bellowed for his brother. His mother cuffed his shoulder with her oven mitt. "You were raised better than that."

After Danny ran reluctantly toward the stairs, Maggie stood on her toes and planted a sloppy kiss on her mother's cheek. "Thanks, Ma. You're the best."

"Away with you now," Maggie's mother admonished as she untangled herself, but her smile was genuine; it always was. "You'll stay to supper, Eudora?"

As usual, it was more of a statement than a question, and Eudora accepted.

The casserole smelled delicious, and there was nothing to eat at her own house.

CHAPTER 6

BY THE FOLLOWING AFTERNOON, the weather had changed. The extended summer weather Charleston had been enjoying for the past few weeks had turned. Overnight, temperatures had dropping to near freezing.

A sudden blast of cold winter wind blew across the street, scattering wet leaves and debris from the previous night's rainstorm. Maggie and Eudora turned their backs against the cold and pulled their shoulders up to their ears.

"I'll be so happy when spring comes." Eudora's voice was muffled by her woolen scarf.

"That's four months from now," Maggie replied.

The gust of wind dissolved as quickly as it appeared. Maggie lowered her scarf and drew a tentative breath. The air smelled like woodsmoke, damp earth, and pine needles. There was so much Maggie loved about this time of year.

"So we have a plan?" Eudora asked.

"We do," Maggie confirmed. "I'm going to Da's office while you go home and try to telephone your father again. We'll meet at Chastains in an hour."

After consulting with her husband, Maggie's mother had

decided to allow Maggie to buy the dress she needed at Chastains, but she was not allowed to put the purchase on Eudora's family account. It was decided, instead, that Maggie walk to the millworks after school to pick up her father's checkbook from the office. Maggie would be allowed to write a check for the dress and her father expected a receipt. He said he'd teach her the correct way to write a check, even though she already knew, and he ended with a warning: "O'Hanlans pay our own way, Maggie-girl. Make do with what you have as you save for what you want. Never use credit; that'll be the end a' ya."

Her father's odd comments were something Maggie would have liked to share with Eudora, but she wasn't sure Eudora would understand. Eudora's world was very different from her own. Maggie doubted Eudora had ever been lectured on saving money.

As if to prove the point, Eudora slowed her pace and asked, "You sure about not using my family account? It seems easier than walking all the way uptown to your father's office."

"Da wants me to use the checkbook," Maggie said as she tucked the ends of her scarf into her coat. "He thinks it'll be good practice for New York."

"Okay, then. I'll meet you in an hour," Eudora said, turning onto her street. "And if you get there before me—"

"I won't go inside. I know," Maggie huffed. Her father had told her twice and her mother reminded her once more before Maggie left for school. Maggie had agreed, but she didn't see what the big deal was.

Eudora blinked. "Don't be silly. Why wouldn't you go inside?"

"I don't know," Maggie admitted. "Parents are weird."

"I was going to say," Eudora continued, "that if you get there before me—" She held up a gloved hand to stop Maggie from protesting. "Don't worry, I won't be late. But if I am a *few* minutes late, Mrs. Tweedy will take good care of you. She'll offer you tea because it's cold outside, but she'll make hot chocolate if you ask. She always did for me. I don't know what she does to it, but it's delicious."

They parted on the corner, Eudora downtown toward her house and the phone call she was trying to make to her father, and Maggie uptown to get the family checkbook.

As Maggie walked up to O'Hanlan Millworks, she thought about the story of how her family came to live in Charleston. She'd made her father tell it a million times and she never tired of hearing his side of it, a story filled with the adventure and excitement of new places. One day her father decided that he'd had enough of cold New York winters and he wanted a fresh start. He took a chance on a dreary lumber-yard because he thought it had potential. Fueled with excitement, he sent a certified check for the down payment and received the keys and title by return mail. It was lucky that Maggie's mother shared her husband's love of adventure. She managed the details and within a month, the children were settled in a new house, attending new schools and meeting new friends. Maggie was happy to know that she shared her parents' love of adventure, happier still that they supported her decision to go off on her own after high school graduation.

If only Eudora would agree to go with her. Maggie had a terrible feeling that Eudora's plan for college would end badly. She'd offered to share an apartment in New York City, but Eudora loved Charleston and refused to leave.

Once at the millworks, Maggie climbed the stairs to the offices and found her father sitting behind his desk, up to his elbows in invoices. He didn't enjoy that part of the business, and he made no secret of it. Both Maggie and her mother helped organize when they could, but it was past time to hire a full-time office manager.

"Da, I'm here!" Maggie called out, despite being the only two in the office.

Carl O'Hanlan looked up from his work, the flash of a smile crinkling the corners of his eyes. "I can see that y'are, Maggie-girl." He pushed away from his desk and stood. Maggie leaned into his hug, feeling the sturdiness of his chest and listening to the beat of his heart. He smelled like sawdust and pipe tobacco, and Maggie felt safe from the chaos of the world. She loved her da more than anything in the world.

"So is it time, then?" His voice rumbled in his chest. "You've come for the checkbook, have you?"

"I'm so excited about this, Da," Maggie said as she pushed away.

Her father scoffed as he pulled open the desk drawer. "I know how much the fancy dresses mean to you, Maggie. And I want you to have every good thing. Now come 'round here'll I show you how to write a check."

"Da!" Maggie was indignant. "I'm almost eighteen years old, you think I don't know how to write a check?"

Her father blinked and his bushy eyebrows drew together.

Maggie continued, though she calmed her tone. "Ma taught me how to write a check when I was twelve. I can balance a checkbook, too."

"Is that right?" He brushed his palm across the stubble of

his chin, then offered her the checkbook. "Okay, then."

"Ma said not to spend more than—"

"You spend what you need; let me worry about your ma," Her father declared. "Eudora will know what to get, and both your ma and I trust her judgement."

Maggie turned to leave, but he called her back.

"Maggie, sit for a second, will you?"

"Da, Eudora'll be waiting—"

"This won't take long." Her father sat in his wooden chair and rolled it to his desk, all set for business. "I want to tell you something. You're old enough to hear it, and I think you should. You know your ma and I love Eudora as if she were our own, but she lives in a different world." He rubbed the back of his neck. "Your mother was supposed to be here to talk to you before you left, but she isn't. She always knows the right words to say."

"I'll be fine, Da." Maggie reached for her father's hand. "I know Eudora's life is different, and I don't want that life for myself. I really am just going to Chastains to see a beautifully constructed dress up close. The stitching, the fabric, the details – that's what's important to me. If I want a career in fashion, I should know a thing or two, shouldn't I?"

"You should." Carl practically sagged with relief. "I'm glad to see that you have a good head on your shoulders."

"I'll be fine, Da." Maggie rose to leave.

"Where is Eudora?" Her father reached for a stack of papers. "You could have brought her into the office."

"I'm to meet her at Chastains." Maggie pulled on her gloves. "She said the shopkeeper would offer me hot tea, but I'm supposed to ask for hot chocolate and that it's very posh."

Her father hesitated, his hand on the pages. "Do me a favor, will ya Maggie-girl? Don't go in there without Eudora."

"Da—"

"I mean it." His voice was stern. It was the tone he used with her brothers but rarely used with her.

"Okay, I won't," Maggie agreed. But on her way out, she couldn't resist calling over her shoulder, "I don't see what all the fuss is about. Eudora had nice things to say about Mrs. Tweedy."

Her parents had never really understood her interest in couture.

Maggie had lived in Charleston long enough to know about Chastains, though she'd never shopped there or even gone inside. Her mother's approach to clothing her family had always been very practical. Her brother's clothes were bought all at once, at the beginning of the school year, and were meant to last until June. On the first day of summer vacation, Maggie's mother would take kitchen shears to the boys' pant legs and transform them into summer shorts, which would be expected to last another three months. Maybe because Maggie was a girl, or because she wore a school uniform most of the time, she was spared the brunt of her mother's practicality. She had a 'good dress' for church and a few more for cotillion events, but nothing like the dresses in the window at Chastains.

Almost an hour later, Maggie rounded the corner to Chastains Dress Shop, but Eudora wasn't there. Maggie was a bit annoyed that she'd have to wait outside for her friend. The promise she'd made to her parents seemed silly now. She was a customer, after all, with money to spend. Why couldn't she go in and enjoy a cup of hot chocolate while she waited?

Maggie knew enough not to press her nose against the shop glass like some little kid. Instead, she stood on the sidewalk outside the shop and contented herself with admiring the dresses in the window. The uniformed doorman didn't even look in her direction.

There were four dresses, equally spaced across the length of Chastains display window, each displayed on a mannequin and all of them lit from above. They were all white, with tiny style variations, and they all appeared to be hand-sewn. Maggie would have bet next month's allowance that any one of them cost more than every wedding dress she'd ever seen. Each of the displays were variations of Dior's New Look, three-quarter length, nipped at the waist with a fitted bodice and a full skirt. The first was designed with a light dusting of sequins along the hemline, and the effect under the spotlight was stunning. As Maggie moved in closer to examine the stitching, the light caught the sequins at different angles, making the fabric sparkle like diamonds. The best element of the second dress was a trail of tiny pink organza roses cascading down the dress. They started at the shoulder then crossed the bodice before falling elegantly down the skirt to the hem. She'd seen that design before, in the fall issue of a magazine, and it was wonderful to see such a thing up close.

But it was the third dress that made Maggie ache to go inside the shop for a closer look.

The dress itself was quite plain, with a round neck and tucked waistline. The fabric was a sturdy dupioni silk, delicate cream and seamed with practically invisible stitches. The detail that made the dress mesmerizing was the woven silver capelet draped around the shoulders. The capelet itself was short, attached to the dress at the shoulders and falling to the waist; any longer and it would have overwhelmed the dress. The material was too thick for an ordinary hook-and-eye closure and there didn't seem to be anything else to draw it closed – no ribbon, no tie, nothing. It was puzzling.

Maggie stepped back and considered her next move. She'd been standing outside the shop for a while now. Eudora still hadn't arrived, and the wind *did* seem to be picking up a little bit. Surely her parents would not expect her to continue to wait outside in the cold.

The bell overhead tinkled delicately as Maggie pushed open the door and crossed the threshold. Inside was even more elegant than Maggie could imagine. She wanted to remember everything so she could recreate something as memorable inside her own shop someday. She closed the door behind her, crossed the marble-floored entrance and descended two steps to the sales floor. The air smelled of old money and privilege, and she allowed herself to imagine what it would feel like to be part of such a world.

Her footsteps were muffled as she crossed the carpeted floor to the reception desk. Surely the clerk could tell her the secret of the dress's capelet. It wouldn't hurt to ask, anyway. She passed an assortment of summer dresses displayed under a sign that read "Resort Wear," Just beyond that was the largest selection of tweed suits Maggie had ever seen. They appeared to be variations on the same theme, with similar fabric, neckline, and length. It struck Maggie as a bit odd; a selection of plain suits in a shop with those dresses in the window.

"May I help you?" A thin, smartly-dressed woman appeared from behind a curtained office. She wore a black sheath dress, set off with a crisp white Peter Pan collar and wide French cuffs. Her only jewelry was a delicate pair of pearl earrings and a gold watch around her wrist. The whole effect was classically understated. And with her hair swept away from her face and fresh red lipstick, she reminded Maggie of a younger Wallis Simpson.

This was a woman who appreciated fashion.

"You must be Mrs. Tweedy."

"I am." The woman's voice was cool. "How may I help you?"

"I'm Eudora's friend. From school. Your dresses are beautiful." Maggie heard herself gush and she cringed. She sounded like a child, and it was exactly the wrong impression.

"Are you picking up something for the Gadsden family?" The woman's gaze cut to Maggie's shoes, then back up to her face.

"No, I'm not. I'm here to—" Maggie began as she felt her face flame.

The bell on the top of the shop door interrupted them.

Posey Chalmers and her mother swept into the shop on a gust of wind. Mrs. Tweedy excused herself to greet them, offering an embrace and a kiss on both cheeks. They murmured greetings as they shed their heavy winter coats and Mrs. Tweedy signaled for an assistant. The assistant, a young woman just a year or two older than Maggie herself, was dressed in a simple black sheath dress but without the white collar and French cuffs. She collected their coats and offered tea.

"Not today, thank you," Mrs. Chalmers replied airily as she smoothed her hair. "We've only come to pick up a few last-minute things. Baxter is waiting in the car."

As their conversation quieted, Maggie stood in the middle of the shop, not understanding what happened and unsure of what to do. Should she go back outside and wait? If she did that, she'd have to cross the shop floor and Posey would see her. Should she tell Eudora she didn't want a dress from Chastains after all? If she did, what reason would she give?

She decided to leave, without saying hello to Posey or her mother and without saying good-bye to Mrs. Tweedy. It was rude to do so, but she didn't know what else to do. Clearly she wasn't sophisticated enough for a high-end shop. If she couldn't navigate her way around a small dress shop in Charleston, what hope did she have of working at Dior or Schiaparelli, or even Bergdorf Goodman in New York City?

As Maggie turned to leave, she saw Eudora outside the front door. She was smiling, her cheeks pink from the cold. She'd paused to talk to the doorman, the same man who had decided that Maggie could open the door for herself. He reached for the door and opened it. The breeze carried a fragment of their conversation into the shop.

"Thank you, Gus. Please tell Mrs. Alberts I said hello."

"I surely will." The man touched the brim of his hat as Eudora moved though the entrance.

"I'm sorry I'm late. I had to wait forever for mother to leave and when I finally called the hotel, Daddy had already left the hotel. I left a detailed message with the front desk, and it took longer than I thought it would." She unwound her scarf and handed it to the assistant who had appeared the moment Eudora entered the shop. She touched the back of her hair, then glanced at Maggie. "Don't you want to take your coat off?"

Maggie had been ready to leave. The sick feeling in the pit of her stomach was still there. Whether she had the money or not, it was obvious that she wasn't the kind of girl who shopped in a place like this.

"Miss Gadsden, how wonderful to see you again." Mrs. Tweedy glided toward them, her face wreathed in a welcoming smile.

"Hello, Mrs. Tweedy. I'm sure you've met my friend

Maggie?" Turning to Maggie, Eudora asked, "You haven't started shopping without me, have you?"

"No, I haven't," Maggie said, though she wasn't able to meet Eudora's eye.

There was a pause in the conversation before Eudora spoke again. "We just need a few moments, Mrs. Tweedy."

Maggie looked up in time to see a flicker of concern cross Mrs. Tweedy's face, then disappear.

"Of course," she said as she pressed her palms together. "I'll just finish helping Mrs. and Miss Chalmers."

"Posey's here?" Eudora said, as she tucked her gloves into her purse. "We'll have to say hello."

The moment Mrs. Tweedy left, Eudora turned to Maggie and hissed. "What happened?"

Maggie tried to shake it off. "Nothing. It's nothing."

"*Something* did," Eudora insisted. "I bet you came in the shop and ol' Tweedy Bird was snappy." She snorted as she snapped her purse shut. "That woman is the biggest snob I've ever met. The more important you are, the nicer she is. She hates everyone else."

"I think we should go."

"What?" Eudora tilted her head and frowned in genuine puzzlement. "Why would we do that?"

"Because I changed my mind. I don't want to buy a dress here." Maggie pressed her lips together as she held back a swelling of emotion. "Wearing it will only be a reminder of how much I don't belong."

Eudora's expression turned to stone as her gaze cut to the shop woman's. "What did she do? Tell me exactly what she said."

"It doesn't matter. I was crazy to think I could—"

Maggie allowed herself to be led to a pair of white upholstered chairs in an alcove of the shop, because she didn't know what else to do. As they crossed the floor, Maggie watched Mrs. Tweedy track their progress.

∾

Eudora led Maggie across the sales floor to a pair of white upholstered chairs in an alcove of the shop. Eudora was careful to maintain a debutante smile, though inside she fumed at the way Maggie had been treated. Someone should have taken Maggie's coat and offered her something hot to drink.

The alcove Eudora chose was the place where women serious about shopping selected their dresses. When Eudora shopped with her mother, they were led across the shop to the alcove as a matter of course. Once seated, they sipped coffee from delicate cups as Mrs. Tweedy offered a selection of outfits, complete with shoes and accessories, for their approval. In fact, Eudora hadn't shopped for a dress from the sales floor since she was ten years old.

"Good morning, Miss Gadsden." It was the shop assistant who greeted them.

"Hello, Martha." Eudora noticed the young woman hadn't yet earned the white cuffs on her dress that would mark her a junior saleswoman. "Take Maggie's coat, please, and hang it with mine."

"Of course," Martha answered. "May I bring you some coffee?"

"No." Eudora shook her head. "Not coffee, thank you. We would like a pot of hot chocolate instead. And maybe a plate of raspberry shortbread cookies. Does Mrs. Tweedy still keep them on hand?"

Martha's eyes twinkled, though her expression didn't waver. "Yes ma'am, she does. I'd be happy to get them for you."

As soon as Martha disappeared behind the curtain, Eudora leaned toward her friend and whispered, "Tweedy Bird specially orders raspberry shortbread cookies from the Italian bakery on Water Street. They're supposed to be for customers, but she never offers them with tea or chocolate. I think she buys them for the shop then takes them home to eat herself."

Maggie's smile was forced. "I know what you're trying to do, and I appreciate it, Eudora. I really do. But I think we should leave."

"We're not leaving." Eudora lowered her voice. "This is a game, Maggie, and you're not playing it right. I don't know what Tweedy Bird did to you before I got here, but I can guess. If you leave now, all you're saying is that you agree with her assessment of you. That you don't belong here. Is that what you want?"

Maggie shook her head.

"Of course not." Eudora laid her hand on Maggie's arm. "And while we wait for our hot chocolate, you should consider the facts. First, you can't find the kind of dress you described from a department store, certainly not from any department store around here. Second – and this is the big one: if you plan to design couture you'll need to know what customers expect. Shopping for couture is an experience, and Chastains is a good place to learn."

Maggie nodded, with more conviction this time. "Maybe you're right."

"Of course I'm right." Eudora raised her chin. "Now sit up straight and act like you belong here."

Maggie snorted just as Martha returned with a tray of hot chocolate and cookies. The scent of warm chocolate and fresh shortbread filled the room as Martha arranged the service on the side table. Two demitasse cups upon squares of lace and tiny silver spoons laid upon the saucer. A tiny silver pitcher filled with chilled cream was placed near the pot and a silver plate in the center of the tray was piled with raspberry cookies.

"This looks delicious, Martha. Thank you."

As Martha poured, Eudora stole a glance at her friend. Maggie had straightened in her seat, her attention on the service in front of her. She looked as if she were memorizing every detail, and that was a good thing.

Encouraged, Eudora pushed a bit further. "Martha, I wonder if you might help us with something else?"

"If I can." Martha's gaze flicked to Mrs. Tweedy, chatting with Posey Chalmers and her mother, then back to Eudora. Eudora felt sure they shared the same thought: if Eudora's mother had been present, Mrs. Tweedy would have been much more attentive.

"My friend Maggie is looking for something suitable for afternoon tea. I wonder if you had any suggestions?" For a moment, Martha looked uncertain, so Eudora added, "It's just that Mrs. Tweedy seems busy with another customer."

Martha glanced back at the shop floor. "I'd be happy to help." She turned to Maggie. "What kind of outfit are you looking for?"

And that was all it took. For the next twenty minutes, Eudora watched her friend chat with Martha about the kind of dress she'd hoped to find. Maggie came to life as she described new trends for fall and the cut and fabrics most appropriate for a debutante tea. By the time Eudora helped herself to a third cookie, they'd decided. Martha knew the shape and color Maggie preferred, her measurements, and shoe size. She disappeared into the back room with a promise to return quickly. Eudora raised the napkin delicately to her lips. "That wasn't so bad, was it?" Without waiting for an answer, she folded her napkin and tucked it under the saucer. "One more thing before Martha comes back."

Maggie had been reaching to pour herself another cup of chocolate. She paused. "What's that?"

"We need to go out there and say hello to Mrs. Chalmers and Posey."

Maggie sagged. "You don't even like Posey. You never talk to her at school."

"You're right, I don't. But that's school." Eudora smoothed the wrinkles from her skirt. "Out here, I have to say hello." She waited until Maggie stood. "It's all part of the game, Maggie. You don't have to like it, but you should understand the rules."

Eudora led Maggie from the alcove back into the main shop, to a new display of evening wear.

Mrs. Tweedy held a sequined cocktail dress aloft with one hand while Posey and her mother looked on. "I can assure you, no one else will be wearing this dress – or anything like it – at the fundraiser."

"I don't know," Mrs. Chalmers demurred, tapping a perfectly manicured finger against her chin as she considered. "The black is nice, but Wallace prefers me to wear navy."

Mrs. Chalmers' face brightened as Eudora and Maggie approached. "Eudora, dear. What a lovely surprise. I didn't know you were here."

But of course she knew. They both did.

Eudora had known the Chalmers family all her life. Caroline Gadsden and Sissy Chalmers had been sorority sisters in college and bridesmaids in each other's weddings. Eudora and Posey had been born the same year, baptized the same week, and were enrolled in the same grade at Santee Academy. When Eudora and Posey were infants, it was convenient for their mothers to allow the girls to play together while they retreated downstairs for coffee and cigarettes. It was a practice the families upheld much longer than they should have, and both girls grew to resent being thrown together.

It was true that Posey was conventionally pretty with blonde hair that hung in soft curls to her shoulders and clear blue eyes that she brushed with mascara and swept with kohl for a perfect cat-eye, but there was nothing more to her than that. No spark. No personality. Not an original thought in her head. Posey obeyed her mother, worshiped her father, and was the envy of every parent whose daughter dared to develop a mind of her own. Posey did moderately well in school because her teachers liked her, and she would do well after graduation because her mother would clear the path for her.

But there was one truth about Posey that was inescapable: Posey Chalmers was popular simply because her parents had money. A lot of it. It was well-known among eligible Charleston boys that upon his only daughter's marriage, Wallace Chalmers would invite his new son-in-law to join his Broad Street law firm and would gift the newlyweds with whatever house Posey and her mother chose. Three children would follow in due time, as would committee membership for Posey and promotions for her husband.

But to Eudora, that future seemed bleak. Never to have an unexpected adventure or forge a path of her own. A life like that seemed suffocating. Which, Eudora supposed, was the reason she'd always tried to be kind to Posey Chalmers.

Posey's mother, however, was a different story altogether. Sissy Chalmers was mean.

In one languid movement, Mrs. Chalmers brought her fingertips to the base of her throat as Eudora and Maggie approached. "Eudora, dear, is your mother with you?" Her gaze swept the shop. "I played bridge with her just the other day and she didn't mention she was coming here today. We could have organized schedules if I'd known."

"No ma'am, she isn't," Eudora answered. "I'm here with my friend Maggie O'Hanlan. I'm sure you remember her. Her father owns O'Hanlan Millworks and her mother chaired the book drive for the public library last year."

Mrs. Chalmers knit her brows together in a feigned moment of uncertainty. It was an act, of course. A deliberate snub to someone Mrs. Chalmers believed unworthy of memory.

Though Eudora's smile didn't waver, she felt her jaw tighten. "Oh, I'm sure you remember. Mr. O'Hanlan *donated* all the building supplies for the music wing at Santee several years ago. I believe you chaired the fund drive?"

"She's in our class at Santee, Mama," Posey added, though she didn't need to.

"Oh, of course. How nice to see you again." Mrs. Chalmers placed her fingertips lightly on the base of her throat, touching the double strand of matched pearls that she never seemed to be without. "And will you be debuting with our girls at Hibernian Hall next month, Maggie?" Mrs. Chalmers smiled, her red-lipsticked mouth stretched across her teeth as she waited for an answer.

It was an obvious attempt to remind Maggie of her place.

It was exhausting, the endless positioning and keeping track of every slight and gesture, and Eudora had no interest in it. But she would meet the jab with kindness and hope Annie would be pleased.

"Actually," Eudora said, "we're here for a few last-minute things before your tea next week. We just stopped by to visit for a minute." Eudora directed her attention to Posey, who Eudora was sure did not understand any of the exchange. "I'll see you tomorrow at school, Posey."

"I'll be with you girls in a moment, Eudora," Mrs. Tweedy offered.

"No need to, Mrs. Tweedy," Eudora said smoothly. "We've asked Martha to help, and she's doing a wonderful job."

Mrs. Tweedy pursed her lips together in a thin smile. "Please give your mother my best."

"Of course, Mrs. Tweedy," Eudora assured her. "I'll tell her everything."

In the end, she and Maggie spent the next two hours looking at afternoon tea dresses and discussing the merits of each. It turned out that Martha had a surprisingly fresh eye for fashion and knew right away what shapes and colors would look best on Maggie. In fact, she had a few unexpected suggestions for Eudora too.

As Martha wrapped the boxes in signature Chastains green grosgrain ribbon, Mrs. Tweedy appeared once again.

And though it was catty, Eudora could not resist. "Martha, thank you again for all your help. I didn't expect to buy anything and here I am leaving with two dresses of my own. I'll surely be asking for you next time I come in."

CHAPTER 7

As they did every year, Eudora's maternal grandparents invited Eudora and her parents to spend Thanksgiving at the horse farm in Aiken. Usually her mother declined without explanation, but this year, with Eudora's father still away on business, her mother accepted. Also without explanation.

Eudora looked forward to the freedom the farm would allow. She'd planned to study Jackson's textbook in the evenings, but that still left whole days away from her mother's watchful eye.

They arrived the day before Thanksgiving and Eudora spent that time in the stables, exercising the horses and helping her grandfather with the mares. As far as Eudora could tell, her mother and Aunt Evelyn spent their time huddled in the kitchen, smoking cigarettes and avoiding both their parents. Then, early Thanksgiving Day, her mother called Carter to bring the car around and all of them left the farm before dinner. Eudora and her mother spent Thanksgiving in Columbia, with Aunt Evelyn, having cold cheese sandwiches and grape soda for dinner because the staff had gone home to their own families. Eudora and her mother left for Charleston early the next day.

No explanation was given, and Eudora didn't expect one.

Now they were home.

"Annie, we're back!" Eudora opened the front door and called into the house as Carter saw to the luggage.

"Eudora, please stop shouting. You must know Annie's not returned yet." Her mother pressed her fingertips to her temples. She hadn't taken her sunglasses off or spoken a word during the entire drive back from Columbia.

"Sorry, Mother." Eudora's reply was automatic as she shed her coat and hung it in the foyer closet.

"Somebody should have seen to the mail while we were gone." Her mother nudged a scattering of envelopes that had been delivered through the mail slot.

Eudora's gasped softly as she recognized the Charleston College seal on one of the envelopes. The letter had come already.

"What is it?" Her mother frowned.

"Nothing, Mother." Eudora gathered the envelopes from the floor and slipped them under her arm. "I'll take care of them. Why don't you go upstairs and rest? I'll bring you a cup of hot tea and a sleeve of Goody's powders."

But her mother hesitated. "I'm sure some of those envelopes are invitations that require responses. The Chalmers' tea is Thursday and after that the Season starts."

"I'll bring them up with your tea."

Her mother slipped off her coat and slid the scarf from her head. She handed them both to Eudora. "That might be better. I do have a crippling headache. Let me deal with Carter first—"

"I can do that, too."

Her mother sagged with a relief so genuine that Eudora almost felt sorry for her. Almost, but not quite. After all, it was her mother who cut their trip to Aiken short and refused explanation, as if Eudora was a child. They drove to Aunt Evelyn's home in Columbia, then ten hours later drove home. Eudora had spent her entire Thanksgiving weekend in the car next to a woman who refused to speak.

After her mother headed up the stairs to cloister herself in her room, Eudora dismissed Carter. "We won't need you again today. You missed Thanksgiving dinner with your family. You should go home to see them."

"Thank you, Miss Eudora."

Eudora thought again about the way her mother had insisted Carter drive them all the way to Aiken and then remain in the staff quarters above the stables until Caroline decided it was time to leave. He didn't expect to spend Thanksgiving away from his family but he was forced to for no reason other than Caroline wanted it that way.

"In fact," Eudora amended. "Take tomorrow as well. And the day after." And because Carter seemed uncertain, she added, "You've certainly earned the time away, and I'm sure Mother would approve."

In the end, it wouldn't matter that Carter was sent home because Caroline Gadsden would not venture from her room until Annie arrived the following afternoon. Annie would spend the whole day preparing whatever food she thought Eudora's mother might like to nibble on. Annie would have carefully prepared trays sent to Caroline's room only to have every one of them rejected. Her mother would emerge from her room when she was tired of pouting and then things would return to normal.

"There are things about your mama you don't know,"

Annie had told her once, during the one time her mother had locked herself in her room for almost a week. But Annie had refused to explain further. She said it wasn't her place to tell.

Now, her mother's cloister worked in Eudora's favor. With Carter gone and her mother in her room, Eudora had the house to herself. She started with the mail, delivering almost all of it to her father's office. She walked to the kitchen as she flipped through the rest, mostly invitations from other debutante families. Those would go on her mother's tray.

That left the letter from Charleston College.

She filled the kettle and set it on the stove to boil, then turned her attention back to the college letter, trying to decide whether to open it. Although she had expected Mr. Hendricks letter around this time, she didn't know what the contents of this particular letter was. If it was simply a form letter, a donation request, Eudora could throw the letter away and her father would never know.

But.

There was still the matter of the calculus final exam: Eudora still didn't have the details. What if this letter contained the time and place for Euodra's test? If Eudora put that kind of letter on her father's desk, he would know she'd applied to Charleston College and might forbid her attending. No, it was better to approach her father with a *fait accompli*, her acceptance to college as a demonstration of her initiative.

The kettle tapped as the water inside simmered and a puff of steam rose from the spout.

Eudora smiled as the idea formed. The perfect solution.

It was surprisingly easy to steam open the flap. The moisture warped the paper, but that could be put right with a warm iron.

The letter was personal correspondence from Mr. Hendricks, so Eudora could not throw it away. He opened by saying that he hoped the Gadsden family had enjoyed a nice Thanksgiving holiday and ended with asking if he could call upon Mr. Gadsden in the coming week. Said he'd welcome a chance to describe the college's upcoming expansion plans, and he ended by extending a personal welcome to the Alumni Auction. The postscript said that he'd have his secretary telephone the Gadsden business offices on Tuesday to follow up.

Eudora held the letter to her chest as she imagined the chaos Mr. Hendricks' letter would cause. Her one saving grace was that her father really had been detained with a client in Philadelphia. Even Eudora hadn't been able to speak with him, so there was no chance that his secretary would bother him about a letter from Charleston College.

That bought her time.

Unless Mr. Hendricks insisted on leaving a message when he telephoned. Myra was diligent about delivering all telephone messages. If that happened, her father would want an explanation. And the only explanation was that Eudora may have stretched the truth a little during her interview with Mr. Hendricks.

She told Mr. Hendricks her father planned to attend the Alumni Auction. The truth was that her father knew nothing about the auction.

She said Edward Gadsden fully supported Eudora's intention to go to college. The truth was that he knew nothing about Eudora's intention to apply.

She promised her father would write a letter of recommendation to the Admissions Office on her behalf. Of course he wouldn't.

A twist of nervous energy sent Eudora up the stairs to her mother's room, the tea tray in hand. As she climbed the stairs, it occurred to her that all she really needed was time. Surely her father would understand her desire to work for the family company if she explained it to him, but she needed to get to him first. To face him as she talked.

The best way to do that was to send Mr. Hendricks the recommendation letter he'd asked for.

Only it wouldn't be written by her father. It would be written by Eudora, in her father's name.

The house was quiet when Eudora opened her bedroom door. She poked her head out of her room and peered down the hallway. Her mother's room was dark, the tea tray left untouched beside her door. Eudora moved toward the stairs, feeling the carpet give beneath her bare feet and the notebook paper flutter in her hand.

She would not get another chance.

Annie was expected to return tomorrow afternoon and there wasn't a thing that went on in the Gadsden home that she didn't know about. Eudora wasn't sure that Annie would approve of what she was about to do, so whatever she did had to be done tonight. Padding down the stairs and through the foyer, Eudora stood outside her father's office. As she reached for the doorknob, her heart began to thump in her chest.

Once she had her acceptance letter in hand, this part of her story would become a footnote, a silly detail hardly worth mentioning. She'd explain later, if she needed to, how she came to write this letter, and her father would appreciate her initiative.

Eudora entered her father's office, carefully closing the door behind her. A pair of bookcases flanked her father's desk at the far end of the room. The books on display were mostly first editions, a gift from a grateful rice planter whose fall crop her father had saved years ago. Her father's desk, an imposing piece of hand-carved oak, had been in the Gadsden family for generations and was one of the few things that survived the war. Eudora navigated the office, guided by a shaft of pale light cast from the streetlamp outside. As she rolled out her father's chair and sat down, she surveyed the contents of his desktop, his pipe in the ashtray, a scattering of spent tobacco leaves in the glass, handwritten notes tucked into the corner of his blotter, his calendar opened to the day he left.

The typewriter was kept on a side table, hidden from view and rarely used. Eudora slipped off the dust cover and dropped it to the floor. The letter itself would be short, just two paragraphs. The first thanked Mr. Hendricks for his time and his interest in Eudora, adding his personal guarantee that she would be an asset to the business college. The second paragraph was just a bit harder because Eudora had to be careful with the wording. Though she'd implied that her father was looking forward to both the Alumni Auction and the college's building projects, she didn't actually know the details. After several attempts, Eudora made vague promises of donations to both the Building Fund and attendance at the Alumni Auction in the spring. Contingent, of course, on Eudora's acceptance to Charleston College in the fall.

She withdrew a sheet of her father's stationery and slipped it into the typewriter.

Using her father's fountain pen, she reproduced his signature exactly, a talent she'd developed by signing his name to countless business letters she'd written on his behalf over the years.

Finally, she addressed the envelope and sealed the flap. She'd deliver it to the post office tomorrow and with a dusting of luck, it would be on Mr. Hendricks' desk the day after.

Replacing the dust cover, Eudora rose from the desk and rolled the chair back in place.

Then returned to her room, satisfied with a job well done.

CHAPTER 8

"WE SHOULD TO TAKE A BREAK, EUDORA." Jackson Legare pushed his hands toward the ceiling and stretched. Six feet tall, with an athletic build and a rower's confidence, he was considered quite a catch among girls in their social circle and had been the subject of more than a few cat fights. Add that to his enviable pedigree, stretching as far back as the Chalmers', and it was no wonder that Jackson had caught the attention of every matron on the peninsula.

Eudora and Jackson had been friends ever since their mothers promised to pair them for Miss Emily's cotillion classes when they were still toddlers. After a lifetime of friendship, they knew everything about each other and kept each other's secrets. Eudora told Jackson about her frustration with Charleston Society and her mother's attempt to force Eudora into it. She'd talked to him about her hopes for joining her father's company, the college degree she needed, and the fears she wouldn't be admitted. It was Jackson who suggested they meet for private tutoring, citing the limitations of Santee's curriculum. And they had, at a corner table at Reed's drugstore, for an hour, every week, for the past six months. For her part, Eudora recognized the pressure he was under, as the only son of a prominent family, to marry well and have children. As they approached the Season, she saw the burden was almost too much for Jackson to bear. She'd known for years that he preferred the company of men to the company of women, but she'd just begun to understand the repercussions of that choice, repercussions that she suspected he'd known all along.

"Are you sure?" Eudora flipped from the chapter test to the answer key in the back of the textbook. "I think we should go over this part one more time. The final is Thursday."

"I'm sure." Jackson slipped his hand underneath the cover of her book and flipped it closed. His gold signet ring glinted in the sunlight. "You'll be fine."

"I need to be better than 'fine,' Jackson." Eudora frowned. "Do you realize that in a few days I'll be sitting for a Calculus final exam?"

"I do."

"And the other boys – in that very same class – will be taking a midterm?"

"I know."

"They created a special test just for me, Jackson, with material from this entire book." She fumed. "They *want* me to fail."

"Of course they do." Jackson crossed his arms over his chest. "Your application has created quite the problem for them. Your father is a distinguished alumnus and they can't risk upsetting him. Their only way out is to give you a test and hope you fail." He reached for a sugar packet and tapped it against the table's surface. "You can count on that test being hard because if you fail, they can say you're unprepared, and they will have protected their business school from invasion for another year."

The waitress came to refill their tea glasses. The ice cracked as she poured the freshly brewed tea from her pitcher. "Can I get you anything else?"

"Thank you, I think we're finished." Jackson reached for his wallet and pulled out a few bills.

When they first decided to meet at Reed's, Eudora tried to pay. After all, it was Jackson who was doing her a favor. But he refused, saying he was happy for people to think they were dating.

The waitress attempted to make change for him, but Jackson smiled and waved her away.

"But you'll be fine," he repeated. "You're a tough girl, Eudora, and you're not afraid to learn new things."

For the briefest second, Eudora allowed herself to relax. If Jackson said she was prepared, it must be true; there was no one better to judge education than Jackson Legare. When Jackson was born, his father, Emmerson Legare III, laid out his son's career and had been directing his life toward that end ever since. The elder Legare hired the best tutors to guide his son's education, enrolled Jackson in sports teams to demonstrate his ability to lead, and finally, had sponsored membership to socially advantageous clubs. In all of his eighteen years, Jackson Legare barely had a moment to himself. But it worked. His entrance to any college his father chose was all but guaranteed. Furthermore, his son had proved so capable that the elder Legare intended Jackson to join his law firm, opening a second office in Columbia after graduating from law school there.

To Eudora's knowledge, Jackson had never been asked what he wanted, and that made the two of them equal.

Still, a tendril of doubt touched Eudora's spine, making her shiver. "What makes you so sure?" she pressed. "*I'm* not even sure I'm going to pass, and the thought of failing keeps me up at night."

"Because I know you. You always know what you want, and you're not afraid to work hard to get it." His eyes twinkled as his smile widened, and Eudora felt the knot of tension loosen. She knew what was coming; it was a story he told often. "Third grade kickball," he declared, as if he'd summed up Eudora's entire life with one phrase.

"I was nine years old, Jackson." Even though Eudora rolled her eyes, she appreciated the story because it gave her courage. "Why do you still bring that up?"

He ignored her and started the story. "A regular Saturday morning and a bunch of us boys are playing kickball in Mr. Parson's field – which we think is hidden from view, by the way. Up walks this bratty little girl, dressed in rolled dungarees and an old sweatshirt."

"I was not bratty." Eudora interrupted at the same point that she always did. "You always say bratty."

"What else would you call it?" Jackson shrugged. "I can still picture the ball you brought to the game: brand new with a perfect bounce. But you had the nerve to tell us that we could only use it if we let you play. The ball we had was lopsided because it had been taped so much. For the life of me, I don't remember why we never bought a new one. Every half hour we had to stop the game just to pump air into the ball." He shifted his position, pushing back against the red vinyl of the booth. "I always meant to ask: how did you know we needed a new ball?"

"I watched you," Eudora replied, as if the answer was obvious. "Mother slept late on Saturday mornings, and Annie didn't care if I went out as long as I was back before noon. I'd been watching your games for weeks and I knew you wouldn't let me play unless I had something to offer. It took a month's allowance to buy that ball, but it was worth it."

"That's how I know you'll be okay." Jackson reached toward the plate of fries in the center of the table, selected one from the top and swirled it in ketchup. "It's been a while, but I've meant to ask: have you heard anything from the college?"

"Just details about the final exam," Eudora lied. "It's on Thursday morning."

"Isn't that the day of Posey's tea?" He popped the fry into his mouth.

"My test is in the morning. Tea's in the afternoon." Eudora closed the cover of the textbook Jackson had loaned her and slipped it into her bag. "How do you know about Posey's tea?"

He raised his tea glass in a mock toast. "First tea of the Season. I know all about it."

Eudora narrowed her eyes. "Posey's mother asked you to be her escort again, didn't she?"

"Not directly. That would be terribly rude." He smirked. "But she did ask my mother if I'd consider being Posey's escort for the other cities. The ones you're not going to."

Ever since she was little, Eudora had known that she would make her debut into Society at the St. Cecilia Ball at Hibernian Hall, after Christmas. Her father was a member of the Society and her mother made her debut there. A few of the girls who debuted there also ventured beyond Charleston to Assembly Balls held in cities spread across South Carolina: Columbia, Greenville, Orangeburg, and Florence. Posey was one of them.

"What did she say?"

He shrugged. "I wasn't told. But if things work out the way I want them to, it won't matter anyway."

"Did your parents agree to let you go to Europe?"

One of the benefits of years of boarding school and private tutoring was that Jackson was able to skip classes if he worked hard. To motivate him, his parents promised him a reward of his choice if he continued with his tutoring over the summers. He accepted the challenge, studied hard, and had graduated high school six months early. For his reward, he'd asked for a trip to Europe.

Jackson had wanted to be a novelist for as long as Eudora had known him. He wanted the freedom to travel and write, to go wherever inspiration took him and to be alone with his thoughts. Since he had six months before he had to report to his college dorm in Columbia, he asked for six months away. His parents flatly refused, saying no good would come of so much unstructured time. So Jackson changed his request from six months to three, asking for time in London and Paris to visit museums and art galleries. He wanted to start his trip in January, when his duty as her chaperone to Society events would be over.

"After much deliberation, the decision's been made." He twisted the signet ring on his finger. "Actually, my father decided and my mother went along with it, as usual."

"What did they say?"

"They said 'No' and that was the end of it." His expression turned sour. "And they didn't appreciate it when I told them they'd broken their promise. I've been instructed to report to Emmerson's office in February to 'learn the ropes,' as it were. I'll be working there until I leave for college at the end of the summer."

"But they promised." Eudora was stunned. "Didn't you tell them you needed a break?"

"I did." Jackson pressed his hands together. "To make the pill easier to swallow, they've allowed me three weeks in Europe – with a chaperone and an itinerary."

"I'm so sorry." Eudora tried to meet his eye but he kept his gaze averted. "I know that's not what you wanted."

"But it's what Emmerson wants, and Emmerson always gets what he wants." He shrugged and slid from the booth. "Doesn't matter. My path's been set, just as yours has."

Eudora reached for his arm. "What if you talked—"

"Talked to who, Eudora? My father?" Jackson's voice was unexpectedly bitter. "You must know that I can't talk to my father any more than you can talk to your mother."

"What do you mean?"

He pointed to the table where they'd been studying. "You have this big elaborate plan to enroll in college behind your parents' back. Did *you* ever consider talking to your parents to tell them you want a career? Don't tell me if you're not willing to do the same thing."

"That's impossible," Eudora sputtered, seeing the reason in his argument but not wanting to face it. "You know what Caroline's like. It's my father who'll be on my side when the time comes."

Jackson reached for his scarf and wound it around his neck.

It twisted in the back and Eudora reached to straighten it. "You're right. I'm sorry. The thing is, I want both. I want to cross the stage at Hibernian Hall. It's a great honor, and all the women in my family have done it. I just want to be allowed to choose what comes after."

CHAPTER 9

EUDORA POUNDED up the back stairs on her way to the kitchen, her book bag thumping against her hip as she ran. The Calculus test had taken longer than she'd anticipated, peppered with instructions and breaks she didn't expect. But it was over and she was home now. And while Annie would certainly not approve of Eudora running through the kitchen, she wouldn't fuss. And Eudora's mother was almost certainly at the beauty parlor or upstairs in the bath, so Annie might even allow Eudora a snack to bring to her room as she got ready for the tea. She'd been too nervous to eat this morning before she left.

Without thinking, Eudora pushed the back door open and let it slam behind her. "Annie?"

"Eudora?" Her mother called from somewhere near the foyer. "Is that you?"

"Yes, Mother." Eudora dropped her bookbag to the floor and kicked it under the table.

"Where have you been?" Her mother's voice grew louder as she approached the kitchen.

Eudora pulled a scarf from the pocket of her coat and

wrapped it around her head, tying it under her chin as her mother entered the room. She fabricated a lie from the first thing that came to her mind, the beauty parlor. "I realized I hadn't made an appointment to get my hair done before the party today, so I went to the salon early hoping they could fit me in."

"Honestly, Eudora." Her mother sighed as she brought the tips of her fingers to her temple. "Why didn't you let me book your appointment eight weeks ago, when I scheduled mine? I told you then how busy the salon would be."

The truth was that Eudora didn't know the time or the room number for her test eight weeks ago so she couldn't have scheduled anything. But she couldn't tell her mother that. Better for her mother to think she was absent-minded.

"How bad is it?" Her mother reached for a corner of Eudora's scarf. "Maybe I can call the salon personally."

Eudora clamped her hand to her head but it was too late.

"Eudora," Her mother dropped the fabric and stepped back. Her face flushed with anger. "Your hair is a fright, and is that perspiration on your forehead? Eudora Grace Gadsden, the Chalmers party is in less than three hours. What on earth are you thinking?"

"Nothing, Mother." Eudora backed away. She didn't dare pick up her books as she retreated. "It won't take me any time at all to get ready, you'll see."

"You'd better be, young lady," her mother warned. "You'd better be."

"Shall I park, ma'am?" The Gadsden family driver, Carter, glanced at Eudora and her mother through the rearview.

"I think you'd better." Eudora's mother frowned as she turned in her seat to look out the car window. "On a day like this, one would think that Sissy, of all people, would know to provide valets, but I don't see anyone."

Overnight, a cold, misty rain had rolled down from the midlands, and a wintery mix of sleet and rain had begun just after mid-day. Eudora suspected her mother was annoyed because the weather would ruin her entrance.

"Pull up to the front of the house, Carter. I suppose we'll have to walk the rest of the way."

Had this been any other Society party in any other Charleston home, the weather would not have been an issue. Most homes in Charleston had been built close to the street, and it would have taken just a moment to cross the sidewalk to the front entrance. But the Chalmers home was different from all the others. When Wallace Chalmers emigrated in 1650, he was flush with family money, so he had the means to settle anywhere he wanted. But it was his wife's family who had funded their marriage, and it was his wife who took it upon herself to design the family home.

Margaret Chalmers came from money; her husband did not.

While her husband busied himself with commerce in the shipping offices, Margaret went about making a home for her family. And she started with a parcel of land. When Charleston was new, it was accepted practice for merchants to buy and build on a narrow wedge of land to be near the waterfront. Margaret rejected the waterfront, the noise, the smell, the chaos, choose instead a large parcel of land in the upper part of the peninsula. Her selection was not well received. Wallace predicted that living that far from town would destroy his business; her new friends warned they would never be allowed to visit.

She ignored them all and proceeded to design the house and gardens herself, though she allowed her husband to claim full credit in the end.

Hiring architects whose aesthetics aligned with hers, and who did not mind working with a woman, she set to work. In a city where houses tended to be tucked into narrow parcels, the Chalmers home, like the Gadsden home, was one of the very few in Charleston that faced the street, with a wide expanse of lawn separating the two. The main house was three stories, crafted from sturdy brick, with a dramatic two-columned entrance. Upper and lower piazzas spanned the length of the house and overlooked the formal gardens, a thing unheard of at the time. The largest of three formal gardens was placed in the front of the house, and it was the location of the gardens that annoyed Caroline's mother on the afternoon of the tea.

As the Gadsden car pulled to the curb in front of the Chalmers' home, her mother's frown deepened. She smoothed a curl that had been tucked behind her ear and Eudora knew what she was thinking – that the mist would ruin her hair and the rain would splatter the suede on her pumps. "Carter keeps umbrellas in the trunk, Mother," Eudora ventured. "I'm sure—"

"Never mind, Eudora."

Carter pointed to the gate house. "Look like someone's coming."

Two young men dressed in crisp white shirts and dark pants met the car, snapping open umbrellas as they opened the curb-side door.

"What a clever solution." Her mother's expression had

changed, reminding Eudora of the sun emerging from behind a storm cloud. But it didn't feel sincere, as if the storm still lurked, waiting, and the thought made Eudora uneasy.

"May I escort you to the door?"

"Thank you." Eudora crossed the sidewalk from the car to the gatehouse.

The slate path from the street to the front door had been swept clean and decorated for Christmas, with evergreen boughs studded with pears, apples, and walnuts, and magnolia wreaths laced with gilded leaves. A length of carpet had been laid over the stones as a courtesy to women arriving in heels, and it was one that Eudora appreciated. While it was true that she didn't enjoy Society parties as much as her mother did, Eudora did enjoy them.

As they approached the house, it occurred to Eudora that had the weather been nicer, this tea may have been set up in the front garden. There was more than enough room between the reflecting pond and the knot garden for at least a dozen tables. The crepe myrtles would have provided shade and color and the pond would have been a nice diversion. But not today. Today, the lawn glistened with a skim of ice and the boxwoods were sprinkled with a dusting of snow, so the tea was held inside.

After seeing the women safely to the entrance, the escorts wished them a good afternoon and returned to the gatehouse.

The front entrance of the Chalmers' home was meant to impress visitors, and it did. The Chalmers family coat of arms had been cast in brass and embedded on a marble slab on the ground. Intertwining ropes hand-carved on either side of the great mahogany door were meant to give the impression that Chalmers money came from shipbuilding, which it did. However, a fight with Posey led to a rainy afternoon spent researching Chalmers family history and a very different story. Eudora had found dusty bills of lading that showed Chalmers cargo had not been tea and silk from China, but something entirely different from the West Indies. She'd never been able to look at the family in the same way again.

Eudora's mother raised the heavy brass knocker and let it fall onto the plate, then stepped back and smoothed her dress with gloved fingertips. Caroline Gadsden carried herself with an easy elegance that Eudora would never possess. She reminded Eudora of Grace Kelly. Today, for example, her mother wore a navy Dior afternoon suit with a slim skirt and a wide belt cinched at the waist. A fur collar circled her throat, framing the Gadsden pearls, a triple strand of perfectly matched pearls that Caroline liked to believe were the envy of all her friends.

Eudora was not as lucky. Where her mother was tall, lithe, and graceful, Eudora took after her father: short and sturdy, with a tendency toward near-sightedness. From a very young age, Eudora had sensed that it was her mother's ambition to transform her into something more acceptable to Society, and today was no different. The girdle Eudora wore under her afternoon dress was a size too small, which allowed the belt of her dress to be cinched to an acceptable size. In addition, the sleeves were too tight, the collar poked her neck, and she hated the color, a dreary navy blue. Eudora endured it because the tea was important to her mother and Eudora's debut was important to her family.

A uniformed maid opened the door. "Good afternoon. May I take your coat?"

"Yes, thank you." Her mother shed her wrap, pausing at the foyer table to place her calling card on the silver tray with the others. It didn't matter the Chalmers women would be hosting all afternoon; leaving a calling card was proper etiquette.

Eudora's cards had been ready for months, though this was the first occasion she'd had a chance to offer one. Both Eudora's and her mother's cards were similar in that they were engraved with simple black script on thick cream stock with the Gadsden crest in the upper corner. But because Eudora was a debutante, her card was meant for her Season only, so it contained only her name, nothing else. After her marriage, she would be expected to order new cards, with her husband's name and her new address. Those cards were meant to last the rest of her life. Eudora understood the expectation even though she didn't agree with it.

She followed her mother through the foyer, where they joined the receiving line at the entrance of the grand parlor. The Chalmers' tea marked the beginning of the debutante Season so the atmosphere was formal. There was a receiving line and guests were greeted by the Chalmers women in order of importance; Sissy Chalmers first, followed by Sissy's new daughter-in-law, whose name Eudora could not remember, and finally, Posey.

"Sissy, your home looks lovely, as ever." Her mother air-kissed Sissy's cheek, slipping into company manners as smoothly as a chameleon changes color. "And Christmas decorations already, how festive."

"Thank you, Caro." Sissy Chalmers' smile slid into place. "It was quite a scramble, I must say. This winter weather came out of nowhere. Right up until the last minute, we'd hoped to have at least a few tables outside." She gave a delicate shrug. "But we can't control the weather, can we?"

"Well, you've made the right decision." Caroline's tone

matched her friend's, smooth and light, reminding Eudora of water gliding over river stone.

Turning her attention to Eudora, Mrs. Chalmers clasped Eudora's hand in her own. Her hands were warm, and her nails polished a bright Christmas red. "Eudora, how nice to see you again, and what an exciting time for you. I just know that you and Posey will renew your friendship in the coming months."

There had been a time, years before, when both mothers had hoped their daughters would be friends. But Eudora's patience for dress-up and dolls was limited, so one afternoon she left the playroom and wandered into Mr. Chalmers' library. Hours later, after a frantic search of the house, Eudora was found in the library, with a dozen rare and first-edition books spread across the floor. She had a vague memory of wanting to show her mother the pictures she found in the books, illustrated drawings of animals and flowers unlike anything in her children's books at home. But her mother had been furious and Eudora hadn't understood.

After that, Eudora remained at home with a nanny while her mother visited the Chalmers alone.

"Thank you, Mrs. Chalmers. I'm looking forward to it." The reply was automatic, but to Eudora's surprise, she realized she was. She was proud of her family's heritage and she appreciated beautiful things; she just wanted more from her life than that.

Eudora and her mother joined the party in the grand parlor.

Margaret Chalmers had designed this room to be the centerpiece of the house, and it was. At least as large as the Gadsden ballroom, it was paneled with dark cypress, furnished with rich carpets and overlooked a finely landscaped winter garden. Today, a fire crackled comfortably in the hearth, scenting the air with applewood and casting a warm glow across the room. The holiday decorations were understated, a swag of pineapple studded with walnuts stretched across the mantle and simple evergreen wreaths hung from the window panes on wide red ribbons.

It was the tea service that took center stage.

The sturdy round table was covered with a heavy damask cloth, with a full tea service on one side and coffee on the other. The pieces were sterling, polished to a mirror-shine and placed on an engraved silver tray. In the center of the table were platters of food: a tiered plate of scones with a chilled bowl of clotted cream, ramekins of pimento cheese, a bowl of stuffed cherry tomatoes, baskets of crisp cheese straws. A side table offered a selection of desserts: a lead-crystal bowl filled with hot-house strawberries, a platter of iced petit-fours, and lemon tarts.

It was all for show, of course. No one here would dare fill a plate with any of it.

"Would you care for some tea?"

"Lemon only, please," her mother answered as her glance swept the room.

"Yes, ma'am." The attendant poured the tea with gloved hands and added a sliver of lemon.

Eudora's plan was to decline the tea and go in search of Maggie, who had mentioned she would arrive early. Eudora hesitated because she wasn't sure her mother would let Eudora leave her side.

After thanking the attendant, Eudora glanced at the cup and saucer in her hand. The cup was etched with the Chalmers' coat of arms, the saucer a ring of palmetto fronds, the South Carolina state tree. Taken together, the implication was clear: Chalmers family sat squarely in the heart of Charleston. Eudora thought the boast was ironic, given the family history, but doubted her mother would agree.

When Eudora was allowed to leave her mother's side, she mingled. Circling the room, she accepted good wishes for her upcoming debut and chatted with her classmates' mothers as she looked for Maggie but couldn't find her. It was still early yet and Eudora wasn't worried. She settled into a group with a good view of the entrance, chatting with her school friends about last-minute changes to the flower arrangements they planned to carry across the stage at Hibernian Hall. It seemed Charleston's cold snap had affected the flowers brought in by train, bruising the petals and wilting the stems. With St. Cecilia less than three weeks away, everyone was scrambling for replacements.

"My mother's having my bouquet flown in, week after next, especially for the ball," Denise Addison announced, proudly. "Daddy said it'll cost a fortune to buy a plane ticket from Atlanta for a bunch of flowers, but Mama said calla lilies are a tradition and we're lucky to get them. Let's just hope the florist here knows what to do with them."

The other girls in the group had the grace to ignore such a self-serving statement. Money was never discussed in polite society, but Denise couldn't be expected to know that. Everyone knew that her connection to St. Cecilia was tenuous, a great uncle on her father's side. It was further said that her mother had pushed for a Charleston debut, not because of the history behind it, but because she was afraid Denise would never become engaged otherwise.

Eudora excused herself from the group and went to look for her mother. She'd been asked not to stray too far from her mother's side because connections would be made here that would lead to important committee assignments later.

Eudora approached her mother's group just in time to hear one of the women hiss, "Who is that woman talking to Sissy? And *what* is she wearing?"

Eudora turned to see Maggie and her mother in the receiving line, and her heart sank.

While Maggie had dressed for the party in the outfit they'd selected at Chastains, it appeared that her mother had not. Every woman here understood that because this tea opened the 1953 Social Season, it was vital to present one's best self. Complete outfits – dress, hat, heels, jewelry – had been planned months before, with military precision. Mrs. Tweedy's record-keeping ensured duplicate outfits would not appear at the same function, and it was not unusual for her to gently suggest a woman rethink her ensemble. Eudora watched her mother agonize over her pattern, fabric, and accessories for almost two months before deciding on her outfit.

But it seemed that Mrs. O'Hanlan hadn't given the same thought to her outfit. She appeared to be dressed for work in a belted gray shirtwaist and a thick black cardigan, the sleeves of both rolled to the forearm and pushed to her elbow. Instead of a smart clutch in a matching or contrasting color, her purse was one that Eudora had seen many times, an over-sized black leather with a chipped metal clasp that bobbed on her forearm as she shook hands with Sissy Chalmers.

Mrs. O'Hanlan didn't seem to know what to do after coming to the end of the receiving line, so Eudora crossed the room to greet Maggie and her mother.

"Hello, Mrs. O'Hanlan."

"Eudora, dear. Don't you look lovely?" Mrs. O'Hanlan

stood in the center of the Chalmers formal parlor, the weekend's epicenter for Charleston's elite. Though she must have been aware of the furtive glances cast her way, she gave no indication that she cared.

"Thank you, Mrs. Chalmers." Eudora turned to Maggie. "You look amazing, Maggie. Just like Cinderella."

And she did. Maggie O'Hanlan looked as if she could take her place in any home in Charleston. Her dress was a deep burgundy wool with a matching crocodile belt and delicate embroidery along the collar and cuffs. Nipped at the waist, it flared dramatically to her calves. The perfect choice for an afternoon tea.

"Did you *see* that silver coffee service? It's monogrammed," Maggie whispered.

It wasn't monogrammed. It was engraved with the Chalmers family coat of arms, but Eudora thought it best not to correct her friend.

"So this is what all those Wednesday afternoons were about, is it?" Mrs. O'Hanlan glanced around the room, and then at the buffet. "Maggie's right, that silver is beautiful, but I wouldn't want to be the one to polish it."

"It's dreamy, Ma. This party is *exactly* as I imagined it would be," Maggie gushed.

"I'm glad you're happy, Maggie-girl, but I'll thank you to remember that there's more to life than fancy parties." Mrs. O'Hanlan's voice was wistful, even as she leaned in to kiss her daughter's cheek. Then she straightened, clutched her purse to her side and the mood was broken. "You girls have fun – behave yourself. I'm off."

Eudora froze.

The Chalmers invitation had been sent to both mother and daughter, with the indication that they were to arrive and depart the tea together. Not dressing appropriately was one thing, but Mrs. O'Hanlan was preparing to bring her daughter to a debutante reception and *drop her off*, as if Chalmers' tea were a child's party. Leaving her daughter alone at this party would have been an unforgivable breach of etiquette and the O'Hanlan's the topic of gossip at every social gathering for weeks to come.

Eudora would not let that happen.

She laid her hand on Mrs. O'Hanlan's arm. "Can't you stay a little longer?"

Had she had been looking at Eudora, instead of gathering her things, Mrs. O'Hanlan might have picked up on Eudora's expression. But she missed it.

Instead, Maggie's mother shook her head. "I'm afraid I have to go. Mr. O is way over his head with the accounts. I'm afraid he's completely muddled the receivables, but he refuses to admit it."

Of course, it was impossible to get someone to stay if they were determined to leave, but Eudora tried anyway. For a moment she considered introducing her to the other women at this party, then dismissed the idea as ridiculous. As a working-class Yankee, Marie O'Hanlan would be chum in the water for Eudora's mother and her friends.

There was nothing she could do.

In the end, Eudora watched two dozen women's heads swivel as they tracked Marie O'Hanlan's departure.

That Mrs. O'Hanlan thanked the hostess before she left mattered not at all.

CHAPTER 10

AFTER THE PARTY, Eudora couldn't sleep. For the whole of her life, she'd had a vague awareness that the trajectory of her life was headed for things that would happen "someday."

Someday, she would meet a boy and fall in love.

Someday, her mother would plan her wedding, which would include a ceremony at St. Michael's and a garden reception at home.

Someday, Eudora would manage a household of her own. There would be women to cook for her and to clean her house, men to tend her gardens and a driver to take her anywhere she wanted to go.

And if she married well – someday – there would be vacations in Europe, a summer house on the coast, and dinner parties for the rest of her life.

Eudora had never questioned that part of her life because it was always there and because the events were so far in the future, they didn't seem real.

All of that would all happen "someday."

Now, it seemed, "someday" was closer than she thought. And Eudora didn't like the way it looked, not entirely, anyway. The life Eudora wanted included college and a place in the family business. For a time it seemed as if she was headed that way, with all the work her father asked her to do for the family business. But then her mother took charge and nudged her life in a different direction.

But there was no reason Eudora couldn't manage social obligations and the family business. Mrs. O'Hanlan did. She managed her husband's accounts and cared for her family. Why couldn't Eudora do the same?

For years, Jackson had listened to Eudora complain about her mother, calling her old-fashioned and stubborn, which she was. And for years, Jackson had patiently suggested that Eudora hadn't given her mother a chance.

"After all," he'd told her, "she has no idea what you want. You've never told her."

Maybe now it was time.

It was that thought that allowed Eudora to finally drifted off to sleep in the early hours of the morning.

Eudora woke the next morning to a sky smudged with pink and a lace of frost edging her bedroom windows. She snuggled deep into the warmth of her bed until she remembered the conversation she needed to have with her mother. Caroline Gadsden was not an early riser, but this conversation was too important to put off, so Eudora decided not to wait. Maybe Annie had come and would make breakfast. Pushing the duvet aside, she climbed out of bed, dressed quickly and made her way downstairs.

To Eudora's surprise, her mother was awake. She was seated at her usual place in the dining room, wearing a blue silk dressing gown. In front of her, the newspaper was open to the Society page. A tendril of steam wafting from the spout of the teapot at her side, and a slice of dry toast on a plate nearby.

"Hello, Mother. May I join you?"

"Of course." Her mother gestured to the tea service on the sideboard. "Would you like a cup of tea? I'm afraid Annie's not in yet, so we're on own own."

"No, thank you." Eudora couldn't remember the last time she'd sought out her mother for casual conversation. Their exchanges were transactional – appointments to keep, a fitting after school – and Eudora was unsure how to proceed now.

Her mother slipped off her reading glasses and leaned back in her chair. "I was just looking at the newspaper for a mention of the Chalmers' tea. I thought Annette's 'About Town' column surely would have mentioned something, but I don't see it."

"I've got something I want to talk to you about."

"Yes, what is it?" Her mother gestured to the chair opposite her as she stubbed her cigarette into the ashtray. "Has Jackson finally declared his intention toward you?"

"Declared his what?" Eudora was taken aback. "It's not like that at all. Jackson and I are just friends."

Her mother scoffed as she reached for her gold cigarette case. "They all think that. It's up to us to show him differently. You just have to know what to do."

"I want to talk about the Chalmers' tea," Eudora interrupted. It seemed like a good place to start.Her mother reached across the table. "If you're upset about how some of the other women treated Maggie and her mother, you should understand what an occasion the tea was and how insulted

Mrs. Chalmers must have felt when your friend and her mother arrived looking as though they'd just stopped by." Her mother opened the monogrammed case and withdrew a cigarette. "Well, it's just not done, that's all."

"That's not it." Eudora's voice was sharper than she intended. Her mother's friends had judged Mrs. O'Hanlan even before she walked into the foyer. With glances and whispers, they made sure she knew she wasn't worthy or welcome. It was petty, and it made Eudora furious. But she could never make her mother understand, and it was pointless to try.

"Very well, Eudora. What did you want to discuss?" The tone of her mother's voice changed. As she withdrew her hand, Eudora recognized the chameleon change. The part of her mother that might be reasonable was retreating into icy politeness, and Eudora didn't know how to reach her.

Finally, she blurted. "I don't want the life you're planning for me."

Her mother reached for her lighter and touched the flame to the tip of her cigarette. As she inhaled, she fixed Eudora with an unwavering stare. "And what is it that you think I'm planning?"

"You want me to be like the women at the Chalmers' tea, and I don't want that. I want to do something else."

"Do you?" Her mother blew a rope of smoke toward the ceiling. "A bit late in the game for that, but tell me: what is it you'd rather do?"

"I want to go to college."

"College?" Her mother tapped the silver ash into the ashtray. "Is that so?"

"Yes."

"Whatever for?"

"I want to work with Daddy. I want a job at his company." Eudora squeezed her hands together in her lap. Her words came out in a rush. "I've been working with Daddy for years and now that I'm old enough, I want an official job. Daddy requires all Associate Brokers to have a business degree. So I thought Charleston College—"

"You thought Charleston College what?" Her mother interrupted, arching a perfectly shaped brow.

"Charleston College would be a good place to start."

"Does your father know about your plans? Has he offered you a job?" Another inhale, another column of smoke rising from her mother.

"No, but—"

"No," her mother finished as she ground her cigarette into the glass of the ashtray. "Nor will he. When you marry, it is your husband who will expect your support and encouragement, not your father."

"But what if I didn't get married right away?" Eudora pressed. "What if I waited until I finished college? What if I married someone who would support my career?"

"No man worthy of respect will allow his wife to work unless he has no other choice. Even then he will be ashamed of himself for not supporting his family, and quite rightly, I might add."

"Then I don't have to marry right away. There's no boy I'm interested in, anyway."

"There's Jackson. With the right encouragement, he'll come around."

"Jackson?" Eudora stuttered. Was it possible that her mother didn't know?

"Yes." Her mother smiled coyly. "Your Aunt Evelyn and I have great plans for you and Jackson. In fact, it's your 'friendship' with Jackson Legare that allows you to skip the five-city circuit."

"Skip the circuit?" Eudora repeated stupidly. She felt as if all the air had been sucked from the room.

"Of course." Her mother scoffed as she reached for her toast. "You must have wondered why Posey Chalmers will be in Spartanburg at the end of the month and you won't."

Did she wonder? Eudora had known that many of the other girls had planned an extended circuit while she was allowed to stay home, but she assumed it was because they liked receptions and dances and cocktail parties. Now, it seemed that the reason her debut ended at Hibernian Hall was because her mother assumed she and Jackson would marry.

Eudora gaped at her mother. She watched her mother calmly sip her tea and replace the cup on the saucer.

"Your debut at St. Cecilia, if managed correctly, will shape the rest of your adult life. Your Aunt Evelyn and I agree that if everything goes according to plan, your debut is just the thing to bring Jackson to his senses."

"Mother," Eudora began.

"Please let me finish." She picked up her lighter and rolled it in her hand. "You already know that my two sisters and I grew up on the horse farm in Aiken, South Carolina, miles from Charleston. Daddy had connections, but Mother didn't, and he was content to live out his life there." She glanced at Eudora, her eyes flinty and full of memory. "What you don't know is that Evelyn and I were not."

"We debuted at St. Cecilia, each of us in turn. Your Aunt Evelyn went first. She followed Great Aunt Addie's instruction to the letter and played the game perfectly. Now, as you know, she's married to a state senator and lives in Columbia, the state capital. When my turn came, I followed Great Aunt Addie's instruction and married your father, a man with excellent prospects, whose family was firmly established in Charleston Society. I got the house I wanted and a generous allowance."

"Your Aunt Dorothy wasn't as fortunate. She chose the boy she *wanted* instead of a boy who would support her. As you know, things have not turned out well for her." Eudora's mother grimaced, as if her younger sister's life was too awful to think about. "The point is, I don't want that for you. You're the only daughter of a prominent Charleston family, and you can make the greatest match of the Season if you—"

"Mother," Eudora interrupted, her voice firm. She couldn't listen to another word. "I don't want to marry a senator, and I don't care about living in a grand house. I think Aunt Dorothy's life is fine. She's married to a man she loves and they're building a life together." Her hands trembled in her lap, but she kept her mother's gaze. "There is more to life than a good marriage."

"Of course there is, Eudora." Caroline folded the cuffs of her dressing gown and smoothed the edges flat. "You'll have committee work and friendships with other young brides. My work on the hospital committee is very rewarding, and many of my best friendships started after my marriage. Those women are married to influential men, who are able to help your father in his work. So you see, we do work together, in a way. It's all connected; it's all important. Let your husband worry about business; you can be the power behind his throne."

Eudora sat at the table, gaping at her mother. How could this woman know nothing about her? Eudora explained the most important goal of her life and her mother hadn't heard a word of it.

Or maybe, her mother had heard and didn't care.

The unfairness of it was staggering. Hadn't Eudora done everything her mother had wanted? Hadn't she cooperated with every instruction? Attended every appointment? She thought that by being a dutiful daughter, when the time came, her parents would listen to what she wanted, maybe even help her get it. Apparently, she was wrong.

But Eudora would not have it.

"You're not listening to me." Eudora learned forward, her words coming out in a rush. "I don't want any of that. I'm not like you. In fact, I don't *want* to be."

"Oh really?"

"That's right. I don't want to spend my days with the same group of women who do nothing but drink coffee and gossip about their friends."

"Is that what you think I do, Eudora?" Her mother's voice was cool, a warning which Eudora would ignore. She wasn't a child who should be afraid of her mother.

Eudora continued, desperate to make her mother understand. "Do you even care what's important to me? Did you know that I've been working for Daddy's company, *doing things that matter*?" She drew a deep breath, past the pounding of her heart. "Of course you don't. You don't know anything about me. You only care about yourself."

And in the silence that followed, Eudora waited. In all her life, she'd never raised her voice to anyone, much less her mother.

She waited.

"I'll not argue with you about this, Eudora." She pushed her chair back and stood. "I've already explained why your

debut and your continued engagement with Society is important, for you and this family. I consider the matter closed."
She hesitated, her hand resting on the back of her chair.
"Except for one thing: I intend to speak to your father about
misleading you. I didn't realize you were still working for
him but I'll see to it that working for him ends immediately.
From now on, I expect you to focus on your Season."

Caroline watched Eudora run from the dining room, and her
heart went with her. She listened to the kitchen door slam and
the sound of her daughter's feet pounding down the stairs,
and felt an overwhelming sadness. If Annie was here, she'd
know what to say. Annie had always been able to talk sense
into Eudora when Caroline could not.

She reached for another cigarette to calm her nerves and
held the flame to the tip. The paper caught immediately and
Caroline drew a breath and pressed her back against her
chair.

Eudora was just afraid, that was all. But she was strong
and she would be fine. In the spring, when she and Jackson
were engaged to be married, she'd understand the importance of her Season.

And she'd be grateful.

CHAPTER 11

ON THE EVE of the St. Cecilia Ball, Caroline stood outside Eudora's bedroom, summoning the courage to knock. She'd made a point of being dressed and ready early, in case Eudora had called for help fastening a bracelet or choosing the right shade of lipstick. Her own debut, and Evelyn's too, was an explosion of chaos at Great Aunt Addie's Charleston home, with squeals of laughter between the sisters and cousins, borrowed jewelry, and great clouds of hair lacquer. One of the happiest times in Caroline's life. While it was true that Eudora was an only child, Caroline had always wanted her to have a similar experience.

But the call from Eudora never came, and Caroline had been left to wait hours in her own room. If she were honest, Caroline might admit that she was relived Eudora hadn't asked for her help. Ever since that morning in the dining room, when Eudora brought up the ridiculous notion of wanting to work for her father, things between them changed. Eudora begun to look at Caroline strangely, as if she could peer into Caroline's very core. As if her daughter did not like what she saw.

It was a terrible thing to be judged by one's own daughter. Worse to be found wanting.

In any case, Caroline had passed the time in her room constructively. She had time to decide whether her diamond cuff bracelet or gold chandelier earrings were a better match for her lavender gown. She couldn't wear both, of course. Eventually Caroline decided she liked the sparkle on her wrist instead of on her ears. She'd spent a bit of time, too, selecting her shoes, changing them twice before deciding the delicate silver sandals were a better compliment to her outfit. Though it was still winter and sandals were not strictly correct, the silver was just the bit of color the dress needed. And so, by keeping herself busy, she was able to push away comparisons of the joy of her debut ball and starkness of her daughter's.

Were it not for the box she had to give to Eudora tonight, Caroline wasn't sure she'd have anything at all to say to her. But traditions must be observed, so Caroline summoned her courage and gently tapped her daughter's door. As she waited for Eudora to answer, Caroline drew herself up to her full height and brushed her fingertips across the waist of her gown, taking comfort from the fact that her figure had not changed in twenty years. Not many of her friends could say the same.

"Come in." Eudora was seated at her vanity in her girdle and her slip. Nearby, her gown was hanging and ready, not a wrinkle to be seen.

Caroline remembered the shopping trip with fondness. She and Evelyn had chosen a white gown for Eudora, as was customary, with a long tulle skirt and a nipped waist. They traveled to Atlanta, insisting the trip was necessary to ensure Eudora's gown was unique, but really it was because Caroline couldn't bear another trip to Chastains. Although Mrs. Tweedy was the soul of discretion, Caroline wanted to spare her daughter the embarrassment of finding a dress that would flatter her cinderblock shape. It was Evelyn who suggested a sprinkling of seed pearls along the neckline would deflect from the waist. But in the end, they decided a capelet would offer more coverage. With the right foundation garments – which they bought immediately – Eudora would look perfectly acceptable.

"Posture, Eudora." Caroline's good humor deflated with a sigh. Honestly, it was almost personally insulting the lack of interest Eudora showed in her own debut. Caroline and her sister Evelyn had strapped yardsticks to their backs to train their posture for weeks before their debut and had practiced their curtsey until their legs ached.

"I've come to give you these." Caroline crossed the room, silent except for the gentle swishing of her gown.

The offering was tucked inside a slim leather case, the edges long since worn with age, the once deep black patina faded to a dull muddy gray. On the inside of the lid, gilded with gold leaf on a background of black silk, was the Gadsden family crest, and on nestled black velvet was a single strand of pearls with a delicate gold clasp and matching stud earrings. It was one of the very few possessions to survive the fire after the war. It had adorned every Gadsden debutante for generations, and now it was time to pass it to Eudora.

Eudora glanced at the contents and set it on her vanity. "Thank you."

Caroline waited for more of a reaction, some hint that her daughter understood the magnitude of the occasion, but none was forthcoming. She felt a swell of anger fill her chest but she tamped it down, refusing to let anything unpleasant spoil Eudora's evening.

Caroline and her sisters would have loved a mother's guidance during their formative years. Great Aunt Addie was helpful, but her social connections were weak, and there was so much Caroline and Evelyn had to learn on their own. When Eudora was born, Caroline vowed that she would guide Eudora whenever possible, smooth the way as Caroline wished the way had been smoothed for her.

And she had fulfilled that promise to herself.

Wasn't it Caroline who paired Eudora with Jackson Legare when the children were young, even though it meant socializing with that awful Legare woman for years? It was such a coup that Sissy Chalmers was fit to be tied when she discovered the opportunity she'd lost for her daughter Posey. Even then, Eudora hadn't realized what Caroline had done for her. Tonight, with Jackson as Eudora's escort, this evening was Caroline's triumph as much as it was Eudora's. And years from now, when Eudora looked back on the evening of her formal debut into Charleston Society, she would remember that Caroline had tried to be helpful.

"These aren't your wedding pearls," Caroline said as she lifted them from the vanity. "Your grandmother left you those to wear on your wedding day. The Gadsden pearls are a triple strand of perfectly matched, larger pearls, with a gold and diamond clasp. For your debut, something simpler is more appropriate, don't you agree?"

"Thank you, Mother." The pearls felt heavy on her skin and

cool to the touch. Eudora forced a smile as her mother looped the strand around her throat.

After she fastened the lock, her mother clasped her hands together, her voice light and carefree. "I loved my time as a debutante, and I know you will too. Have I ever told you the stories?"

"Many times."

Though Eudora had known since she was a little girl that she would debut before the St. Cecilia Society, she had also known the event was more important to her mother than it was to her. It was her mother who had pushed for extra instruction – outside of Wednesday afternoon cotillion classes – obviously giving Eudora and Jackson more time together. In fact, her mother had arranged shopping trips, introductions, and private instruction, mostly without asking Eudora's opinion on any of it. And Eudora had gone along, without protest.

That had been her mistake.

Her mother adjusted the diamond cuff on her wrist, then ran her fingertips across the fabric of her sleeve. "My dance card for St. Cecelia was filled – all sixteen dances, mind you – even before many of the other girls had crossed the stage. Not giving the other girls a fair chance was terrible breach of etiquette, but…" Her mother's voice faded, and the twinkle in her eye hinted that she didn't care at all about breaking rules if it had gotten her what she wanted.

After a moment, Caroline continued. "And the morning after—" She brought her hand to her chest and laid her fingertips gently over her heart. "Well, there were just so many arrangements and calling cards that the front hall looked like a flower shop." She leaned forward. Eudora flinched, but her mother seemed not to notice, lost as she was in her memories. Her voice dropped to a whisper. "Your Aunt Evelyn and I argued about that for years – who had the most arrangements from admirers the morning after our debuts."

She seemed to come to herself then. Sighing, her mother's gaze focused on Eudora. "Are you nervous?"

"No."

Truthfully, Eudora was more concerned about the results of the Calculus exam she'd taken twelve days before. Jackson had warned her to take her time, so she was one of the last to finish, but the uncertainty of the outcome still made her uneasy. She had expected to receive the results by now.

"Your bouquet arrived; it's downstairs waiting for you." Her mother's words pulled Eudora from her thoughts.

"Good."

"I've spoken to Jackson's mother. He'll be waiting for you after you cross the stage."

"Okay."

It was the shrug that did it. After Eudora shrugged, she saw her mother's smile falter, saw the crack in the light-hearted façade. Eudora had learned to recognize it as a sign that she'd done something she shouldn't have. When she was younger, Eudora tried very hard to please her mother until she realized she never could.

Her mother drew herself up, as Eudora knew she would. "We have traditions, Eudora, a way of doing things that go back hundreds of years, and we have an obligation to uphold those traditions," she said, a sentiment Eudora had heard many times before. "Tonight, everything you do will impact this family. You are a Gadsden, Eudora, and I expect you to behave like one."

"Yes, ma'am," Eudora replied, but she didn't mean it.

Acquiescence seemed the only way to get her mother to leave Eudora in peace.

As expected, Caroline turned to leave, then hesitated at the door, her hand on the knob. Her voice softened, something Eudora did not expect. "You'll see, Eudora. You'll see we only want what's best for you."

CHAPTER 12

SLEET SPATTERED against the windshield and the wipers flicked it away. Inside, the windows fogged with moisture and the air crackled with tension as the car inched forward. Eudora's mother had insisted a late start because it would allow Eudora to make an entrance, but it seemed that every other Society matron had the same idea. The line of sleek black cars carrying debutantes and their parents to Hibernian Hall stretched at least three blocks down Queen Street. Eudora sat in the back seat, between her parents. Their conversation had long since ceased.

Carter glanced at the rearview mirror. "Should I try to go around, ma'am?"

Eudora's mother leaned forward, narrowing her eyes and glaring out the window, as if force of will would allow her to speed past the other cars.

"No." Her answer was curt. "We need to be on the right side of Meeting Street so you can pull up to the Hall properly." She snorted, like a bull in front of a red cape. "No one walks across the street to St. Cecilia. Honestly, Carter, you've been with us long enough to know that."

"Yes, ma'am."

Eudora's father shifted in his seat. Eudora knew he didn't like the way her mother spoke to the staff, but good manners prevented him from correcting his wife in front of them.

"I don't know why they didn't just cancel the ball tonight and reschedule for tomorrow instead," her mother continued as she glared at the traffic.

"Caroline, there's nothing we can do about the weather." Her father's tone held an undercurrent of reproach that Eudora heard but her mother did not.

"Eudora needs to make an entrance," her mother insisted.

"I'm sure we'll be there in plenty of time." Her father's voice was steady, but he was losing patience. Eudora glanced at her mother. Why couldn't she see that?

Finally, Eudora's mother turned her attention from the window to her husband, her hands held tight in her lap. "You don't understand, Edward." Her gaze flicked to Eudora, seated between them. "There are accommodations that need to be made. We must take advantage of every opportunity."

Eudora felt the shame rise from her core and flood her face.

Eudora's mother drew a breath to continue, but Eudora's father stopped her. "Caroline. That's enough." Her father leaned in to whisper. "You'll be fine, Eudora,"

Knowing her father was on her side was enough, at least for now. Her moment to shine would come later, when Eudora showed him her acceptance letter from his alma mater. They'd celebrate then. She could wait.

Eudora turned her attention to the bouquet she was meant to carry across the platform. That too, her mother had arranged, reserving a half-dozen calla lilies in one of the few shipments from Atlanta. Callas were a traditional flower for debutantes, and Eudora had to admit the flowers were beautiful: creamy white and unblemished. But while most girls would carry a simple bouquet, a few stems of the same color wrapped with a white satin ribbon and fastened with a matching pin, Eudora's mother had gone beyond that. Eudora's bouquet started with six white callas but hers surrounded a bright green lily in the center. And instead of a plain satin ribbon, hers was adorned with a gold medallion etched with the Gadsden family crest. It was an odd choice for her mother to make, jarring in its contrast and unwieldy to carry.

After what seemed like an eternity, it was their turn. Carter slid the car along the curb of Hibernian Hall and Eudora glanced out the window. The wrought iron gates in front of the building had been decorated with delicate vines of green smilax, the tender leaves dripping with moisture. And someone had thought to erect an awning over the walkway from the gates on the sidewalk to the double staircase that marked the Hall's entrance.

"You see, Caroline? Nothing to worry about." He wanted to smooth over the tension from the drive, and Eudora was grateful for the gesture. Her mother was wrong. Eudora *had* been looking forward to her debut, but not in the way her mother had hoped. Eudora's debut would not determine her life's direction.

The car door opened with a whoosh, letting in a blast of cold December air. Her father exited the car first, sheltered by an attendant's oversized umbrella. Eudora followed and took her father's arm. Together they walked into the building.

Eudora would have two escorts for the evening, her father

and Jackson. Her father, as a member of the St. Cecilia Society, would present her to the committee, and by extension, to Charleston Society. As her escort, Jackson would be the first to welcome her after she crossed the stage, and he would be awarded the first dance.

She felt the warmth of her father's arm through his jacket and drew reassurance from it.

Despite a twinge of nerves, Eudora felt prepared to walk across the platform at Hibernian Hall. She'd attended seven years of cotillion classes and years of private dance appointments with Jackson because her mother was convinced she would stumble. The shopping trip to Atlanta was tedious, but Eudora went anyway, not understanding why a gown from Chastains wouldn't be acceptable. Posey had bought her gown there, so it was good enough for the Chalmers women.

Eudora had always known she wasn't attractive, not in any way that mattered to her mother. Her mother told her so in a million different ways: posting the latest reducing diet in the pantry as a reminder of what Eudora couldn't eat, or dragging Eudora to a foundation fitting the week she turned thirteen. Of course all of it bothered her, but Eudora had long discovered that no matter how hard she tried, she would never get her mother's approval.

So she stopped trying.

It was her father whose approval she wanted. She had been dying to tell him of how she managed to talk her way in to see Mr. Hendricks and about the final she'd been forced to take. But because he was away on business when she sat for the test and exhausted when he finally arrived home just a few days ago, Eudora decided to surprise him with her acceptance to his alma mater. It would be a nice belated Christmas present for him. And

Mr. Hendricks seemed satisfied with the letter she'd sent in her father's name, because he hadn't replied. So all was well.

It would all work out, this plan of hers, and that thought was what made her smile as she passed through the double doors of Hibernian Hall.

The foyer glowed with the light of a hundred beeswax candles, reflecting off the polished wood floor and the tall entry windows. The fireplace in the ballroom had been lit, threading the air with the delicate scent of applewood and cloves. In front of her, the wide Greek columns that graced the foyer were wound from floor to ceiling with even more smilax vines, the tender green leaves a stark contrast to the fresh white paint.

As she stood next to her father, waiting for their turn to register with the host committee, Eudora felt an unexpected surge of excitement. It felt as though she were part of something bigger than herself or her family. She imagined all the women who had come before her, to this hall, about to enter Society as she was. Hundreds of them, crossing the same stage and making their curtsey to the committee. And Eudora felt deeply honored to take her place among them, to be a thread in the tapestry of the city she loved.

"Edward, how nice to see you." One of the men at the long table in the foyer stood. Dressed in white tie and tails, he offered his gloved hand and her father shook it.

"Nipper, I didn't know they'd have you at the registration table," her father said with a smile before turning to Eudora. "Of course, you remember Eudora? Eudora, this is Mr. Nipper Hamilton. We were in school together."

"Oh, our paths have crossed a few times since then, I imagine." Her father's friend seemed nice, roughly the same age and build as her father, but with a bit less hair and a bit thicker around the middle.

"Indeed they have, old man," her father agreed. "Indeed they have."

Mr. Hamilton turned his attention to Eudora. "This is a big night for you, young lady. You must be very excited."

"Yes, sir," Eudora replied. "I'm honored to be here."

Maybe because of all the rules restricting membership, the registration process was surprisingly brief. As soon as her father signed his name to the register, Eudora was given her dance card. Fashioned from ivory cardstock with gilded edges, it opened like a book. The page inside was divided into sixteen numbered lines, for sixteen partners, one partner for each dance. A silver pencil was provided, attached to the card with a narrow silver ribbon. It was beautiful, even better than the cards Miss Emily supplied for dance practice. Remembering Miss Emily's instruction, Eudora tucked the card behind her bouquet. It was not appropriate for a debutante to display her dance card until after she was presented.

Eudora and her father ascended the stairs to the ballroom the same way they entered the building, with Eudora walking tall and resting her hand lightly on her father's arm.

Eudora hesitated as they reached the ballroom, amazed at the transformation. Last fall, Miss Emily had taken the girls who planned to debut to the hall so they would be familiar with the process. Back then, the ballroom was empty, with a few stacked chairs in the corner and tabletops rolled to the side. Now, it looked like a fairy garden, with delicate green wreaths hanging from the window on fat white ribbons, and greenery draped across curtain rods and stretched along the fireplace mantle. Throughout the room was the soft yellow glow of beeswax candles. Polished silver candelabra on either side of the mantle held tall tapers, with small votive candles scattered on tabletops. And the hearth crackled with fat logs, tuxedoed attendants flanking each side of the fireplace to watch for stray embers.

"Not yet." Her father paused to correct Eudora. He pressed his arm to his side to slow her pace. "We don't enter the ballroom until you've been presented." He gestured to a second room on the side of the ballroom. "That way."

"Of course," Eudora mumbled, feeling stupid after years of instruction. "I knew that."

Her father placed his hand on top of hers. "I think you look beautiful, Eudora, and you've made me very proud."

"Thank you, Daddy."

They moved to the back hall, where the line of debutantes threaded. Just past the entrance to the committee, the girls were met by a gaggle of matrons who fussed. They straightened hems, fixed wilting flowers, corrected posture, and soothed frazzled nerves. Officially, the ball wouldn't begin until all the girls had crossed the stage, and the room hummed with nervous anticipation.

"You'll be fine." Her father placed his hand over hers. "You're not nervous, are you?"

"Not at all," Eudora lied. The truth was that she hadn't been nervous until she arrived backstage. That was when everything felt real. Her mother predicted she'd fail, and her mother knew more about this process than anyone. A hiss of doubt snaked up Eudora's spine, raising goosebumps on her skin.

To distract herself, Eudora turned her thoughts to Maggie and how much she would have loved this – the white dresses, the gloves, the pearls. Eudora would memorize every detail and would bring back stories to Maggie. She'd repeat every one, no matter how many times Maggie asked, because there was no one in Charleston would who have reveled in the ceremony more than Maggie O'Hanlan.

Except Maggie wasn't allowed to attend.

Eudora was jolted from her thoughts by someone announcing her name. And the rest of the presentation was a blur.

She remembered her father offering her arm and had a vague memory of climbing the stairs to the platform. Her father squeezed her hand against his arm once before letting go. And when he stepped back, she was alone on the stage in front of the members of the St. Cecilia Society.

For a moment, she forgot everything she was supposed to do. When she finally was able to move, she wasn't sure of her balance. Her mouth went dry and her heart thumped in her chest.

Her mother was right, and her father would be ashamed of her.

Summoning every bit of courage she had, Eudora drew a deep breath. She smiled to the committee and inclined her head as if she were royalty. Then she dropped into a flawless curtsey, sweeping her arms gracefully to her side and touching her forehead to the floor. After rising to her feet, she thanked the committee and exited the stage, feeling the prickle of goosebumps on her arms as she walked. She felt triumphant.

Her mother was wrong after all.

"Good evening, Mrs. Gadsden." Jackson nodded to Eudora's mother and shook her father's hand. "Mr. Gadsden."

Jackson stood before them, in white tie and tails, wearing fresh white gloves and a white lily boutonniere to match the bouquet that Eudora carried. His brown hair was sharply parted, the sides combed neatly around his ears. Handsome and refined, Jackson would have been a perfect catch for any debutante who didn't mind that he preferred the company of men to the company of women.

He complimented Eudora's mother and asked about her father's business, but the twinkle in his eye was Jackson's tell. All of this was a game to him. It always had been. Eudora remembered the cotillion classes they skipped just to see if they could get away with it, and the times he mis-counted dance steps in her ears just to slip her up.

It was hard to believe all that had come to an end.

"I believe the first dance is mine?" He looked pointedly at her dance card, and Eudora hid her smile.

"I believe it is," Eudora answered as she removed her dance card from the ribbon of her bouquet and wrote his name on the first line.

She and Jackson were play-acting, but Eudora didn't miss the gleam in her mother's eye. She'd always wanted them to be a couple.

"Come, Edward." Eudora's mother leaned in to her husband, her whisper loud enough for them all to hear. "We should let them have a moment alone."

Eudora watched her parents make their way across the ballroom, then turned to Jackson. "She never stops trying, does she?"

"Not since we were children," Jackson answered. "But I'm afraid you're going to have to get along without me for a while, so break it to her gently, will you?"

"You're going?" Eudora was thrilled. Not that Jackson was leaving – she'd miss him terribly – but she was happy that he was finally starting the adventure he'd dreamed about for years.

"I am."

"How did you get your parents to agree?"

Jackson hesitated, and Eudora reached for his arm. "What happened?"

"Nothing I can't manage," Jackson's smile was brittle. He wouldn't admit it outright, but Jackson saw his father's blessing as a vote of confidence in his ability. Not getting it was the same as predicting failure. "I've accepted their graduation gift – a month's tour of Europe."

"When do you leave?"

"Tomorrow." Jackson dropped his gaze. "The benefit of working hard and graduating high school early is that I can leave as soon as my chaperone duties to you are fulfilled. At least I'll beat the tourist crowds to the monuments."

"What about when you come back?" Eudora's head buzzed with questions. "Does your father still expect you to go to law school and open a second office in Columbia? I thought you didn't want any of that."

"I don't. I've accepted the trip, but what they don't know is that I'm not coming back." He lowered his voice. "I'm meeting friends in Italy and we're getting an apartment. If Florence is good enough for Dante, it's good enough for me."

"Please tell me you've thought this through." Eudora held his gaze. "What if your parents demand you come back? What will you do for money if they cut you off?"

"Don't worry about me; everything will work out. I'm going to cash in the return ticket; that should hold me for a while. After that, I guess I'll get a job. I'll figure it out as I go." His expression shifted, becoming serious. "Honestly, Eudora,

I don't see that I have a choice. If I stay, their plans will break me."

The first notes of a waltz began to play, interrupting their conversation. As a debutante, Eudora and her escort were expected to be on the dance floor.

Jackson bowed his head and offered his arm. "Shall we?"

CHAPTER 13

CAROLINE WOKE to the slam of a car door. Sweeping aside the duvet, she rose from her bed. She crossed the room and managed to look out the window in time to see a white delivery van pulling away. She recognized the logo on the side of the vehicle and felt the tension lift from her shoulders. It wasn't until this moment she realized that she was afraid Eudora wouldn't receive any flowers at all. But of course, the thought was ridiculous. Eudora was a Gadsden, after all.

Caroline reached for her silk wrapper and slipped it on as she frowned at the narrow bed next to her own. The rumpled blankets on his bed signaled that her husband had already started his day, completely oblivious to the importance of this day. Every debutante's mother knew the morning after St. Cecelia was equally as important as the night before.

The fabric of her robe fluttered behind her as she padded down the stairs. She'd ordered the foyer table cleared to make room for the arrangements, but as she moved down the stairs, she wondered if one table was enough. Caroline herself had received more than could be displayed in the foyer of Great

Aunt Addie's Charleston home. Evelyn received at least as many.

Caroline expected to see minor arrangements from friends and family to congratulate Eudora on her debut. Those Caroline would dismiss. They meant nothing.

What mattered was the type of bouquet sent by Jackson Legare. Caroline had spent much of the night watching her daughter's interaction with Jackson. There were together for at least three dances and the midnight supper. In between, there were several trips to the punch bowl. Successful marriages had started with less.

As she descended the last few steps into the marbled foyer, Caroline's pace slowed. She gripped the banister as she surveyed the bouquets on the front table. There were at least a dozen, in every shade of ivory and white scattered across the mahogany tabletop. But ivory and white flowers were from family friends and relatives; they meant nothing.

It was color she was looking for – anything pink would be a good start, even red might be acceptable, if one considered that Jackson and Eudora had been 'together' for years. The flowers Jackson sent to Eudora the morning after her debut, especially as her escort, would be an expression of his feelings for her. Of course it was old-fashioned to declare his intention with flowers, but St. Cecelia itself was old-fashioned, steeped in tradition, and morning-after flowers were expected. But there was nothing.

Caroline descended the last few stairs, calling for Annie as she went.

Annie emerged from the kitchen, wiping her hands on her apron. "Good morning, Miss Caroline."

"Where are the other flowers?"

"Other flowers?" Annie echoed, stupidly.

"Have you put them all out?" Caroline felt her heart begin to thump. "Surely there were more than these delivered."

"Nothing come to this house but what's here." She pointed to the table. "And I put them out the way you told me – expensive arrangements up front." She moved toward the table. "There was something else, though. You didn't tell me what to do with wrapped flowers, so I put them in water and set them in the back."

Caroline circled the table in search of the 'something else.'

Off to the side, under the shadow of another arrangement, was a slender crystal vase of pale pink freesias. An interesting choice, pink for innocence and freesia for admiration.

"Flowers with color are to be placed in the front," Caroline instructed as she cleared a spot for the vase. "I was very specific."

Reaching for the card, she sliced the envelope open, ignoring Annie's frown. She scanned the script.

You've made quite an impression.
Brock Rutledge.

The wording made her cringe, so formal and stilted. And she wasn't familiar with the Rutledge family, so she'd need to rely on her contacts for information on his family's background. Caroline skimmed the card again before slipping it into her pocket and turning to Annie. "Has Mr. Gadsden left the house?"

"No, ma'am. He's in his office, last I saw."

Caroline waved her away. "Fine, Annie. Thank you."

She scooped the morning mail from the basket as she left the foyer and made her way to her husband's study.

~

"Wake up, baby."

Annie's voice was gentle, and Eudora pushed it away, burying her head deeper into her down pillow. It had been such a long night. She just needed a few more minutes of sleep.

But Annie was insistent.

"Eudora." Annie squeezed her shoulder, her tone firm. "C'mon now. Your daddy want to see you."

"Daddy?" Eudora blinked as she sat up in bed. Her father never asked for her.

"Uhm-hum. And he don't sound pleased." As Annie pulled the duvet back, a rush of cold air chased away the pocket of warmth inside. "Best get dressed now."

"What's wrong?" Eudora groped for her robe. "Why does he want to see me?"

"Not that." Annie pointed toward the closet. "He wants to see you in his office. You can't go in your bedclothes. Hurry now."

Eudora stepped into a plain tweed jumper and ran a brush through her hair. She pushed her feet into her shoes and grabbed a cardigan from a shelf, buttoning it up as she moved down the hallway. Only when she was standing outside the office to her father's study did she pause to catch her breath, her heart pounding, her head still fuzzy with sleep. Her mother's summons could be mostly ignored because her anger was like brushfire, quick to blaze but tended to burn itself out quickly. Her father was very different. She'd only seen him truly angry a handful of times in her life, and it was frightening. His anger was a slow burn that erupted very rarely and was best addressed before it blazed.

She knocked.

"Come in."

As Eudora stepped into her father's office, she scrambled for anything she may have done to deserve being called to his office. He'd only just arrived home, so maybe the reason had to be work-related. She thought about everything she'd done to help with his trip but came up with nothing. His correspondence was up to date, as was Palmetto Exports' invoices and receivables. She hadn't had a chance to suggest the itinerary for the next business trip, but he didn't plan to travel again until the New Year and that was weeks away. Plenty of time for scheduling.

Her father sat behind his massive oak desk dressed for work in a dark suit, crisp white shirt and striped tie. Unnerving, because he never wore a suit when he worked from home.

Goosebumps rose on Eudora's arms.

"Sit." He looked up from his work and gestured to the guest chair in front of his desk.

Eudora straightened her back as she crossed the room, a whisper of defiance touching her spine. Everything was in order and she'd done nothing wrong. She didn't deserve to be called to her father's office as if she were a first-year employee.

Eudora smoothed a wrinkle from her dress before looking up. "You wanted to see me?"

Her father capped his fountain pen and set it on a stack of papers on the side of his desk. Then he leaned back in his chair. "Who is Mr. Hendricks?"

"Mr. Hendricks?" Eudora echoed, though she could feel her pulse surging.

"Charleston College," he supplied.

"I believe Mr. Hendricks is the Admissions Officer." This was not the way Eudora wanted to tell her father.

"So I gathered. But why is he writing to me?" Her father lifted a sheet of paper and read from it. "'...pleased to welcome you to the head table at our Alumni Auction.'" He set the page on his desk and leaned forward in his chair. "Let's start with that."

Eudora wanted to wait until she had the acceptance letter in her hand, but it seemed that she had no choice now. Maybe it would be better to get everything out in the open. Then she and her father could begin to work together to find a place for her in the company.

So she told her father everything.

To demonstrate her initiative, Eudora described how hard she'd worked to prepare for the exam, studying with Jackson in secret and borrowing textbooks from the library. She even mentioned leaving school early to meet with Mr. Hendricks. She finished her story with confidence, predicting that she would receive a formal acceptance letter in the spring.

"I see." His expression unchanged, her father read another section of the letter. "'...based on your recommendation, we don't foresee a problem with the committee.' Why does Mr. Hendricks say I recommended you? I don't remember writing any such letter."

Eudora shifted her weight in the chair, crossing her legs at the ankles. She'd left that part out of her story.

She swallowed but discovered her mouth was dry. "I wrote it." Her voice caught so she cleared her throat and continued. "I wrote the letter – my recommendation – on your behalf."

"I see. And did you sign it as well?"

"I did."

"In my name?"

"Yes, because they weren't going to let me in otherwise." Eudora leaned forward. "I called you several times at your hotels and left messages. I even left messages with Myra asking you to call me, but you never did." She finished weakly. "So I thought—"

Eudora's father shifted his attention back to Mr. Hendricks' letter as if what Eudora said mattered not at all. As he read, she heard a sharpness to his voice that she didn't expect. "'We are grateful for your generous donation and pledge of support to our Alumni Auction in the spring.'" He dropped the letter and it floated to the desk. "Is that your doing as well?"

"Yes."

He moved his hands to his desktop, clasping them together so tightly that his fingers were white. An anger that Eudora had never seen before gathered behind his eyes.

When he finally spoke, his voice was low and dripped with disgust. "It occurs to me that your mother knows nothing about what you've been up to, is that correct?"

"No sir, she doesn't."

"No, she doesn't," he repeated. "Because she would have stopped you."

There didn't seem to be a way to answer that, so Eudora remained silent.

"Just so I understand the full scope of what you've done..." He drew a deep breath and leaned back in his chair, crossing his arms in front of his chest. Fury radiated from him. "Not only did you offer Charleston College a letter of recommendation in my name, you took it upon yourself to make what appears to be a substantial donation? Also in my name."

"I used your stationery and wrote them a letter, yes."

"My personal stationery?" He lifted an eyebrow.

"No." Eudora dropped her gaze to the floor. "Your business stationery."

"So by your actions, Palmetto Exports is not only buying a table at the Alumni Auction, but I am also seated at the head table. Is that everything?"

"Yes," Eudora replied as she stared at the floor. Her father made everything she'd done sound so deceptive. All she wanted was to work for his company, and everything she'd done was done with that in mind.

Her father slapped his hand on the surface of his desk and she jumped.

"*Look at me, Eudora.*" His face was red with fury, his voice booming against the walls of his study. "What you did was unforgivable, using company resources for your personal gain. If you were an employee, you'd be fired on the spot. More than that, I would seriously consider filing criminal charges against you for forging my name. Do you understand?"

"Yes." As Eudora's vision blurred, her voice broke. "No – I mean no, I don't understand."

He seemed astonished by her reply, and in the silence that followed, Eudora gathered her courage. She straightened in her chair and found her voice. "I have always wanted to work for Palmetto Exports." She pointed to the corner of the study. "When I was ten years old, I added columns of numbers for you on a little table you'd had set up by the window. I remember it very clearly, and I remember thinking that some-day, I'd work by your side, maybe even one day take over when you decided to retire."

"Your mother has other plans for your life. She always has."

"Why did you give me work to do if you had no intention of—" Eudora's voice cracked and she paused, squeezing her hands together in her lap. "Why did you have me do all those things?"

"It kept you busy," he answered, simply.

In the silence that followed, the grandfather clock in the foyer chimed the hour, the deep gong echoing throughout the house. Eudora counted them for something to do, a distrac-tion so she wouldn't have to think about what her father had just said. It occurred to her that when the gongs stopped, he would pronounce sentence and his decision would be final. When the clock stopped chiming, her father's life would go on as usual, but hers would be over.

And she was right. When the gongs stopped, it seemed that her father had composed himself enough to pronounce sentence upon her.

"You used my company's reputation for personal gain." He spit out the words, as if he couldn't bear to be in the same room with her. "You took advantage of my standing as an alumnus and a member of the business community to get what you wanted."

"But—"

"Do not interrupt me, Eudora." Her father's voice was poison. "Your actions have forced me into a difficult situation with both Mr. Hendricks and the college. A situation that was precarious to begin with." He leaned forward, clenching his hands together on his desk. "I had thought your mother had raised you to value reputation and honesty, but I can see that I'm mistaken. From this moment forward, you will have nothing further to do with Palmetto Exports. I wash my hands of you."

Abruptly, her father turned his attention to the papers on his desk.

Before she rose, she tried one last time. "Daddy, can't we talk about this?"

"We already have."

CHAPTER 14

EUDORA LEFT the house in a blur of tears and fury, pushing past Annie in the kitchen and her mother in the dining room. Her father had completely misunderstood her intentions, and she didn't know how to fix things.

But Maggie would.

Eudora had run a full three blocks toward the O'Hanlan house before remembering Maggie's family had traveled to Brooklyn to visit relatives over Christmas break and the house would be empty. Then she walked another two blocks before deciding to go there anyway. The key to the back door would be under the mat, and she was sure Maggie wouldn't mind. She'd spend time in Maggie's room, sit in the O'Hanlan kitchen and she'd feel better. She might never go home again.

Then she thought about the gossip her disappearance would generate and she reconsidered. Something as spiteful as running away the morning after her debut would humiliate her parents, and she wouldn't do that to them. She thought about walking to Jackson's house. That would have been acceptable, but he'd already left for Italy and wouldn't be home either. Annie would help, try to smooth things over with her parents, but even Annie couldn't fix this. The things her father said to her could never be taken back. What was worse was that Eudora wasn't sure he'd ever try.

She slowed her pace. Her breath rose as mist in the chilly air before melting into the morning.

The streets on the upper peninsula were quiet this early, the traffic lights on Meeting Street blinking from green to yellow to red despite the absence of traffic. The sidewalks near the harbor were fringed with ice. Overhead, the sky darkened as a puff of wind carried salty air in from the harbor. Eudora shivered as she secured her collar firmly around her neck. She ran from the house not thinking, grabbing an overcoat from the foyer on her way out. It was one of her father's.

"You there! Stop!"

Ahead, a young girl ran from the train depot clutching a seagrass basket to her chest, the cloth fluttering in the breeze. Closely behind was a man in a dark blue uniform carrying a baton, his face masked in rage.

Eudora ran behind them for several minutes, calling out once as she struggled to keep up. She lost sight of them at an intersection and she stopped running. Charleston had begun to wake, with shopkeepers unlocking their doors and turning on lights, and there would be questions if Eudora was seen, disheveled and out of breath, so she ducked into a narrow side street. Though there were a few houses nearby, the street was more of an alley, protected and quiet with wrought-iron fences surrounding private gardens. It would be a good place to think. She dropped onto a low brick wall, not caring if the rain pooled in the crevices of the bricks or the mud on the ground ruined her sweater.

She'd never seen him so furious.

There was a solution somewhere, she just couldn't see it yet.

Leaning her head against the wrought-iron bars, she closed her eyes and listened to car tires hiss over the wet pavement as they drove by. In a tree overhead, a bird called out and in the distance another answered. Slowly, her body relaxed and she drew her first full breath since leaving home.

Somewhere in the distance, she heard what sounded like muffled puffs of air, sometimes so faint that Eudora couldn't tell if it was real. It seemed to come from further down the alley. Pushing herself to her feet, Eudora moved toward it.

There, slouching against the wall and tucked behind a fern, was the running girl, pulling in breath as fast as she could. At Eudora's approach, the girl turned, her eyes widened in fear.

Eudora froze, holding out her hands. "I'm not going to hurt you. I just want to know if you're all right?"

"This time." Her voice was strong; behind the fear was anger. Beside her on the cobblestones was the seagrass basket she'd been carrying. She wore a gray wool dress, cinched at the waist with a narrow black belt and a cardigan threadbare but large enough to wrap around her thin frame twice over.

"He didn't catch you."

"And he never will," the girl answered, "'less you tell him my hiding place."

"I won't." Eudora shook her head. "But the ground is wet. You should get up."

"I'll be fine."

"Well, you look cold to me," Eudora pressed. "If you get sick you won't be able to outrun the Health Department man."

After a moment, the girl conceded. "True enough."

"We can share my sweater until you warm up. Then you can be on your way."

The girl rose to meet Eudora, but her gaze was wary. "How is it you happen to be sittin' in the very same alley as me?"

"It's a long story," Eudora said, bitterly.

"Looks like I got a bit of time with nothing much to do until that man stop looking for me." The girl raised her chin. "Name's Letty."

"I'm Eudora." Eudora removed her coat and offered it to the girl. "I've seen you at the train station before, selling food to the passengers."

"That's true," Letty allowed. "Best fried chicken in the state."

"That's what my friend Maggie says." The chilly air bit through Eudora's clothing. She ignored it. If the girl saw her shiver, she might return the coat, and there was something about Letty that made Eudora want to open up. "Most of the women I've seen at the depot work in pairs. Is there someone I can find for you?"

Letty shook her head. "I work alone. But we ain't talking 'bout me."

"Fine." Eudora crossed her arms in front of her chest to conserve warmth. "I did the wrong thing for a very good reason but no one seems to care about why."

The sound of a whistle, shrill and close, startled them both. The inspector was back, red-faced and winded, at the mouth of the alley. Letty tensed. The seagrass basket was hidden under a fern and wouldn't be noticeable unless he looked closely.

He cracked the baton against the palm of his hand as he approached them. "Don't you run from me this time, girl." His eyes narrowed, his voice low and gravelly. "M'done chasing after you."

Eudora felt Letty gathering her strength to run, and Eudora stepped forward. The cobblestones were slick with frost, and the man was close enough now to overtake her. He was just looking for an opportunity to use his club.

Eudora stepped forward. "What seems to be the problem?"

"Been after this one for a while." He snatched at Letty's arm, but she slipped through his grasp. He was close enough that Eudora felt his breath on her skin. He smelled of tobacco and sweat. He glared at Eudora. "You just step aside now and let me do my job."

Furious, Eudora pushed the man's hand away. "Let go of her."

"This don't concern you." He sneered.

"It most certainly does." Eudora drew herself to her full height. "My name is Eudora Gadsden, and this girl is employed by my family."

"She's not." The man challenged. His eyes narrowed as the muscles of his jaws clenched. "She's one 'a them women sells chicken at the depot. Lot 'a people getting sick off 'a that chicken. It's my job to round 'em up."

"I believe you have her mistaken for someone else." Despite her fury, Eudora softened her tone, giving Letty time to kick the seagrass basket deeper under the ferns. "Because I can assure you, she made me tea this morning at my family's home."

"If that's true, what are you two doing in this alley?"

"It's a short cut back home." Eudora spun the lie easily. He faltered but remained standing, so Eudora pressed. "My family is home, holding Sunday breakfast for me. I'm sure they'd appreciate it if you let us pass."

After another moment's consideration, the man retreated down the alley and back toward the station.

When they were sure he'd gone, Letty bent to retrieve her basket. She straightened her dress before turning to leave. "Thank you," she said.

"Wait, you can't leave yet."

Letty paused.

"We have to leave together. What if he's still out there and sees you walking alone?"

"He won't find me."

"How can you be so sure?" Eudora glanced toward the mouth of the alley.

Letty shrugged.

"Why don't you come home with me? You'll be safe there, and warm."

"You think I'm some homeless dog in the street?" Though her tone was respectful, Letty's eyes sparked with defiance. "I got my own home. My family's waiting for me, same as yours."

"But you heard what that man said," Eudora countered. "He'll be looking for you at the depot and won't stop looking until he arrests you. It'll be hard to sell your food now."

"You think I don't know hard?" Letty challenged, her eyes flashing. "I do. Known it a long time."

"Okay, then." Eudora sighed, turning to leave.

"Miss Eudora?"

Eudora turned.

"I 'preciate your kindness. You ever need a favor, you just ask."

"You're welcome, Letty. Good luck to you."

To Eudora's surprise, Letty snorted. "Thanks just the same, but I make my own luck."

They parted ways on the corner, Letty headed uptown and Eudora back home to resolve what awaited her there.

CHAPTER 15

WHILE THE REST of Charleston celebrated a successful debut, Caroline was forced to deal with her daughter's failure. And it was almost too much to bear. She crushed another cigarette into the ashtray and tossed the stub to the side with the others. Only now, after three full hours of planning and telephone calls, did she feel prepared for the enormity of the project that lay ahead of her. The boutique in Atlanta was expecting them next week. The manager had promised to gather a selection of debutante dresses in Eudora's size and have the seamstress and her assistant available for the alterations that would no doubt be needed. Evelyn had agreed to come too, for moral support and advice.

How could she refuse, after what had happened? It was still so much to take in.

"Another cup of tea, Miss Caroline?" Annie appeared at the entrance to Caroline's sitting room. Though it was Sunday morning, a time Annie usually reserved for church services, she'd agreed to stay because the family needed her.

Annie, bless her, had kept the house quiet all morning while Caroline worked. She'd answered the telephone and the doorbell, taking messages and making excuses for the family's absence. And she'd kept the tea coming, hot and strong, to ease the pounding in Caroline's head.

Caroline dropped her pen on her notepad and pushed her shoulders back. "Just one more, I think. Then I'll be ready to speak with Eudora."

Annie hesitated, then nodded. "I'll get y'tea."

After Annie left, Caroline allowed herself to lean back in her chair, stretching her arms overhead. What had happened to Eudora was a nightmare and entirely unexpected. Imagine, that Jackson boy leaving for Florence the morning after Eudora's debut.

The first hint that Caroline had of anything going wrong was when she'd been called into Edward's office earlier that morning. He had been frustratingly indirect, as usual, but he seemed to imply he'd been disappointed with his wife's management of his daughter's Season. "Too much free time," he'd said. Caroline had explained that free time was part of her plan to allow Eudora time with Jackson. In fact, Caroline had been so sure that Jackson was going to propose to Eudora after her debut that she hadn't bothered to arrange a longer Season. She thought she'd be planning a spring wedding instead.

Apparently, that was not to be.

The details of Eudora's failure, and the reason that Edward knew about it before she did, were unclear, but his directive wasn't. Caroline was to plan an extended Season for Eudora and spare no expense in doing so.

It was Sissy Chalmers who had provided details in a hurried telephone call earlier that morning. Apparently, Jackson Legare had shocked everyone by leaving that very morning for an extended trip to Florence. The first thing that came to Caroline's mind was that Eudora had somehow offended him, but she didn't see any evidence of that at the ball. In fact, their attention seemed to be entirely focused on each other. In Eudora's defense, her daughter had said that she and Jackson weren't an item, but Caroline didn't believe it; not with the amount of time they'd spent together.

What was clear was that Jackson was firmly out of the picture, for whatever reason. The more immediate concern was that Eudora had been left without a Season and without any prospects.

Thankfully, Sissy Chalmers had provided a bit of other information, assistance in solving the mystery of the Rutledge family. Caroline wasn't familiar with them, but Sissy was.

The Rutledge family was an established, respectable Charleston family. Brock's father, William Rutledge II, had been a federal judge. He was an older man whose first wife had died shortly after giving birth to a daughter, who Sissy thought now lived in one of the northern states. After a brief period of mourning, he did the only honorable thing, and married again to give the girl a mother. Not much was known about the second wife, Sissy had said, other than her name was Lenore and she was significantly younger than her husband. Their only son, Brock, had been a cadet at The Citadel until the elder Rutledge had fallen ill the year before last. The family brought him to a private hospital in Switzerland and remained by his side during treatment. Unfortunately, he didn't recover, and the family moved back to their home near The Battery last year. They'd been in mourning for the past year, so their social engagements were limited.

In a strange twist of luck, Eudora seemed to be the only debutante he sent flowers to. Now that Jackson was apparently out of the picture, Eudora at least had something she could work with. The situation was dire, but not a complete loss. With careful management and guidance, this time next year Eudora could preside over a home almost as grand as the Gadsden home.

The deep gong of the grandfather clock broke the stillness of the house. Caroline glanced at the slim gold watch on her wrist, surprised to learn that she'd worked through lunch. And wasn't Annie supposed to return with tea?

There was a noise in the kitchen and Caroline caught a glimpse of her daughter. "Eudora, is that you?"

"Yes, Mother," Eudora called from the kitchen, her voice toneless.

"Come in here so we can have a talk." Caroline lightened her tone. It was possible that Jackson's disappearance had come as a surprise to Eudora as well. "It's been so long since we talked, don't you think?"

It was strange that Eudora was already dressed in street clothes the day after her debut. Caroline herself had been exhausted after St. Cecilia's and allowed herself to stay in bed the entire day. Eudora, however, was different. She preferred fresh air and movement when something bothered her, so she must have been out walking. Jackson leaving must have been such a blow. Caroline made a mental note to make sure the onus for Jackson leaving sat firmly at the Legare's doorstep; it wouldn't do to have people think Eudora was in any way responsible.

In the meantime, Eudora would take comfort in the fact that Caroline had her future firmly in hand.

"Things will move quickly for you in the next few months," Caroline began, then hesitated as she looked at her daughter's face. The light behind Eudora's eyes, the spark that had both infuriated and secretly pleased Caroline, had dulled. Her face was pale and she looked as if she were on the verge of tears. Jackson must have meant more to Eudora than she'd let on. A swell of anger filled Caroline's chest, but she pushed it away. She would deal with Kitty Legare and her wayward son later. Right now, it was important to give Eudora hope, something to look forward to.

So Caroline drew a breath and began. "First, you should know that it's not your fault the foyer table isn't overflowing with flowers from admirers. Apparently, no one, not even Posey Chalmers, got more than two bouquets this year. I think we can all agree that it's been a disastrous start to the Season." She paused a minute, hoping for a response but not expecting one. Eudora was clearly not herself. It occurred to her that passing along a bit of gossip would bring them closer. She lowered her voice to a whisper. "And, bless her heart, Joannie Fletcher didn't even get flowers from her escort."

"I'm very tired, Mother." Eudora's voice was flat. "I'd like to go upstairs and rest. Can we talk later?"

"Not until I tell you about your Season. Everything from this moment forward has been carefully planned, so you needn't worry." Caroline flipped to the first page in her spiral pad and checked her notes. "We leave for Atlanta on Wednesday, for at least a full week of shopping. Three shops I called assured me they will have a selection of gowns ready, with accessories to match and outfits for the remaining week." Caroline tapped a fingernail against the page. "Though I have my doubts that a gown shop will carry what we need for every occasion." She frowned. "Evelyn said she'd help, but she's only available for a short time, and with the Assembly Ball in Columbia just a few weeks away, we need to hurry." It had been decided that the Wednesday morning train from the

Charleston depot to the Atlanta terminal would be the most efficient choice. Carter had acted so put-out over Thanksgiving when she'd had him drive them to Aiken, she'd just as well avoid the drama. Caroline placed a crisp checkmark next to the travel arrangements box, then moved to the next line. "Orangeburg, Greenville, and Florence are after Columbia, so we have a bit more time to prepare. Although we might want to drop Orangeburg altogether and think about something closer to Atlanta." She tapped the pen against the paper. "Evelyn might have a connection that would allow you to debut in Augusta. I'll have to check. It's probably better if you get out from under Posey's shadow, anyway."

As Caroline scribbled down her thoughts, it occurred to her that getting away from Posey and the Charleston girls was a very good idea. She wasn't sure a competition would end favorably for her daughter, and time was tight.

"Mother?"

"Yes?" Caroline closed the cover of her notebook as she looked up.

"What is all of this?" Eudora swept her hand across the air above the table.

"Why, I thought I'd explained all that. We're expanding your Season to include the entire circuit, though we might—"

"Why?"

"Why what?" Caroline frowned as she glanced over Eudora's shoulder toward the kitchen where Annie seemed to be preparing breakfast. She'd hoped that Annie would address Eudora's concerns about Jackson Legare. Annie was better at drying Eudora's tears than she was.

"Why are you planning a circuit?" Eudora repeated.

"To launch you properly into Society, of course." Caroline pushed away a rising feeling of frustration. Eudora, after all, had just had her heart broken. Caroline should make an effort to be kind. "Your father has permitted us to spend whatever is necessary, so you needn't worry."

"Daddy knows what you're doing?"

"Of course he does." Caroline frowned in confusion. "It was his idea to extend your Season."

Eudora looked away.

There seemed to be nothing more to say, so Caroline continued. "We have a fitting next week in Atlanta. I have sent notes to your teachers, and they'll excuse you from the start of the spring term. I'm so grateful that Santee recognized the value of a full Season."

No reaction from Eudora, so Caroline tried one last time. "And if you find a nice boy at the end of it, we'll consider even that a success."

She rose from the table. "I'm going upstairs to freshen up. Then I have more telephone calls to make. You go ask Annie to fix you something to eat and you'll feel better."

A thought occurred to her as she reached the doorway, and she turned to address Eudora once more. "Something dietic, Eudora. We have dress fittings next week."

Annie lifted a plate from the dish rack and wiped it dry. She hadn't expected much of an explanation when Miss Caroline asked her to stay home from services this morning, and she didn't get one. Look what happened to Carter, thinking he was only dropping them two off in Aiken then being told to stay. His family'd waited turkey dinner on him and everything.

Something was wrong in this house this morning, no

denying that. What with Miss Caroline hunched over train schedules and papers all morning and Mr. Edward locked in his office. No one speaking to anyone on a morning they ought to be celebrating baby girl's success. Oddest family she'd ever worked for, but they paid on time and Miss Caroline could be kind when the mood struck her.

A shuffle of chairs from Miss Caroline's sitting room signaled whatever she and Eudora were discussing had come to an end. Annie hoped Miss Caroline had been gentle with that baby this time. She very rarely was.

Eudora appeared in the kitchen doorway looking pale and drawn, like she'd spent the night being tormented by a boo hag. Annie'd set up a broom tonight by the back door, bristles up, keep that boo hag busy.

"What'd your mama say?" Annie stacked the plate in the cabinet.

Eudora slumped onto the kitchen stool and looked at Annie with such anguish in her eyes that it almost broke Annie's heart. "He doesn't want me."

"Who don't want you? That Jackson boy?" Annie had known for weeks the Legare boy had planned to leave Charleston. Her cousin Tippie worked in their house and didn't hesitate to tell everyone Legare business. Annie was sure Eudora had known he'd left that morning. Known too, the reason why.

Eudora waved the words from the air. "Not Jackson. He'll be fine. He got away. I meant Daddy."

"What about your daddy?"

"He won't have me working for him. Said he never wanted that."

"Oh, honey." Annie opened her arms and moved toward Eudora, her heart hardening against Mr. Edward.

But Eudora stiffened as Annie approached, so Annie stopped and dropped her arms by her side. There were times when this child carried such a burden that it looked like she would shatter at the touch. This was one of those times.

"Can you make me something to eat?" Eudora managed a half-smile.

"You know I will." Annie flopped the dishtowel on the counter and went to the refrigerator. "What would you like?"

"Macaroni and cheese."

Annie eyed her warily. Eudora hadn't been allowed to eat much more than cottage cheese and cling peaches since they returned from Atlanta. "You sure?"

Eudora nodded. Annie thought she saw a spark in Eudora's eye but it was gone so fast, she couldn't be sure.

"And cornbread," Eudora added.

"Your mama might have something to say about that," Annie ventured.

"I think Mother will be upstairs for a good long while."

After a moment, Annie shrugged. "All right then."

CHAPTER 16

AFTER TWO PLATES of Annie's macaroni and cheese, Eudora left the house, though she didn't have a destination in mind. In truth, no one would care where she was until it was time for her to board the Wednesday morning train for Atlanta. Annie went home after the dishes were washed, when it was clear that Eudora's father was in his office for the duration and Eudora's mother had retreated upstairs to her room. And because Eudora could not stand the tension of the house without Annie to dampen it, she left too.

It seemed that Annie was the only one who cared about her, and that was an oddly freeing thought.

It was almost fourteen blocks to Marion Square and Eudora walked all of it. The December wind tugged at her hair and bit at her gloveless hands. She'd had the presence of mind to slip on a coat before she left but had neglected to take gloves or a scarf.

Pushing her hands deeper into her coat pockets, she chose a sheltered bench and considered her options.

She'd never seen her father so angry. It was unfair that he'd rejected her excuse that what she did was well-intentioned, but she knew that his decision was final. He'd never forgive her for what she'd done, and she'd never be part of Palmetto Exports. Her father, whose approval she'd always treasured, had turned on her, and she didn't know if she'd ever be able to win him back. As she sat on the bench, she felt the weight of his judgement press against her until she was unable to draw breath.

And her mother, it seemed, also thought Eudora was a disappointment, though that came as less of a shock. There was comfort in the knowledge that Eudora had tried her best to please her mother but never could. At least now, she could stop trying.

But what to do now?

As the wind blew across the square, Eudora shifted on the bench, lifting her collar against the cold.

"Eudora?" The man standing next to her was about Eudora's age and wore the gray uniform of a cadet from The Citadel. A close crop of sandy blond hair peeked out from beneath his service cap, and the tip of his ears were red from the cold. He paused for a moment, then his smile widened. He looked vaguely familiar, but Eudora wasn't entirely sure. "Eudora Gadsden? I thought that was you."

Eudora's nose had begun to run in the cold, and she sniffed, not caring how it appeared. "I'm sorry, do I know you?"

"Brock Rutledge. We danced last night at St. Cecilia." He reached into his pocket, withdrew a freshly pressed handkerchief and offered it to her. "May I sit with you?"

"No."

He seemed amused by her answer. "At least take this."

Eudora sniffed again. Her only alternative was to wipe her nose across her sleeve, and she couldn't bring herself to do that. She took the handkerchief and nodded her thanks, noticing that he averted his gaze as she indelicately blew her nose into it.

When she'd finished, she wadded it up and stuffed it into her pocket. "Thank you."

"Did you get my flowers?"

"Did you send me flowers?"

He paused again. "I'm sorry, have I done something to offend you?" He seemed genuinely surprised. "I may not be Fred Astaire on the dance floor, but I've been told I can dance fairly well." He sat next to her on the bench. He rested his hands on his knee, sharp white gloves against dark gray wool, and Eudora imagined how warm those gloves must be. "We were together for the fourth dance, I believe. Your escort went to get punch and I took advantage of your free time."

She didn't like him sitting next to her and certainly didn't want to discuss the ball, which seemed so far away now and so unimportant. But she didn't know how to make him leave. All at once she decided she was finished playing debutante games. She simply stood up.

"Thank you for the loan of your handkerchief, Brock. I'll make sure it gets back to you." She turned to leave. Then good manners made her turn back. "And thank you for the dance, I'm sure it was wonderful."

"At least let me walk with you."

"You don't know where I'm going."

"Doesn't matter," Brock said as he offered his arm. "I have three hours left of weekend leave and I'd consider myself fortunate to spend them with you."

Eudora rolled her eyes, but she took his arm because it looked warm and her hands were cold.

"Wait." He stopped and unbuttoned his coat. "Take this."

Eudora felt the weight of his coat, and the warmth spread across her shoulders. "Isn't this coat part of your uniform? Won't you get in trouble for being out of uniform, even on leave?"

Brock shrugged. "Following rules all the time is exhausting, don't you think?"

They wandered across the square and down toward the seawall, with Brock seemingly content to let her choose the direction. The truth was that she didn't know where to go. He'd already asked if she'd like to stop for a hot chocolate to warm up, but she had no intention of turning whatever this was into a date. After they'd walked in silence for a bit, Brock began telling her about his family, and Eudora listened to the sound of his voice as she let her mind wander.

"And we came back a few weeks before St. Cecilia."

In the silence that followed, Eudora realized that she was expected to answer, or at least to comment, but she had no idea what to say. And that she'd been unforgivably rude to someone who'd sent her flowers and lent her both a warm coat and a handkerchief.

She hesitated, stopping on the sidewalk and looked up at him. "I'm sorry, Brock. My mind is somewhere else."

"That's okay," he replied amiably. "I'd skip that part too, if I could."

"Skip what part?"

"My father's funeral. My mother and I are back in Charleston after a long time away." He lifted his shoulder and Eudora noticed his black armband for the first time. "It's good to be home, that's all."

"I'm sorry. My lack of attention was unforgivably rude." Eudora felt herself blush with shame. "Please, continue with what you were saying."

"Not much to tell, really. My father's doctors suggested a private hospital in Switzerland, and that's where we've been living for the past..." His voice trailed off as he thought. "For the past two years, I suppose. Maybe less." He shrugged. "It all blurs together."

"I imagine it does," Eudora replied as she picked up the thread of the conversation. "Was it just you and your mother in Switzerland, with your father? Do you have any brothers or sisters?"

"I have a half-sister, but she stayed in Charleston." She felt him stiffen and Eudora glanced at him for explanation, but let the matter drop when she saw the change in his expression. His jawline was tight, his lips pressed together in anger. "She's moved since, up north."

In a flash, his expression changed back and he changed the subject. "But that's enough about me. I'd rather hear about you. What were you doing on a bench in Marion Square in December?"

"Trying to decide what to do with my life." Eudora was surprised by the bluntness of her statement. Her first thought was that her mother would have been horrified at her candor. She barely knew this boy at all. Her second thought was that she didn't care. The rules she'd been following had made a mess of her life. It might be time to do things her way.

"Oh, really?"

"Yes," Eudora pressed on, not caring if his interest was genuine. It felt good to give voice to the things she'd been thinking. "My parents intend for me to continue the Season, five or six cities in all. I want a job instead – in business. Does that shock you?"

"Not at all." He slowed his pace, turning to look out over

the harbor. "Times are changing. Charleston is growing. Why shouldn't you be part of it?"

Eudora blinked, convinced she'd imagined his response.

He laughed and for the first time, she noticed a dimple on his cheek.

Two hours later, she turned toward home, curious about the type of flowers he'd sent her.

CHAPTER 17

It was a chilly late afternoon in January when Eudora turned the corner toward her home. The shadows stretched across the cobblestones in the pale winter light and summer seemed like a distant memory. Eudora opened the garden gate and slipped though, latching the gate behind her. She stood in the garden, looking at her house, memorizing every detail, because her life was about to change.

And she wasn't entirely sure if she was ready.

On the second floor, the light of her mother's bedside lamp shone through the blue silk sheers of the window. Her mother was reading in bed, most likely with a glass of warm milk by her side; she drank it to help her sleep. In the front of the house, the lights were on in her father's study, and though she longed to see him, she knew the door would be locked and knocks unacknowledged. If only he would let her explain, things might be different. But once Edward James Gadsden made a decision, there was no chance for appeal.

In the kitchen, all the lights were on, even the lamp by the window. Bright and welcoming.

Annie had waited up.

Eudora hurried along the garden path, the gravel crunching under her feet as she ran toward Annie's kitchen.

That girl had worked Annie's last nerve, coming and going these last few weeks without a word to anyone. This time she'd been out so long that she'd missed supper and Annie had almost given up, almost sent Carter and his son out looking. Though neither would know where to look and she didn't know where to send them. Annie might have suggested to start with that nice Irish girl, the one who lived over near Colonial Lake, but she hadn't been around much lately, so Annie suspected Eudora's comings and goings were something else.

So there was nothing to do but wait.

All day, Annie waited and into the night besides, the house creaking and groaning as if every Gadsden ancestor seethed in anger at the treatment of one of their own. And she couldn't blame them. The shards of past arguments and current resentments were embedded in the walls of the house, and unless something was done to fix it, the boo hags would come, bringing company and chaos. It was past time for Annie to step in, set things right.

The kitchen door creaked open and Carter peered in. "You think I might could go now? It's getting late and I like to tuck my boy in at night."

Annie glanced at the clock; it was later than she thought. "You still here?"

Carter nodded. "Nobody said for me to leave. And after what happen' in Atlanta, I don't want to make trouble."

The trip to Atlanta was the week before last and it was a

disaster. Miss Caroline had train tickets in hand until that uppity sister of her called, saying her husband didn't want his wife traveling that far without an escort. As if anyone would be fool enough to tangle with those two women. The tickets were returned and Carter was told to drive them all to Atlanta. Near three hundred miles. Took him all day to drive it, with stops for lunch and such. Good thing Annie had the sense to pack Carter food for the trip, else he would have starved. At the end, Carter unloaded the luggage and made to leave, thinking he'd be back at the end of the week. But no, he was told to stay. Again. Given twenty dollars and told to find a place to stay and be back every morning to drive them around.

When he returned, hungry, tired and near-about sick, Annie boldly gave him money from the coffee can and told him go be with his family. Miss Caroline knew what she did wasn't right; she was just showing off for her sister.

"You g'won. Miss Caroline's gone to bed hours ago," Annie said, feeling the old spark of annoyance threatening to ignite. She smothered it because it would do her no good to feel it. The bad juju would attract things she didn't want in this house.

Carter thanked her and dashed down the stairs, probably hoping to catch his own family before they tucked in for the night.

Annie turned to the stove, lifting the wooden spoon from the yellow spoon rest. Turning down the flame, she gave the perloo one more stir. The argument with her father had changed that girl. Lord knew Caroline had never been Mama-soft, but at least Eudora could depend on her daddy seeing her. But everything changed after that day. When Eudora left for Atlanta, she was stone-faced and serious, looking like a soldier about to go into battle. Which, Annie supposed, wasn't far from the truth. This was a cold house, for all its beauty, and most days it gave Annie chills just to be here.

Just as she was about to turn off the burner and give up on warming this dinner, Annie heard Eudora's feet pounding up the kitchen stairs. Annie whispered a prayer of gratitude for the safe return of that baby.

As the lock on the kitchen door turned, the weight of worry lifted from Annie's shoulders. Her baby was red with cold, but safe. She wanted to rush to Eudora, wrap her in the same kind of hug she'd give her own grandbabies, but she held back because she knew her place.

"Hi Annie." Eudora offered a smile as she shed her coat, but something seemed off. That little girl looked more tired than she ought to be, her face lined with the worry her mama heaped on her.

"I made your favorite, and cornbread besides." Annie pretended to stir the pot as she watched from beneath her lashes. She'd cared for Eudora since she was little bitty and knew her better than anyone.

Eudora heaved a sigh as she slid into a chair at the table. "That sounds wonderful. Thank you." She spread the napkin on her lap and reached for her water glass.

"You catch a chill?" Annie ventured.

"A little bit," Eudora answered.

Annie ladled the shrimp and rice into a shallow bowl, then added a sprinkle of green onions the way Eudora liked it.

"You going to eat with me?"

"Not this time, baby." Annie settled herself across from Eudora. "I want to talk to you."

Eudora stiffened, and Annie knew she'd have to be gentle.

Too many people telling that girl how to be and not enough asking her what she wanted.

Annie turned to the oven and pulled the packet of cornbread out. As she peeled away the tin foil, the smell of warm cornbread filled the kitchen and Eudora perked up as Annie knew she would.

"Is that for me?" Eudora eyed the packet.

"Made it special." Annie smiled as she pushed the crocket of honey-butter toward Eudora.

She waited until Eudora had chewed and swallowed her first bite of cornbread before trying again. Annie set her elbows on the counter and leaned in. "You gonna tell me what you been up to?"

Eudora shrugged. "Not much."

"You're not remembering who you're talking to," Annie said. "Let me remind you that I have kept every secret you ever told me, and I'd protect you with my last breath." She reached across the table for Eudora's hand. "And I'm here to tell you that what'choo doing ain't right. I know you're angry with your mama and daddy, but you're out late, you miss meals—"

"Mother has supper trays sent to her room and I haven't seen Daddy in weeks," Eudora interrupted, her voice sharp. "It's not like I have anyone here waiting for me."

"You have me," Annie said, simply. "And I worry."

For a moment, Eudora sat, her expression blank. Then, slowly, her eyes filled with tears and her lip began to tremble.

Annie gave Eudora's hand a quick pat and let it go. "I need to know you're okay, Little Bit. Right now, what I see is an angry young woman with parents who ain't behaving like they should. That can spell trouble, if you ain't careful." Annie locked her gaze with Eudora's, knowing she'd be able to sift the truth from whatever explanation Eudora offered. "You tell me right now what'choo been doing out so late since that fancy ball a'yours."

"Okay." Eudora's voice was soft and Annie felt her heart squeeze. From the time she was bitty, this girl had always been so eager to do the right thing, to please her parents, and they never once had a kind word for her. Not for the first time, Annie wished she could have taken Eudora home with her and given her the care she deserved. But, of course, that wasn't possible. "I met a boy."

Before she could stop herself, Annie laid her hand over her heart. "Oh honey, no."

Eudora shook her head. "It's not like that, Annie. Nothing like that."

"Then what is it like?"

"It's a long story."

"I got all the time in the world."

As Eudora ate, she told Annie about meeting Brock and not remembering who he was at first. About the dates they'd been on, in groups and chaperoned. Perfectly proper dates that Miss Caroline would have approved of, had she known. Annie listened to Eudora describe what she'd been up to for the past several weeks, but she watched, too. She saw the expression on Eudora's face change. She felt the air around Eudora lift and charge with energy. Eudora's appearance changed, as well. Her hair was still windswept, her cheeks red and chapped, but something was different. Something in her carriage that Annie couldn't identify.

It looked like determination.

CHAPTER 18

"You're doing *what*?"

"Getting married." Eudora dipped her hand to show Maggie the engagement ring on her finger. The diamond was as big as an acorn, square cut and flanked by smaller stones on either side. "Brock proposed and I've accepted."

"Why?" Maggie felt herself drop to the bed. She sat, blinking at the flashy ring in front of her, and her first thought was that her best friend was making a mistake. She couldn't say that outright, of course, so she repeated her question. "Why would you get married?"

"I would think the reason would be obvious." Eudora settled onto the floor. "He asked and I accepted."

"Is this the boy who sent you flowers the morning after St. Cecilia?"

"Yes." Eudora crossed her legs and leaned her back against the wall.

"But that was less than a month ago."

"It was five weeks ago," Eudora corrected, her words clipped.

"Five weeks?" Maggie echoed. "It took you longer to learn

to make a soufflé in home economics. And your soufflés still fall." Maggie's attempt at humor was met with silence. "Are you serious?" she asked, finally.

"Why would you think I wasn't?" Eudora's voice held an edge that Maggie didn't recognize.

"Oh, I don't know, Eudora." All at once the Irish temper Maggie had inherited from her mother exploded. Behind it was weeks of cancelled lunches, missed phone calls, unreturned messages. "Maybe because the last I heard your mother had planned a full Season for you. And the last time we had an actual *conversation*, you were on your way to Atlanta to buy a dress." Maggie felt her frustration rise, the tone of her voice matching the rising panic in her chest. She felt as though she was losing her best friend, that Eudora was turning into something Maggie couldn't recognize. Into Posey. "You barely speak to me at school, you're *never* around anymore and when you finally do come over, you show me *that*?" Maggie flicked Eudora's hand away. "Marriage was the last thing you wanted, Eudora. Have you forgotten? We used to sit right here—" Maggie paused to smack the surface of her bed with the palm of her hand. "Right here and make fun of Posey and the other girls for getting married so soon after graduation, and here you are doing the same thing." She slowed, pressing her forehead with her fingertips harder than she needed to. Maybe this was a dream and when she woke up, everything would be all right.

Then a thought hit Maggie with an almost physical force. She gripped the bedspread to steady herself, the fabric balling in her fist as she squeezed. "Is your mother making you get married? Because you don't have to – you can stay here. I don't even have to ask my parents for permission. I'm sure they'll say yes. In fact, I can go with you right now to help you pack."

"Stop it." Eudora's voice was brittle, forced. "Why can't you just be happy for me? You're supposed to be my best friend."

"I *want* to be happy for you, Eudora, and I'm trying. I really am." Maggie rose from the bed and paced the room. "I just can't help but think you might be rushing things a bit. How much do you know about this boy?"

"I know as much as I need to." Eudora wouldn't meet Maggie's eye. Instead, she focused her attention on a stray thread in the carpet.

That told Maggie all she needed to know. Eudora didn't want to get married. Not really.

"'As much as you need to'?" Maggie repeated, more slowly now. The questions tumbled in her mind, like rocks in a washtub, but if she gave voice to them, Eudora would dig in even deeper, then it would be impossible to get her to see reason, even if she wanted to. Eudora could be stubborn that way. Maggie walked to her desk and sat, giving the impression that she intended to be perfectly reasonable. "Tell me then, because I don't understand how you could abandon plans you've had for years after knowing someone for five weeks."

"I'm not abandoning anything, Maggie," Eudora finally replied. "I danced with Brock at St. Cecilia, only I didn't remember. And he sent me flowers the morning after to thank me. He's different from the other boys I know. He thinks an extended Season is outdated, just like I do. He's as excited as I am that I've been accepted to Charleston College, and he wants me to take classes in the fall. We're even starting a business together." Eudora's eyes sparked with excitement.

"Doing what?"

"We're not sure yet, but he's got really good connections. We're going to spend our first summer as a married couple putting together business plans."

"That's great, Eudora," Maggie said. "But why do you have to marry him? Why can't you just be business partners?"

"Because he believes in me," Eudora said.

"I believe in you," Maggie insisted. "Lots of people—"

"No," Eudora interrupted. "They don't. Not for this." Eudora dropped her gaze and stared at her hands. "I was enrolled in Santee Academy when I was five years old. There was never any question of going anywhere else. All my friends, with the exception of you, are the daughters of my mother's friends, and the sons are the boys who I'm supposed to date. Jackson Legare was selected as my cotillion partner before I even left the hospital. I'm pretty sure my mother called Mrs. Legare to arrange it even before my father was allowed in the room." Eudora laced her fingers together and drew a soft breath. "Almost every article of clothing I've ever owned, every dress, every gown, every suit, has come from Chastains. My world is very small, Maggie, and it's hard to change and impossible to escape. So when I meet a boy who thinks the way I do and believes we can do great things together..." Her voice trailed off to a whisper. "It's hard not to listen."

Maggie listened, not knowing how to reply. If Eudora could only see herself as Maggie did: strong, determined, smart, she wouldn't sell herself into marriage just to escape her parents. Earlier in the year, Maggie had asked Eudora to come with her to New York City after graduation, had offered to share the room in her aunt's Brooklyn brownstone, but

Eudora had refused. She said her heart was in Charleston and she wouldn't leave. And when Maggie offered her own room in the O'Hanlan house, Eudora refused that too, saying the scandal would destroy her parents.

A breeze ruffled the white curtains on the window, pulling in the scent of winter jasmine. Outside, Maggie heard the sound of a metal can skittering along the asphalt road and her brothers calling to each other.

In the end, Maggie said the only thing she could say. "When is the wedding?"

"Right after graduation." Eudora's voice was clear, her tone firm. "I need you to be happy for me."

Maggie nodded, understanding the wheels had been set in motion weeks ago and that she was powerless to stop them. If Marie O'Hanlan were here, she might know what to say to bring Eudora to her senses, but her mother was away and Maggie didn't have her mother's gift, so they sat in silence.

"The engagement party is on Valentine's Day," Eudora offered. "You and your parents are invited."

"Do you love him?" Maggie asked impulsively.

"What?"

"I asked," Maggie turned to her friend, locked her gaze with Eudora's and would not let go, "if you love him."

"Yes, of course."

Eudora's expression was a mask that Maggie had seen many times, mostly when she was lying to her mother. It didn't fool her then and it didn't fool her now.

Maggie narrowed her eyes and offered one final challenge. "Then say it," she insisted. "Say 'I love Brock' – what's his last name?"

"Rutledge." Eudora lifted her chin and held Maggie's gaze. There was determination in Eudora's eyes, but that was all Maggie saw. "Brock Rutledge," Eudora said. "His name is Brock Rutledge, and I do."

That wasn't quite the same thing but Maggie didn't know what else to say.

"I need you to be okay with this, Maggie." Eudora's comment was unexpected, her voice small. "You need to believe this is my choice, and I want my husband and my best friend to like each other."

"I don't even know him," Maggie countered, careful to keep her tone neutral. "I'm supposed to be your best friend, Eudora. Why haven't I met him before now?"

"He's a cadet at The Citadel. They keep him pretty busy and he doesn't get many weekend passes." Eudora reached for Maggie's hand. "You *are* my best friend, and I want you to be my maid of honor."

Maggie hesitated. Didn't being maid of honor imply that she supported this marriage? She wasn't sure she did.

"C'mon, Maggs. My mother suggested Posey Chalmers." Eudora gave an exaggerated shiver. "And I can't have that."

"Your mother knows about your engagement?"

"'Course she does," Eudora scoffed. "Wasn't that the point of my Season? Marrying Brock ends the Season early and gets me into college."

Eventually, Maggie agreed to be Eudora's maid of honor.

It was a decision she'd regret for the rest of her life.

CHAPTER 19

THE EAST BAY Yacht Club was nestled in a sheltered cove at the mouth of Charleston Harbor, overlooking Fort Sumter. A polished brass plaque between a pair of gas lamps at the entrance was the only hint that something existed behind the brick wall. Maggie had walked past it many times on her way to White Point Gardens, but had never gone inside because she and her family weren't members. Today, however, the entrance was open and the gatehouse staffed with uniformed attendants. Today, the O'Hanlan family would be allowed inside because Eudora had chosen EBYC as the site for her engagement party and Maggie and her parents had been persuaded to come.

"Looks like this is the place." Maggie's father turned the car into the entrance, the tires on the station wagon crunching on the white gravel and oyster shells that lined the drive.

A man emerged from the gatehouse. He was dressed in dark pants and a long woolen overcoat, and as he got closer, Maggie could see EBYC insignia embroidered on his epaulet.

"Good evening, are you here for the Rutledge-Gadsden party?"

"Ahoy, young man. We are indeed," Maggie's father chirped.

Maggie winced at her father's attempt at humor. She knew for a fact that her mother had spoken to her father about keeping his comments to himself because she'd overheard their conversation the night before. Her father's point, as usual, was that he couldn't understand why some people thought themselves better than others when everyone 'put their pants on one leg at a time.' All Maggie's mother had to do was remind him that it was Eudora's engagement party and that the event was important to Maggie. He'd agreed to do his best.

From the back seat, Maggie could see her mother laying her gloved hand gently on her father's forearm as a reminder. He cleared his throat and continued in a normal tone. "Yes, we are. The name's O'Hanlan."

The guard checked their name against the list on his clipboard and waved them through. "Thank you, Mr. O'Hanlan, please pull forward to the valet."

The entrance to the clubhouse was marked with a blue canvas awning imprinted with the initials EBYC in large capital letters. Maggie's father pulled the car up and they were met by two other men in similar uniforms who opened the doors for Maggie and her mother.

"Welcome to East Bay Yacht Club." The valet offered his arm and led Maggie from the car.

"What a beautiful place," Maggie's mother commented as she joined her daughter in the alcove.

"It really is," Maggie agreed.

The late afternoon light faded into evening, casting a blue light across the grounds. Beyond the clubhouse was a wide stretch of carefully manicured grass, with gravel paths lined with white painted stones. A flagpole that looked like a ship's mast had been planted squarely in the middle of the lawn; the halyard slapped against the metal mast and a string of burgees fluttered in the breeze. One of the paths led to what Maggie assumed was a boathouse, near a protected cove and a mooring of small sailboats. Another wound around to the back of the clubhouse and the muted sounds of a band playing.

The recent cold snap appeared to be over and winter seemed to be making way for an early spring. The evening air was soft and the air smelled hopeful. As the breeze shifted, it brought sounds and smells from the water. In the distance a squatty wooden motorboat approached the cove, its motor a deep thrumming, its crew scrambling as the captain steered it closer to the dock. Maggie could hear the wood creaking as the dock shifted in the boat's wake and the rope slapping against the pilings as the crew tied-off.

Inside, Maggie imagined, the setting for Eudora's engagement party would be just as beautiful, entirely different from lodge dances her parents attended, and Maggie insisted they all dress for the occasion. Since Maggie had refused to ever return to Chastains, she had designed and sewed evening dresses for herself and her mother. Her own gown was a deep navy velvet with white trim around the sweetheart neckline and fitted at the waist with princess seams. Her mother's dress was a bit trickier because Maggie couldn't get her to stand still long enough to fit the dress properly, and it was only three-quarter length because the cost of silk fabric was dear. Still, Maggie was pleased with the results. The bright green silk perfectly matched her mother's eye color, and the fabric draped softly from her waist to her calves. And her father didn't protest at all when Maggie insisted he rent an evening suit and shoes.

In fact, they were all so elegantly dressed that Maggie could almost imagine herself as one of them, walking the red carpet to a movie star's party. That was, if she weren't positive her father would embarrass them all.

As if on cue, the sound of her father's deep laughter punched through the peace of the evening.

"Ma." Maggie's gaze cut to her father, who seemed to have thumped the valet on the back, then back to her mother. "You promised you'd talk to him."

"You know I did," Maggie's mother said. "I heard you on the stairs last night, listening." She reached into her bag for her compact and flicked it open. "This whole situation with Eudora makes your father uncomfortable, and when he's uncomfortable, he makes jokes. You can't change who he is, we can only hope to temper it a bit."

Maggie scoffed.

"I'm not kidding, Maggie," her mother admonished as she tucked the compact into her purse. "Eudora and this boy seem to be moving very quickly. Your father and I would have liked to have had a chance to meet him before now, maybe have Eudora and her young man over for supper once or twice." She snapped the clasp closed and fixed her gaze on Maggie. "It seems so fast. Are you *sure* you didn't know anything about her engagement before now?"

Before Maggie could reply, her father approached. "My two favorite girls," he said, as he extended his arms for them to take. "If I don't get a chance to tell ya later, I'll tell you now: you're the prettiest ones here."

Her mother scoffed but reached for his arm anyway, and Maggie saw a hint of pink coloring her mother's cheeks.

They continued underneath the canopy, walking on the carpeted path from the courtyard to the club's entrance. Placed on either side were oversized pots of delicately blooming miniature cherry trees. Their branches had been threaded with tiny white lights which cast a warm glow against the delicate blossoms. The front door was dark polished wood and caved with an intertwining rope design. Mounted on either side of the door were heavy brass lanterns, one red and one green. And in an obvious nod to Valentine's Day, a wreath of gilded paper hearts hung over the heavy wooden door.

"We must be in the right place," Maggie's father joked as he pointed to the brass plaque beside the entrance. "In case you were wondering if we lost our way from the entrance to the front door. Says right there, again: East Bay Yacht Club."

"I'd wish you'd stop making jokes, Carl," Maggie's mother chided. "You know how worried we are about Eudora."

Maggie's father immediately sobered. "I know you are, Marie. I am too. But Eudora is a smart girl, and I'm sure she knows what she's doing." He placed his hand around his wife's shoulders and drew her in. "And if she doesn't, I'm equally sure you and Maggie will know how to make things right. Now, let's just enjoy this fancy party."

"Maybe you're right," Maggie's mother allowed, though she hesitated.

"Of course I'm right," he replied. "And would'ja look at these?" He gestured to the brass lanterns. "Donny Joe's been working on the boathouse over on Sullivan's and he told me about these lights. The colors mean something – but I'll be darned if I remember what it was."

"They have to do with navigation," a man behind them

offered. Tall and slender with blond hair, the man reminded Maggie of Fred Astaire from the movie Royal Wedding. He was dressed like the character in the movie too, in a white dinner jacket, shiny black shoes and a gold signet ring on his left hand. He looked completely at ease in his surroundings. "The green is mounted on the vessel's right and the red is mounted on the left. The lights are supposed to help the captain steer around boat traffic by telling him on which side to pass. Information that's vital on the water but completely unnecessary for a building's entrance. In fact; I think they just do it for show." He offered his hand with a smile. "Alistair Rutledge, uncle to the future groom."

Maggie's father accepted his hand and shook it. "Carl O'Hanlan, friend of the future bride. This is my wife Marie and my daughter Margaret."

The conversation continued as they made their way inside the foyer and as the attendant took their coats. As the adults chatted, Maggie took a moment to admire the room and memorize the details. Since she planned her clothing line for a well-heeled crowd, she needed to know what they liked.

The entrance was spectacular, a large circular room paneled in dark wood and tiled in white marble. A large silver vase of spring tulips greeted visitors, and an ivory guestbook and a gold pen invited them to sign their name and leave good wishes for the couple. Antique wooden boats were displayed on wooden cradles placed in glass cases, along with trophies and plaques for races won. Overhead, an enormous crystal chandelier filled the room with warm yellow light. The plaster medallion that held it in place seemed to be set in the center of a ship's compass, with ornate letters indicating the cardinal directions. On the far wall, a pile of birch logs crackled and popped in the hearth, sweeping the chill from the room.

After shedding her coat and handing it to an attendant, Maggie excused herself from the group and went to find Eudora.

A cocktail reception was held before dinner, in a room that occupied most of the first floor. On the far wall were wide bay windows that offered an expansive view of the club's grounds and Charleston Harbor. Tall tables scattered around the room held tasteful flower arrangements in tiny crystal vases. A hundred of Charleston's most distinguished couples dressed in their finest evening clothes gathered to wish the couple well. Maggie recognized a few girls from school, Posey Chalmers, Eleanor Franklin, and Mary-Davis Todd, but didn't rush to join them.

Those were Eudora's friends, not hers.

Maggie accepted a flute of Champagne from a passing waiter and sipped.

Finally, she spotted Eudora on the far side of the room, surrounded by well-wishers. Maggie almost didn't recognize her because she looked exactly like the women who surrounded her. Eudora's hair was swept into the same kind of chignon that Eudora used to make fun of for being stuffy and matronly. The same girl who never gave a thought to her clothes now wore a stunning gown of pale blue, with a darker blue sash that anchored the empire waist and fell gently to the floor. The diamonds at her ears and throat caught the light, sparkling when she laughed. This wasn't the girl that Maggie remembered, but maybe it was the woman that was meant to be.

Maggie glanced at her own dress and felt like a duck in a

room full of swans. No matter what she wore, she would never fit in.

"Maggie, right?" A pair of cadets in dress uniform stood before her. Brock was the taller of the two, with wavy blond hair, a deep voice and a distinctive Charleston accent. She'd met him once before, briefly, and couldn't stand him. She thought he played to his audience, charming and deferential when he needed to be, sarcastic and coarse when it served him. Furthermore, Maggie would stake a month's allowance on a bet that his accent was exaggerated. But she promised herself that she'd try, for Eudora's sake.

"It's nice to see you again, Brock. What a lovely party." Maggie stood stiffly as he leaned in to kiss her cheek.

"It can officially start now that you're here." Brock's voice was smooth, but there was something in his eyes that suggested he didn't like her either. "May I present my good friend, Charles Montgomery? As you can see, we're both at The Citadel, but hope to graduate in May."

Maggie offered her hand. "It's nice to meet you, Charles."

"Hello, Maggie." He accepted her hand and shook it. He didn't look weird at all.

"Charles is my best man and since you're maid of honor, you two should get to know each other." Brock dimpled when he smiled, something Maggie had not noticed before. It looked forced, something he did for effect. "You're both at the head table, of course, with Eudora and me so you'll have plenty of time to talk." Brock placed a hand on each of their shoulders and Maggie resisted the urge to shake it off.

Instead, she tried again. For Eudora. "This is a beautiful club, Brock. I've never been here before."

"My family's been members of East Bay Yacht Club for years. In fact, my father was Commodore for years before he got sick. The club had a dinner dance scheduled for tonight, being Valentine's Day and all, but we managed to persuade them to move their event to next week."

Maggie nodded awkwardly as Brock excused himself to greet his other guests.

"So how do you know Eudora?" Charles asked after Brock left.

"Eudora and I go to school together, Santee Academy. We've been friends since fifth grade." Maggie accepted another flute of Champagne and sipped. "How about you? How long have you known Brock?"

"Not that long, actually." Charles shrugged. "To tell the truth, I was a little surprised when he asked me to be his best man."

The dinner gong rang before Maggie had a chance to reply. She found her parents and followed the crowd upstairs to the ballroom. Her parents were seated with couples they wouldn't know, but they'd make the best of it. It was a running joke with the O'Hanlan relatives that Maggie's father could charm the birds from the trees if he wanted to, and her mother... well, her mother was a good listener.

The soup was a clear broth, the appetizer a selection of spiced shrimp on a bed of Carolina Gold rice, the type of rice Eudora's father exported, and Maggie wondered if maybe this was a signal that Eudora and her father had made up. Maggie wanted to ask, but Brock was sitting between them and it would have been impolite to lean over to ask.

There would be time later, she was sure.

Maggie sipped her wine as the waiters cleared the plates. She caught her mother's eye and smiled, giving the impression she was having a good time, which she wasn't. Brock had barely spoken to her and the woman on Maggie's right seemed in deep conversation with the person on *her* right, leaving Maggie entirely alone.

But that was okay.

All at once a parade of waiters, each holding a silver-domed plate in their gloved hands, appeared from the kitchen and approached the head table. In unison, they set the plates on the table and lifted the covers. The crowd murmured their approval, but Maggie tensed.

Lamb.

On the plate was a lamb chop, rare, with a ramekin of mint jelly, okra salad, and a tuft of parsley.

She turned to Brock and said the first thing she thought of. "This is lamb."

He nodded as he lifted his knife. "Yes, it is."

He didn't seem to understand, so she continued. "Eudora hates lamb."

And it was true. Eudora hated the very *idea* of lamb chops. When they were younger, they'd played the game "What would you never eat?" Eudora's choice was always lamb, and no circumstance Maggie ever thought of would get Eudora to change her mind.

Flood, no.

Famine, no.

Stranded on a desert island and lamb chops was the only thing to eat until rescue.

"I'd rather starve," had been Eudora's firm response.

So why was Eudora's most despised food being served at her engagement party?

"Brock," Maggie pressed. "Why are you serving lamb?"

He offered a smile before depositing a slice in his mouth. "It's my favorite."

CHAPTER 20

EUDORA ROLLED ONTO HER STOMACH, her new princess phone pressed to her ear. Her mother, in a rare display of generosity, had arranged for the telephone company to hook up an extension in Eudora's room. No explanation was given, but Eudora didn't expect one.

"The new course catalog came out today," Eudora reached for the brochure on her nightstand.

"Is that right?" Brock's response seemed noncommittal, but then she wouldn't expect him to be as excited as she was.

"Yes, that *is* right." Eudora tried a bit of flirting but was met with silence. She'd seen Posey reduce a boy to a stuttering mess with a smile and few well-chosen words, but Eudora could never seem to get the hang of it. Brock didn't seemed to notice when she tried, either.

Maybe in time.

She cleared her throat and continued. "I can't decide which business classes to take. They all look so good. Business Accounting is offered on Tuesday and Thursday at eight a.m., do you think that's too early?"

"You're the one'll be getting up, not me."

His reply was confusing. Eudora's father was usually dressed and at his office before either Eudora or her mother woke. She assumed all men had the same work ethic.

"I know we plan to start a business together, but it will take some time for me to finish my degree," Eudora ventured. "Have you decided what you're going to do in the meantime?"

"You let me worry about that," Brock replied. "You have a wedding to plan."

But she didn't. The truth was that Eudora's mother had taken over the wedding planning almost immediately. She and her sister Evelyn met to discuss details, and Eudora was rarely consulted on anything. Her wedding dress had been ordered from a boutique in Savannah based on a picture in a magazine. Mrs. Tweedy was charged with arranging alterations and ordering the bridesmaid's dresses. Eudora hoped they were nice.

Eudora had refused the first time Brock proposed. Then he asked twice more, explaining that theirs would be a modern marriage, a marriage of equals, unlike anything their social set had seen before. He said he admired her dream of going to college and then onto business, insisting that Charleston would welcome progressive thinking like hers. When she told him that she didn't love him, he said he didn't care. That he admired and respected her and that great marriages were built on less.

It was Brock she called after her mother presented her with a train schedule and an extended Season. She'd said they were 'only dating' and there 'might be better fish in the sea.' It was Brock who suggested she accept his proposal and focus her efforts on school instead of Society.

So she did.

And she was able to fool everyone except Maggie.

So she started avoiding Maggie, just for a little while.

In the fall, when she was safely enrolled in school, she'd explain everything, and Maggie would understand. After all, they were best friends, weren't they?

CHAPTER 21

EUDORA SAT at the vanity in the dressing room of St. Michael's cathedral, staring at her reflection. Her bridesmaids had left her alone, promising to meet her in the narthex for the walk down the aisle. Her mother had cried when she saw Eudora in her dress, taken both Eudora's hands in hers and told Eudora how happy she was, how excited for her future. Her father wouldn't meet her eye. She picked up the brush and ran it through her hair, one last time as a single woman. In just a few minutes, she would anchor the veil to the top of her head and descend the stairs.

Was she sure?

She didn't know.

But she believed Brock to be an honorable man, a man of his word, and he'd promised her that marriage was the best step forward for both of them. He'd confided that since his father's passing, his mother had been worried about 'getting him settled,' and now she would rest easier. As for Eudora, she'd have the freedom to choose whatever she wanted to do. That was more than she was allowed in her father's home, debutante or not.

So yes, she was willing.

She glanced at herself in the mirror again. The next time she looked at herself, she would be Mrs. Brock William Rutledge, of the Charleston Rutledges, descendants of the only captive of Blackbeard's crew who made it to shore alive in 1776.

The knock at the door was sharp, pulling Eudora from her thoughts.

"Come in," she answered.

Lenore Rutledge, the woman who was to be her mother-in-law, entered the room, carrying a slim velvet box. She was not much older than Eudora's mother, though William Rutledge had been closer in age to Eudora's grandfather. For the wedding of her only son, Lenore Rutledge wore a dark gray dress with thick black trim along the hem and wrists, indicating a widow in mourning. Her husband had been gone for almost two years, so even in the strictest sense, Lenore would be allowed to wear color. But she didn't. And Eudora couldn't help but take offense, though she said nothing.

Lenore perched on the edge of the chair opposite Eudora. "I will admit that I don't know much about you, other than my son has chosen you to be his wife, and your association with this family begins today. You will become a Rutledge. Our history will be your history, and you will be the one to curate it." She slid the box onto the vanity and opened it. Inside was a perfectly matched triple strand of pearls, with a diamond clasp. "These pearls have been in our family since the beginning, and Brock has asked me to give them to you."

Eudora touched the base of her throat and felt the necklace she'd chosen to wear, the Gadsden pearls. "But I have pearls of my own. They've been in my family for a long time, too."

"Then you must choose." Lenore laid down the box. "I trust you will make the right decision." Then she turned and left the room without another word.

After a moment, Eudora unclasped her great-grandmother's pearls and slid them off her neck. After all, it was just a necklace.

Four hundred guests filled the nave of St. Michael's church on a bright spring afternoon in late April, the weekend after graduation ceremonies at Santee Academy. The recent warm weather had encouraged the azaleas to bloom, and the church grounds were awash in pale shades of pink, white, and red. Large crystal vases had been strategically placed around the nave, each filled with arrangements of spring flowers, lilac, wisteria and tender green ferns. Their fresh scent mixed with the aromas of candle smoke from the altar and beeswax from the pews to perfume the air.

Two flower girls, distant cousins on her mother's side, were outfitted in pale pink dresses with patent leather shoes and dainty lace-trimmed ankle socks. The organ music started, and they began the procession by dropping tiny handfuls of white rose petals from small baskets of woven seagrass as they walked toward the altar. Next came the ring-bearer, a cherubic five year old relation who wandered down the aisle clutching the small ring pillow, awed by his responsibility. Then eleven bridesmaids, three friends from school, the rest daughters of her mother's friends, all dressed in blue and carrying bouquets of white tulips and purple freesia.

The ceremony was over before Eudora realized it. She had

vague memories, but they were splintered and disjointed, not what she expected from her own wedding.

Memories of the opening bars of the Wedding March.

Of the suit fabric on her father's arm as he gave her away.

Of the breeze on her face and smell of candle smoke as Brock lifted her veil.

In no time at all, Brock slipped the ring on her finger and the organist began to play again. Eudora's mother was wrong: Eudora would not remember her wedding day for the rest of her life. In the end, Eudora was left with very little memory of it.

And she wondered what all the fuss was about.

The reception was held on the grounds of the Gadsden home. Eudora's mother had ordered a tent set up in the garden because April weather could be unpredictable, but she'd softened the edges by hanging potted ferns around the perimeter. A string quartet played softly in the background, and there was a hum of subdued conversation, peppered with the clink of serving utensils, and occasional laughter.

Brock squeezed her hand as they walked under the flowered trellis, and Eudora remembered offering him a smile, but a moment later, he was gone. She watched him walking toward his friends. Saw him loosening his bow tie and accept a drink in a wax-coated cup. She heard him laugh.

Then Eudora began to tremble. The edges of her vision blurred as the weight of what she'd done settled into her body. In the space of just four months, Eudora had met and married a man she barely knew. She would move into his house. Share his bed. Become his family.

Unable to move forward, Eudora wondered what would happen if she just ran away.

"Eudora, there you are." The voice was gentle and she turned toward it. "I've been looking all over for you. And here you are." Uncle Alistair offered his arm. "Please allow me the honor of escorting you to the reception." Uncle Alistair's grip was reassuring, his voice soft. "Things are not ever as bad as they seem. And you don't strike me as someone who gives up easily."

It was as if the snap of a rubber band jolted her awake. Everyone was watching, and she was embarrassing herself.

She accepted his arm and found her voice, though it cracked when she spoke. "I've just stopped to admire the wisteria, it's one of my favorites."

"Interesting thing about wisteria. It grows wherever it's planted and blooms in any soil. A vastly underestimated vine, in my opinion," Uncle Alistair remarked.

Eudora let him escort her to the reception and onto the dance floor for the first dance. It was a horrible breach of etiquette, not dancing the first dance at one's wedding with one's husband. But Brock seemed to have vanished, and Uncle Alistair's offer let Eudora save face. Later, Eudora overheard Uncle Alistair remarking to a guest that he had imposed on Eudora's good nature and requested the first dance. That the blame lay entirely with him.

Brock joined her for the third dance, and part of the fourth. He stayed by her side as they greeted guests and chatted with friends and relatives he hadn't met before. He smelled vaguely of alcohol, but he was so charming when he spoke to her that Eudora dismissed his disappearance at the trellis as last-minute jitters. She'd had them herself, hadn't she?

As the afternoon light began to fade into evening, guests started to gather their things. Children were rounded up and carted home, off to bed. For adults that chose to stay, the caterers lit tea light candles inside oversized hurricane lanterns and placed them on tables. As the party wound down, Eudora went to look for her husband. She'd searched the house, the garden, and the courtyard without success. She was about to give up when she saw a flicker of movement in the alley. She turned just in time to see her new husband grabbing one of her bridesmaids by the waist and lifting her up. Posey's dress fluttered around her feet as he picked her up, and she squealed in delight as she steadied herself against his chest.

Someone grabbed her arm, and Eudora's attention was diverted. "Eudora, dear, I'd like to wish you the very best." The woman was older, one of the many guests Eudora did not know.

Eudora murmured her thanks and the woman went away. By the time Eudora looked toward the alley again, Brock and Posey were gone, and Eudora had no idea what to do.

After an hour or two, Eudora saw Posey again, breathless and red-faced. Her updo had fallen, tendrils of blonde hair escaping their bobby pins.

Posey reached for Eudora's hand. Her speech was slurred, her eyes unfocused. "Eudora, I can't believe you kept this a secret! How *exciting*."

Eudora's gaze flicked back toward the sidewalk, to her husband. He smiled as he approached, a few steps behind Posey, his expression guileless, his walk confident. If Eudora had looked closer that day, she might have seen a fissure, a weakness that should have been addressed, but she was young and naive that day and didn't know what to say. It was something she'd come to regret.

"Is Brock really taking you *to Paris* for your honeymoon?" Posey continued, bringing her hands to her heart and sighing. "I've *always* wanted to go to Paris."

"Paris? I hadn't heard," Eudora replied, her gaze on her husband.

"Then it's a surprise?" Posey gasped. "And I've ruined it."

"There you are." Jason Pickney, Posey's steady boyfriend, approached and reached out to Posey to steady her. Eudora had heard they'd met at the Assembly Ball in Columbia. He was a third-year law student, and his people were politicians and federal judges. He hadn't proposed yet, but Eudora's mother had said that Mrs. Chalmers expected a summer engagement, after Jason graduated. Aunt Evelyn had said he was quite a catch, that living in Columbia wasn't so terrible, if one chose the right neighborhood. Eudora wondered what Posey thought of it.

"Jason, good to see you again." Brock offered his hand, which Jason ignored. Instead, he fixed his gaze on Brock just a moment too long, and Brock looked away.

"I better take this one home," Jason continued, pulling Posey close and steadying her against his body. "She's had enough fun for one night." He turned without another word, guiding Posey firmly away from the reception."

Eudora had spent the day smiling and chatting with people she didn't know, and she was tired. After most of the guests had gone and the servers began to clear the tables, she took a moment for herself. Eudora's father had long since retired to his office; she could see his desk lamp burning from where she stood. Her mother and her friends had moved to the sitting room for coffee and conversation. Eudora could see movement behind the silk sheers and imagined the table set with coffee and pastries, as it had been so many months ago when Eudora opened the invitation to the Chalmers' tea.

How different things had been then.

How simple.

Eudora followed the garden path to the reflecting pond, looking forward to sitting on the rock beside it, where she used to sit when she was little. The fish had long since been removed, her mother conceding the fight against neighborhood raccoons, but the fountain remained, and Eudora had always found the sound of splashing water to be peaceful. As she approached, she heard the chorus of evening frogs, creatures her mother had not been able to remove. It occurred to her, at that moment, that after tonight she would have her own house to manage, her own gardens. And she liked the idea.

The smell of pipe smoke pulled her from her thoughts.

It was Uncle Alistair, seated on the bench beside the pond. He seemed utterly relaxed, his arm draped across the back of the bench, his legs crossed at the knee. Though their exchanges had been brief, she liked him and looked forward to getting to know him better, but she was reluctant to disturb him.

She stood on the path, deciding, when he noticed her and called her over. "Eudora, how nice to see you. Please come join me." He laid his pipe in the ashtray on the bench and straightened.

She spread the skirt of her wedding dress across the rock opposite him and sat. "This used to be my favorite place to think when I was little."

"Everyone needs a good thinking place," he replied, amiably, then gestured to his pipe. "Do you mind if I continue? Not everyone enjoys the smell of pipe tobacco as much as I do."

"Please." Eudora waited until he retrieved his pipe, then spoke again. "I'd like to thank you for your wedding gift, Uncle Alistair. It was really very generous." She paused to gather a bit of courage, but still couldn't quite meet his eye. "And I want to thank you, for before. Under the wisteria trellis. And the first dance—"

"You're very welcome for the gift, dear girl, but I'm not sure what you mean about the wisteria." He tapped the bowl of his pipe against the edge of the glass ashtray. "As for the first dance, I am very grateful you decided to indulge me. Many brides wouldn't."

Eudora looked at him with profound gratitude. If the rest of Brock's family was anything like his uncle Alistair, maybe she hadn't made a mistake after all. And for the rest of her life, Eudora would find the scent of pipe tobacco comforting, simply because it reminded her of Uncle Alistair.

For a moment, they sat in compatible silence, listening to the sounds of the evening.

"Brock said we're going to Paris for our honeymoon. Did you know that?" Eudora remarked. "I've always wanted to go."

"Really?" Uncle Alistair raised his eyebrows as he patted his breast pocket and pulled out his packet of tobacco.

"Yes."

"Interesting." Uncle Alistair filled the bowl of his pipe then glanced at her. "Have you seen the tickets?"

The oddness of the question was jarring.

"Brock arranged everything – plane tickets, hotels. Posey let it slip, and I don't think she was supposed to. I think it was meant to be a surprise."

"Is that so?" He flicked a match and held it over the tobacco. "When are you leaving?"

Eudora watched the flame dance as he drew air though his pipe and realized that she didn't actually know the details.

Uncle Alistair seemed oddly preoccupied with his pipe in a way that made her uneasy. It was almost as if he knew something but wouldn't say.

She hesitated, then asked about something that had been bothering her. "I noticed you wrote a check to us for a wedding gift. A generous amount, thank you again. But the check was written only to me, not both of us. And I'm sorry to ask, but was that intentional?"

He blew out his match and turned his attention toward her, his clear blue eyes sharp. "Yes, it was. And I hope you'll allow a bit of advice from a man who has known Brock all his life. I suggest you put it somewhere safe for a little while – without cashing it – just until you settle in."

"Why would I do that?"

"Sometimes things are not as they first appear to be, that's all. But you seem to be a smart girl; I'll wager you already knew that." Drawing sharply on his pipe, he frowned and tapped the bowl against the ashtray. "I see I'm going to need a new pipe."

CHAPTER 22

A SOFT BREEZE from the open window woke her up, cool on her skin in the still of the late August morning. A hint of fall touched the air, and Eudora welcomed it. Raising her chin toward the window, Eudora breathed in the salty harbor air and felt her spirits lift. The Rutledge home was closer to the seawall than the Gadsden home had been, and Eudora had been delighted to discover that when the wind shifted in the early evening, it brought the briny smell of the ocean with it. There was also a piazza off the master bedroom, set with two fat wicker chairs and a glass-topped table. It overlooked the garden, and Eudora had spent quite a few nights sitting on one of those chairs, waiting for her husband to return home.

She slipped out of bed, careful not to disturb her sleeping husband. He'd been out at a business dinner the night before and had gotten home so late that Eudora didn't want to wake him. She crossed the room and dressed quickly in her closet, putting on clothes she'd already laid out. On her way out of the master bedroom, she stopped to retrieve the acceptance letter she'd received from Charleston College. She'd taken the letter out several times over the summer, smoothing the creases and reading text she'd already memorized, just to remind herself that this day would, eventually, come.

Closing the door softly behind her, Eudora slipped the letter into her pocket and made her way down the stairs. In a household that rarely rose before ten o'clock, Eudora had come to appreciate the quiet of the early morning. She'd even started a subscription to the morning newspaper and had come to look forward to her routine of reading the business section while drinking a strong pot of Earl Grey tea. It was a wonderful way to start her day.

Today, however, there was no time for tea.

Today was the first day of registration for fall classes at Charleston College, and Eudora intended be first in line.

Eudora pulled her coat from the front closet and went to retrieve her purse from the kitchen.

"Eudora, what a pleasant surprise." Lenore sat at the head of the table, an open date book before her, a silver tea service on the sideboard behind her. Her diamond ring flashed as she gestured to the chair next to her. "Come sit."

Eudora sat, though reluctantly. On the surface, Lenore had been perfectly welcoming, but she reminded Eudora of a spider lurking on the edge of a web, waiting for one mistake. And she'd resisted all attempts of friendship, something else that made Eudora uneasy.

Lenore rang the bell to summon Flora from the kitchen. "Eudora will be joining me for breakfast. Set another place, please."

The Rutledge home was run very differently from the Gadsden home, and it took some getting used to. Lenore didn't entertain the way Eudora's parents did. There hadn't been a dinner party since Eudora's arrived, no cocktails parties and only a handful of afternoon bridge games. Even family dinners were small, bland, and served early, giving Lenore time to 'digest.' Eudora missed Annie – her cooking and her conversation.

The breakfast Flora brought from the kitchen was identical to the one in front of Lenore, a scoop of cottage cheese and a sliver of melba toast.

"Thank you, but I don't have time for breakfast today. I have an early appointment and I don't want to be late."

Lenore frowned. "I had hoped for a chance to review the menu and the seating for the dinner tomorrow night. Uncle Alistair will be joining us, as will Brock's stepsister and her husband."

As a new wife, one of the things that Eudora was expected to do was assume management of the Rutledge home. Among other things, she was to plan the family's meals, hire and direct the staff. Up until now, Lenore had been reluctant to release control, so including Eudora in the planning of a dinner party, however small, was a good step forward.

Thanks to her training at Santee, Eudora could plan a dinner party in her sleep. "So a total of six?"

"That's right."

"I'll arrange something very nice, and I'll speak to Flora about it on my way out." Eudora rose with an apologetic smile. "Please excuse me, but I really do have to go. I don't want to be late."

Eudora left Lenore in the dining room and made her way to the kitchen for a conversation with Flora, one she was not looking forward to. It was customary for a new wife to arrange her kitchen the way she wanted and that sometimes included replacing the old cook with someone new. Knowing that she would be preoccupied with schoolwork, Eudora had planned to keep Flora on. Flora knew the routine of the household, and it was easier for Eudora to assimilate than it was to bring in someone new. But because Flora had been hired by Lenore, her allegiance remained with Lenore. She made it very clear that she took orders from Lenore alone and Lenore did very little to dissuade her. Still, Eudora tried.

Eudora pushed open the door to the kitchen and found dirty dishes on the countertop and a tub of cottage cheese dripping with condensation. Flora was seated at the table with her feet propped up and a Hollywood gossip magazine in front of her.

"Flora, I'd like to speak with you about the menu for tomorrow night's dinner party." Eudora pulled a glove from her purse and slipped it on.

Flora flicked the page and glanced up. "Now?"

"Yes."

"Mrs. Rutledge has the menu planned already, and it's best not to change it."

Eudora snapped her purse shut. She crossed the kitchen to retrieve a pencil and a pad of paper. Then she made her way back to Flora. She closed the magazine cover and set the pad and pencil on top.

"*This* Mrs. Rutledge is giving you a new menu," Eudora said. "Use my family's recipe for Perloo. Call Annie for it – ask for the name of our seafood man and be sure to order from him today. He'll deliver fresh shrimp early tomorrow morning." Eudora slipped on her other glove. "Oh, and borrow some of Daddy's Carolina Gold rice from Annie, too. Though she'll probably offer you some when she finds out what you're making. Use that rice only; please don't use instant." Eudora paused, then pointed to the still-untouched paper. "I think you should write this down."

"I was planning on serving lamb chops," Flora challenged. "Mr. Brock likes lamb. They both do."

"I expect he'll live if the menu is different." Eudora took the checkbook from the drawer and slipped it into her purse. We'll start with beef consommé. Make a green salad to serve with the Perloo. Order the vegetables from the man on Tradd Street. He's got the freshest."

"We have our own vegetable man." Flora sniffed. "Been serving this family for years."

Eudora tucked her acceptance letter into the checkbook and continued as if Flora hadn't interrupted. "For this dinner, I'd like you to follow my directions. Annie can give you the number."

"If you say so."

"I do say so." Eudora turned to leave. "Tell the gardener we need yellow flowers for the table, something bright that won't drop pollen. Ask him to have them ready tomorrow afternoon and I'll arrange them. I'll do the seating tomorrow afternoon as well."

Then she left before Flora had a chance to argue.

CHAPTER 23

AFTER MONTHS OF WAITING, years of preparation, and a few missteps along the way, she'd finally made it. Eudora stood at the entrance of the auditorium and took it all in. Spread across the length and width of the floor were dozens of tables with pages of class listings, and Eudora could sign up for any class that interested her. All she had to do was register. She'd practically memorized the fall catalog; she'd leafed through it so many times the pages were dog-eared and marked with notes. Several of the accounting classes looked interesting, and it was hard to choose between them. Eudora wondered if they'd allow her to take more than one.

She took a deep breath and walked to the information table. "Excuse me."

A man with short cropped hair, a friendly round face, and dark-framed glasses looked up from his stack of papers. "My first customer. Good morning. How can I help you?"

"I'm not sure where to start."

He unfolded a paper map and slid it across the table. "First thing you do is get to the registration table – right here." He tapped a spot on the map. "After they check you in, you'll get your packet. That allows you to choose your classes. Pick five, then write your check at that table all the way over there." He stood and pointed to the far side of the room. "Every year they pick the farthest corner." He shook his head as if the complexities of the finance department were beyond him.

Eudora said a quick 'thank you,' grabbed the map and crossed the room to get her packet.

Though the line at the registration table was short, the man at the table wasn't nearly as friendly as the information man had been. He didn't even look up from his papers.

"ID." He extended his hand.

Eudora produced her driver's license from her wallet.

He stared at her license, comparing it to the list of names in front of him. Then he frowned.

"Is there a problem?" Eudora asked.

"Your name has changed."

"Yes, it has. I was married in April." She reached into her purse for her acceptance letter and presented it to him. "I was accepted to Charleston College under my family name, Gadsden. Eudora Gadsden."

She expected him to switch to the "G" list of names and wave her through. She was anxious to register for classes and the auditorium was filling with students.

"Does your husband know you're registering for college?"

"Does my—" Eudora blinked. "Yes, of course he knows, but I don't see why that matters."

"I'm going to need a note from him before I can allow you to register." He turned to the woman next to him. "Debbie, you got one of those married permission forms with you?"

The woman shook her head. "Sorry, they're all in the office. I just packed what was necessary."

Turning back to Eudora, the man continued. "You're going to need to go to the main office—"

"You have my letter of acceptance, isn't that enough?"

"All married women need their husband's permission – in writing – before they register for classes. There's a form for it around here somewhere. Ask your husband to sign it and return it to us."

"That's ridiculous."

"School policy. Has been for years. You can either spend all day arguing or get the paper signed. Only one of those things will get you a seat in class." He motioned to the next person in line. "Next."

"Excuse me." The boy behind her shouldered his way to the table and Eudora had no choice but to leave. Her heart sank as she glanced at the lines forming in front of the business classes.

She gathered her things and regrouped. According to the map, the registrar's office was fairly close. How hard would it be to walk there, collect the paper, sign Brock's name to the bottom, and return to registration? She and Brock had talked about college, and they'd agreed she would attend. So there was nothing dishonest about her signing his name to an agreement he already knew about and it would save her time.

"We check." The woman's face was kind but her tone was firm. She gestured toward the empty office behind her. "He calls every one of the husbands personally to ask if they really want their wives in school instead of at home."

"Please tell me you're kidding." Eudora slumped against the countertop.

"You think you're the first one to forge her husband's signature?" The woman at the counter arched an eyebrow. "Child, please."

"What am I going to do now?"

"You're going to pick yourself up and go find your husband." The woman pushed the paper toward Eudora. "Get him to sign this. Then you march back here and register for classes. Don't let them take that from you."

"But the classes I want will be full by the time I get back." Eudora cringed at the sound of her own whining.

"Then don't come back." The woman returned to her chair and her typing. "I guess it just depends on how bad you want it."

Eudora stood outside the registrar's office with no idea where to find her husband. He didn't go to an office every day because, he insisted, he was too busy meeting people and making contacts to waste time behind a desk. Honestly, Eudora wasn't sure how Brock spent his days, and he wasn't forthcoming with answers so she might never know for sure. A period of adjustment was expected as any newlywed couple got used to each other's ways, but Brock didn't seem to care if he got to know her better. If anything, he seemed to be pushing her away, and Eudora didn't know why.

As Eudora walked back up the path, she passed the auditorium, now packed with students eagerly selecting classes for the fall. She imagined all the classes she wanted filling up and closing, and her chest filled with anxiety. Signing Brock's name to the paper in her hand would be an easy thing; harmless, really. They'd talked about her attending; he'd given his word.

But she couldn't do it.

Her father had never forgiven her for signing his name to

that letter, and she didn't want to invite retribution by signing Brock's name to this form. Their relationship was strained enough already.

Twenty-four

Outside, the weather threatened a late summer thunderstorm. Overhead, lightning flashed across the sky. The humidity was oppressive and every movement took effort.

"Do you think it'll rain tonight?" Eudora asked as she watched the sky for another flash. Heat lightning, she thought. Annie used to say that a night sky full of heat lightning was a bad omen, a warning of trouble to come. Eudora hoped it wasn't true.

"Don't know." A drop of water fell from Brock's freshly washed hair onto his shirt as he reached into his closet for a necktie. He pulled out two, frowning as he decided.

"I like the blue," Eudora offered.

After only four months, their conversation had distilled to little more than an exchange of information. She wanted to talk to him about her classes. She needed him to sign that paper. But his moods were unpredictable. Sometimes he wouldn't give her what she wanted, just because he knew she wanted it. This was too important to be one of those times, so she proceeded carefully, gauging his mood as she spoke.

He tossed the yellow one back into the closet and faced the mirror.

"Are you going to be late again tonight?" Eudora picked a thread from the bedspread, a brown matelassé she didn't care for. The pattern was heavy, the material stifling.

"Yes. Don't wait up."

"Where are you going?"

"I'm entertaining potential investors, Eudora." Brock turned up his collar and slid the tie around the back of his neck. "I told you that."

"Shouldn't we be working on your business idea together?"

"We could have been, but we didn't get the funding we needed now, did we?" The muscles in Brock's jaw locked as he looped one end of his tie around the other. "You could have at least helped with that."

Sunday dinner with her parents had gone badly. Her father joined them only for dinner then retreated back to his office, leaving her mother to entertain them. Eudora had been humiliated, and Brock seemed to blame her.

"My father never discusses business during Sunday dinner."

"So you've said." He pinched the knot of his tie and slid the fabric to his throat.

"It's a rule he's always had, Brock, for as long as I can remember," Eudora explained. "Sunday dinner is reserved for family at my house. My father warned you that he wouldn't discuss business at the table."

"When else am I supposed to see him, Eudora? He's not exactly welcoming me into his office."

"Maybe if you and Tommy J start more modestly, you won't need so much money up front." It was spiteful, but she couldn't resist adding, "Then you won't need my father."

Brock either didn't hear or ignored her. Either one was equally possible these days. "We have a solid business plan, Tommy J and I." Brock splashed cologne into his palms and touched his cheeks and neck with the scent. "With all the road work they're doing, everyone in this city will want a car, and the closest place to buy one is all the way up in Goose Creek." He stepped back to admire his reflection. "Setting up a dealership in the city is money in the bank, Eudora."

Eudora said nothing, though the words pushed against her throat. The car dealership was Brock's third business idea in a month and the one Eudora thought most likely to fail. The space required for inventory was massive and land on the peninsula was expensive, which was why the nearest dealership was eighteen miles away. But Brock wouldn't listen. He never listened.

She changed the subject before she said something that would start a fight, something that had been happening more and more lately. Brock could stew for days after a fight and she didn't want that. She rose from the bed and went to the dresser, where she'd left the registration form. "Classes start soon. I tried to register today, but they wouldn't let me. They said I needed your permission."

Brock turned from the mirror. "What do you mean, my permission?"

"Charleston College won't let married women attend classes unless their husband says it's okay."

She saw him smirk as he turned back to face the mirror, and the ember of resentment she'd been pushing back flared, bringing memories of all the times he'd dismissed her. But this was a fight she didn't want. She'd learned enough about her husband in the last few months to know that he needed to feel in command. If he felt pushed, he would never give permission. College was too important to her, so she swallowed her pride and played his game.

She offered him the paper and pen. She even managed to smile. "Would you mind signing their silly form, please?"

"Sure." To Eudora's great surprise, Brock shrugged and scribbled his name at the bottom of the page.

"I'll bring it to registration tomorrow." Eudora tucked the page under the lace doily on the dresser. "One more thing – I'll be writing a check for tuition. Just so you know."

Brock crossed the room to lift his new sport coat from the hanger behind the chair but didn't answer, so Eudora repeated. "Did you hear me, Brock? I said—"

"I heard you, Eudora. I'm not deaf," Brock snapped. He sat on the chair to slip on the shoes he'd had delivered from Chastains the day before. After tying his shoes, he sat back and looked at her. "I'm not sure college tuition is the best use of our money right now."

"What do you mean?"

"It takes a lot of money to get a business up and running, Eudora," Brock said. "Tommy J and I have been entertaining potential clients—"

"What clients?" Eudora asked, the ember in her chest flaring again, this time stronger. "How do you have clients already if you don't have a business?"

"It's business, Eudora. You wouldn't understand the specifics." Brock rose from the chair and smoothed his tie. "What I'm telling you is that money is tight right now—"

"It shouldn't be," Eudora countered. "We set aside money from our wedding specifically for college tuition. My father gave us a very generous check three months ago. What happened to it?"

"That was for our honeymoon." He reached for his suit jacket and slipped it on.

"Which we didn't take." Eudora stood, her heart thumping in anger. Outside, heat lightning flashed across the sky.

Instead of the wedding trip to Paris that Brock had promised and her father had funded, they'd spent a rainy month in Augusta in a boarding house with Tommy J and an assortment of Brock's friends. Brock said they needed time to develop a plan for their new construction business and this was the best way to get it done. Eudora would have believed him, were it not for the fact that Brock and his friends knew nothing about construction. Or about landscaping, the business idea they'd had before construction. Or about the women's fur salon, or about antique shops, or nightclubs.

"We've had unexpected expenses starting this business." Brock shrugged as if it didn't matter, though his expression was guarded. "Things will be better in the spring. You can go then."

"But we planned for fall," Eudora sputtered, not believing what was unfolding before her. "You promised. College is the only reason I—"

"You what, Eudora?" Brock spun around, his expression hard. "The only reason you married me? I know."

"As long as we're telling the truth," she demanded, "why did you marry *me*? Surely you had your choice of other women."

"I did." He snapped his watch to his wrist. "Posey, for example. She was a very good choice."

"Then tell me. Why did you ask me to marry you? Why me instead of Posey?" Eudora moved to the vanity and sat on the bench, steeling herself against whatever reason he offered.

"Your father."

She blinked. "My what?"

"Your father." Brock bit the words and spit them at her. "You're an only child, Eudora. There's no place for your father's money to go *except* to you. He was supposed to take me under his wing and show me the business. Sponsor our membership to his clubs, pave the way for my success. But he didn't do any of that, did he?"

Brock snatched his keys from the leather tray on the dresser top. He reached the door, his expression granite. "I thought marrying a Gadsden would be good for business. Not only is that *not* true, but you're actually holding me back. At least Posey's father has connections."

The door slammed behind him. Soon after, Eudora watched his car headlights as he pulled out of the courtyard and drove away.

~

She'd had enough. Enough of her husband's tantrums, his unpredictability, his lies.

More than enough, actually.

Unable to tolerate another second in her husband's home, Eudora left. She grabbed her keys and sweater on the way out the front door, though she had no direction in mind. She needed fresh air. She needed to think.

The humidity of the day had lifted, and Eudora felt as though she could draw a deep breath, her first in days. It was a welcome contrast to the stuffiness of the Rutledge home, with Flora's obstinance and Lenore's judgement. Eudora had walked several blocks aimlessly, and another six on her way to the O'Hanlan home. She and Maggie hadn't had much to say to each other since the wedding, and Eudora blamed herself. Maggie might have been right about everything, and Eudora would not have been able to bear the pity in her friend's eyes if she learned how tense things really were.

The O'Hanlan house was dark but Eudora approached

anyway, unlocking the front gate and circling to the back of the house. In the yard was a tall chinaberry tree that Maggie had taught Eudora to climb when they were girls. Back then, Eudora was scared to climb, placing her foot on every branch and waiting for Maggie's encouragement to proceed. That day Eudora had climbed higher than she ever thought she would, not stopping until she was level with the roofline. She remembered the summer sun on her face, the scratches on her legs, the sticky tree sap on her fingers, and the feeling of accomplishment feeding her soul.

She was proud of herself that day, of finding a store of courage she didn't know she had.

She needed to find that courage again.

As Eudora stood in the O'Hanlan's backyard, staring up at the tree, she felt the damp grass soaking through her shoes. The leather would be ruined and Brock would be annoyed at the expense of a replacement pair, but Eudora didn't care about that right now. She stepped toward the tree and reached toward the trunk, feeling the roughness of the bark, ridged and raised over time, against her fingertips. A longing welled up in her. A longing for Maggie, who Eudora had been avoiding since her wedding. And a longing for the girl Eudora used to be not so long ago, courageous and unafraid.

"Okay, then," Eudora muttered to herself. It took her just a moment to make a plan. Then, reaching down, she dug a few pebbles from the dirt and slipped them into her pocket. She kicked off her wet shoes, peeled off her stockings and hiked the skirt of her dress up above her knees. "You can do this," she said as she reached for the first branch.

She took her time, placing her bare foot carefully and testing each branch before she placed her weight on it, as Maggie had taught her. About halfway up, her grip slipped on a wet branch, and she nearly lost her footing. But she righted herself. With her heart pounding, she grabbed another branch, feeling the rough bark scrape against her palms. Still she continued, tearing the fabric of her dress free when she felt it snag. She didn't stop, wouldn't let herself stop, climbing higher and higher as if reaching the top of the tree would prove her worth.

But the tree had grown in the years since Maggie had taught her to climb. It seemed so much taller now than she remembered. She reached the top because she wouldn't let herself give up, but neither would she let herself look down. When the branches finally became too thin to support Eudora's weight, she finally stopped. Across from her were the dormer windows of Maggie's attic bedroom. She honestly didn't think she'd make it this far; she'd slipped the pebbles in her pocket just in case.

Movies and books made it seem so easy, tossing a pebble against the glass pane to get someone's attention, but it wasn't. Eudora would have to free one of her hands to dig the pebble out. The branches were slippery with dew and it was such a long way down.

She'd have to think of something else.

All at once, she was unsure. Turning her head slowly, she looked toward Maggie's window. As usual, it was open just a few inches to catch the evening breeze. Eudora prayed Maggie was home.

"Maggie," Eudora called, a stage whisper only loud enough for her friend to hear. "Maggie, wake up!"

She could feel the mosquitos buzzing around her face. One of them landed on her leg, but she didn't trust her balance enough to slap it away. With no other choice, Eudora looped her arm around a branch and dug into her pocket. She tossed the pebble toward Maggie's window but it fell short, bouncing against the roof and falling to the ground.

She tried again, pulling another stone from her pocket and tossing it toward the house. That one came closer, but still fell short.

Eudora raised her voice. "Maggie, wake up! It's me!"

No answer.

In the silence, Eudora realized that she had climbed the tree without stopping to consider what she would do if Maggie wasn't home. Eudora tightened her grip and glanced at the ground, hoping she wouldn't have to wait until morning. A fireman rescue would be humiliating.

She pulled the last stone from her pocket and threw it toward the window with all her strength. It hit the glass with a sharp crack.

Almost immediately, Maggie's bedroom light flicked on.

Maggie cranked open her window and poked her head outside. "Eudora? What are you *doing* out there?"

"Maggs, let me in." A trickle of perspiration slid between her shoulder blades. A mosquito buzzed in her ear.

"Why didn't you just ring the doorbell? I would have let you in."

"It's late. I didn't want to wake anyone."

Maggie leaned out the window and looked at the ground. "That's a long way up."

"I *know* that."

"And a long way across."

"I know that too." The bark bit into Eudora's palm as she shifted her grip.

"Can you climb down? I'll open the front door."

Eudora shook her head. "I don't think I can. It's too slippery."

"Okay, give me your hand." Maggie leaned out her window and reached her hand toward Eudora. They didn't connect. "Wait a second, I'll be right back."

A mosquito buzzed around Eudora's face. She puffed it away.

Maggie returned with the quilt from her bed. She pushed it out the window and spread it across the roof. "Use this for traction and climb across – but be careful."

There didn't seem to be any other choice.

Eudora crept out as far as she could on the branch, then stretched toward the quilt, still warm from Maggie's room. It smelled like the detergent Mrs. O'Hanlan used, and Eudora breathed in the scent for courage.

"Can you reach my hand now?" Eudora had managed to straddle the roof and the tree, but her legs felt like rubber and she wasn't sure she would make it the rest of the way without help.

Maggie's grip was strong, and a moment later, Eudora tumbled through the window and onto the floor.

Maggie eyed the scratches on Eudora's shins and the bark chips on her knees. "Hang on a second – you're soaking wet." She went to her closet and pulled out a pair of jeans and a sweatshirt. She pointed to the closet. "You can change in there."

Eudora pushed herself to her feet and moved toward the closet. The bites around her ankles had risen to welts. The hem on her dress was ragged, and there was an irreparable tear across the back, but she didn't care. She'd done it: she'd climbed the tree. She stripped to her skin and toweled herself off, feeling the tension uncoiling from her shoulders as she dressed in the clothes Maggie had given her.

"You gonna tell me what's so important that you had to

climb up a tree in the middle of the night?" Maggie called into the closet.

Eudora leaned her head against the wall and allowed the tears to come, unchecked.

"Eudora?" Maggie stuck her head in the doorway, her eyes squeezed shut. "You decent?"

Eudora sniffed and nodded. "I'm fine."

"You are not," Maggie declared. "Come out of there and tell me what's wrong."

Eudora exited the closet and Maggie handed her a box of tissues. Eudora dropped to the floor and Maggie joined her, pulling a blanket from her bed.

"You were right, Maggs. About everything." Eudora sat on the floor and leaned her head against Maggie's bedframe. "I married too fast to someone I barely know and don't even like anymore." Her nose started to run, and Eudora sniffed. Finally, she swiped her nose with the back of her hand. "He's out almost every night but won't tell me where he goes or who he's with. He spends money so fast that it scares me. His mother hates me, the house is haunted and I miss Annie." She ended with a deep sigh.

"I had no idea. I really didn't."

"No one does. Brock can be charming when he wants to be. He fools a lot of people. He fooled me." Eudora pulled a tissue from the box. "Not you, though; he didn't fool you. You've never liked him, have you?"

"No, I haven't." Maggie shook her head. "I've seen his type before, in Brooklyn. He reminded me of a man my Aunt Eileen dated. He was bad news."

Eudora pulled a tissue from the box and began to shred it.

Maggie broke the silence, her voice gentle as a whisper. "Does he hit you?"

"Why would you ask that?"

"Because Aunt Eileen's boyfriend hit her, three times, before Da found out," Maggie said. "Da went over and had a talk with him. We never saw that man again. So I'll ask one more time, and I want you to know there's no shame in the truth: Does Brock hit you?"

Eudora closed her eyes and shook her head. "No, but he gets so angry. It seems like he wants to."

"What does your father say?"

"He doesn't say anything," Eudora said. "Daddy hasn't talked to me since I signed his name to that letter."

"If you're in trouble we can ask Da—" Maggie began, but Eudora cut her off.

"We can't, Maggie. I'm married now and my job is to pretend to be happy so I don't embarrass my family or Brock's." Eudora lifted her head from the bedframe and looked at her friend. "It's what I deserve, I guess. The truth is that I married the first boy who asked because I didn't want to be a debutante. I thought I was outsmarting my mother." Eudora snorted. "It's funny – I'd give anything to have that time back. All of it – tea parties, social committees, and railing against my mother – seems so much easier than my life now. If I could go back, Maggie, my path forward would be different."

Many of Eudora's friends were just now finishing their extended Season, and every conversation buzzed with stories Eudora wasn't part of. When conversations turned to engagements and marriage, Eudora felt pressured to pretend hers was perfect. Eventually, the pretense was too much for her so she declined social invitations and counted the days until college classes started.

Eudora felt as if she were a hundred years old, though she

had just turned eighteen. She couldn't imagine spending the rest of her life this way. She felt trapped, desperate. Closing her eyes, she rested her head against the bedframe and melted into the quiet of Maggie's room. Outside, the leaves of the chinaberry tree rustled in the breeze, and the clock on Maggie's bedside table ticked softly.

Finally, Maggie's voice broke the silence. "I leave for New York City in two weeks."

"That's great, Maggie." Eudora opened her eyes and smiled at her friend. "Did you find a job in a fashion house?"

"Not quite." Maggie laughed. "Aunt Eileen found me a job at Bamberger's, with her. You're looking at the new junior sales clerk in Women's Sportswear."

"But that will lead to something better, Maggie. You've been designing outfits since you were eleven years old, and they're beautiful. It won't be long at all until they discover how talented you are." She straightened. "In fact, I still want to be your first customer. As soon as I figure out how we can afford it."

"Come with me."

"What?"

Maggie leaned forward, her eyes bright with excitement. "Come with me," she said again, her voice rising. "I'm leaving for Brooklyn in two weeks. I'll have my own room at Aunt Eileen's house, and she won't mind if we share it. Aunt Eileen helped me find my job, and she'll help you, too. I know she would. You don't need to stay in Charleston, and you don't *ever* need to go back to Brock."

It was a tempting offer, and for a moment, Eudora considered it. A fresh start in a new city with no one to worry about except herself. She would never be subjected to Brock's anger or her father's silent treatment. Would never have to please her mother or explain herself to her mother-in-law. She could leave Charleston with Maggie and never come back.

That was when she realized she couldn't.

Charleston was a part of her. She was born here, went to school here. All her relatives and friends were here. She was part of the fabric here, a way of life she couldn't imagine giving up. It was difficult now, so very difficult, but there had to be a different solution. Eudora couldn't imagine living anywhere except the Lowcountry.

After a moment, she shook her head. "I can't, Maggs. Running away is what got me in this mess in the first place. I want to stay. I need to stay."

To Eudora's surprise, Maggie smiled. "Good."

"You don't want me to come with you?" Eudora gaped. "You weren't serious?"

"Oh, I was serious," Maggie said. "But I agree that your life is here. You've been talking about Charleston College since forever." Maggie reached for her hand. "You were never one to run away, Eudora. Don't let that man dictate your life."

"But—"

"You made a mistake. One mistake." Maggie raised her forefinger in the air. "That doesn't translate into a life of servitude. Come to think of it, Brock made a mistake too, if he thinks he married a pushover." Then her expression sobered and she pursed her lips as she considered her words. "But I need you to do something for me, Eudora, and I'm not kidding."

"What is it?"

"I want you to *promise* me that you'll come to my house for dinner once a week with my family while I'm away. My mother will keep an eye on you, make sure you're okay. No one else needs to know why you're coming. You just come."

"Okay, I promise," Eudora agreed, feeling as if she could finally breathe. She and Maggie were friends again, and Eudora felt a bit of her courage return.

She tucked the blanket under her legs and leaned against the bed, grateful for Maggie's friendship. They talked as if no time at all had passed. As if they were schoolgirls again, catching up on each other's lives, until the birds began to wake and the sky lightened. Downstairs, Eudora heard feet pounding across the floor and the muffled slam of a door.

Maggie shrugged. "My brothers fighting for the bathroom. Happens every morning." She pushed herself to her feet. "It's Saturday, so Ma's probably making pancakes. You should stay for breakfast."

"I'd love to," Eudora began, then stopped. "But won't your mother think it's strange that I'm coming downstairs with you?"

"Have you met my brothers? They'll distract her." Maggie scoffed. "She won't even notice you're here."

Eudora's stomach growled as she thought of Mrs. O'Hanlan's strawberry pancakes. She rose from the floor. "Thanks, Maggie."

"What are best friends for?" Maggie shrugged. "Come over any time." She paused at the door, her hand on the knob. "But Eudora? Next time?"

"Yes?"

"Use the front door."

Not only did Eudora stay for breakfast at the O'Hanlan home, she had lunch there as well and was even invited to stay for dinner. She would have accepted if it wasn't for the dinner plans with Brock's Uncle Alistair that night. The perloo she'd instructed Flora to make was easy. Eudora had been taught to make it when she was ten years old, and with Annie's guidance, there was nothing that could go wrong. The flowers and the seating chart needed her attention, but that could wait until after lunch.

Eudora allowed herself an entire morning with Maggie to catch up and wrap herself in their friendship. She put all of her problems aside while they spent the day sifting through memories as they decided what to pack for New York City and what to leave behind. In the end, they had three suitcases of clothes and four cardboard boxes of essentials, including Maggie's sketch pads and designs and the sewing machine she'd gotten for Christmas the year before. On her days off, Maggie planned to call on fashion houses because, as she said, "you never know."

Eudora left the O'Hanlan house just after lunch, feeling refreshed and almost optimistic.

She walked up to the gates of the Rutledge home with a much-improved outlook. She'd allowed herself plenty of time to prepare for the dinner guests' arrival and would take her time seeing to the details. She pushed open the garden gate and entered, scanning the gardens to see which flowers had been selected for the arrangement. Yellow blooms would look best against Lenore's antique green tablecloth, and Eudora could pair them with white tapers in silver candlesticks.

She crossed the garden and climbed the back stairs with a light step, looking forward to a meal that reminded her of Annie. Pushing open the door to the kitchen, Eudora entered the house. She found her mother-in-law waiting for her and an explosion of chaos all around.

"Eudora." Lenore stood in front of a pyramid of soup cans

with an apron secured around her waist, her face red with fury. "I thought I'd made myself clear this morning when I asked you to help plan tonight's dinner."

Behind Lenore was Flora, stabbing a lamb roast with the point of a knife and stuffing the holes with cloves of garlic. She didn't look up from her work when Eudora entered the kitchen.

"You did." Eudora dropped her purse on the table and rushed toward them. "What happened?"

"*What happened* was that you weren't here this morning to provide Flora the instruction she needed for the recipe you requested. So she had to resort to a recipe she knew." Lenore huffed. "Honestly, Eudora, if you ever hope to manage a household of this size, you need to learn to provide direction. I don't know why your mother didn't teach you that."

"Perloo is a gumbo," Eudora said. "There's nothing to it."

"I'm not going to argue with you." Lenore drew a long breath as she untied her apron. "Flora told me your recipe called for special ingredients, which we didn't have. She was left without direction, coming to me only when she didn't know what else to do."

"She wasn't left without direction. I told her to call Annie."

Realization dawned slowly as Eudora watched the corners of Flora's lips curl into a sneer.

"If you can't bring order to a kitchen, Eudora, you have no hope to manage a household with a staff as large as ours." Lenore continued as she dropped the apron on the chair. "Now if you'll excuse me, I need some time to get ready. Alistair will be here in less than an hour, and these dinners are tedious enough without you adding to it."

Even after Lenore left the room, Flora refused to meet Eudora's eye, focusing instead on her work.

"I see what you did, Flora, and it was a mistake." Eudora gathered her things and went to dress for dinner.

Twenty Five

Upstairs, Eudora dressed quickly, sweeping her hair into a quick chignon. She chose a simple black dress from her closet and the triple strand of Rutledge pearls from the velvet box. She added a bit of red lipstick and a spritz of perfume, then heard the doorbell chime downstairs. Because Brock hadn't come upstairs to dress, Eudora assumed that he must be downstairs entertaining Uncle Alistair.

After taking a moment to compose herself, she made her way downstairs to the front parlor.

Uncle Alistair stood by himself in the front parlor, mixing a drink at the bar.

"Uncle Alistair, how nice to see you again." Eudora crossed the room, flicking on table lamps as she went. Flora should have turned them on before their company arrived. "I'm sorry no one was here to welcome you."

"Ah, Eudora. I'm delighted to see you, as always." Uncle Alistair planted a papery kiss on Eudora's cheek.

"May I finish fixing that drink for you?"

His smile was quick. "Oh, no thank you. You'd be shocked at how much gin I allow myself. My grandmother made the best gin and tonics I've ever tasted. But then, she distilled the gin herself, so that might have accounted for the taste."

Eudora blinked and Uncle Alistair chuckled at her expression.

"She sounds like a formidable woman." Eudora said, finally.

"She was, indeed." Uncle Alistair twisted a lemon peel and dropped it into his drink. "Her name was Frances Lynne Rutledge. And it was her husband Jerome who married into the family and took the Rutledge name as his own. It caused quite a scandal, back in the day. You remind me a little of her, in fact." He paused to stir. "In fact, the Rutledge family history has always been more working-class than aristocracy, but as matron, Lenore gets to shape the narrative into whatever suits her."

Eudora poured seltzer into her own glass. Brock and Maggie had never gotten along, and Eudora had begun to suspect that part of the reason was because of the O'Hanlan's working class background. Lenore had questioned why Eudora hadn't kept up her debutante friendships and Brock had even gone so far as to suggest she see more of Posey.

"So Brock never told you? That's not surprising, really. He shares his mother's opinion that earning a living is something other people do."

"No, he never told me," Eudora murmured.

Uncle Alistair lifted his drink and sipped. He closed his eyes as he swallowed, then sighed with contentment. "Lenore has very good taste in gin, I must say."

He opened his eyes and regarded Eudora for a moment. "My Gram was a formidable woman. She carried this family through the war and the hunger that followed. She distilled gin in the attic, poured it into fancy bottles and sold it to the Yankee occupiers. She entertained the officers' wives and sold them tea from leaves she'd picked herself." He chuckled at the memory. "Mostly, chicory, I think, so it did no lasting damage. My point is that if it weren't for Frances Lynne

Rutledge doing what needed to be done, there would be no Rutledge family."

Eudora glanced at the portrait of Xavier Rutledge hanging over the mantle. "Is there a portrait of her in this house?"

"Oh, no." Uncle Alistair snorted. "That would be an acknowledgement of an unseemly past. Best not to broadcast that. Sad, though, because I believe that if Gram hadn't been constrained by the customs of her time, she would have done great things." He went back to the bar and filled a fresh glass with ice. "Forgive my bluntness, but it is my feeling we are at a similar crossroads in Rutledge history. While this family has not exactly fallen on hard times, we are in need of a new direction, and I don't believe my nephew or his mother are up to the task."

He glanced up from his drink and locked eyes with her, then he smiled. His blue eyes twinkled with mischief. "I believe *you* are. And oh, won't it be lovely to watch." He reached for the tonic water and added a splash to his drink. "It would be my great pleasure to assist you, should you ever need advice."

"Thank you, Uncle Alistair, but I don't have any great plans."

"Not yet," he countered as he screwed the top back on. "But you strike me as someone who will, when the time is right. You don't know me well enough yet to trust me, but I hope you will in time."

Eudora opened her mouth to reply, then closed it again.

"These dinners can be quite trying, and this gin is delicious." Seeing her expression, Uncle Alistair gave a bark of laughter. "Forgive me, my dear. One of the freedoms of growing older is that one can express whatever thought one has."

But he wasn't that old. As William's younger brother, he couldn't have been more than sixty.

His blue eyes twinkled as he watched her. "Let me help with your calculations. William was my older brother by two years. He was fifty when Brock was born, so that makes me sixty-eight years old, in September."

"I'd heard that Brock's father was a bit older than Lenore."

Uncle Alistair laughed again. "That's putting it mildly, my dear. Lenore was William's second wife and was not as embraced by the Rutledge relations as she'd hoped to be." He gestured to the empty room. "As you can see there, is no love lost between us."

"Why is that?"

"Because I told him not to marry her. And I was very adamant about it, too, as I recall."

"Why would you tell him that that?" Eudora struggled to process all this new information.

"I'm afraid the details are a little sordid." Uncle Alistair pursed his lips as he considered his words. "Let me say that William and I had a very different opinion of what Lenore wanted – and I'll leave it at that." He paused to sip his drink. "Come to think of it, maybe William knew but didn't care. She had quite a hold on him, if I recall correctly."

Eudora felt herself blush and she looked away.

Uncle Alistair clucked his tongue. "Now, now. It's not as bad as all that. This family is no different than any other family in Charleston." He lifted his thin shoulders in a delicate shrug. "So many families paint our ancestors in the best possible light, don't you agree? But all of us have skeletons in the closet, things we wished would remain hidden. When you get to be my age, deciphering what is real from what is presented becomes a delightful way to pass the time. A puzzle to solve during the more tedious social gatherings."

Eudora felt strangely protective of her mother-in-law and felt the need to defend her. "You say Lenore doesn't care for you, but she was very insistent that she wanted this dinner party to go well. Why would she go to that kind of trouble if she didn't?"

Uncle Alistair finished the last of his drink and returned the glass to the bar. "Tonight isn't just a beloved relative coming for dinner. It's a financial check-up, if you will."

"I'm sorry, but I don't understand."

Uncle Alistair frowned. "They haven't told you?"

Eudora shook her head.

"I have been given charge of the family finances." Uncle Alistair set his glass on the bar. "Lenore needs a firm hand, and that's where I come in." He frowned. "Although she has yet to appreciate my guidance."

"How did you come to be in charge of the family finances?"

Uncle Alistair lifted the silver nut spoon and scooped a few cashews from the silver bowl, then deposited them into the palm of his hand. "One of the things my brother did before he died was protect the family from the free-spending habits of his new wife. The family investments are staggered to allow a modest income while protecting the principle for future generations. That was my doing." Uncle Alistair lifted his hand, in a mock toast to himself. "And though my brother and I have never gotten along, he made me the executor of his estate. So for the remainder of my life, I will direct the Rutledge family finances, meeting quarterly to explain to Lenore why she can't have more money."

He popped the cashews into his mouth. "So I guess my brother really did get the last laugh."

The first course of the dinner Flora had prepared was canned pea soup, bland and cold. Eudora pushed her spoon through it once before giving up and setting her spoon on the plate. This dinner party was not what she'd intended. Flora had ignored Eudora's instructions and was serving inedible food. Brock's stepsister and her husband had cancelled at the last minute, but the table was still set for six. Brock was sullen because Uncle Alistair sat at the head of the table. Lenore's job as hostess was to keep the dinner conversation light and flowing, but she wasn't good at it and Eudora's attempts to fill the silences were met with one-word responses from both Brock and Lenore.

Lenore rang the silver bell for service and Flora came to collect the soup bowls and present the next course.

Uncle Alistair turned his attention to Brock. "Now that you're back from your honeymoon, you must have some thoughts for your future. Tell me your plans, my boy. As a Citadel graduate, you have your choice of military placement."

"Brock doesn't want to be in the military," Lenore was quick to answer for him. "He's been looking at opportunities in Charleston instead."

"Is that so?" Uncle Alistair smiled but Eudora noticed that it didn't quite reach his eyes. "Well, that might be a better choice. Charleston is growing. Lots of opportunity."

Flora returned with the main course, serving Brock first, then Lenore and Uncle Alistair and finally Eudora. It was such an egregious breach of etiquette that Eudora assumed the slight was purposeful.

Eudora picked up her cutlery and looked at her plate.

Lamb.

On the plate in front of her were three medallions of red meat, stark and bloody against the white bone china, the juices pooling on the plate and staining the potatoes pink. She wasn't prepared for the revulsion she felt. Eudora's stomach rolled as she pushed the plate away. She would deal with Flora later.

"Brock, what is it you plan to do in Charleston?" Uncle Alistair asked. "Which opportunity interests you most?"

"I don't think this is the time, Alistair, do you?" Lenore interjected.

"Remember why I'm here, Lenore." Uncle Alistair's voice was steady, his attention on Brock. "This meeting is long overdue."

"May I remind you that we just lost William, Alistair," she countered. "Allow us time to grieve."

Uncle Alistair's reply was soft, but firm. "I am well aware of the loss, Lenore; William was my brother as well as your husband. But I would not be doing my job as executor of his estate if I let things continue as they are." He turned again to Brock, his tone firm. "What is this business you'd like to develop?"

Lenore drew breath, and Uncle Alistair's gaze cut to her. "Please allow the boy to answer for himself."

Eudora waited for Brock to describe the car dealership. She hoped Uncle Alistair would point out the problems with his business plan, because there were many and Brock wasn't listening to her.

"I'm glad you asked, actually." Brock leaned forward in

his chair, looking first toward his mother, then to his uncle. "We've come across a rare opportunity. This one can't miss."

From the corner of her eye, Eudora thought she saw Uncle Alistair stiffen, but she couldn't be sure.

"It seems the Charleston Parks Department ordered too many palmetto trees for a project on the west side of town and the summer sun is drying the burlap around the roots." He shrugged as if the details didn't matter to him. "The trees are dying. It's gotten so bad that the city is paying a crew just to water the burlaped roots every day."

He paused to pick up his fork, then glanced at his uncle.

"Anyway, Tommy says we can probably buy them cheap." He shrugged. "Maybe take a few for ourselves. The city has so many, they won't notice if a few are missing."

Seemingly unaware of the silence that followed, Brock sliced into his lamb and chewed.

Uncle Alistair was the first to recover. "I was under the impression that you had wanted to open some sort of car dealership?"

Brock nodded, then swallowed. "That's still in the works, but selling the surplus trees will give us immediate income. Fully grown palmettos can be sold for a lot of money."

Eudora glanced at Lenore, who had focused her attention on the lemon floating in her glass of tea. Then Eudora turned her attention to Uncle Alistair, who seemed stunned. She thought of the check her father gave them to fund their honeymoon, a trip that Brock insisted they postpone while he focused on his business. And this was the business opportunity he chose.

"There are no surplus trees, Brock." Eudora straightened in her chair, tamping down the anger she felt. "I've read articles in the newspaper about this project. The city drained a large section of marsh on the west side of the peninsula to make room for roads and housing. The palmettos are meant to line both sides of the main street, with a few extra planted around the neighborhood."

Brock shrugged then speared another piece of meat. The blood dripped onto his plate. "So?"

"They're *trees*, Brock. Fully grown palmetto trees and they're huge, thirty feet tall – at least. They're lying on the side of the road, right where the city intends to plant them when construction is finished." Eudora glanced at the faces around the table to see if anyone was following her logic, but only Uncle Alistair seemed to be listening. She continued anyway. "Don't you think they'll notice if some are missing? How will you steal them? They're too big to pick up without special equipment. You have nowhere to store them, and I can't image who would want to buy one."

Brock's lips tightened into a thin white line, and Lenore rushed to his defense. "I would think you'd be more support-ive, Eudora. Every business needs time to grow, and there are always details to work out. Nothing is perfect."

"How do you know so much about these trees?" Brock scoffed, wiping his mouth with his napkin and leaning back in his chair as his mother rang the bell for coffee.

Eudora met Brock's petulant tone with quiet confidence. "The project you're talking about has been in the newspaper for weeks. I've been following the stories and reading the editorials. The project they've planned is massive; it's going to change the shape of the city, but not everyone wants it. The palmettos were a compromise, a way to appease the people who wanted the marsh to remain."

"I've been following the story myself, and it's quite inter-esting," Uncle Alistair said as he returned the creamer to the tray with a gentle tap. "I didn't realize the Post and Courier was delivered here."

"I started a subscription just after Brock and I were married," Eudora offered, in case he objected to the cost. "I've been reading it every day. I especially like the business section."

"Good for you." Uncle Alistair's eyes twinkled. He lifted his cup and turned his attention to his nephew. "Eudora's points are valid, Brock, and you would do well to listen to her."

Brock's fingers tightened around his cake fork, though his attention remained on his plate.

"Eudora." Lenore set her coffee cup down and dabbed her mouth with the linen napkin. "I'd like to throw a small luncheon tomorrow, to introduce you to a few of my friends. Several committees in my club are still in need of volunteers, and this is a wonderful way for you to make connections. With the right amount of persuading, I'm sure we can find a place for you."

So nothing had changed after all. Eudora was still expected to take her place in Society.

In the silence that followed, Eudora thought of Maggie and the adventure she was about to embark on. Maggie had always known what she wanted, and she never let anything stop her. In a few short weeks, she would be leaving for Brooklyn, to start a new life there.

It took courage to claim that kind of freedom, and it was about time Eudora found hers.

"I'm sorry, but I'm not free tomorrow," she said. "And I won't be joining any committees."

Uncle Alistair looked amused, hiding his smile under cover of his napkin. "And what are your plans for tomorrow?" Uncle Alistair asked.

"I'm going to find a job." Eudora's plan unfolded as she spoke. "I'd planned to attend college classes next week, but I was told there is no money for tuition. So I'll defer my enrollment until the spring and earn the money for tuition myself."

Brock responded first, his voice whiney. "No wife of mine is going to work."

Eudora ignored him and she addressed her thoughts to Lenore, who seemed surprised by Eudora's plans. "Before we were married, Brock and I agreed that I would attend college in the fall. I'm sorry that no one told you."

"No, no one did." To her surprise, Lenore simply inclined her head. "An interesting choice for a woman, I think."

"Maybe we can find the money for your fall semester," Uncle Alistair offered. "Would you consider a personal loan?"

"Thank you for the offer, but I'd like to do this myself." To her surprise, Eudora meant it. If she earned the money herself, no one could take it away from her.

"Then I wish you the best of luck, my dear." Uncle Alistair tucked his napkin under his plate and rose from his chair. "Lenore, Brock, we have things to discuss. Let's adjourn to William's office, shall we?" He turned to Eudora. "Eudora, you're welcome to join us if you'd like."

"Thank you, but no. I'd like to prepare for tomorrow."

"In that case, it was a pleasure to see you again."

Twenty-six

Eudora woke the next morning and dressed quickly while the rest of the household slept. She was on the front steps when the morning paper hit the sidewalk, intending to return to the kitchen and browse the classified ads as she drank her tea. But at the threshold, she heard a stirring from the master bedroom and abandoned her plans. Brock had made it very clear that he didn't want her to work, and he wouldn't make it easy for her to find a job. So Eudora fetched her purse and left the house, making her way to the breakfast counter at the drug store. There, she would find peace.

Because it was still early yet, the breakfast counter had few customers. The waitress led Eudora to a large booth, and she made good use of the space, spreading the newspaper across the table's surface and reading every classified ad. It didn't take long for her expectation of finding work quickly to turn to frustration. The jobs that sounded interesting required skills Eudora didn't have. From childhood, Eudora had been trained for life as a Society wife and was qualified for little else. There were no ads for the things Eudora could do.

But it was early yet; she'd find something.

Then it occurred to her: maybe the best way to find a job was to ask.

Eudora drank the last of her tea and paid the bill. She slipped on her gloves and gathered her things. It was best to start with what you know and work from there. Chastains seemed a fine first choice. After all, Eudora had been a customer all her life. She knew the clientele and what they liked. She was familiar with every social event and outfits suitable for all of them, and she'd always gotten along well with Mrs. Tweedy. Eudora would have no problem working there.

She arrived at the shop before it opened. She stood before the wide picture window, watching the clerks prepare the store for customers. Their tasks seemed simple enough, though it hadn't occurred to Eudora until now that someone had to ready the shop before the customers came. As she watched the women work, Eudora fiddled with the edge of her glove, smoothing the leather around her fingers. What would she do if any of the women from her social circle – her mother, her mother's friends, Lenore's friends, or the girls from school – came in for an outfit? Would she be expected to serve them? Would they think that Eudora, working, was beneath them or would they admire her fortitude? Except for that one time with Maggie, Eudora barely gave a thought to the girl who rung up her purchases or wrapped her packages.

This wouldn't do at all; there were too many complications.

With a sigh, Eudora turned from the window.

"Eudora, how nice to see you again." Mrs. Tweedy opened the door wide and flipped the sign, indicating the shop was open for business. "Please, come in."

Because it would have been rude to refuse, Eudora followed Mrs. Tweedy into the shop.

"How was your honeymoon? Was Paris as romantic as I've heard?" Mrs. Tweedy rounded the corner of the reception desk and stood behind the counter.

Eudora's reply was automatic now. A practiced response she'd given to friends who had begun to ask. "Brock and I have decided to put off our honeymoon trip until later this fall. The summer crowds can be so overwhelming. We're rather go at a time that's less hectic."

Mrs. Tweedy nodded as she reached under the counter for the account book. "I've been meaning to speak with you about something, Eudora, so it's good you're here early. We'll have a bit of privacy."

"What is it?"

"Well, this is a bit awkward, I'm afraid." Mrs. Tweedy

frowned as she tapped the ledger with a manicured finger-nail. "It seems that your house account – the Rutledge account – is in arrears. Badly. My attempts to collect the balance have gone, shall we say," she pursed her lips as she considered her words, "'Unnoticed'."

"I don't understand." Eudora watched as Mrs. Tweedy opened the book and flip the pages.

"I know this must be uncomfortable for you, Eudora." Mrs. Tweedy rested her thin hand on top of the page. "But I don't seem to have a choice. The Gadsden account has always been up to date. I'd hoped that you, as a Rutledge, would be able to use your influence to make things right." She ran her finger down a column of numbers. "As you can see, some of the charges go back six months or more without a payment. Our policy has always been to send a bill at the end of the month, with the expectation that we will receive payment in full within a few days. That hasn't happened with the Rutledge house account in quite some time." She gave a tight smile, her lips stretching across her teeth. "We've always valued your patronage, Eudora. I hope we can work together to resolve this matter."

Eudora drew herself to her full height. "Thank you for bringing this to my attention. If you'll make a note of the balance, I'll see that you're paid."

"I knew that you would, my dear."

"In the meantime, would you close the account, please? There's no reason to allow new charges if the old charges aren't paid."

Mrs. Tweedy withdrew a sheet of stationery from beneath the desk. After jotting down the total, she folded the page and offered it to Eudora. "No need. The Rutledge account has been closed for several months. Though one or two purchases seemed to have slipped past, I'm afraid we can't allow any others."

"I understand."

～

Eudora left Chastains utterly humiliated.

How many other shop accounts had been left unattended? Did Uncle Alistair know about them? Was this the reason for Uncle Alistair's visit and ongoing quarterly financial meetings? Surely her parents would not have allowed her to marry into a family that was destitute.

The heels of her shoes pounded against the pavement as Eudora fled King Street, away from shops and owners who might want to pull her aside for another whispered conversation. As she walked, conflicting emotions rose and fell as she tried to unravel what happened and her part in it. Some of her anger was directed at her parents, who should have known about the Rutledge finances and warned her. It seemed that her mother's social circle had failed them both. And her father. Wasn't it his job to protect his only daughter or was he still so angry about the letter that he didn't bother to look into the Rutledge family at all?

But Eudora saved the harshest judgement for herself. She'd convinced herself that the choice to marry Brock was her way of asserting her independence, of rejecting her mother's vision for her life. But Eudora had outsmarted herself. And that wasn't even the worst part. The worst part was that she hadn't even given herself a chance.

Eudora peeled off her gloves and stuffed them into her purse. The cool of the September morning had given way to mid-day heat. The sun baked the pavement, making her uncomfortable in her suit. She paused under the shade of a magnolia tree to catch her breath, withdrawing a handkerchief from her purse to dab the perspiration from her face. She hadn't intended to walk this far or be outdoors this long, but the thought of returning to the Rutledge home kept her from turning back.

Looking around, she recognized the neighborhood as being part of the upper peninsula, near the train depot and relatively close to O'Hanlan Millworks. She and Maggie would sometimes walk this way after school to see the Halloween decorations in the neighborhood. A few of the houses were famous for their decorations, with scarecrows, carved orange pumpkins, and dried corn stalks against the front entrance. On impulse, Eudora decided to see if Maggie was free for lunch. She would be leaving for Brooklyn soon and Eudora wanted to see her.

Cheered a bit by the thought of seeing Maggie again, Eudora crossed the street to walk in the shade and made her way to the millworks, allowing her thoughts to wander and not paying particular attention to where she was. She'd lived in Charleston all her life and wasn't likely to get lost.

Until she turned a corner and everything looked unfamiliar.

She'd been in this neighborhood before, many times. The house in front of her had been one of her favorites, two stories with a deep front porch with columns on either side and a widow's walk on the roof. Eudora remembered a carpet of green grass across the front yard and window boxes filled with flowers most of the year. Just last Christmas, the owners had decorated with pinecone-studded garland across the roofline, candles in every window and a Christmas tree in the front parlor.

Now it was different. Now, the property was surrounded by a chain link fence scattered with bright yellow "No Trespassing" signs. The front garden had been scraped clean, the grass uprooted, the urns gone. In their place was a sheet of gravely dirt imbedded with tractor marks and footprints. Great sheets of plywood covered the first-floor windows, nailed to the side of the house and marked with bright neon spray paint. One of the window boxes had been knocked loose; its front panel shattered.

"Look strange, don't it?" The man who stood before her was tall and lean with dark skin and a kind face. He'd taken off his suit jacket and draped it across his arm and had loosened his thin dark necktie.

"It does," Eudora agreed. "What happened?"

"They came and did this all in one day. They call it progress." The man frowned as he pointed to the dump truck parked on the far side of the street. "A bulldozer'll come tomorrow and tear it all down. Trucks come after that and haul it away. Next week you won't even know a house stood here."

"But the house was beautiful. I'm sure someone would want to buy it. Why didn't they put it up for sale?"

"'Cause they wanted the land." The man's eyes blazed for an instant before he looked away. If Eudora hadn't been watching his face, she would have missed the anger there. "So the city condemned it. They said the wiring was bad, though no one inspected it, and they gave George Fraser a week to fix it. They would'a made the deadline if they'd been allowed to use their own electrician. City electricians cost more than double. No way could George come up with that much money in a week."

The man fell silent and both he and Eudora stared at the house behind the fence.

Eudora dropped her gaze to the carriage block buried in the grass at her feet. Her family's home had a block just like this one on the far side of the front entrance. On both stones, the surfaces had been worn smooth, with a dip in the middle where hundreds of feet had stepped to exit their carriage.

"What happened to the family who lived here?" she asked.

"Moved away," the man said simply. "Too sad to think about and can't do nothing about it anyway, so I'm afraid I'll have to bid you a good afternoon." He offered a sad smile, then tipped his hat and walked away.

Eudora remained where she was a few minutes after the man left, wondering who bought the property and what they planned to do with it. And why the city didn't allow the Fraser family more time to replace the wiring.

Twenty-seven

Eudora had been to O'Hanlan Millworks a few times, but that was years ago. Mr. O'Hanlan had just become the new owner and was busy sorting the place out. He'd bought a sleepy little building supply company, but he always said he had big plans for it. The times Eudora visited, the loading dock was littered with garbage, wooden pallets lay splintered and forgotten in the corner, and ragged canvas tarps hung from the inventory shelves.

As Eudora approached, she was awed by the changes. The driveway had been widened and paved to accommodate two trucks abreast. Two flat-bed trucks parked side by side as forklifts loaded pallets of plywood and brick from the warehouse. Another set of smaller trucks waited behind them for their turn. Men with clipboards shouted across the yard to men in hardhats, directing what appeared to be barely organized chaos. A wooden sign nailed to the side of the building pointed the way to the office, up a set of wooden stairs to the second floor. Eudora climbed to the top, avoiding the freshly painted walls and the bins of hardware that lined the hallway. The office was behind a glass-paned door. Inside, a bank of file cabinets stretched along the far wall, with small wooden desks nestled between them, and an oversized dining table strewn with papers. Somewhere, a phone rang.

"Eudora! Well, aren't you a sight for sore eyes?" Maggie's mother rounded her desk. Her arms opened and pulled Eudora in for a hug. "What brings you all the way up here?"

"I wanted to surprise Maggie by asking her to lunch. Is she here?"

"'Course she is," Maggie's mother answered as she squeezed again. "She's downstairs checking on an order, but she'll be up in a second." After a moment, Maggie's mother let go. She grasped Eudora's shoulders and held her at arm's length while she took Eudora's full measure. "We haven't seen you since your wedding," she said, her eyes sharp. "You look tired," she finally decided, releasing her grip on Eudora's shoulders. "Are you getting enough sleep?"

"I'm fine, Mrs. O'Hanlan, really." It felt terrible, lying to Maggie's mother, but Eudora was so used to the automatic reply that everything was fine that the words came out before she could stop them. She finished with a practiced smile. "I've just been busy getting used to married life."

"Well, you've been away, too." Mrs. O'Hanlan nodded, even as she searched Eudora's face. "The adjustment to

Charleston time must be hard, with you so recently returned from your honeymoon. Was Paris as lovely as I've heard?"

Mrs. O'Hanlan's smile broadened as her head tilted, and it occurred to Eudora that Maggie's mother expressed more of an interest than her mother had. Except for two Sunday dinners, Eudora hadn't seen her own parents since her wedding.

Without waiting for a reply, Mrs. O'Hanlan continued her questions. "Did you see the Eiffel Tower? Is it as beautiful as the pictures? I bet it is. I'd love to hear all about—"

The outer office door opened with a bang and Carl entered the office, reading from a stack of pages and muttering to himself.

"Carl, look who dropped by to see Maggie." Mrs. O'Hanlan draped her arm around Eudora's shoulders. "Isn't that wonderful?"

"Welcome back, honey." Mr. O'Hanlan brightened when he saw Eudora, and he leaned in to kiss her on the cheek. He brought with him the scent of sawdust and fresh air. "Maggie'll be up in a minute. She's trying to find a bill of lading for hardware we need for a project. I can't find it anywhere."

Mr. O'Hanlan turned his attention back to the papers in his hand. He scrubbed his fingers across his cropped hair and heaved a long-suffering sigh. "Marie, Kilgore Construction's in the yard. They want to order another load of lumber, but I ain't letting 'em have it until I see where they pay the bill from last time. Donny says he paid, but I don't see a receipt—"

Mrs. O'Hanlan pressed her fingertips against her temple and squinted as she glanced at the stacks of papers scattered across three separate desktops. "Something from Kilgore arrived in the mail just the other day. I had it in my hands.

Give me just a minute, I have to remember what I did with it."

"Kilgore's *waiting*, Marie. I won't let them load without a receipt and they say they're not moving until they load." Carl's voice rose as his face reddened. "Their truck is blocking the driveway."

Mrs. O'Hanlan ignored her husband's outburst as she sifted through a stack of pages, setting one paper down and reaching for another.

"Jeeze. Marie, ain't you got a system?" Carl rubbed the back of his neck. "They're waiting down there."

Finally, his wife had enough. She paused her search just long enough to glare at her husband. "You do remember that my help is given out of the goodness of my heart? That you should have hired a professional bookkeeper to track your accounts and straighten out this mess? Maggie's leaving for New York City in a few days and you'll be left with no one to help you."

"I'll do it," Eudora blurted.

"Do what, doll?" Mrs. O'Hanlan's gaze flickered to Eudora, then back to the papers on her desk.

"I'll do your books." Eudora took a deep breath and continued. "Mr. O'Hanlan, if you're planning to hire someone to do your accounts, I'd like to apply for the job."

As both Mr. and Mrs. O'Hanlan gaped at Eudora, the office door banged open and Maggie stepped inside the room. She looked from her parents to Eudora, then back again. "What'd I miss?"

Maggie's mother was the first to recover. She moved back to the desk she had been occupying, opened the desk drawer and pulled out her purse. "I'll tell you what you missed." Her voice was light as she snapped her purse open and removed her gloves. "Your father has finally taken our advice and hired someone to help with his books. And it's about time, I'd say."

Carl blinked, his expression blank.

"Da hired you?" Maggie gushed and she walked toward Eudora. "That's wonderful, Eudora. I don't know why I didn't think of it myself."

"Looks like I just got the afternoon off." Mrs. O'Hanlan's smile broadened as she pinned her hat to her head "I'm going to go home and put a roast in the oven. Then I'm going to put my feet up and listen to my programs on the radio."

"Marie, what about Kilgore's account?" Carl sputtered. "Have they paid for their last order or not?"

His wife kissed him on the cheek as she moved toward the door. "You'll have to ask Eudora, dear. She's in charge of your books now." She paused as she reached Eudora. "The job pays forty dollars a week." She hesitated, then frowned as if another possibility just occurred to her. "If you can't manage full time, we'll take you when you're free. In fact, we'll work the details out as we go along."

"Mrs. O'Hanlan, please. Just a minute." Eudora reached out to stop her, catching her just before she left the room. She wasn't sure who to address her comments to, but it seemed that Maggie's mother was the one in charge. "I have to tell you that I'm entirely self-taught. Everything I know about accounting I either learned from my father or read about in a college textbook."

Her comment was met with silence, so she continued, hoping the job offer wouldn't be rescinded. Taking a deep breath, she explained. "I wanted to be prepared for my business classes, so I borrowed textbooks from the library and I've been reading them. They're really quite interesting." Instead of dropping her gaze, she met Mrs. O'Hanlan's eyes. Her words came out in a tangle. "I'm not going to college this fall, as I thought I was. So if you think I'm not qualified to do your books, I'm happy to work for free until you think I *am* ready." She paused, steeling herself against the answer that might come. "I'd like the job for the chance to work. I don't need to be paid. I'm happy to work for free until you're satisfied with my work."

At some point, Eudora realized she had been repeating herself, so she stopped talking altogether. She stood in front of both Mr. and Mrs. O'Hanlan, holding her breath and hoping they wouldn't take her up on her offer to work for free. The millworks would be a perfect place to learn about business while earning money for tuition.

Mrs. O'Hanlan was the first to speak. "I haven't been to college either, Eudora, and I figured out Mr. O'Hanlan's accounting system just fine. You will, too." Then Maggie's mother frowned, her expression firm. "First rules of business, my dear: never undervalue yourself and never work for free."

"Marie!" Carl called as he sifted through the pages on the table. "Kilgore?"

His wife smiled as she pulled on her gloves. "I'll speak to them on my way out."

As the door behind her mother closed, Maggie reached into a desk drawer for her purse. "Eudora and I are going to lunch now, Da." She flashed a brilliant smile. "We'll be back in an hour."

Twenty-eight

Eudora sat at the kitchen table, the pot of Earl Grey tea

growing cold by her side. She'd been at her new job at O'Hanlan Millworks for several weeks, untangling the accounts and using her textbooks as reference. The work she couldn't finish during the day, she brought home at night, decoding the entries and what they meant as the rest of the household slept. She began to slip her alarm clock under her pillow, rising at four-thirty to study. The pot of Earl Grey was a comforting companion, and the work helped her forget how much she missed Maggie.

Some of the work was overwhelming. More than once Eudora wondered about her ability to learn the system. Mrs. O'Hanlan had noticed Eudora's struggling and had suggested breaking it down into more manageable parts, so Eudora's goal became learning one new accounting concept every day. She'd become a regular fixture at the college library, studying textbooks she wasn't allowed to buy and learning everything she could. Eventually, Eudora had the idea to use the Rutledge household accounts as a working example. After all, Santee Academy had trained Eudora to manage a household – what was a business, really, but a household on a larger scale?

Eudora was horrified at what she'd discovered.

The Chastains house account wasn't the only one overdue. She'd discovered past-due notices from the silversmith on King Street and terse letters from a haberdashery on Tailor Street. So, with Uncle Alistair's blessing, Eudora had begun to make payments, redirecting a portion of her paycheck to bringing these accounts current. Shop owners seemed surprised at the unexpected attention from a Rutledge.

One of the accounts, however, confused her – the grocery bill from Fredrickson's.

As the housekeeper, part of Flora's job was to plan meals

and order what she needed from various grocers, who would deliver orders three times a week. Except for Lenore's bridge afternoons and an occasional dinner party, the Rutledges didn't entertain often, so the invoice from Fredrickson's should be fairly consistent. But they weren't. No matter how many times Eudora tried, she just couldn't reconcile the statements with the invoices. And that would mean a conversation with Flora.

She and Flora had never warmed to each other, despite the fact that Eudora was technically mistress of the house and was within her rights to organize it however she chose. But household duties had never interested Eudora, so she was content to let Flora run things as she chose. Eudora directed most of her energy to the O'Hanlan business instead of the Rutledge household because the work energized her and she was proud of the progress she'd made.

Eudora sighed and pushed the account books away. Outside, the sky had begun to lighten, washing the sky in shades of pink and casting the garden in soft gray shadows. The city had begun to stir, and it was time for Eudora to get ready for work. She poured the rest of the tea into her cup and drank it cold, surprised again at how much time she'd spent working. Gathering her invoices and stacking the cash envelopes, she tucked everything inside her ledger book, closing the cover and slipping it into her bag.

A short time later, showered and dressed for work, Eudora returned to the kitchen. Flora had arrived for work. She stood in front of the refrigerator, unpacking the day's groceries from a box on the floor.

Now was as good a time as any for a discussion about the Fredrickson's bill.

"Good morning, Flora." Eudora reached inside her bag for

the September grocery invoice. "Can I see you a minute please, over here?"

"I need to get breakfast started," Flora answered without turning. "Mrs. Rutledge likes her tray on time."

"It won't take long, and I'm sure she won't mind waiting." Eudora pulled out a chair from the kitchen table. "Over here, please."

With a huff that Eudora chose to ignore, Flora abandoned her work and made her way to the table, wiping her hands on her apron as she walked.

After Flora sat, Eudora opened her notebook and ran her pencil down the statement until she found what she was looking for. "This statement shows an order for a large roast beef, a bag of potatoes, and a half-bushel of green beans on the twenty-first."

"That's right."

"But Mr. Rutledge, his mother, and I dined at the Yacht Club that evening. And were away the next. When did you serve the roast beef?"

Flora flicked her hand over the invoice and scoffed. "Those people over there, they make mistakes all the time."

"I telephoned Mr. Fredrickson to ask about this charge and several others. He said you signed for the delivery. You always sign for delivery."

"I can't be expected to know when I served a roast. Just know I did." Flora's expression hardened as she looked away.

Eudora held her place with her fingertip as she pulled another book from her bag. "That's what I thought too, until I compared my datebook with the orders. There have been several large orders placed on days the family was away." She looked at Flora, careful to keep her expression neutral, though her heart was pounding. "I was hoping you could explain that."

"Flora, didn't you hear me ring?" Lenore breezed into the kitchen in a light blue dressing gown, her hair tied in a soft yellow scarf. "I'd like my coffee now." Eudora was struck by how young she looked without her face made up.

Flora glared at Eudora before rising from the table. "I'll get it right now."

"No. You won't." Eudora's voice was sharp, causing both women to startle. "Flora, I asked you a question, and I'd like an answer. I want you to explain these charges from Fredrickson's."

"What's all this? What charges?" Lenore gestured to the open account book, then moved toward the table for a better look. Turning the statement toward her, she scanned the contents.

The change to Flora's temperament was immediate. Her face softened as crocodile tears gathered in her eyes. She pleaded with Lenore. "I've been working in this house a long time, Miss Lenore. I know how you like things done and I do my best. Always have." Flora's expression hardened as she pointed at Eudora. "That girl is accusing me of stealing."

Eudora straightened. "You will address me as *Mrs. Rutledge*, Flora," Eudora replied, her tone even, despite her fury. "I haven't accused you of anything. I've simply asked you for an explanation. You are, after all, the one who places the Fredrickson's order and the only one who signs for deliveries."

Lenore looked up from the statement and frowned. "Flora?"

Flora pushed her arms to her side, her hands curled into fists. "I've been with this family for twenty years, and in all that time, you have never once questioned my character like *she* is."

If Flora expected to find an ally in Lenore, she was mistaken.

Lenore paused for the briefest of moments, then her gaze sharpened. "I believe you've been asked a question, Flora."

Flora reached for Lenore's arm and seemed surprised when she backed away. "Over the years I've had Fredrickson's deliver a few of my own orders here so I can take them home with me when I leave. Saves me a trip to the Piggly Wiggly on my way home. I always tell them to bill me separately, but they must have made a mistake—"

"If I'm not mistaken, you live with your daughter and her husband?" Eudora asked. "Not a very big household, is it?"

"No, it isn't." Flora shook her head sadly. "They're the only family I got."

Eudora glanced at the items she'd checked. "So why would you need to order a bushel of oysters, an entire ham shoulder, or six-pound beef roast?"

The room was silent.

"You're selling the food, aren't you?" Eudora asked, though she didn't need to. Flora looked away. "You charge the food to us and sell it to who, your neighbors?"

Lenore gasped. "Flora."

"You're fired." Eudora rose from the table, taking the Fredrickson invoices with her. "The amount you've stolen will be deducted from your last paycheck. Give me your house key and leave immediately."

But Flora remained where she was, her last appeal directed at Lenore. "Mrs. Rutledge, please. We go back a long way, and you know I wouldn't steal from you. Not on purpose. Don't let this woman ruin years of friendship."

"Oh, Flora." Lenore's reply was soft. "How could you?"

The grandfather clock in the front hall softly chimed the hour.

"Flora. You must see that you've got no choice," Eudora said. "We could have you arrested for theft, but we'd rather not."

Flora dropped the keys on the counter, turned on her heel and left the room without another word.

Eudora and her mother-in-law watched until they heard the back door slam.

Then Lenore turned. "Eudora?"

"Yes?" Eudora turned with a smile. Maybe this would be a fresh start for them. Maybe they could grow to be friends.

"I am hosting a small luncheon today." Lenore rose from her chair. "Since you fired the housekeeper, I'll expect you to have it ready by one o'clock."

Twenty-Nine

Eudora could have put something together for Lenore's luncheon, but she didn't want to. What she wanted was a more permanent solution, the feeling that this kitchen was run under her direction. She wanted someone whose work ethic she admired, who she could trust, and who might grow to be a friend. And she could think of only one person who would fit that bill.

Eudora called for a taxi because she didn't have time to waste. As the car drove up Meeting Street, she tried to think of what to say. As they crossed Columbus, she began to worry that no matter what she said, the young woman might not want to help. And when the car finally slowed to a stop along the curb at the train depot, Eudora was convinced the whole trip was a waste of time. But if she was here anyway, she might as well try.

Eudora leaned forward to give the driver the fare. "Would you mind waiting? I'll be right back."

"Sure." He shrugged and pulled a newspaper from under the seat. "It's early yet. I've got a few minutes."

Eudora crossed the sidewalk and climbed the stairs to the depot. The departure board announced the first train of the day was bound for Columbia. It was a relatively short trip and one where passengers might not want to buy food, so Letty might not be there. Eudora jumped from the platform to the tracks and walked along the far side of the train.

In the distance, Eudora saw her.

Small and slight, walking the length of the train, she carried a sweetgrass basket in front of her body and had tied a jug of coffee to her waist. The jug appeared to weigh more than she did; the vibration of it bumping against her leg as she walked shook her entire body.

Eudora stepped over the tracks and went to meet her.

"You come back for more chicken?" Letty shook her head. "Don't have any yet. Biscuits only, this early in the morning. But I got sausage and ham. Just made. Coffee's hot, too."

"I'm sure it's delicious," Eudora replied. "But I didn't come here for that; well, not specifically."

Letty's brow lifted. "Oh?"

"I just caught our housekeeper stealing, so I fired her. The problem is that my mother-in-law is hosting a luncheon this afternoon, and I can't cook. I was hoping you'd come to my house and help."

"Help you cook lunch?"

"Well, I wouldn't really be helping. I guess I meant 'would you make lunch?' All of it. Yourself."

"Today?"

"I hoped you would, yes."

"You don't know nobody can cook 'side me?"

"I do. My mother's housekeeper could help, or I could have something delivered from a restaurant. But I remember how good your food is, and I wanted to offer you a job." Eudora sat on a tree stump next to the tracks.

What Eudora thought she was offering was stability. The stability of working in a big kitchen instead of walking a set of train tracks. The stability of a regular paycheck instead of coins collected from train passengers.

To her surprise, Letty refused.

"Thank you, but no," Letty said. "My Auntie Mae worked in a big house for a time and didn't like it. She here now, at the depot selling chicken with us, and no one tells her what to do. The money she makes is her own. No one threatens to take it away 'cause they mad at something she done." She shifted the thermos of coffee against her body. "So I thank you for your offer, but my answer got to be 'no'."

"Did you know the Health Department plans to increase patrols around here? The newspaper says they won't stop until they've either arrested y'all or driven you from the depot."

"'Course I know that. I come here every day." Letty lifted her chin. "But I'll be fine."

"What if I paid you in cash, every day? You can leave any time you want."

Letty untied the coffee jug from her waist and set it down with a thump. "Why you want me to come work for you so bad?"

"I met you before, several months ago," Eudora began. "I don't know if you remember—"

"The alley? 'course I do. I still have y' sweater."

Eudora pulled a leaf from a nearby branch and began to shred it. "The thing is, you seem nice. I liked talking to you, despite our circumstances, and I could use a friend in my husband's house. Things have been… difficult there for me."

In the distance, the train whistle blew. The conductor called for all passengers to board.

Letty glanced at the depot. She stood. "Thank you all the same, but I got biscuits to sell."

"I'll buy it all." Eudora blurted the first thought that occurred to her.

Letty turned back. "What'd you say?"

Eudora drew herself to her full height, all five feet two inches. "I said 'I'll buy it all.' And I'll pay you for your time, too, if you come to my house and fix lunch for my mother-in-law's friends."

A smile tugged at Letty's lips. "She that bad?"

"You have no idea."

Letty shrugged. "Let's go, then."

She and Letty settled on a fair price for an afternoon's work as they walked to the waiting taxi. Then she removed two wrapped biscuits and handed them to the driver. "Thank you for waiting for me. I've brought you breakfast."

"Hey, thanks." The driver hurriedly folded his newspaper and tossed it on the seat next to him. "You didn't have to do that."

"My pleasure." Eudora scribbled a quick note explaining her absence from work, tucked it into the basket and handed it all to the driver. "Do you know where O'Hanlan Millworks is?"

"Sure I do."

Eudora pulled a few bills from her wallet, enough to cover

what she owed and the fare to the millworks. "Please bring the basket and the coffee to Mr. O'Hanlan. Tell him I've sent breakfast for his crew."

Letty watched the exchange, but it wasn't until the taxi drove away that she spoke. "I might could come a few days more, just 'til you get someone."

"Really?" Eudora felt her chest fill with the first full breath she'd had since confronting Flora. "That's great news. I'll pay you, of course."

"Every day?" Letty asked. "In cash?"

"Yes, of course."

"And I can fix the kitchen how I like?"

That request was new, but seemed minor to Eudora, so she agreed.

"Then it seems we got ourselves a deal," Letty said.

By mid-morning, Letty had settled in the kitchen. Eudora had offered to buy Letty any ingredients she needed, but, after surveying the contents of both the refrigerator and the pantry, Letty declared there was more than enough on hand to feed a few ladies who probably didn't eat anything anyway. Then she went to work, chopping and mixing. Eudora stood by, expecting to help, but Letty shoo'd her out of the kitchen, saying Eudora was just getting in the way.

So Eudora decided to report to the millworks after all. She gathered her things, slipping one of her budget envelopes from her ledger into her purse. There was one stop she had to make before reporting to work.

Chastains was empty when Eudora approached the front

door. The silver bell jingled as she pushed open the sleek glass door and stepped inside the shop.

"Eudora, how nice to see you again." Mrs. Tweedy emerged from the office behind the register, both hands reaching for Eudora's and clasping them in hers. "I was so afraid that you might have been offended by our last conversation."

"Not at all. You were forced into an uncomfortable position," Eudora replied as she pulled an envelope from her purse and placed it on the counter. "I'd like to pay off the house account. I'm afraid I only have cash, so I'd like a receipt, please."

"Of course, dear." Mrs. Tweedy counted the bills and made a note in the account book. "This is admirable, what you're doing." She reached for her receipt book. "You are a blessing for the Rutledge family, Eudora."

"Thank you, Mrs. Tweedy." Eudora folded the receipt and slipped it into her purse.

As she turned to leave, Mrs. Tweedy stopped her. "Oh, Eudora, wait a moment, will you?"

Eudora stopped.

"Would you like to look around a bit before you leave?" Mrs. Tweedy gestured to a display of evening dresses. "The Yacht Club dinner dance is Saturday after next, and I have some very nice gowns. I'm happy to reinstate your house account and post the charge there."

"Thank you, but I'm afraid I don't have time to shop right now. I'm expected at work." Eudora lifted her chin. "I work now."

It felt good to say.

Mrs. Tweedy nodded. "I understand. Maybe another time."

"Yes, another time. I'll look forward to it."

Thirty

Letty had decided to stay several days more. The meals she cooked and served seemed to have lifted everyone's mood until Flora, and her bloody lamb roast, became a distant memory. Eudora had offered to help cook on more than one occasion, but Letty shoo'd her out of the kitchen. Letty had said, "Some people just don't have the talent for cooking. You one of 'em."

And when the days turned into weeks, Letty declared her intention to reorganize the kitchen. Eudora was thrilled.

Though Eudora wasn't allowed to actually cook anything, Letty had allowed her to brew one pot of tea only because Eudora rose so early in the morning to work on the mill-works' ledgers. Sometimes, Eudora dared to toast a single slice of wheat bread, but that was all. She'd come to love having Letty in the house, and following her rules was a small price to pay to keep her.

This morning, Eudora woke early, dressed, and brought her ledgers to the kitchen. She pushed open the kitchen door to find Letty standing in the middle of chaos, her hands on her hips and a scowl on her face. The sleeves of her dress had been pushed above her elbows and her cardigan draped across a chair. At her feet, half a dozen cardboard boxes lay scattered across the kitchen floor, some empty, some not. A few cupboard doors opened wide, and the pantry had been emptied entirely, with various cans and boxes stretched across the length of the countertops.

"You're getting an early start on the day," Eudora

commented as she reached for the kettle and filled it with water.

"Yes, I am." Letty glared at the mess on the floor. "Decided I couldn't sleep another lick 'til I banished that woman from this kitchen. So I came over to do it."

"What woman? Flora?"

"Yes, Flora." Letty turned her glare on Eudora, then back to the mess. "No wonder she cook the way she did."

Is there anything I can help with?" Eudora flicked on the burner, then made her way to the table.

"That." Letty pointed toward a pile of appliances stacked in a pile near the door. Eudora recognized an electric skillet, several aluminum pots, and an ice crusher that appeared to be brand new. "I'll tell you right now: good home cooking does not come from a can or a fancy gadget."

"I've said that you can fix this kitchen any way you want. Order whatever you need to cook." The kettle whistled, and Eudora went to see to it.

"Not sure how long I'ma stay," Letty replied. "But I can't cook with what you got, and I can't keep bringing bags of essentials with me every day."

"We can buy whatever you need. All you have to do is tell me." Eudora settled into a chair with her tea. She opened her notepad and turned to a fresh sheet of paper. "If it'll help, I'll start a list."

Letty crossed her arms. "You won't like what I have to tell you."

"Try me."

"Knives. They need to be sharp. Every one you got is as dull as a rainy Tuesday."

"That seems easy enough." Eudora scribbled on the pad.

"I'm sure we can find a knife man to come out and sharpen them."

"Meat delivery."

"What?"

"We need a meat man who delivers, a good one. The one you have delivers like you don't know any better. His cuts are cheap and he's charging too much."

"Really?"

"Yes."

"Is that all?"

"No ma'am, it is not." Letty's scowl deepened. "I told you you wouldn't like it."

"I didn't say anything." Eudora waited for her to continue.

"Produce," Letty said, simply. "You need a produce man."

"Don't we have one?" Eudora looked up, her pen poised over the page. "Who did Flora use?"

"Supermarket, near's I can tell."

"What's wrong with the supermarket? It's new, it's close, and they can deliver anything you need."

Letty scoffed. "The greens old, the okra soft, and they wouldn't know a ripe tomato if it bit them."

"Fair enough," Eudora agreed. "Annie has a produce man she likes, but you can use whoever you like."

"That's not all." Letty lifted her chin, as if her list were a test. Which, Eudora finally realized, was what it was. "I can't find a seasoned iron skillet anywhere in this kitchen, and I can't cook without one. Cornbread don't taste right if it ain't baked in iron. And chicken can't be fried in anything else."

"Flora never made cornbread," Eudora explained. "Or fried chicken."

"You got me now, and things gonna change."

Eudora bit back a smile at the idea that Letty planned to stay longer than a few days. "I'll order you a skillet and have it delivered today."

"Delivery won't get you a good one." Letty rolled her sleeves down and fastened the button at her wrist. "You can't order something like that over the telephone. I need to pick it out myself, feel the weight of it to know if it'll last."

"I understand. Is that all?"

"No, it is not." Letty strode back across the kitchen, to the pantry, and pulled out a bag of flour. She wrinkled her nose as she set it on the counter. It dropped with a thud. "Flour's off." She swept her hand across an assortment of baking supplies on the counter. "All'a that needs replacing. I can't think of cooking without fresh." She crossed the room and opened the refrigerator. Except for a tub of cottage cheese on the top shelf and a few of Brock's beer bottles in the door, it was bare. "We need real food in this kitchen. Vegetables – okra, peppers, onions, beans, and good cornmeal," Letty crinkled her nose as she pointed to the mixes that Flora had used, "not that boxed nonsense." She took a breath and continued. "We need a good fish man, a chicken man, and a butcher who'll deliver sausage until I can see my way clear to making it myself."

"And I'm guessing our house account at Fredrickson's won't do?" Eudora put down her pencil.

Letty shook her head. "No m'am, it won't."

Eudora rose from her seat and walked to the desk. She opened the top drawer and removed a budget envelope, money she'd set aside for her textbooks. She withdrew all the bills inside, counted them and placed them on the counter in front of Letty. "I have sixty-five dollars saved. If you can start with that, you can have it, but please spend carefully. I'll have a little more next week and a little more the week after."

Letty's gaze shifted from the envelope to Eudora's face. Eudora felt her cheeks burn as she realized that Letty understood the Rutledge family was not well off and that Letty might not want to work for them.

After a long moment, Letty nodded. "That be fine."

"Thank you." Eudora turned to leave the room, then paused at the doorway. "Letty?"

"Yes?"

"Does this mean you're going to stay?"

Letty snorted. "I ain't decided yet."

Thirty-one

By January, Eudora had her own office.

Mrs. O'Hanlan found her a desk, and Mr. O'Hanlan instructed a work crew to build walls around it. Eudora brought a plant from home, a squatty brown teapot, and a graduation picture of her and Maggie. The accounting textbooks she'd consulted many times a day during her first month on the job were shelved because she rarely needed them anymore. Mr. O'Hanlan had remarked that his accounts had never been so organized. In fact, he'd been so pleased with the work she'd done on receivables that he wasted no time in handing over payables and payroll as well. The big project for the New Year was to be inventory, predicting what they needed, finding ways to use what they had, and negotiating price for what they had to buy.

The millworks itself was flourishing, too. The city was draining marshland on the west side of the peninsula to make way for a new stadium and medical center. The naval yard couldn't hire workers fast enough. The city awarded so many contracts for roads and infrastructure that construction companies were forced to look to Savannah and Orangeburg for help. Workers came to Charleston and brought their families, and everyone needed a place to live. Builders arrived to fill the need and O'Hanlan Millworks was happy to supply the materials. In the last few months, they'd doubled the number of workers in the yard and added much-needed loading docks and storage for inventory.

Eudora was thrilled. Her work kept her busy and she liked earning a paycheck. She'd used it to pay off several of the house accounts and managed to put aside enough for spring classes, too. When the spring catalog arrived in the mail, Eudora was thrilled to realize her foundation was more solid that she thought, that her time in the library had been wisely spent. She'd already learned most of the information in the introductory classes, so she decided a more advanced single class on Thursday morning made more sense.

Pounding feet on the wooden stairs to the offices pulled Eudora from her thoughts. Only one person moved that fast. She bit back a smile and turned toward the door to wait.

Jimmy McCallister, the new office boy Mr. O'Hanlan had hired to run errands and deliver messages, rushed into the office, his thin chest heaving and his hairline damp with perspiration. When Mr. O'Hanlan hired Jimmy back in December, he said that he expected Jimmy to hustle, and Jimmy had taken his warning very seriously.

"You don't have to run everywhere, Jimmy. I think Mr. O'Hanlan may have been exaggerating, just a bit."

Jimmy leaned over to catch his breath and placed his palms on his knees as he drew air into his lungs.

Eudora went to the water cooler and filled a paper cup. She waited until he'd caught his breath to offer it to him and waited again while he gulped down the contents. The boy was maybe twelve years old and a classmate of one of the O'Hanlan boys. She'd been in the office when he came in, wearing a crisp white shirt and a necktie, to ask for a job. He wanted to earn money for Christmas, he said, and he promised to work very hard.

"Jimmy, has Mr. O'Hanlan gone to lunch yet, do you know?" Eudora asked, mostly to give Jimmy time to recover. Since his first day, she'd never seen him do anything but run.

"He's right behind me – told me to catch you before you go to lunch – wants you to wait for him."

"Did he say what he wanted?"

"Not to me." Jimmy straightened, then flicked his gaze toward the outer door. "He sent me to get the year-end inventory reports. Guys in the yard want to place an order."

"Right here." Eudora lifted a folder from a wire basket on her desk.

They heard footsteps on the stairs, heavy and slow.

Jimmy's eyes widened as he rushed to the door. "Thanks!" He was gone in a flash, slamming the door behind him.

A moment later, Mr. O'Hanlan appeared, red faced and out of breath. "I told that kid about slamming doors," Mr. O'Hanlan grumbled. "Boy's like a jackrabbit."

Eudora followed him to his office. "Weren't you the one who insisted he run everywhere?"

"Yeah. Maybe that was a mistake." Carl rounded the corner of his desk and dropped to a chair. "I'll talk to him."

"I've got checks for you to sign," she said, finally, as she laid the folder on the desktop.

"Paychecks already?" he asked as he drew the folder close

and opened the cover. He unscrewed his fountain pen and signed the first with tangled and hurried script, then pushed it to the side and started on the next one. "You got those quarterly income statements for me? I'm thinking about giving year-end bonuses, and I need to know what we can afford."

"In your inbox. I put it there this morning."

"Good work, thanks." Carl finished signing and tapped the stack against his desktop. Then he flicked his chin toward a pair of green vinyl chairs in front of his desk. "Sit down a second, will ya? I want to talk to you."

Eudora froze. The thought of losing her job took the breath from her body.

When she didn't immediately sit, he glanced at her expression and rolled his eyes. "Eudora, you gotta stop looking like someone who's been called to the principal's office when I say I want to talk to you. It's not always bad."

"I know," Eudora said as she shook the tension from her shoulders. "I just want to do a good job."

"And you are," Carl assured her. "That's why I want to talk to you." He drew a breath and reached across the desk for his pipe. "I spoke to Donny over at Kilgore this morning. He said you were right about that bookkeeper. Been with them for twenty years and stealing from them for at least half that. What made you suspicious?"

Eudora was hesitant to tell him that she'd discovered Flora doing almost the same thing earlier in the year and had never forgotten it. One action made her suspect the other.

Instead, she shrugged, as if it were nothing. "She wasn't too careful about covering her tracks. It wasn't hard to unravel."

"Well, it was good work you did. Saved them thousands, and he's grateful," Carl said as he tapped the bowl of his pipe against the edge of the ashtray. He frowned, as if trying to gather his thoughts, then he put his pipe down and looked directly at Eudora. "Tell me, Eudora, how are things at home for you?"

She felt her body tense, though her smile remained in place. A credit to her years of cotillion. "What do you mean?"

"No easy way to ask, Eudora, so I'll just come right out with it." Averting his gaze, he focused his attention on tamping down the tobacco. "Sometimes, a man doesn't like his wife to work. I'd like to know if Brock is that kind of man." He lifted his shoulders, then frowned as he lifted his gaze. "If Marie were here, she'd know a better way to ask, so I hope you'll overlook the gruffness of the question."

"Of course." Eudora stalled. She wouldn't lie to Carl, but neither did she feel comfortable telling him the truth.

The truth was that it had been a mistake marrying Brock, and she regretted it. In the last few months things had deteriorated to the point where they had dropped all pretense at civility and they seemed content to live vastly separate lives. Brock was out when she came home from work, still out when she went to bed, and she was careful not to wake him when she left the following morning. She didn't know where he was much of the time, and he didn't volunteer the information. For her part, Eudora did the same, keeping the scope of her work from him and hiding her paychecks because she didn't trust him.

It wasn't the marriage she wanted.

It wasn't the marriage he'd promised.

But Eudora refused to consider divorce because of the disgrace it would bring to her family. So she was stuck.

"On second thought, you don't have to tell me anything, Eudora," Carl said, breaking into Eudora's thoughts. "I didn't mean to pry. I have an opportunity for you, that's all, and I wanted to make sure it doesn't cause you trouble at home."

Curiosity got the best of her. "What kind of opportunity?"

Carl visibly relaxed as she settled into the chair across from his desk. Eudora bit back a smile. He was always more comfortable with business. Any hint of emotion, any workplace drama, would be left to Marie to manage. "Donny Kilgore fired that bookkeeper a' his last week and needs a new one fast. He wants to know if you'll help him hire someone permanently and if you'll do his books in the meantime. Whole thing shouldn't take more than a month or two, but he pays well and he'd owe you a favor when it's over."

"But what about my work here?"

"You'd continue to do that, of course." Carl's wooden chair creaked as he leaned back. "I'm not letting you go, no matter what Donny needs. He's okay with you taking work home. He doesn't care where you work, he just wants his accounts straightened out, same as you did for me." As he paused, his gaze sharpened. "But what I am going to suggest is that you bring his ledgers here. I'll give you a key and you can work in your office, lock everything up when you're done. That way no one but you will know what you're doing."

Eudora felt the heat rise to her cheeks and she understood what Carl was implying. That her husband couldn't be trusted. Eudora was embarrassed because she agreed with him.

"Another thing: I'm sure Donny wouldn't mind paying you in cash." He shrugged, as if it didn't matter to him, but Eudora suspected the cash payments were his idea. "That way no one would know if you brought home a little extra. 'Mad money,' I think Marie calls it."

"And you don't mind me using your office?"

He leaned back, his relief evident in the wide grin unfurling across his face. "Lemme tell ya something, Eudora. You got a bright future ahead 'a you, and it'd be nice if I could tell everyone that your empire started right here."

"Thank you, Mr. O'Hanlan." It had been a long time since anyone had told Eudora that they were proud of her. Unexpectedly, Eudora felt tears beginning to form, and she bit the inside of her cheek to hold them back. "Please tell Mr. Kilgore that I'd be happy to help him."

Mr. O'Hanlan snorted. "That's another thing."

"What is?"

"We work construction. Enough with the 'Mister' already, wouldja? Call me Carl."

"I'll try to remember," Eudora said.

Thinking their conversation was over, Eudora turned to leave, but Carl called her back. "Sit down a minute, willya? Got something else I want to talk to you about." He set his unlit pipe in the ashtray and turned to retrieve a battered folder from a shelf.

Opening the cover, he lifted one of the pages. "I've been keeping this for a coupl'a weeks, and I was only going to bring it to you if you were interested in doing the Kilgore books."

He slid the page toward her, tapping it with his finger as it crossed his desk. "He said to think of it as an incentive to get you to do his books."

Scribbled on the page was a single address. She wasn't familiar with that part of town, but the address seemed to be on the upper peninsula, west of Marion Square. Next to the address was a dollar amount, circled in thick red marker and underlined twice.

"I don't understand." Eudora looked up.

"It's an opportunity, Eudora, something you need to think long and hard about. Only you can decide if it's right, no matter what Donny Kilgore says." Carl pulled a map from the shelf behind him and unrolled it across the length of his desk, anchoring the edges. Fishing a carpenter's pencil from his shirt pocket, he leaned over the map. "Lemme show you something. See this? Here and here?" He circled big swatches of land near the Ashely River. "The city's draining the marsh-land on this side. They've got a new stadium but didn't figure on space for cars, so they're building roads like crazy. The new medical center is here, with new houses being built here, here, and here." He tapped the page for emphasis. "This is where the city's building, and everyone's following."

Eudora remembered a bit of conversation she'd overheard a month or so before. Brock and his friend Tommy J wanted Lenore to finance their newest business idea – a construction business. "We'll make a fortune filling marshland, Mother," Brock had said when he asked her for collateral to secure a business loan. "All we need is the money to buy dump trucks – the city's practically giving the contracts away."

In the end, Uncle Alistair intervened and refused to allow another mortgage on the house. Brock had been furious for weeks afterwards.

Eudora glanced at the address and then again at the map spread across the desk. "But the stadium construction is over on Barre Street. This address isn't anywhere near that."

"You're right." Carl's chair creaked as he leaned back in it. "Donny says the building has been neglected."

"I still don't understand what he wants."

"He's giving you an opportunity, Eudora. And it might be a good one." Mr. O'Hanlan reached for his pipe and knocked the bowl against the side of the ashtray. The tobacco that tumbled out was still fresh, and Eudora hid a smile. Mrs. O'Hanlan had forbidden her husband from smoking his pipe, but apparently that didn't stop him from filling it. "One thing I learned right off is that you don't chase profit," he continued. "By the time the newspaper reports the building projects, the bids are out and the contracts are mostly decided. Unless you've already got connections, like Kilgore and some of the others, you don't have a snowball's chance of getting rich off city contracts."

Reaching into his desk drawer, he removed the pouch of tobacco he kept there. As he opened it, the scent threaded the air. For the rest of her life, the smell of pipe tobacco would make Eudora happy because it reminded her of Mr. O'Hanlan.

"Filling it isn't smoking," he warned as he glanced at her.

"I won't say a word," Eudora promised.

Carl nodded then continued, his attention on his pipe as he spoke. "The thing is, if everyone's running in one direction, the smart money will always go a different way. The property at that address been in the Walker family for generations. Donny says the family tried to sell it a few years back, had it up on the market for months. No one wanted to put in the work because it's easier to buy a brand-new split-level on the other side of town."

"Are they still living in the house?"

"It's not a house." He withdrew a pipe cleaner from his shirt pocket. "Which made the property trickier to sell, from what Donny told me. Anyway, the number circled on that page is the tax balance – money the state wants in exchange for releasing the property." He glanced up. "Donny said you might want to buy it."

"Buy it?" Eudora breathed. "Me?"

"Yes, you," he confirmed with a twinkle in his eye.

"What am I supposed to do with a condemned property?"

"It could be a nice investment property for you. Or you might want to tear it down and build something new." He shrugged. "It's up to you. But first, you need to go look at it. See what you think. Then come back, and we'll talk about it."

"But I don't know the first thing about restoration. Or construction."

"You didn't know about running an accounting department either, until you learned." He shrugged as he sucked on the end of his pipe. "You've worked here for less than six months and you've straightened years' worth of accounts. You've collected payment on invoices that I didn't even know we had and organized timecards so the boys downstairs know where to punch in. You're smart, Eudora, and you learn quick. 'Side that, Donny and I'll be around to help."

Eudora leaned back in her chair. This was something she'd never even considered.

Mr. O'Hanlan leaned forward, toward the jar of pipe cleaners on the edge of his desk. "But it won't be easy; construction never is."

She turned her attention back to Carl, who had been watching. He shrugged. "It's up to you, Eudora. It's an opportunity that just happened to come up. No shame in letting it go, either, if this ain't the right time. Donny still wants you to do his books. That work might lead to other work, who knows? Could be the start of a nice business. Accounting is what you wanted to go to school for, isn't it?"

"Yes. I'm registered for one class this spring, but I haven't paid tuition yet," Eudora replied absently as she tried to make sense of what Mr. O'Hanlan was saying.

Mr. O'Hanlan poked the end of the pipe cleaner into his pipe as he waited for her to gather her thoughts.

"Let me make sure I understand," Eudora began again, glancing at the address on the page. "The city of Charleston is selling an entire building for two hundred and seventy-six dollars. Whoever pays that amount will own the property outright."

"That's right."

"Have you seen this building?"

"I haven't. You should keep in mind that if the city's selling for back taxes, that probably means no one wanted to buy it. So you should look carefully before you decide anything."

"Really, Mr. O'Hanlan," Eudora protested again. "I don't know the first thing about construction."

Carl dismissed that concern with a wave of his hand. "Donny Kilgore is an excellent contractor and he owes you a favor. This millworks supplies building material to some of the best subcontractors in the city, and most of them owe me a favor – heck, most of them owe *you* a favor. Now might be a good time to call in your marks. Assuming, of course, you want to pursue it."

Eudora's mind raced with possibility. "Do you think Donny might agree to trade my accounting services for construction labor? I could use my salary here to pay for materials."

"Which I'm sure you can get at cost," Carl finished with a smile.

Eudora remembered the money she'd been saving to pay for spring tuition, a little bit each week from her salary tucked into an envelope she'd hidden in her jewelry box. Maybe this was a better investment.

"Does this sound like a good investment idea to you?" Eudora asked, finally. "Buying this building to fix it up?"

"It might." Carl nodded. "Donny's been doing pretty well for himself lately. He seems to find the good ones."

"Would you want to partner with me? We can buy the property together."

"Sorry, Eudora, I can't. The timings not right for me." Carl shook his head. "Now that the accounts are straight, I want to think about expanding this place instead. Maybe branch out into the retail market. There's the space downstairs that I'd like to turn to a place where customers can buy hardware or lumber in amounts smaller than the contractors order."

It was probably too good to be true, anyway. The safest plan would be to continue on the path she'd started.

"I'll have to think about it," she said, just to be polite.

"'Course you will. But don't take too long," Carl warned. "Donny gave me this lead two days ago and if he knows about it, you can bet other people do too."

There was something in his tone that tugged at her. If Donny went to the trouble of giving her a business lead and she never bothered to look at it, would he ever go out of his way for her again?

"I don't suppose it would hurt if I went to look at the place now." Eudora rose from her chair. "I was about to head out to lunch."

"That's a good idea. Go look. You can decide after you see it." Carl turned his attention to a stack of papers in his in-box.

"Can I bring you something back for lunch?" Eudora collected her purse from her desk drawer and slipped on her coat.

"Nah." He scoffed. "Marie'll be here later and she's

bringing me lunch." He frowned, miserably. "She's started to watch what I eat."

Eudora hid a smile. "I'll see you after lunch, then."

Carl called after her. "Remember to keep an open mind. That place ain't gonna be pretty. If it was, they'da sold it by now."

When the taxi pulled up to the curb, Eudora almost didn't get out of the car. The property wasn't at all what she'd imagined. When Mr. O'Hanlan described the building as having retail space on the first floor and living space on the second, Eudora imagined one of the sweet little shops along King Street, the front windows filled with lace or linens or silver.

But she was mistaken.

The property before her now, the building that Mr. Kilgore had suggested as an 'excellent investment,' appeared to have been condemned. The chain link fence surrounded the building and the small lot beside it was posted with warnings and No Trespassing signs. The front door had been padlocked, and every window on the first floor was covered with warped plywood. What was more, a weathered tax notice had been nailed directly into the front door.

"Should I wait?" The taxi driver leaned across the seat and peered at the building through the passenger window.

"No, thank you," Eudora said firmly, even as she double-checked the address. "This is the right place."

She paid the driver and opened the car door, but it took a few more minutes of discussion to convince him to drive away. It annoyed her a little, how overprotective he seemed. The walk home back was manageable and it occurred to

Eudora that if she were a man, the driver would have left her at the curb without a second thought.

Remembering her promise to keep an open mind, Eudora crossed the few feet of blue slate sidewalk separating the curb from the shop's front door. The padlock on the front door held firm when Eudora tugged it, and at first glance there appeared to be no way in. Then she noticed a gap in the plywood that covered the picture window. Intrigued, Eudora moved in for a closer look, carefully stepping around the shards of broken glass and lumps of crumbling stucco that littered the property line.

As she glanced inside, her spirits lifted.

Inside, there were possibilities.

The transom window above the front door let in enough light that Eudora could see into the large front room, and she felt her imagination begin to stir. The floor was hardwood and grimy, but the size and shape of the planks suggested they might be heart pine. A bucket of oil soap and a good scrubbing would bring them back to life. The windows were wide, and Eudora imagined the light they would let in. On the far wall there was an outline of what appeared to be a fireplace. She stepped back from the building and followed the roofline to a stubby chimney near the front. So it was a fireplace after all.

Eudora smiled.

From the outside, the second floor appeared to be in better shape than the first. The windows on the second floor were narrow, maybe six feet tall and three feet wide and outlined with brick. Although a few of them had been broken, none were boarded up and only a few patches of stucco were missing from the façade, which was encouraging. The most exciting discovery was the earthquake rods threading the length of the building, four of them, just below the roofline. Eudora squinted at the plates anchoring the rods, but couldn't see a stamped date. Even so, she felt a shiver of excitement as she considered how old the building might be. This could be a forgotten piece of Charleston history.

Returning her attention to the front room, Eudora imagined the shop with a silver bell over the door, chiming whenever a customer entered. And she saw the fireplace lit, smoke rising from the chimney and drawing people in from the cold. She closed her eyes and saw a restaurant, with delicate lace curtains in the windows and flowers on every table. Or maybe something better than a restaurant – a tearoom, with sturdy mugs and chunky knit tea cozies to keep the pot warm. Eudora did love her tea.

Her heart thumping, Eudora left the front window and walked to the side of the property. There, she saw a scrap of yard that had been shaded by a latticed trellis planted with wisteria. But the vine had been allowed to grow unchecked, and the weight of the vine pulled the structure loose, leaving it a splintered heap on the ground. A wisteria that old could be saved, of course, and the trellis easily rebuilt to make room for a patio shaded from summer sun.

She ignored the weeds that choked the flower beds, the garbage in the yard, and the kudzu vines that stretched across the lot and up the side of the building. All of that was cosmetic, an easy afternoon of garden gloves and determination.

Stepping back, Eudora surveyed the entire property in front of her, the sweet little building, the sheltered patio for summer, the convenient parking. She felt the pulse of adrenaline as she allowed herself to imagine what it would be like to hold a piece of Charleston in her hand. And what it would feel like to breathe life back into it.

Her father had built a thriving business from less than this. Mr. O'Hanlan had bought an entire lumberyard without even looking at it. Both of those men took a gamble and it paid off.

Maybe this was her gamble. A chance for something big.

Mr. Kilgore believed she could do it, or he wouldn't have given her the address. Mr. O'Hanlan said it was a good opportunity. One she should not let slip away.

Eudora looked again at the price scribbled next to the address. For the past six months, she'd been putting aside a chunk of her paycheck for spring tuition. She'd registered for one class instead of five, so there was still plenty of money left in her tuition envelope.

Maybe this was meant to be.

She jotted down the address of the tax office, then started walking toward it.

Thirty-two

"You what?" Carl scrubbed his head with his fingers. "You didn't get a survey first? An appraisal? Nothing?"

"You said the property was a good investment," Eudora countered, sinking into her chair.

Far from being delighted with her initiative, Carl had been pacing the floor of his office for the last twenty minutes, peppering her with questions about the property she'd just bought.

"I told you to go *look* at the property, not buy it." Carl

circled around his desk and dropped to his chair. "And you didn't even go inside?"

Eudora shook her head. "It was fenced and padlocked."

Carl just sighed.

Then he picked up the phone and dialed a number. "Donny Kilgore, please." He closed his eyes and rested his forehead on his fist. "Donny? This is Carl over at O'Hanlan's. You got a minute?"

Thirty-three

Once the city accepted her bid on the Walker property and signed over the title, there was no turning back. A walk-through revealed even more historic treasures, like crown glass in the interior transom windows and the original hinged shutters wrapped in sheets and stored in the cellar. Back in February before any of the work began, Donny Kilgore suggested that it might be easier to raze the building and start over, but Eudora would not hear of it. She'd already imagined a tearoom in the front room, with a crackling fire in the hearth and a scattering of warm wooden tables and comfortable chairs.

Although work for Eudora was going well, her marriage had been deteriorating for some time. The atmosphere in the Rutledge home crackled with tension whenever Brock was there. Eudora responded by spending more time at the millworks. When construction began, Carl had suggested Eudora use the millworks office as her base, explaining that he'd be there to answer her questions whenever she needed him.

But the truth was that neither of them trusted Brock.

He and Tommy J had yet to find a profitable business idea,

and when Brock's frustration turned to anger, he took it out on her. He noticed her extended work hours and demanded to know how she spent her days. Evading and deflecting his questions had become exhausting and when he didn't get the answers he wanted, he turned mean.

This morning, however, Eudora had been given an unexpected respite. Brock had decided to escort Lenore to Monday morning brunch at the yacht club. No one had thought to include Eudora, but that was fine with her. She had work to do. Eudora had the luxury of spreading her books and ledgers across the table because, except for Letty, Eudora had the house to herself. On one side of her was a stack of construction bills, on the other a ledger from the account Carl O'Hanlan had opened for her. She'd funneled money into it from the accounting work she'd done for Donny Kilgore and one or two others, and she'd used the money to pay for materials. Although the balance seemed substantial, there were several large invoices coming due at the end of the project.

Over at the stove, the skillet popped as Letty added a knob of bacon grease to the cast iron pan. "You want one egg or two?" she asked.

Convincing Letty to work in the Rutledge household was the best thing Eudora had ever done. Letty was the closest thing to a friend Eudora had in the Rutledge house, and Eudora was grateful that Letty had decided to stay, even if the arrangement was still temporary.

"I'm not very hungry," Eudora answered without thinking. Her attention was focused on the stack of paperwork she was expected to file at the tax office in the morning and she wanted to make sure there were no mistakes.

"Two eggs, then." Letty nodded as she cracked a shell on the side. "Gots t' keep your strength up, all this running around you doing. Sausage or bacon? I got both ready, right here."

When Eudora failed to answer quickly enough, Letty decided for her.

When it was ready, Letty crossed the room and set a warm breakfast plate on the table, filled with cheesy eggs, a sausage biscuit, and fried tomatoes. It smelled delicious and Eudora felt her stomach rumble.

"You gonna figure it all out, you know." Letty gestured to the stack of papers as she pulled out a chair for herself. "You always do."

"I hope you're right, Letty."

Letty gestured to the stacks of money stuffed in envelopes scattered on the table. "This look like a bootlegger's haul."

"Final payments for the restoration." Eudora speared a bit of sausage. "That envelope goes to the tax office. That one goes to the millworks for materials. The rest goes to Donny Kilgore's contractors; they're doing the finishing work this next week."

Letty sipped her coffee then set it down. She eyed the envelopes on the table. "Dangerous to have that much cash in this house."

"You're right, I know." Eudora put down her fork and pushed her plate away, her appetite gone. Sometimes the anxiety of hiding things from Brock and his mother was too much to bear. "The tax office won't take cash, anyway. I need to write them a check and the check needs to be in my name. I don't have a business account, and I can't put that much money through the Rutledge house account." She hesitated. "Lenore might not notice, but Brock absolutely will and I don't know how to answer the questions it will bring up."

"You thought about asking Mr. O'Hanlan?"

"I really want to do this part myself, Letty. If I ever want a business of my own, I need a checking account to pay for things." Eudora leaned back in her chair. There had to be a solution. She just wasn't seeing it yet. Then a thought occurred to her and she glanced at Letty. "Did you ever need to write a check when you sold your food at the depot?"

Letty peered over the rim of her cup. "Can't image me, or any other women from the depot, asking to open an account at one of your banks." Her expression hardened. "We have our own bank," she said, finally.

They sat in silence for a moment, then Eudora noticed the light outside had changed. Lenore and Brock would be back soon. She gathered up the envelopes and slipped then into her bag. Then folded the tax papers and the work invoices and added them to the cash.

Letty looked up, surprised. "You got an idea?"

"No," Eudora said. "But I've come this far without one and the tax office won't wait." She rose and gathered her things. "Thank you for breakfast, Letty. I'm sorry I didn't eat much of it."

To Eudora's surprise, Letty smiled. "You will. You're gonna figure out the answers to your problem and when you get back, that building will be yours. I'll fix you a special dinner to celebrate."

Eudora snorted. "Lenore will think the dinner is for her."

Lenore had been invited to join a fundraising committee to benefit the newly built hospital on the edge of town. It seemed the Rutledge reputation was improving. Then again, maybe the invitation had come because Eudora had just recently paid the house account at the silversmith shop owned by the chair of the hospital committee.

Letty rose from the table. "Let her think what she wants while you go about your business."

~

The heavy wooden door at the Charleston Commerce Bank opened with a soft whoosh.

The idea to open an account at CCB came to her as she walked up Meeting Street. Her father had done business with that bank for years. Thomas Rawlings, an executive director and member of the bank's board of directors, had overseen the Palmetto Exports account for decades. He could be counted on for his discretion and his loyalty to the Gadsden family. What was more, he was familiar with the work Eudora had done for her father, and he would understand that she needed a checking account for her own business.

It was a perfect solution.

Eudora stepped into the dark-paneled lobby, the heels of her leather pumps clacking on the marble floor as she made her way to the reception desk. She'd accompanied her father to this bank several times, and it was reassuring to see that nothing had changed. The same crystal chandelier graced the entrance. The same oil paintings of horses and fox hunts stretched across the far wall. In fact, the only change appeared to be an updated framed photograph of a newly elected President Eisenhower displayed beside the bank's own president.

"Good morning," Eudora smiled at the receptionist. "Would you please let Thomas Rawlings know that Eudora Rutledge would like to see him?"

"Of course." The girl behind the desk didn't seem much older than Eudora. She lifted the telephone receiver and glanced at Eudora before dialing a number. "What time was your appointment?"

"Oh, I don't have one." It didn't occur to Eudora to make one. She'd never needed one before.

The girl's smile slipped.

"I'm sure he'll see me," Eudora assured her. What banker would refuse a new account? "Tell him Eudora Gadsden is here to see him. I was recently married, and he might not recognize my new last name."

The girl looked doubtful but dialed the number anyway. After a hushed conversation that Eudora could not hear, the receptionist glanced at Eudora, her smile tight. "Mrs. Baldwin would like to know if this is regarding Palmetto Exports."

Mrs. Baldwin was Thomas Rawlings' personal secretary and had been a guest at Eudora's wedding. Eudora knew for a fact that her office was less than ten feet away from the lobby. Why wouldn't she come to speak with her?

"Palmetto Exports is the name of my father's business." Eudora tamped down an uneasy feeling that coming here had been a mistake. She cleared her throat and drew herself up. "I'm here on business of my own, not connected with my father's."

The receptionist swiveled her chair away from Eudora and cupped her hand over her mouth as she whispered into the phone. The exchange was brief, and when it was finished, the girl replaced the receiver on the cradle.

"Mr. Rawlings will be out shortly," she said, her demeanor changed. She gestured to a cluster of chairs near a wilted plant. "Please have a seat over there."

Fifteen minutes later, Mr. Rawlings entered the lobby and Eudora rose to meet him. Short and portly, clean shaven with black-rimmed glasses and a wisp of dark hair combed across his bald head, he'd been her father's banking manager since before Eudora was born.

"Eudora! Look at you, all grown up now. I haven't seen you since the wedding. How was your honeymoon, my dear?" He clasped both of her hands in his.

"Wonderful, Mr. Rawlings." By now, the lie slipped easily from her lips. "Thank you for asking."

"So what brings you to our little bank this morning?" he asked, his tone jovial, his expression expectant. "Business must be brisk if your father has you doing errands for him? How nice of your husband to allow you to continue to work for your father."

Eudora bristled. "As I said to Mrs. Baldwin, I'm here on business of my own. It not connected to Palmetto Exports. In fact, my father doesn't know I'm here."

"Oh?" His brows furrowed.

"Yes," Eudora continued, surprised to be discussing business in the lobby. In the past, she and her father were whisked directly to Mr. Rawlings's office where Mrs. Baldwin would have a coffee service waiting.

"You're not here on behalf of your father's business?" he repeated, blinking behind his glasses.

"No, I'm not."

"Nothing to do with your family?"

"Nothing."

"I see." His smile froze as he adjusted his eyeglasses. "I'm afraid you've caught me at a bad time. I was actually on my way to another meeting. I'll be sure to ask one of our senior associates to take care of you." Without waiting for a reply, he leaned in to kiss her cheek as he did when she was a child. "It was good to see you, my dear. Please give your father my best."

Clearly, she'd been dismissed. Stunned, Eudora returned to her chair in the lobby and waited. Some time later a man appeared from the bank of offices to the left of the lobby. The executive offices, and all the men she and her father had ever done business with, were behind the oak door to the *right*.

"Mrs. Rutledge?" The man approached Eudora's chair and offered a benign smile. His brown hair was sharply parted and combed to one side, with a crisp white Oxford, dark navy suit, monogrammed cuffs, and a tan line visible just under his collar. "I understand you'd like to open an account?"

"That's right," Eudora replied. "Business checking."

"Let's step into a conference room, shall we?" He placed his hand lightly on her back and steered her through the lobby. He pulled the chair out for her and waited until she was seated before claiming a chair across the table from her.

As Eudora set her purse on the table, she glanced at the wall clock near the door. She still had to go to the tax office today. She'd hoped that opening an account would be a brief errand.

The man templed his fingers in front of him, an oily smile spreading across his face as his college fraternity ring glinted in the light. "This is a commerce bank, the oldest and most respected in Charleston. Our customers are some of the finest business owners in the state."

"I know what type of bank this is, Mr—" She arched an eyebrow and waited.

"Sheely. Skip Sheely."

"Mr. Sheely." Eudora's temper flared and she cut him off. "I *know* what kind of bank this is. My family has been doing business with this institution for decades. I'm here today because I've started a business of my own and I need a business account."

Skip leaned back in his chair, his expression no longer accommodating. "Then you should know Charleston Commerce Bank deals with amounts much larger than anything a home business might generate. I'm surprised your father didn't tell you that."

"I'm not operating a home business," Eudora said, feeling her cheeks flush, annoyed that he might mistake her anger for embarrassment. She paused to take a breath and steady her nerves. However condescending this man might be, this bank was the solution to her problem and she didn't want to lose it. She began again. "I am prepared to open the account with a sizable deposit—"

Eudora went to unclasp her purse, but Skip interrupted, his voice sharp. "Let me save you some time, Mrs. Rutledge. I'm afraid we're not going to be able to help you."

"I can't imagine why not." She held his gaze. "I have a cash deposit to open the account."

"I had hoped not to be this blunt with you, Mrs. Rutledge." He crossed his arms in front of his chest. "As the oldest commerce bank in the state, we must have the highest standards. We're very particular about whom we choose to service, and I'm afraid you don't meet those standards." He rose, the meeting clearly over. "Your father should have explained this to you."

Without another word of explanation, Eudora was guided back to the lobby. This couldn't be happening. She had cash in her purse, and her family had been customers of this bank for decades. Mr. Rawlings and his wife were frequent guests in the Gadsden home. They'd hosted Eudora's family at his summer house on James Island for many years.

Why was she being turned away?

"Eudora?"

Several feet away, near the oak door of the executive offices, stood Uncle Alistair. He was in the center of a group of bank executives whom Eudora vaguely recognized. She returned his greeting, offering a wave of her hand but unable to summon the energy for anything more.

His brow furrowed, then he turned to the executives and said something Eudora could not hear. Nodding in response, they shook his hand and retreated through the oak door to their offices. As Uncle Alistair crossed the lobby toward her, Eudora's heart sank. He would want to know what brought her to this bank, and what reason could she possibly give?

"You look like a woman who could use a slice of pie," he said unexpectedly. "I know just the place."

She shook her head. "I'm sorry, Uncle Alistair, I'm just not up for it. Another time, perhaps."

He sat in the chair next to her and appeared to be choosing his words carefully. "Things aren't as dire as they appear. They never are. I would be happy to help sort them out."

Eudora looked at him, wondering how much he knew and what he would say to Brock and Lenore. He'd promised business advice before, but Eudora hadn't needed it.

Until now.

She nodded and he offered his arm. Eudora rose from her chair and together they left the bank.

The diner was a short walk away, another restaurant Eudora had never been to. On the way, Uncle Alistair carried the conversation by himself, chatting about the weather and the upcoming Master's Golf Tournament. He seemed to be allowing her a chance to collect her thoughts, and Eudora was grateful for his chivalry.

He held the door open for her and she walked inside.

"Mr. Rutledge, welcome. I haven't seen you in here lately. How ya doing?" The waitress' nametag said "Betty." A tuft of brown hair was pinned under a paper cap, and her smile was wide and genuine.

"Can't complain," Uncle Alistair answered as she led them to a table near the counter. "How is your family?"

She scoffed. "Husband invited me to go fishing with him and his buddies this past weekend." She slowly shook her head. "Should'a known something was up, 'fore he asked."

"Why's that?" Uncle Alistair asked as they settled into their chairs.

"I's the only wife there. I did the cooking." She shrugged, good-naturedly. "I got a trip to the beach out of it, 'fore I cooked anything. Made him promise a trip up to Myrtle Beach before the summer's out."

Uncle Alistair laughed. "Good for you."

"Can I bring you the usual, Mr. R?"

"Yes, please. And the same for my niece, too."

After Betty left, Uncle Alistair unrolled his utensils from the bundle in front of him and smoothed the paper napkin across his on his lap. "I hope you don't mind me ordering for you, but this pie reminds me of the ones my grandmother made."

Eudora followed suit, unrolling her fork and setting it on the edge of her placemat. "You know every diner on the peninsula, don't you?"

He laughed again. "Only the good ones."

The food came almost immediately, two slabs of pecan pie

with a mountain of whipped cream on the side. And two thick mugs of hot coffee.

"I'm under strict instructions from my physician to eliminate sweets, but I'm afraid pecan pie is something I can't give up." Uncle Alistair sipped his drink and grimaced. He set the mug back on the table and added a generous pour of cream to his coffee before pushing the container toward Eudora. "The coffee is very strong here. I suggest quite a lot of cream."

They sat in silence for a while and ate their pie. Eudora suspected he was giving her time to gather her thoughts. On impulse, she decided to trust him.

"Uncle Alistair, about the bank," she began, and the story unraveled slowly. By the time Betty came to clear their plates and refill their mugs, Eudora had told him everything. When she got to the part about using her salary from the millworks to pay off delinquent charge accounts, Uncle Alistair grimaced but said nothing. He didn't know she'd been working to pay off the debt.

When she'd finished, Uncle Alistair shook his head in disgust. "Lenore opens accounts without telling me sometimes, Eudora. I don't always catch them all, and I'm sorry you were put in that position. But what were you doing at Charleston Commerce? I can't imagine they'd concern themselves with house accounts."

"I was at the bank this morning, hoping to open an account for my business. I have the cash in hand for a deposit and even had a name for my company – Palmetto Holdings." Eudora sighed. "I've been using the millworks account for most of the restoration, but it's come to the point where I need checks in my own name to finish this job." She reached for her empty mug and felt the weight of it in her palm. "I'm so close."

Uncle Alistair signaled for the check. "I'd like to share something with you, if I may?"

Eudora nodded.

Betty dropped the check on the table. "Always nice to see you, Mr. R. Take care."

"The pie was delicious, Betty, thank you," he replied.

Then he returned his attention to Eudora, his gaze focused on hers. "I was born in Charleston and have lived here all my life. I love it here, but I don't imagine this city is perfect. It has flaws, like anywhere else, and one of them is that many of its citizens are not eager to embrace change, particularly those in power." He unfolded his wallet and laid a few bills on top of the check. "You should understand that bank was never going to open an account for you, no matter how much money you offered. You're a woman, my dear. And you cannot begin to compete with the boys who run things over there."

So that was the end of it. Eudora felt her shoulders sag as she slumped against the back of her chair.

"Now, don't give up," he admonished. "If you're set on that bank, you still have options. I'm happy to open an account for you in my name, with you as a signatory. You can use the account freely to conduct your business however you like. I can offer advice, or not, your choice."

It was the same offer Carl gave her, and Eudora refused, politely. "I really want to do this by myself. It's my business, and I want my name to be on the letterhead. And on the checks. And on the business license."

"Knowing exactly what you want is a very admirable trait for a business owner, Eudora." Uncle Alistair reached into his breast pocket for a small spiral notepad and scribbled something on a slip of paper. "But sometimes we all need a bit of help to get there. If you insist on having your name on the checks, you'll need a different bank. Go to that address and talk to Morley Babbich, and only to him. Tell him you're my niece." He corrected himself. "Better yet – I'll call him to tell him you're coming."

He raised his hand to signal to Betty.

"A slice to go, Mr. R?"

"Not this time, but thank you." Uncle Alistair smiled. "I would like to borrow your telephone, if I might?"

"Sure thing. You know where it is," she said as she lifted the check from the table and scooped the bills into her palm. "Nice tip. Thanks, Mr. R."

"You are very welcome, my dear."

As he rose to leave, he turned to Eudora. "One more thing: I don't know who you spoke to at the commerce bank, but you should know that many of the junior executives who work there were cadets at The Citadel. Chances are very good that Brock will know about your visit by the end of the day, if he doesn't already."

Eudora drew a sharp breath, but Uncle Alistair held up his hand. "A good offense is the best defense, or so they say. I suggest you have a plausible story ready, because you'll need it. You can say that you were doing an errand for me, for the family, and I'll confirm it."

"Thank you, Uncle Alistair."

He shook his head. "No need." He pointed to the paper he'd given her. "Bring all your paperwork to that address. After that, you should have everything you need for the tax office and just enough time to get there. Mr. Babbich will be expecting you."

Thirty-four

As Eudora unlocked the door and stepped into the house, she felt the weight of the day slip from her shoulders. In the kitchen, Letty was at the stove tossing bay leaves into a stock pot. The rich scent of a shrimp stock threaded the air. Over the past several months, it had become obvious that the kitchen would be exclusively Letty's domain – if she decided to stay – and that was fine with Eudora. Letty reminded her a little of Annie in the way that she took over, making a big house feel more homey.

Eudora breathed in Letty's cooking as she slipped off her coat and dropped her work on the table. "That smells like perloo, Letty."

"Close to it." Letty poked the stock with a wooden spoon. "Been so long since you stayed home long enough to eats a decent meal, I knew I'd have to make you something you'd want to stay home for." She smiled before turning her attention back her skillet. "And 'fore you ask: yes, I'm using garden tomatoes. Annie lent me a quart of the ones she put up last summer."

"Well, it smells delicious." Eudora moved to the kitchen table, pulled out a chair and fell into it. She allowed herself just a moment to catch her breath, then reached for the work in her bag.

"What time Miss Maggie comin' tomorrow?"

"Said she'd be here before lunch." Eudora glanced up from the ledgers she'd spread across the table. "Would you mind making us some grilled cheese sandwiches for lunch? She said yours are the best."

"I surely will," Letty replied. "Be nice to see her again."

Eudora and Maggie had kept in touch since Maggie moved to New York City earlier that fall. But letters and phone calls were not the same as seeing her friend in person, and Eudora was excited for the visit. Excited, too, for the surprise party the O'Hanlans had planned for the next evening to celebrate the incorporation of her business. She wasn't supposed to know about it, but she did, and she was touched by their thoughtfulness.

As Letty bustled about the kitchen, Eudora turned her attention back to the property's accounts. Construction had taken longer than she'd planned, and had claimed all of her savings and most of her sanity. But the project gave back, too. Eudora felt as if she had found a piece of history, polished it, and returned it to the city she loved. And that made her very happy.

"You 'bout done fixing up that building?" Letty flicked off the burner and pulled the bacon from the pan.

"Almost."

"How much work you got for tonight?"

"Couple of hours, not much," Eudora replied. "Uncle Alistair finished the rental agreement for the new tenant, and I need to look it over one more time before I present it to the tea store people tomorrow."

Eudora was proud of herself for having found the tenant and pitching them the idea of expanding their business to Charleston. It turned out that they had been considering the idea but had yet to find a suitable location. They were intrigued when Eudora told them about her building, and when she offered to let them choose the fixtures and finishes, they agreed to sign a ten-year lease. In the end, they would have the shop they wanted and Eudora would have a happy long-term tenant. It worked out for everyone – or *would* work out for everyone, as soon as they signed the contracts.

"Hmmm." Letty's reply was non-committal.

Eudora looked up, surprised at Letty's reaction. "What is it?"

"How long you fixin to keep this empire of yours a secret?" Letty pulled two green peppers from the icebox and laid them on the counter. "You know that Mr. Brock getting suspicious already, askin questions I don't want to answer."

"Questions? Like what?"

"Like where you go all day. Who you meet with and what you do. I don't like his tone when he ask, neither," Letty huffed. "Sounds like he know something."

Because Brock still hadn't found a job he liked or a business to buy, Uncle Alistair insisted that Eudora incorporate her company as soon as the tenants were signed. He said her name would be hidden in the paperwork and only the bankers would know the building belonged to her. Everyone else would think the property was Uncle Alistair's and that Eudora was doing him a favor by checking on its progress. Eudora would have preferred that everyone know she started Palmetto Holdings, but she let herself be convinced, if only to protect what she'd created.

"Well, it doesn't matter now," Eudora replied. "Both he and Tommy J are in Savannah and won't be back for another week."

"That's something else you don't seem to know." Letty frowned as she reached for a cutting board. "If that man finds out about what you did to get him there, he won't forgive you."

Eudora's breath caught. "How did you know about that?"

"I know just about everything goes on in this house, and I'm tellin you: do not underestimate that man."

It was a great idea; even Maggie thought so when Eudora explained it to her.

As subcontractors and workmen finished their projects, Eudora needed the freedom to leave the house whenever she was called to inspect the jobsite. For a while, Eudora worked around Brock's schedule, hiding bank records and ledgers under the clothes in her closet and reconciling the accounts at night while he was out. There had been several close calls, too. One night Brock came home unexpectedly to find Eudora working on her ledgers. At first, he didn't seem to notice or care, and her invented explanation of becoming treasurer for the library committee seemed to satisfy him, but she knew she wouldn't be able to fool him for long.

Then a family friend extended an invitation to Lenore to spend a month at their home on Sullivan's Island, and it seemed like the opportunity Eudora was looking for. She had hoped Brock would go with his mother. Without a job or the prospect of a job, there was really nothing to keep him in Charleston. Certainly their marriage wasn't a reason to stay. She and Brock could go days without seeing each other, and Eudora found that she preferred it that way. Brock stayed out late, slept late, and Eudora suspected that his friendship with her friend Posey might have become something more.

They'd been married less than a year and had already lost all interest in each other.

Eventually, Eudora brought the problem to Carl. He said he'd take care of it. Three days later, a letter arrived from a plumbing contractor in Savannah, inviting Brock and Tommy J to discuss a business opportunity. No investment required. Guaranteed profits. Brock left the next day, and Carl's friend promised to keep them busy for a week.

That left plenty of time to sign the new tenant and incorporate her business. Brock would never know that the property, or the newly formed Palmetto Holdings, was hers.

"What's done is done, Letty. Let's not think about it anymore." Eudora set her pencil down and stretched the tension from her shoulders. "I'd rather tell you about the building, anyway."

"Okay, then. Tell me." As the shrimp stock simmered, Letty reached for a bowl and set it in the sink to catch the onion peels.

"Like I said, we found a tenant. That is—" She glanced at Letty, working at the sink. "if you sure you don't want the shop space for yourself? I did promise you first refusal, and that space would make a nice diner."

Letty shook her head as she chopped the peppers and celery. "I'm fine right here, for a time."

"You said you'd tell me. If you decide you want to leave."

"I ain't forgotten."

"You think you might want to move in? We have more than enough space, and you can have any room you like."

"I'll let you know." Letty turned the knife in her hand and frowned at the blade. "All this sneaking around makes me nervous," she said finally. "How much longer 'til you're done?"

Eudora drew a deep breath and let it out slowly. "Everything happens on Friday."

"Tell me again how that man can't swoop in at the last minute and take everything you worked so hard to get."

"Because Palmetto Holdings will be incorporated and my name will be hidden," Eudora replied. "Uncle Alistair is drawing up papers for that, too."

Letty scoffed.

"We're in the home stretch, Letty," Eudora assured her. "This is all good news."

"I'll feel better when your name is hid."

"I will, too."

~

After a while, the rich scent of sizzling onions, celery, and green peppers filled the room, distracting Eudora from her work. She looked up from the ledgers and projections spread across the table just in time to see Letty add a handful of ham to the skillet and adjusted the flame on the burner.

"Annie adds bacon to hers," Eudora offered.

But Letty scoffed. "And I felt like adding ham. You might like it if you keep an open mind." Letty chopped a pile of greens and dropped them into a cast iron skillet. "This knife is duller than I'd like. It needs to be looked at."

"Didn't the knife man come this week?" Eudora asked, her attention on the landscaper's final invoice. He'd under-charged again, and this time he included a scrawled, hand-written explanation at the bottom of his bill that she couldn't quite decipher.

"Ow!" The knife clattered to the floor as Letty yelped. She stepped back and wrapped her hand around her fingers. Blood seeped from between her fingers and dripped down her wrist.

Eudora was up in a flash, crossing the kitchen to Letty's side. She grabbed a towel from the countertop and wound it tightly around Letty's hands.

"Don't let go," she said. "Press your fingers against the cut, hard as you can."

Eudora opened the back door and shouted across the garden to the carriage house, hoping the gardener was still there. "James, we need help! Bring the car around – hurry!"

Eudora steadied Letty against the counter and turned off

the oven and the burners on the stove. "You're going to be fine."

James swept Letty into his arms and carried her to the car.

"Take us to Dr. Bunting's office – right away," Eudora said.

James put the car in gear, then hesitated. He glanced through the rearview mirror at Eudora. He said nothing, but his meaning was clear: He and Letty had their own doctors and would not be welcome in Dr. Bunting's office.

"Your doctor is too far away, and Letty's bleeding. I will make sure that Dr. Bunting helps us." Eudora's tone was steady and confident, but she wasn't at all sure Letty would be treated by the Rutledge family's physician.

Fortunately for all of them, the doctor happened to be working late. And because his waiting room was empty of regular patients, he allowed Letty inside. After cleaning the wound, he said it wasn't as bad as it looked, and he went to work dressing the cut with butterfly stitches and a gauze wrapping.

They drove Letty home and two hours after they left, returned home themselves.

James pulled the car into the courtyard and opened Eudora's door. "You need me to go inside and turn the rest of the lights on?"

Eudora glanced up at the house. There was a single light burning in the kitchen, which struck her as odd. She thought she'd turned off all the lights, but she must be mistaken.

Finally, she shook her head. "You go on to bed, James. And thank you. I can manage from here."

"Yes, ma'am."

Eudora walked to the front door, sagging against the frame as she dug for her key. She still had a mountain of work left to do, ledgers and statements she'd left spread across the table. But first, a shower and a change of clothes. And maybe a cup of tea.

Eudora's mind was on her work as she made her way down the hall toward the kitchen, the paperwork she had to file, the tenant lease to review.

Pushing against the door, she stepped into the room.

Then she froze.

"Quite a little empire you've got here." Brock sat at the kitchen table, her books, receipts, and building notes spread out before him. His lips stretched across his teeth as he hooked his foot around the leg of the chair next to him and shoved it across the floor toward Eudora. "Come. Sit. I want to hear all about it."

Eudora's heart pounded in her chest, though she was careful not to show it. She set her purse on the counter and slipped off her jacket, moving slowly to gather her thoughts. "There's nothing to tell. I have a bit a free time, and I've been doing a favor for Uncle Alistair, that's all."

"That's not what this looks like." Brock jabbed his finger against a page of the ledger. "These expenses are from construction. When did dear old Uncle Alistair buy a building on King Street? And what is Palmetto Holdings?"

"I really don't know. That's his business, not mine." She shrugged as she reached to remove the papers.

Brock slapped her hand away.

Eudora resisted the urge to rub away the sting.

His voice dropped to a growl, a warning that took her breath away. "These papers are for incorporating a business, and your name is on them."

His eyes smoldered as he waited for an explanation.

"I don't know anything about it; I told you that." Eudora met his gaze. "Ask Uncle Alistair if you don't believe me."

She reached for the ledgers, but he swept them off the table. The books fell to the floor with a clatter and the papers drifted across the room like fall leaves.

"I bust my butt every day looking for a way to support this family, and it seems that *my wife* has already hit the jackpot." A vein in his neck budged as he roared. "*How* does that happen, Eudora? I'd like to know."

"I've already explained and I'm not telling you again," she began.

His eyes narrowed and he raised his hand, slapping her across the mouth.

Eudora felt her head snap as stars exploded in front of her eyes.

"Don't you *dare* lie to me." Brock pounded his fist on the table. "What do you think people will say when they find out that my *wife* is the breadwinner?" His voice dropped to a whisper. "You have one more chance to tell me what this is – just one."

Eudora swallowed and tasted blood. Her lips trembled as she pressed them together. It had taken everything she had to get to this point, and she wasn't about to give it all away. Not to him.

"Everything okay in here?" James poked his head in the kitchen, his eyes widened at the scene he had just witnessed. "Sorry, ma'am, I heard a noise and I thought you might could need some help."

Eudora straightened her back, then turned toward the back door where James stood. "I'm fine, thank you. It's nothing."

Brock glared at James, and then at Eudora. "This isn't over, Eudora."

Despite the weight he'd gained in the past year from late-night drinking, his body was still solid. It connected with her and she fell, sprawling onto the floor in a heap.

James reached for her, but Brock pushed past him, too.

He pounded down the back stairs. The car engine revved and sprayed gravel across the courtyard as Brock drove away.

Eudora felt herself begin to tremble, then shake. The floor underneath her was cold. She had a vague idea that she should get up, but she didn't remember how. Couldn't get her legs to work.

James pulled her to her feet. "I'd like you to come home with me, Miss Eudora. You'd be doing me such a favor."

"A favor?" Eudora repeated.

"Yes, ma'am. My Ginny's been asking after you. I bring you home, she'll fix you a cup of tea and give you a soft place to sit."

Eudora felt a sob take shape deep in her chest, so she cleared her throat to push it away. "Thank you, James. A nice visit with Ginny is just what I need."

James' house was on the edge of town, beyond the train depot, near Newmarket Creek and the marshes. It was a tiny clapboard house with a kitchen in the back, a sitting room, and a bedroom shared by five children. James' wife, Ginny, had greeted them at the door, her eyes widening at the sight of Eudora's face. She ushered the children to bed before returning with a warm blanket, a damp towel and a few precious ice cubes. She'd offered the bundle to Eudora with her gaze averted. The gesture was kindly meant, but Eudora had never felt more humiliated.

They wanted to give Eudora their own bed. James offered to sleep in the car, so there wouldn't be talk. Ginny said she'd make up a pallet on the floor of the children's room. But the offer made Eudora uneasy. The house was small and she knew her staying would put at least one of them out of their beds. She tried to refuse but both Ginny and James had insisted. In the end, she accepted, grateful for their hospitality.

Much later that night, while the rest of the house slept, Eudora sat at the kitchen table, trying to make sense of what happened. Trying to understand how her life had veered so far off course. Eudora Grace Gadsden – cosseted only child of Caroline and Edward, celebrated debutante with a bright and hopeful future. The only female student in the business program at Charleston College.

How could a life filled with such promise crumble so completely?

As the night wore on, Eudora's head throbbed and her bruises ached, but the real pain went deeper than that, all the way to her core. She'd proven herself. Despite all the obstacles, she'd created something she was proud of. And all of it was about to be taken away.

She wasn't going to let that happen. But she didn't know how to stop him.

Early the next morning, as the birds were waking, the house began to stir. Murmurs from the bedroom, little feet hitting the floor. When James emerged, Eudora asked him to drive her home.

There was no time to waste.

In the blue light of morning, James pulled up to the curb in front of the Rutledge home. He snapped off the headlights. If James was worried about alerting Brock to their presence, he needn't have bothered. Brock's car was missing from the courtyard and the house was dark.

"I'll wait right here," he said, turning off the ignition. No amount of persuading would convince him to change his mind. "No, ma'am. I will not leave. Not til I know."

Eudora promised to be quick. She planned to gather a few clothes and go to Maggie's house. The O'Hanlan's would take her in until she decided what to do, even if her own parents wouldn't.

Eudora unlocked the front door and pushed it open. Kicking off her shoes, she padded down the hallway toward the front staircase.

"Eudora? Is that you?" Lenore called from the dining room.

Eudora retraced her steps and entered the dining room. Lenore was seated at the table, a pot of tea in from of her. A cigarette burned in an ashtray littered with stubs. It looked as though Lenore had been seated for quite some time. If she were expecting breakfast, she'd be disappointed.

"I'm afraid Letty won't be in today. We're on our own for breakfast."

"Thank you just the same, but I didn't come to eat."

"Why did you come?"

"Letty called me."

"Letty?" Eudora repeated. "Why?"

Lenore studied Eudora's face, then lowered her gaze to Eudora's arm. Finally, she lifted her chin. "Did my son do that?"

"Yes."

"Brock is weak, and weak men make the worst bullies," Lenore said as she leaned against the back of her chair. "But I thought you knew that."

Eudora felt a surge of anger at her mother-in-law's blithe attitude. "How would I know that? And why would I marry him if I'd known?"

"Because stupid men are easily manipulated. I thought that's what you wanted, but I seem to have been mistaken," Lenore answered easily. She rested her hands on the table, lacing her fingers together. She had quite a collection of diamond rings on her fingers, and they sparkled in the early morning light. She tapped her wedding set, still on the third finger of her left hand. "I picked the engagement diamond out myself, did you know? I told Brock's father I wouldn't marry him without a ring all my friends would be envious of, and I insisted on something new. A demand unheard of from someone like me, someone without breeding or background."

Her gaze shifted to Eudora, her eyes sharp. "If you haven't heard how I came to be part of the great Rutledge dynasty, you haven't been paying attention."

"Uncle Alistair—"

"Yes, Alistair." Lenore inclined her head as she reached for her tea. "Alistair. The man I would have preferred to marry."

Eudora blinked. She must have misheard.

"But that's a story for another time, I think." Lenore twisted the wedding ring on her finger. "I owe you an apology, Eudora. I seem to have misjudged you, and that doesn't happen often. People don't usually fool me."

Eudora didn't have the time or the patience to untangle the riddles her mother-in-law laid before her. She moved to leave the room and was too exhausted to excuse herself.

"You have quite a fight before you, Eudora," Lenore

added, stopping Eudora in her tracks. "My son won't surrender easily."

Eudora froze. "How did you—"

"Know that something other than a service committee had claimed your attention?" Lenore scoffed. "Please. It wasn't difficult. And if that son of mine cared about anything other than himself, he would have noticed as well."

"Well, he did notice," Eudora retorted, her anger rising to the surface once more. "And he plans to take it all from me. Everything I've worked for."

Lenore leaned back in her chair. "And I've come to help you keep it."

Eudora opened her mouth to respond, then closed it again. Surely she'd misheard.

"I thought that might get your attention." A smile played across Lenore's lips. She lifted the teapot and refilled her cup. "My son is a buffoon, like his father. In the beginning, I was sure you'd shared that same sentiment. Why else would you have married him so quickly?" She gave a delicate shrug as she replaced the pot on the warmer. "But given recent events, I'm not as certain you have what it takes to manage a man like that. Luckily, I do."

Eudora pulled out a chair and sank into it. There was too much to take in, too much to process.

"Careful," Lenore warned. "You don't have much time."

"I don't know what to do." A wave of exhaustion washed over Eudora.

"Dower rights."

"Excuse me?"

"Dower rights are what allowed me to keep this house, even as Alistair tried to sell it from under me just days after William's death."

"Uncle Alistair wanted to sell this house?"

"Alistair Rutledge is not the man you think he is, Eudora. He can be just as ruthless as the rest of them," Lenore said offhandedly as she rose from her chair. Crossing the room, she retrieved a sheet of paper from the drawer of the buffet. "What saved me from Alistair Rutledge was hiring an attorney of my own, someone who was loyal to me and only me. Men will always stick together, like serpents in the garden, especially in a town as small as this. So it's essential that a woman understand her options." She scribbled a name on the page and slid it across the table. "Daniel Brown is the man I hired. Telephone him and tell him who you are. Be sure to mention my name and insist he see you right away. After he helps you – this one time – hire an attorney of your own. On retainer, and pay him well."

Eudora pulled the paper close to her and read the name on the page. Could the answer really be as simple as that? She curled her fingers around the paper, heard it crackle and felt the weight of it in her hand, but still wouldn't allow herself to hope.

Not yet.

Lenore returned to her seat. "Go now, my dear. You have a lot to do and not much time to do it." Then she smiled. "Good luck."

Thirty-five

Eudora opened the heavy wooden door and strode across the marble floor toward the receptionist desk. Of course Brock had chosen the Charleston Commerce Bank for the meeting.

He thought he'd won.

"Good morning, Mrs. Rutledge." Eudora recognized the receptionist at the desk, the same girl who radiated disinterest on Eudora's last visit. Now, it seemed, the girl wanted to help. She beamed as she gestured to a bank of chairs along a far wall. "Mr. Sheely said he'd be out in a moment. He'd like you to wait over there."

"Thank you, but I'd rather not wait. I don't have time." Eudora slipped off her gloves and tucked them into her purse. "I assume they're all in the conference room?" Without waiting for an answer, Eudora crossed the lobby and pushed open the oak door to the executive offices.

She assumed that Brock would have told the bankers to expect a large account, and that they'd gather around the conference table like ravens on a gravestone, and she was right. She heard the men talking before she entered the room. She recognized Brock's deep baritone, this time light and jovial as he made a joke, and the chorus of forced laughter from the bankers. It seemed the celebrations had begun. Wouldn't they be surprised? She curled her fingers around the strap of her purse and continued down the hallway, drawing even breaths as she walked. Turning the corner, she entered the room, but when she saw the men seated around the conference room, her courage wavered. There were so many of them.

Brock sat at the head of the table, a position unearned. He appeared to be utterly relaxed, with a folder of papers in front of him and the staff of the Charleston Commerce Bank surrounding him, ready to do whatever he asked.

Skip Sheely was the first to notice her. He rose and extended his hand, an oily smile slithering across his face. "Mrs. Rutledge, how nice to see you again. Please come in."

She would not shake his hand. Instead, she stared at him

until his smile faded and his eyes clouded with doubt. Then she nodded. "Mr. Sheely."

The other men stood as she entered the room. Eudora's heart pounded in her chest as she passed the chair meant for her and made her way to the head of the table. Brock would not surrender his chair to her, but neither would Eudora yield.

The banker's smiles faded as they watched the struggle.

Eudora pretended not to notice.

Skip was the first to recover. He returned to his chair and tipped back, brimming with confidence. "Mrs. Rutledge, let me be the first to congratulate you. You've done a fine job helping Mr. Rutledge restore the property on King Street."

"Have I?" She glanced at Brock, but his attention was focused on the packet in front of him.

"Yes, and let me assure you that had I known the King Street property was the reason for your visit to us, several months ago, we would have—"

"Found time to meet with me?" Eudora asked.

"Yes, well." He cleared his throat. "You're here now, so let's proceed. I'd like to introduce—"

Eudora held up her hand. "I have no interest in who these men are, Mr. Sheely."

Brock glared at her. She held his gaze and did not flinch. How brave would he be in a room full of men?

Skip gestured to the chair next to him. "Would you be more comfortable over here, Mrs. Rutledge?"

"No, I don't believe I would."

Eudora's temper flared as she looked at the men surrounding the table. All of them gathered to take what she'd built.

"Let's just begin the meeting," Brock said.

"Very well." Skip opened the cover of his packet and the other men followed suit. "The value of the King Street property has increased substantially because of the work your husband put into it. Our real estate department has appraised it and are confident they can secure a buyer. In fact, they already have someone in mind. Isn't that right, boys?"

Several of the men nodded, but the energy of the room had shifted and Eudora could feel it. They weren't as confident as before. Several of them glanced at Eudora and then at Brock.

Skip passed a folder to her and offered a pen. "A quick signature in the places we've marked is all we need from you, Mrs. Rutledge, and then you can be on your way."

Eudora accepted the pen, then closed the folder and set the pen on top. "I will not sign your papers because I have no intention of selling my property."

Then she waited.

The men shuffled their paperwork and whispered to each other in quiet voices, but Eudora kept her gaze focused on her husband.

Skip cleared his throat to speak but Brock interrupted, his voice low. "Eudora, you may sign or not, I really don't care. We'd like your signature, but it's not required. I can sell the property without your consent."

"I'm afraid that's where you're mistaken," Eudora replied. "There's a little thing called 'dower rights,' which in this state means I retain thirty percent of the property. Unless I relinquish them, you can't sell. And I don't intend to relinquish them."

"That's an old law," Skip scoffed, even as his voice rose. "So archaic that it's not even recognized anymore."

"I'm afraid it's very much recognized," Eudora said. "My

attorney is very familiar with it. So, you won't be selling my building today."

Eudora held her breath as she watched Brock's face redden. Neither Eudora nor her attorney were entirely sure that dower rights applied in this case, and she hadn't given him much time to research, but they were betting that no one else at this meeting would be sure, either. Brock's position as head of the family was stronger than he realized, though he didn't know it. Eudora had staked everything on the premise that no one at this table would be interested in pursuing it further.

In short, she was bluffing.

After a moment of murmured discussion, one of the older men stood, leaving his folder untouched on the table. "This is distasteful business, and I don't want to be a part of anything that casts an unfavorable light on this institution. If you'll excuse me, gentlemen. Mrs. Rutledge."

Two others stood in agreement and followed him out the door. But three stayed, their greed making them hungry.

"You should be proud of yourself, Eudora," Skip spoke in soothing tones, as if Eudora were a child. "You've done well, but your husband knows what's best for your family." He reached for the pen and opened the folder. "Sign the papers and you can..." He fumbled for the right words. "Go back to your life."

There wasn't much difference between the two men, Skip and her husband. And at that moment, Eudora loathed them both.

"I'd like to speak to my husband alone, please."

Skip rose, reluctantly. "I'll be right outside, Brock. Then we can get started on ideas for your car dealership. I've got the loan papers all drawn up. All we need is the down payment, and the King Street property will qualify."

So that was it. That was why a team of bankers filled the room. That was why several stayed, despite threats, despite knowing Eudora did not want to sell. It was a trade. Brock had promised them something in return for seizing her property. Eudora clenched her fists until they cramped.

Brock waited for her to speak. His gaze flicked to the bruise on her cheek, barely visible under a thick coat of cosmetics. Eudora thought about not covering it up, proving of how far her husband would go to get his own way. But in the end, she spared him because she wanted something from him.

"I have a proposal for you."

He scoffed. "What could *you* possibly offer?"

"What I did – finding an old building and restoring it, then finding a tenant and using the rent as capital for the next project. That wasn't a one-time thing. I plan to do it again. Many times, in fact."

That part was true, at least. There was a sweet little two-story brick near the train station that looked interesting. She couldn't wait to see the inside.

But first, Brock. Her husband was a liability she couldn't afford.

"I plan to focus my attention on the business, acquiring properties and restoring them. Nothing else."

He scoffed. She ignored him.

Eudora withdrew a document from her bag and slid it across the table to him. "These are the papers that have incorporated my business, Palmetto Holdings. That part is done." She pointed to a line on the page, though it almost killed her to do so. "Your name is here, Brock Rutledge, Chairman of Palmetto Holdings."

He looked at the page, then at Eudora. Finally, he asked, "Why?"

"Because I want to start over, Brock. We were friends once; we can be again." Though the words were offered with a smile, they burned in her mouth. She meant none of it, but she needed him to believe she did.

The truth was that Eudora would have been very happy divorcing Brock Rutledge, but she knew what would happen to her if she did. As the woman, Eudora would become a pariah, an outcast in Charleston Society. Worse, the fallout from her decision would affect her parents. Social and committee invitations would be withdrawn or not issued at all. Her father's business would suffer, and her mother would crumble under the weight of Society's judgement. Eudora would not let that happen.

"You would be paid a salary," she continued. "Small at first, then increasing as the business grows. Other benefits will follow, of course. In a year or two, we can add club memberships and maybe a travel allowance."

"And what do you get?" Brock seemed interested, but petulant, like a child who had to make sure no one's share was larger than his.

She shrugged, as if what she got was inconsequential. "I build the business. I choose the properties, the contractors, the tenants, all without interference from anyone. You get a generous salary and I get to do the work."

Brock shifted in his chair, unsure, and Eudora's patience dissolved.

The carrot had been offered. It was time for the stick.

"My offer is generous, and I suggest you take it." She

leaned forward, folding her hands on the conference table and leveling her gaze at him. "If you don't, I will uncover the bruises you inflicted and everyone will know how they came to be. Then I will divorce you." Her voice was cold. "And I will tell everyone that our marriage ended because of your affair with Posey Chalmers-Beechum. Think of how powerful her family is, her husband's family. Think of what they can do to you."

Eudora saw his eyes lose focus as he considered her words. Then color drained from his face and his expression hardened. She held up her hand before he could speak.

She didn't care what he had to say.

She pressed the pen into his hand and he signed.

"LADIES AND GENTLEMEN. DISTINGUISHED GUESTS." Mr. Hendricks stood at the podium and leaned toward the microphone, his voice breaking the hum of conversation at the luncheon. "Thank you all for coming."

As the conversation dimmed, Eudora scanned the crowd for her friends, returning their smiles with one of her own.

Maggie was there, at a table filled exclusively with O'Hanlans. She sat next to her fiancé, a brilliant designer she'd met at work. They seemed to love each other fiercely, and Eudora was happy for them. Maggie had recently been promoted to senior buyer for Better Dresses and seemed very at home in New York City, though she returned to Charleston, often, to visit. Carl and Marie O'Hanlan had started looking at property in Savannah because they'd hoped to retire in a few more years. The pace of the building industry had gotten to be too much for Carl. He was happy to sell his business to his sons and spend his time on the golf course with his wife. Eudora could not imagine Charleston without them, and Maggie even predicted he'd be bored in a week and stir-crazy in a month. She would be sad to see them go, and she planned to visit Savannah every chance she got. Maybe even open a branch office there.

At a table closer to the front, Brock sat next to his mother. Lenore had moved to a beach cottage on James Island, relinquishing control of the Rutledge home to Eudora. In the past few years, they'd grown surprisingly close. Because the cottage was a bit secluded from her neighbors, Eudora hired a companion to look after her mother-in-law and a small staff to see to her daily needs. Lenore seemed happy, especially when she visited her grandchildren in Charleston.

Eudora's own parents were not present. Her father never forgave her for forging the letter years ago. And except for a brief flicker of interest in Eudora's debut, her mother's attention turned back to her own life. She missed them terribly at first, but the passing years seemed to have dulled the pain.

While Letty hadn't formally agreed to work for the Rutledges, she did decide to move in when it became clear that Eudora needed help with her babies and Brock wasn't willing to provide it. Despite being offered any room in the house, Letty tucked herself into the small room off the kitchen because she wanted to "keep an eye on my kitchen." The Rutledge house was better for Letty being in it, and Eudora thanked her lucky stars every day that she had been at the train depot that day.

Uncle Alistair passed just last spring, taking all his secrets with him. Eudora was anxious to hear more about Lenore's interest in him. Why she married William instead of his brother, but Lenore never brought it up again. And it would have been unforgivably rude to ask.

"And so," Mr. Hendricks continued, "it is my great honor to introduce Mrs. Eudora Rutledge, of Charleston's very own Palmetto Holdings. You might not know that Mrs. Rutledge was the first woman to be admitted to the business program at Charleston College. She has chosen to remember us with an endowment to the business college. The Rutledge Scholarship for Women in Business will make it possible for more women to attend the business program, and I, for one, welcome them." He glanced at her and nodded. "Ladies and gentlemen, Mrs. Rutledge."

Eudora rose from her seat at the head table. She left her napkin on the chair and crossed the dais to the podium. Then she unfolded her speech, smoothed it against the wooden surface, and began to speak.

ACKNOWLEDGMENTS

I'm so grateful to everyone who helped bring this book to life.

First, to the readers of THINGS WE SURRENDER who wanted to know more about Eudora's life. I hope you like where this story takes you.

To the research staff at the Charleston Public Library. You have superpowers and I'm in awe of the information you found for me. Truly, you are the best thing about Charleston.

To David Anderson, who read the worst first draft I've ever written and still managed to find some good in it. Eudora would have liked you.

To Laurie, Sandy, Heather, Liz, and Ann for keeping me focused and off the internet. Your encouragement carried me to the finish line. I will always be grateful.

To Elisa, Alison, Susie, Debra, Mike, and Elizabeth, for loving my novels. It's a pleasure to write for such enthusiastic readers. You keep me going.

And finally, to Emmett. If you stopped barking at everyone who walks by our house, I'd get a lot more writing done. But you're still a good boy. The best boy.

Heidi writes about quirky small communities, imperfect families, and the power of second chances. All her stories have happy endings, though it might a little while for the characters to get there.

She divides her time between the beautiful Pacific Northwest, where her Inlet Beach novels are set, and Charleston, South Carolina, the setting for her Lowcountry collection. She's currently at work on a new series, set in a small beach town on the New Jersey Shore.

She loves to hear from readers and answers every letter. Drop her a note at Heidi@HeidiHostetter.com, visit her website at www.HeidiHostetter.com, or find her on Facebook.

Things We Surrender

Family has to take you in, no matter how many mistakes you've made. At least that's what Joanna Rutledge Reed thought.

At eighteen, she left her family's ancestral home in Charleston, South Carolina, despite promising to stay. For years, she did whatever she wanted, barely giving her family a second thought. But a string of bad decisions results in heartbreak, forcing her to return home, her life in tatters.

Set against the rich tapestry of Charleston, South Carolina, three generations of strong Southern women share a history and not-quite-forgotten secrets. Will the bonds they forged years ago be strong enough to give them a second chance at being a family?

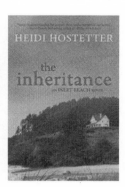

The Inheritance

If you like the Gilmore Girls' Stars Hollow, you'll love Inlet Beach. When three sisters arrive to claim the oldest house in town for themselves, you can bet the residents of this tiny beach community will have something to say about it.

The Inheritance is filled with the quirkiness of a small town, the craziness of an imperfect family, and the hope of a second chance.

Pacific Northwest Writers Association 2015 Literary Contest Finalist.

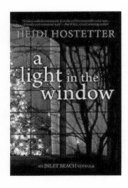

A Light in the Window

At Inlet Beach, storefronts are draped with garland, sprinkled with fairy-lights and dusted with Christmas magic.

But things are not as perfect as they seem.

As a blustery Pacific Northwest Christmas draws near, can the community of Inlet Beach help a boy with a shattered past find a home for the holidays?

A Light in the Window is a heartwarming tale of community, family, and second chances.

Made in the USA
Middletown, DE
23 September 2020